TRUST
NO ONE

BOOKS BY ROGER STELLJES

ROGER STELLJES

TRUST
NO ONE

bookouture

Published by Bookouture in 2025

An imprint of Storyfire Ltd.
Carmelite House
50 Victoria Embankment
London EC4Y 0DZ

www.bookouture.com

The authorised representative in the EEA is Hachette Ireland
8 Castlecourt Centre
Dublin 15 D15 XTP3
Ireland
(email: info@hbgi.ie)

ISBN: 978-1-83618-365-5
eBook ISBN: 978-1-83618-364-8

PROLOGUE

Ana kept her head low, two hands gripping the steering wheel, the Honda bouncing and rattling on the rough, uneven driveway as she raced away from the cabin. She peered up just over the dashboard and the pavement and white lines of the road suddenly appeared.

She yanked the steering wheel hard to the right and swerved, then accelerated on the tight two-lane road carved like a tunnel through the dense woods. She glanced up to the rearview mirror and her heart skipped a beat. A set of headlights flashed behind her.

But only briefly.

Then the vehicle turned into the driveway she'd just emerged from.

Get away. They'll come chasing.

She needed to put distance between herself and the cabin. She looked up every few seconds as she sped along. But there was nobody behind her now, just... the darkness of a Sunday night.

Letting out a cleansing breath, she sat more upright in the driver's seat. Ahead, a yellow sign with an arrow pointing left was coming up. And as the headlights illuminated the road ahead, she saw it was a sharp turn.

Ana pumped the brakes. Her tires squealed, her right-side wheels feeling as if they barely held the edge of the paved road.

Slow down before you kill yourself.

A green road sign on the right said Manchester Bay, ten miles. She had hoped coming here would solve their problems. It had only made them worse.

As she clenched the steering wheel, her question was: *What do I do now?*

Where do I go?

Who can I trust?

Those were questions she didn't have answers to. However, given what she knew, and all the people that were already dead who had possessed similar information, she knew they would keep hunting for her until they eliminated her as a threat. They had been for eight years. Now that it was just the two of them on the run, they wouldn't stop now. They were more vulnerable than ever.

"Momma?"

Ana looked down between the seats to see a terrified five-year-old Emma, lying on the floor in front of the back seat just like she'd told her to do.

"Honey, are you alright?"

"Mommy, where's Daddy?"

She couldn't answer that question either.

How do you tell your daughter that her father was dead?

ONE

"THAT WAS THEN, THIS IS NOW."

Five Hours Earlier

Braddock took one more look at his target, the pin one hundred and five yards away. His playing partner said he only needed to hit the ball ninety yards.

"It's in the rough but sitting up some," Koz said, taking a drink of his beer. "It won't have much spin when it lands so land it on the front of the green and it'll release the rest of the way. Just get it up and over the tree."

"Right," he said with a chuckle. "Got it."

As if I have that kind of control.

He'd been playing golf regularly for four years and was happy to say he was improving. The game was becoming more natural. He set his grip, relaxed his shoulders, and centered the club face right behind the ball. He slowly took the sand wedge back, paused for just a split second at the top and then brought the club down and through.

The club face made a crisp thumping sound on the ball and then turf, his long arms swooping through the hitting zone, his head and eyes turning left with his shoulders, looking up to see the ball elevate up and... just over the tip of the pine tree high into the sky, fading just a bit to the right of the flag. The ball landed on the green and rolled out a few yards. It was the closest of the four balls on the green. "Huh."

"Yes!" Koz exclaimed with a fist pump. "Fifteen feet. Gives us the nearie."

"I'll take it," Braddock said happily as he stuffed his sand wedge back into his golf bag and sat down in the golf cart, reaching for his beer and swigging down the last of it as they drove ahead to the green. The nearie was a point in their Scotch game, the bet they had against the other twosome, which was Eff'n Jones and his partner Bon.

"Who knew a fucking pigeon like you could hit that shot," Jones moaned. "I expected you to hit a fucking piss missile into the pond from there."

"Big-time players make big-time shots," Braddock retorted with more confidence than he really had.

Jones always knew where the Scotch game was at, would call it out shot-by-shot, and right now he and his partner were behind on the hole and behind in the game overall. He was very much in what they all liked to call the ATM position, i.e. the pay position. Braddock had been in that spot more than once.

But now, because of his higher golf handicap, if he got down in two putts, they would win the hole and a bunch of points on the bet. Braddock took one last look at the hole and then hit the putt, watching the ball trundle up toward the hole, just missing a few inches to the left and then stopping a foot away.

"Well, shit," Jones bitched.

"That's good," Bon said dejectedly, conceding the putt, disgustedly hitting the ball back to Braddock. "Four net three for a birdie. *Fuck!*"

"Mini sweep on level six baby," Koz chortled and then turned to Jones. "Pay, bitch."

"Yeah, yeah, yeah," Jones muttered.

"Winners buy the first round," Bon declared.

"That's fine," Braddock said and then with a sly grin, "I'll be buying it with *your* money."

"Nyeh, heh, heh, heh," Koz needled with a big grin. "I love taking motor mouth's cash."

The four of them grabbed a table on the clubhouse patio, had another beer, paid out the bet and ordered burger baskets, relaxing on a warm late August Sunday night.

"When does Tori get back?" Bon asked, stuffing fries in his mouth.

"Tonight, though it'll be after midnight," Braddock replied. "Her flight lands at ten thirty and then she has the drive up here from the Twin Cities, so I'd imagine she'll get home at one, one thirty, somewhere in there. Maybe later."

"And then it'll be post time," Jones declared loudly, miming as if he was riding a horse. "You'll be smashing that ass of hers."

"Geezes, Jonesy. Could you be any louder? Or cruder? Or just... not verbalize your lewd thoughts, hard as that would be for you."

"Seriously?" Koz replied, shaking his head, looking around at people staring at their table. "I don't think the elderly couple on the other side of the patio heard you. They probably haven't had post time in twenty years."

"It's an absolute mystery why you're not married," Braddock said, rolling his eyes, wiping the corner of his mouth with a napkin.

"Neither are you."

"Yeah, well... that may be true. But I get to go home to Tori every night because I don't behave like you. You go home to who, exactly?"

"Whoever I want, whenever I want," Jones bellowed. "All it takes is a call."

Koz laughed. "In your dreams, half pint."

Jones pulled out his phone. "We'll see about that. You want me to send pictures later."

"*No!*" they all replied in unison.

"Why are we friends with him?" Bon said.

"I provide fuckin' entertainment is why," Jones cracked with a smile. "I make you laugh."

"Today, we made you pay," Braddock needled, tapping the two twenty-dollar bills still lying on the table. "I might frame these."

Koz waved to their server. "Can we get the check before Jones says something else stupid?"

"Credit card roulette for the bill?" Jones suggested.

"Sure, I'll take more of your money," Koz retorted. Bon nodded.

"Braddock?" Jones prodded.

"Man, one day, just one day, I'd like to go home ahead," he moaned ruefully. "But, yeah, let's go."

* * *

It looked like Will Braddock. At least he thought the man did.

Julio watched the tall man with mostly black hair come up the fairway with his playing partners and then after sit on the patio with them for another hour, another round or two of beers, plates of burgers, a relaxing Sunday night at the course. He was certain the burger he'd watched him eat had been far superior to the lukewarm fast food one he'd choked down a few hours ago.

They'd never met in person, though he'd seen him from some distance back in the day when Braddock was poking around the docks where Julio once worked. That man had been tall with wide shoulders and shorter black hair, wearing a dark suit, NYPD detective's shield and gun on his belt.

The man he was watching now too was tall and angular. He looked a bit thinner than he remembered, although that could be due to the navy-blue golf shorts, bright lime-colored golf shirt and bright white golf hat with sunglasses perched on the brim. Then there was the thin stubbled beard, and his hair had some gray streaks and wavy flow to it now. A man who would be comfortable on a golf course, or dressed in camo in a deer stand, common hobbies of people in this part of the world. He'd seen plenty of that in the past few years living in northwest Wisconsin.

The server arrived at the table and one of the men held up the four credit cards. They were asking her to pick one.

She did.

The short one wearing the bright yellow golf shirt grimaced. The other three laughed and clapped loudly.

"It was *your* idea!" one of them bellowed.

* * *

Lange parked close to a cart path and was watching through the cover of a grouping of mature trees. He could see Julio in the car parked in the back of the parking lot, binoculars to his eyes. From behind his sunglasses, he looked in the distance to his left and saw Braddock sitting on the patio, relaxed with friends.

It had been a long time since he'd seen Braddock. His phone buzzed.

"Cardi."

"Where are you?" his partner asked.

"I'm at a golf course outside of Manchester Bay. I'm watching Julio. He's watching... Braddock."

"And... how does he look?"

"Julio?" Lange smirked.

"Funny, Ray."

"Braddock looks like Braddock. Tall, some gray in his hair now, something of a beard but otherwise as you'd remember him. You'll probably see for yourself here in a day or two."

* * *

Braddock had his wrist draped over the steering wheel, Mellencamp's "Pink Houses" playing on the Power Loon when the dashboard screen lit up. Tori. He answered.

"Hey there." He could hear hustle and bustle in the background. "Where are you?"

"Pittsburgh. I'm in line for an iced coffee."

"How was the conference?"

Tori had spent the past several days at an academic conference at the Greenbrier in West Virginia. All part of her new life as a professor. "It was surprisingly good. Picked up a few things. I also reconnected with two old Bureau colleagues who were mentors, Oliver and Connie Reid. They live in New York. One teaches at NYU and the other at Fordham."

Braddock laughed. Tori still loved New York City and visited it any chance she could and spoke wistfully on occasion of living there again one day. A native New Yorker himself, these days he didn't mind the occasional short trip back, though he was quick to dismiss any thoughts of a permanent return. He was not leaving the lake. "Let me guess, that's triggered in you a desire for a visit to the city that never sleeps."

"I was thinking about a weekend trip. See Tracy and my goddaughter."

"We can talk."

"What are you up to?"

"Just finished golf. I'm heading home."

They chatted for a few minutes about her trip, friends and then Quinn and how he was spending his last days of summer. Labor Day was in a week, then school started. "He's sleeping over at a friend's tonight. It's just Boomer and I."

A voice called out in the background: *Now boarding.*

"They're calling my flight. Gotta go," Tori declared. "I'll be home really, really late. I'll try not to wake you."

"You can wake me *all* you want," Braddock said, thinking back to Jones. Not the crudeness, but he had missed her.

"Well, I have been gone five days," Tori replied, taking the hint. "Are you feeling just a *wee* bit neglected?"

"Why yes, yes, I am."

"I'll make it up to you. Maybe, just not tonight."

Tori hung up and Braddock turned off the H-4, making his way around the north end of the lake when his phone rang again. A 715-area code number. That was Wisconsin.

Bob Seger's "Night Moves" started.

The phone kept ringing. It was probably some telemarketing call. He hit cancel, turned up the volume and started singing along.

Two minutes later the phone rang again. The same 715-area code.

Persistent. He was ready to deny it again and then thought it wouldn't be the first time he'd gotten a call from an out-of-state jurisdiction looking for help or information. He cut the music and tapped the screen. "Will Braddock."

"Is this the Will Braddock who was once a detective with the NYPD?"

He sat up a little straighter at the NYPD reference. "Who's askin'?"

"Hector Ramirez."

"And I should know you why, Hector?"

"Well, you knew me as Julio Gonzalez. Hector was my middle name back then. I had to change my name."

"And Hector or Julio, why would I know you?"

"Dan Guerero."

Braddock froze.

"Braddock?"

That Julio Gonzalez.

"Braddock?"

Why after all this time?

"Braddock?"

"Yeah." He could tell the man was in a vehicle. He suddenly checked his rearview mirror, but it was clean other than a set of taillights way, way back, barely visible in the near darkness.

Dan Guerero.

He'd long dreaded hearing that name again. When he'd first moved to Minnesota, it would pop into his mind almost daily though he'd be quick to try and think of something, anything else. Those momentary thoughts had diminished with the passage of eight years' time. An old problem, long put away.

"I thought Guerero's name might throw you for a loop."

Braddock checked his rearview mirror again but now it was clear; the tailing headlights had disappeared. He refocused. "How did you get this number?"

"I've had it for some time. You know, just in case I needed it. It pays to have a plan."

"And you're calling me why?"

"I need your help, man. Something serious."

"Well, Julio, or Hector, or whatever you're going by now—"

"Like I say, I go by Hector, but you can call me Julio if you want."

"Well then, Julio. I was maybe interested in *your* help eight years ago. Dan was killed, then my informant Malik was murdered, and you disappeared. To be honest, I figured you were either dead or you set up Malik and blew town before I could track your ass down."

Julio snorted in disgust. "Malik was my friend."

"So you say. You weren't around to speak to about what happened to him or for him. That doesn't exactly scream friend, Julio."

"I ran before I ended up like him."

"And that's been what? Eight years. Why would I help *you* now?"

"Because maybe I know some things about what happened to Guerero. To what happened to Malik."

"Nobody wants the Guerero case out in the open again. Nobody."

"Don't be so sure," Julio replied with a derisive snort. "The Guerero case is active again, man, way active. I've got NYPD detectives hunting for me now. One showed up in Superior, where I work. I ran before he got to me, or the other cops did."

"What *other* cops?"

"The ones that killed Guerero! You know other cops did him dirty. That's why I need your help, man."

Braddock closed his eyes for a brief second, a flood of thoughts and emotions long in slumber instantly at the front of his mind.

Julio beckoned, "Braddock, you still there?"

"What makes you think you can trust me?"

"Malik once said I could. And best I can tell, you haven't been hunting for me the past eight years."

Braddock exhaled and shook his head. "I'm not interested."

"You wanted to know what I knew eight years ago."

"That was then, this is now."

"I'm right here, man. I just want to talk."

"It's not my concern, even if it is yours. I got away from it, and I don't want back in."

"Come on, man. You're leaving me hanging."

"Talk to the NYPD detectives. If they reopened the case, those detectives are probably on the level."

"Probably?"

"You want protection, tell them what you know and tell them who you're afraid of. Get the hell away from here and leave me out of it. I want nothing to do with any of it."

"You don't get this, do you? I can't trust the NYPD. It's the cops who killed Guerero, who killed Malik, who will kill me if they get the chance."

"That's not my problem and I'm not going to make it my problem."

"Look, Braddock," Hector pleaded. "I'm going to be at the Halfway Highway Diner at eight a.m. tomorrow. Just come and hear me out. Then you can decide if you want to help me."

"If you're in trouble, you'll have to get out of it on your own."

"Malik once told me you were a stand-up guy, someone I could trust. Sounds like he was wrong."

"I don't know you and I don't owe you anything."

"I'll be at that cafe in the morning," Julio said. "Or I'll just show up at your work and you'll have no choice but to talk to me."

"You do that, Julio, and I'll put your ass in a jail cell and call NYPD myself."

Braddock dropped the call. He checked his rearview mirror again as he drove home.

* * *

Julio parked his car around the back of the hunting cabin and entered through the back door. Ana was sitting on the area rug on the floor, playing with their five-year-old daughter Emma.

"What happened?" Ana asked anxiously.

"He turned me down," Julio said as he sat down at the table. Emma walked over to him and climbed up onto his lap and he hugged her. "Has she had her meds?"

"No. Let me get the bag." She reached inside a duffel bag and brought over a large Ziploc bag that held a smaller plastic bag with tablets, and another with vials and syringes. She took a tablet out, filled a juice cup and handed both to Emma.

Emma swallowed her pill and washed it down. That was her nighttime medicine. Ana would give her an injection in the morning.

"I'll get her to bed," Ana said.

The hunting cabin had two bedrooms. One room had two sets of bunk beds in it. Emma took a lower bed. They unfurled her pink sleeping bag and tucked her in, leaving her with her favorite dolls. Ana closed the door, and Julio handed her a beer.

"You're not meeting him in the morning?" she asked.

"No. I should have just walked up to him at the golf course or in the parking lot and forced it. Instead, I waited to call him, and he told me to go away. He wanted nothing to do with me."

"What do we do now? I mean, what?"

"What we've been doing."

"We've been moving for eight years," Ana complained. "I'm tired of it. This is no way for us to live."

"I am too, which is why we finally came here but Braddock, he won't help us." Julio dropped his face into his hands. "I should have never gotten involved. I should have never been an ... informant."

"You need to try him again."

"Ana—"

"Force it. If he doesn't show at that restaurant, then we go to the sheriff's department. Make him step his ass up. If you go there, he has to talk to you. And if he won't, we go to the sheriff and tell her what we know. We've come this far. We're not taking no for an answer."

"Maybe..."

There was a flash of light through the curtains of the large window at the front of the cabin.

Julio grabbed his gun and went to the front window, peering out the gap in the curtains. A four-door tan Ford sedan pulled to a stop. A man got out. It was the same police detective looking for him in Superior at the plant on Friday.

How did he find him?

This was his friend's hunting cabin. Heck, cabin was generous, it was a shack though it had electricity and running water. Nevertheless, the detective had found him.

Dressed in a dark sport coat and white dress shirt, he was out of the car, standing behind the opened driver's side door, peering about the cabin, and appeared to be alone. He made eye contact with Julio and held up his identification. "Julio, I need to talk with you."

"Maybe you should talk to *him*," Ana suggested. "Braddock won't and he's here."

"He's a cop."

"We're here to find a cop, for crying out loud. Talk to this one."

Julio opened the door a crack. "Who are you?"

"Detective Ray Lange. NYPD. I'm with the Cold Case Squad. I'm investigating the murder of NYPD Police Detective Dan Guerero eight years ago and I need to speak with you. May I please come in?"

Julio peered outside, beyond Lange's car, and up the driveway before it disappeared back into the dense woods where it eventually came out on a paved county road.

"I've come alone."

"You detectives always have partners."

"Mine is in New York City. She's not here. It's only me."

Julio looked back at Ana.

"Let him in," she said. "See what he has to say."

"Julio!" Lange called, his gun in his left hand dangling on his index finger. "I'll come in unarmed. I'll leave it in the car. I'll leave my phone in the car."

"Do that."

Lange leaned down and stuffed the gun under the driver's seat. He approached the house with his arms held out.

Julio slowly opened the door, his gun still hanging low in his right hand.

"You're not going to need that," Lange said, gesturing to the gun. "I'm not here to arrest you, to take you into custody, anything like that. If I were, I'd have local law enforcement with me, and you would have had no choice but to surrender. Do you see any of that out here?"

Julio didn't. *Did that make him less nervous, or more?* "Maybe it would be safer if I did."

"I can do that, though I'm not sure that would make you safer. I'm unarmed. I just want to talk."

"Alright, come in." Julio waved with his gun.

He let Lange inside and closed the door. "I'm still going to pat you down."

"Fair enough." Lange turned around and put his hands up against the wall and spread his legs.

Julio handed Ana the gun. She held it, pointed at Lange while Julio frisked him. Lange had a wallet and a badge and nothing else. "No cuffs? No cell phone?"

"They're all in the car," Lange replied. "I'm just here to talk."

Julio stood up and took the gun back from Ana. "No cop is ever here to *just* talk. I'm keeping my gun."

"That's fine, Julio. Or is it Hector?"

"It's Hector now, at least in Superior. If you want to call me Julio instead, I don't really care."

Lange nodded and looked over to Ana. "Ma'am, I'm sorry for the late hour." He stepped to the small round kitchen table and sat down. Julio followed him over. "Julio, keep the gun, but put it in your pocket, stuff it in your pants, something. Waving it around makes me nervous."

Julio stuffed the gun in the back of his pant line but kept his distance from Lange.

"You have any training using that thing?"

"Enough." Julio looked over to Ana. "Keep a look out."

"I'm alone," Lange insisted and then looked at the two beers on the table. "You got an extra one of those?"

"Sure," Julio replied and retrieved a beer from the fridge.

Lange twisted the cap off and took a long swig. "Ahh. Thanks."

"You're here about Guerero, right?" Julio said, taking a drink of his own beer. "I had nothing to do with what happened to him."

"Come on," Lange said, shaking his head, leaning forward on his elbows, both hands on the beer bottle. "Then why disappear eight years ago? Why change your name? Why be on the move all the time? Why sneak out the side door at the refinery on Friday afternoon when I showed up with Superior Police to speak with you? Clearly you either know something or are guilty of something. I tend to think it's you *know* something."

"I had nothing to do with his murder."

"And Malik?"

"Malik was my friend. I had nothing to do with that either. I ran before I ended up like him. Like I said, I didn't have anything to do with what happened to Guerero. I didn't have anything to do with the shooting."

"If I had any questions about that, you just allayed them with how you handled that gun."

Ana chuckled, looking back from the front window. "I've told you to be careful with that thing."

Lange continued, "Julio, I think you have information about *who* was responsible and *why*. That's what I want to know."

"How is it *you* have my name to begin with?" Julio replied.

"You wouldn't be running all these years if you didn't know something."

"That's not my question. My question is how do you have my name? Why do you even think I have information?"

"I'm a detective, I detect."

"You're a detective, you had a source. Who?"

"Let's just say that information that went missing years ago has turned up."

"What information?"

"Guerero had an investigative file of his own that was recently discovered. Notes mostly about what he was looking into, and you're name features—prominently."

Julio shook his head in frustration. "Why should I trust you? Why should I trust anyone with the NYPD?"

"You must trust Will Braddock, right?" Lange replied, sitting back, folding his arms. "I mean, you're here in Manchester Bay to see him, correct?"

"I identified him. I followed him from his house to the golf course."

"Did you talk to him?"

"He called him. Tonight," Ana said, looking back again. "Braddock won't see him. Told him to go away."

"He did," Julio affirmed and then slowly shook his head. "It looks like he has a good life here. Maybe I can't blame him."

"Hmpf." Lange chuckled. "I am not surprised. Braddock's name shows up in this new evidence too, which is how I found you after you fled Superior. I suspected you were coming here, perhaps for this reason. Unfortunately, your trust in him may be entirely misplaced."

"Because of how he shows up in this new evidence?"

Lange nodded. "This might have been the worst place for you to come, which is another reason why I don't have any local police with me."

Julio narrowed his eyes. "Braddock is dirty?"

"If you want to get free of all this, you need to work with *me*. My squad is trying to get answers."

"Then look inside your own house," Julio asserted.

"I know," Lange said, nodding. "Which is why I'm here... *alone*."

"I'm not so sure about that," Ana called from the front window.

"What?" Julio said, shoving his chair back.

"I think I saw someone out there," she said.

"There shouldn't be," Lange said. "Let me see."

* * *

Two men—Vooch and Conn—pulled masks down over their faces and made their way down the left and right sides of the driveway in the darkness, guided by the dim light through the curtains of the picture window.

On their left flank, a third, Boo, was deep in the woods, working his way forward.

Vooch shuffled ahead, crouching as they approached the cabin. The curtains moved. They'd been spotted.

"We're blown."

* * *

Lange rushed to the window and peered around the right edge. "I make two men coming up the driveway."

"Who are they?" Ana asked.

Lange looked to Julio. "Do you know?"

"I don't. I only had one name I gave Guerero back then, and it wasn't even a cop."

"Who?"

Julio paused, peering out the window, trying to spot the men who were coming.

"Julio, who?"

It took Julio all he had to say the name. "Stagliola."

"Stagliola? Wait. Carmine Stagliola? You gave Guerero the name of Carmine Stagliola?"

"You look surprised."

"I... I... I am."

Julio nodded. "And he had a cop buddy or two. I didn't know

those names, but one showed up in a silver sedan at least a half-dozen times, always wearing a dark suit, tie, had a big round head, black hair combed back. And then two times there was another man with him, bigger guy, shaved head, burly, had a menacing look about him. Stagliola seemed to know them both pretty darn well."

Lange's eyes widened. "You're absolutely sure?"

"You know who I'm talking about?"

"I think I do. Shit."

"Stagliola and this guy would watch for a specific container, track it being loaded onto a trailer and then be hauled away. I saw Guerero brace Stagliola once down on the docks just as I was clocking in for my shift. It wasn't but a day or two after that he was gunned down."

"You ever tell Braddock about any of this?"

"Never got the chance back then and he didn't want to talk about it a few hours ago either."

"And now these guys show up."

Lange reached for his phone and grimaced. It was in the car, along with his gun. The two approaching men spread apart and raised their guns.

"Get down!" he yelled, tackling Ana to the floor.

Crack! Crack! Crack! Crack!

The window shattered. The sheetrock and paneled walls were punctured.

"Mommy!" Emma cried out.

Ana scrambled across the floor toward the bedroom.

"Julio, give me your gun," Lange said.

Julio tossed it over. Lange peeked over the edge of the windowsill, caught sight of one of the men on the left, popped up on his right knee.

Pop! Pop! Pop!

He dropped back down. "Julio, whether you know what you're doing or not, you're going to have to fight this with me.

I'm going for my car and my gun. You need to cover me while I do. A short burst of four shots, two left, two right."

"Okay."

Lange crawled across the floor to the door and reached for the knob and looked back to Julio. "Now!"

Julio turned around the corner and fired.

Pop! Pop! ... Pop! Pop!

Lange scrambled out the door, keeping low, rushing to his rental car.

Crack! Crack! ... Crack! Crack!

They'd seen him. Shots pinged off the car.

He opened the driver's side door and pulled his gun from under the driver's seat along with the spare magazine. *Where was his phone?* He peered around but couldn't find it. He'd put it under the seat but now, where did it go?

Ping! Ping! Ping!

Shots rattled the car.

They were coming, fast.

The phone would have to wait.

He shifted to his right and peeked over the trunk. He glimpsed one of them behind a tree on the right side, maybe a hundred feet away, turning at him. He ducked.

Crack! Crack! Crack!

The shots pinged off the passenger side.

He shuffled to his right to the back of the car and snuck another peek.

Come on, you son of a bitch. Show yourself. Stick your head out.

* * *

"Lange's at the car!" Conn exclaimed.

Vooch gestured for Conn to move forward.

"Cover me," Conn said. He slid to his right and rushed ahead.

* * *

Julio peeked around the corner and saw the man move ahead. *I have an angle on him.*

Boom! Boom! Boom!

* * *

Atta boy, Julio. The man came into Lange's sights, and he had a decent angle to fire on him. He rose just enough.

Pop! Pop! Pop!

* * *

Vooch stepped to the right and unloaded at the front of the cabin.

Bap! Bap! Bap!

"*Ahrg!*"

Conn's left shoulder recoiled. He fell hard on his left side.

"Conn!"

Conn rolled back to his right off the side of the driveway and leaned up against a tree, cradling his left arm.

"Conn!" Vooch called.

"I'm hit."

* * *

"*Oh... oh...*"

Julio collapsed to the floor. Instinctively he reached with his left hand, and it was instantly moist. His belly was on fire, the burn searing through his body.

"Julio!" Ana called as she started to crawl to him.

"No. Stay there. I'm... I'm... done for," Julio replied, gasping. "Take Emma. Go while you still can, baby!"

"No!"

"They'll kill you if you stay. You have to try and go!"

Boom! Boom! Boom!

The gunshots punctured the paneling and sheetrock above their heads.

"I love you. Be careful who you trust. Go! *Now!*"

Ana scrambled across the floor to the bedroom door as another barrage of gunshots zoomed overhead puncturing more of the sheetrock, the paneling and windows. She reached up and opened the bedroom door.

"Mommy! Mommy!" the five-year-old Emma screamed, sitting up, her blanket wrapped around her.

"Get down! Get down!" Ana replied, dragging her daughter to the floor. "Come on, we have to go!"

At the door, Ana took a quick peek toward the front to see her husband standing with his back to the wall to the left of the front window, trying to eject the magazine from his gun, gasping for breath, the front of his shirt a bloody mess.

"Go! Go!" he gestured. "You have to get out of here."

"What about you?"

"Get Emma out of here."

"Daddy!" Emma wailed and tried to break free of Ana to crawl to him.

"No! You go with Mommy!"

Boom! Boom! Boom!

Bap! Bap! Bap!

Emma screamed in terror. Ana dragged her with her right arm to the back of the cabin.

"Daddy! Daddy!"

"Stay down," Ana said, pulling her daughter to the floor as glass, sheetrock dust and chunks of paneling debris filled the air.

When they reached the kitchen table, she reached up and grabbed her purse and then kept crawling across the aged linoleum floor of the kitchen to the back door and yanked it open. Staying low she lifted Emma into her arms and ran out the door, across the deck and down three steps to the Honda. She opened the back passenger door for the CR-V and shoved Emma inside along with her purse. "Stay on the floor."

* * *

One down, one to go, Lange thought. He peered around the rear of the car, hunting the left side of the driveway. Julio fired.

Boom! Boom! Boom!

The other man was low, behind the trunk of a tree, returning fire.

Bap! Bap! Bap!

The back door to the cabin was flung open and he saw Julio's wife and daughter scrambling for the Honda. She had only one way out and needed cover. He shuffled a step right.

Pop! Pop! Pop!

The man ducked right. Lange shifted another step right and raised up.

The car started and he heard the wheels spin in the gravel. Ana zoomed around the north side of the cabin. A moment later she came around the front and raced ahead to the driveway.

The man jumped out from behind the tree and fired at her.

Bap! Bap! Bap!

She turned to the left, driving straight at him.

Atta girl.

The masked man dove left into the trees just before she hit him, the little SUV ricocheting off the tree and swerving, but she somehow kept it on the driveway. The man rolled to his feet, pivoted and fired at her as she raced away.

It was a mistake. He was exposed.

Lange aimed. *I got him.*

Bam! Bam!

"Oh!" Lange felt the two shots in his back, his legs instantly buckling beneath him.

He collapsed against the rear of the car. He looked left to see the red taillight of the car, Julio's wife turning right, racing down the road. At least she had gotten away. He slowly turned his head to see the outline of the approaching figure and started to raise his arm.

Bam! Bam!

The shots hit him in the center of his sternum.

His gun dropped from his hand as he gasped for air, resting against the rear of the car, unable to move, his body no longer responding to his brain's commands. A hulking figure wearing a mask emerged from the woods, slowly walking toward him, gun up. The man pulled his mask up. Then a small beam of light from the cabin hit his face.

"You..." he gasped. "Boo."

"Sorry, Ray."

Bam!

* * *

"What took ya?" Vooch exclaimed, running to Boo.

"You two went early. And the woods were thicker than hell."

Stag pulled up in the SUV, skidding to a hard stop. "What the hell happened?" he asked, letting the driver's side window down.

"They saw us coming. And I'm pretty sure that was Julio's wife who got away."

"I could have chased—" Stag started. "But you guys..."

"Shit," Boo bitched.

"She won't get far but we best get the hell out of here," Vooch said.

"First things first. Stag, help Conn. Vooch, come with me," Boo ordered.

The two of them approached the cabin and peered inside. Julio was lying against the wall just below the front picture window. Vooch approached and picked up Julio's gun. The man's eyes looked lifelessly up at him. Nevertheless, he made sure.

Bap!

Boo searched the cabin quickly. In one of the bedrooms, he found a cell phone. He used Julio's face to open the phone and went to recent calls.

"He called Braddock. A couple of hours ago."

"We have to get the hell out of here," Vooch said. "Conn is going to need help."

"Come on." Boo ran back outside and reached into Lange's pockets.

"What are you looking for?"

"Keys." He found them in a pocket and hit the trunk release. "Help me get both bodies into the trunk."

That done, they drove to Conn, who was propped up against a tree on the right side of the road. They helped him into the back seat of Lange's car.

Boo looked at the oozing hole in Conn's shoulder. He took off his own outer shirt and pressed it against the wound.

"Ahh, Fuck! Ahh, Fuck!" Conn screamed. "Something's broken."

"We need to stop the bleeding. Hold the shirt on it with your right hand. As much pressure as you can bear," Boo said and then to Vooch, said: "I'll make the call, see if we can get him some help and we'll have to dump this car. If we're lucky, nobody finds this place for a few days."

"And if they do?" Vooch replied.

"Braddock will have to hold up his end of the bargain."

TWO

"TO SEE IF A STORM COMES."

Tori parked her Audi Q5 next to Braddock's pickup truck. Getting out of the car she stretched, stiff from the flight and then the nearly three-hour drive. She ran her tongue over her lips, tasting and feeling the sweater-like mixture of Diet Coke and coffee on her teeth. *I need a good brush.*

She retrieved her luggage from the back of the Audi, walked to the house and smiled. Their neighbors Joe and Leslie had company. Four people were sitting around the firepit, music playing lightly, a cooler visible. Leslie gave her a wave which Tori returned.

"Tori, do you want a nightcap?" Leslie called out, holding up a Yeti that was no doubt filled with an alcohol concoction of some kind.

Tori laughed. "I'll take a rain check. It's been a long one. I need some sleep."

"Well, we'll keep it down."

"Oh, no worries," she replied with a wave. "Have one for me."

"Will do."

She stepped quietly into the house though the door chime went off.

Ding! Ding! Ding!

She stepped into the entryway and a happy puppy looked up at her from his crate, wagging his tail eagerly despite his sleepy eyes.

"Hey, Boomer, how are you, buddy?" she said, opening the crate door and then scratching him behind the ears with her right hand while he licked her left one. "Such a good boy, you big fur ball." He still had some puppy softness to him. She closed the crate door. Boomer looked back up at her, his tail slowly wagging.

In the master bedroom, she stepped softly into the closet, stripping off her clothes and slipping on a long T-shirt. After a thorough brush of the teeth, she slipped out of the bathroom to find Braddock lying in bed, on his back, his eyes open, staring vacantly at the window, the curtains drifting lightly in the night breeze.

"Hey," she said as she slid into bed and leaned over to kiss him. "What are you still doing up?"

"Can't sleep," he said, throwing his right arm around her, drawing her close. "I'm glad you're home."

* * *

Boo got ahold of the doctor just after 1:00 a.m. After detailing Conn's condition, the doctor said he could do it if they could get to his clinic within the hour and pay his price.

"He wants twenty-five grand," Boo said, placing his hand over the phone.

"Pay it," Vooch replied. "He needs treatment, now."

They arrived at the clinic, and all pulled on their face masks again. The doctor let them in the back of the clinic just before

2:00 a.m. Conn a bloody mess, his right arm around Vooch's shoulder, hobbled inside first to the imaging room. The doctor examined the wound and shoulder area, poking and prodding in various places, eliciting several loud grunts and groans from Conn.

"What do you think?" Boo asked.

"It's not just the wound," the doctor replied. "I need to take an X-ray to confirm but I think his clavicle is broken. If it's shattered, I can stabilize him, but he'd need surgery with a plate and screws. I can't do that. If it's just a regular fracture, we can use a sling and figure-eight brace."

"How long?"

"A couple, three hours either way. I need to get started, but I don't treat until—"

Boo handed the doctor an envelope. "That's half. You get the other half when you're done."

The doctor considered the offer for a moment. "Deal."

"I'll be back in a few hours after I take care of our other piece of business," Boo said to Vooch.

The doctor went into the back of the clinic to a safe, tapped in a combination and the safe opened. The doctor stuffed the envelope inside. Then he looked at Vooch. "You're going to have to help me with him."

After the X-rays, they moved Conn to a treatment room.

"What's the story with the shoulder?" Vooch asked the doctor, who slid on a pair of glasses and evaluated the X-ray.

"The clavicle is broken but not shattered." He gestured to the image. "No fragmentation, just a clean break. More like it broke from a fall."

"He went down hard, after he was shot."

"Then he's lucky."

"I ain't feeling so lucky," Conn moaned.

"So, what then?" Vooch inquired.

"I treat and sew up the wound."

The doctor shot Conn up with a local and had him take two Valium.

"You need to lie still. I have to get the bullet out and then stitch up the wound."

"Is it going to hurt, Doc?" Conn asked.

"More than a little, but with the local and two Valium you're not going to give a shit." The doctor looked at Vooch. "Keep him steady."

* * *

Boo left the back door of the clinic and drove across the street to find Stag waiting in the convenience store parking lot. He had a map up on his phone.

"You find a spot?"

"Here," Stag said. "It's about a half-hour north."

Boo looked at the location on the map. "Not much for population around there."

"That's what I'm thinking. No prying eyes, especially at this time of night. Get in and get out."

"Stay close behind me until we get there. I don't want anyone seeing this license plate."

Boo drove north on Highway 10 and placed another call to New York.

"You get to the doctor?"

"Yeah, he's treating him now," Boo replied. "How'd you know about this guy?"

"I made some calls to some old contacts in Minneapolis. The man I spoke to said this doctor is dealing with his second divorce. Needs cash he doesn't have to tell anyone about. We can all relate." He paused. "Was killing Lange necessary?"

"It couldn't be avoided, and you know it couldn't be avoided. It was a must and eliminated two problems."

"What about Braddock? Did Julio make contact with him?"

"Yes. Or at least his cell phone shows that they spoke briefly."

"No other reason to go to Manchester Bay than to make contact. No other reason to go there than to see Braddock."

"Which is why, when Lange showed up—"

"You had no choice."

"What now? You know this is going to stir shit up."

"Maybe."

"No. It will. And you know it will."

"You let me worry about that. You just make sure you get rid of those bodies."

* * *

The whole procedure took just over three hours. It was now just after 5:00 a.m., still fully dark outside. The area around the clinic and strip mall was quiet, the large front parking lot empty.

Together, Vooch and the doctor gently eased Conn off the examination table, letting him get to his feet. He was a pale ghostly white, sweaty, wincing, careful with every movement. Vooch wrapped a white hospital blanket around him, his left shoulder bandaged, a figure-eight splint for the broken collarbone and his arm in a sturdy black sling tight to his body to help ease the pressure on the fracture.

The doctor looked at Vooch's left forearm, wrist and hand. "That looks dry."

"It's been itchy lately. I use some cream sometimes when it gets like this but don't have it with me."

"Hang on." The doctor went to a cabinet, hunted through the shelves and retrieved a small white container. "Apply this moisturizer to it once or twice a day. It'll reduce the irritation."

"Thanks. His prognosis?"

"Fractured clavicle and tissue damage. It could have been

much worse. He's lucky. The collarbone should heal normally in eight to twelve weeks. He needs to keep the shoulder immobilized in the brace all that time and in the sling for the next several days. The wound will heal sooner but he'll have a jagged scar. You saw it, the way the skin was shredded apart. I sewed him up best I could but I'm not a plastic surgeon." He reached for a blank pill bottle on the counter. "Have him take these for the pain but don't let him take too many. Easy to get hooked and you don't want that. The most important thing is he gets some rest. It'll all heal with time."

"Understood," Vooch said and then handed the doctor an envelope, the second half of the payment. "You never saw us."

The doc looked inside the envelope and nodded. "Not very good for this business if I remember who I saw and treated."

"Exactly."

"You better get out of here before the sun comes up."

Vooch peeked out the small rear window on the back door to see Boo and Stag back waiting for them in the distance, leaving a good walk for them. He helped Conn make the long walk to the waiting SUV and helped him up into the back seat. As Stag pulled away, he asked, "Where to?"

"Back to Manchester Bay," Boo said.

"Why?"

"To see if a storm comes."

THREE

"I'M A MAN OF ACTION AND INTRIGUE."

Despite the late hour of her arrival home, Tori's body clock had her up at the crack of dawn with Braddock. As they often did in the summer, the two of them took a morning swim down the shoreline to his in-laws' dock and then back.

Braddock had been a college basketball player, but Tori often thought he could have been a better swimmer. He had a swimmer's body, with wide shoulders, long windmill-like arms, and a lean body. And he was determined to keep it that way. Most men his age had gone well soft in the middle but there was hardly an ounce of fat on him. Nor her for that matter. The two of them were active, followed a rigorous exercise regimen and ate healthily, at least most of the time. Hockey season parent "safety" meetings filled with pizza, wings and beer were proving an ever-greater annual challenge to overcome. Each spring there was work to shed the added winter coat.

His six-foot-four frame covered the first half-leg of their swim quicker than she could, being nearly a foot shorter. That said, she was a former triathlete and had a good stroke and would only be twenty seconds or so behind him. Usually, he would wait at Roger and Mary's dock for her, and they would float in the cool water and talk for a few minutes, easing into their day before they swam back. Not today. When she reached the dock, he immediately shoved off for the return leg.

"Okay then," she said with a mild chuckle. Sometimes he was just in a hurry. Maybe he had something on his calendar.

She took a moment to rest. It was a nearly perfect morning, the sky a clear blue, hardly a breath of wind, the water like glass. But it would be a warm one for later August, temp in the eighties. She watched Braddock, his arms moving powerfully through the water, his feet kicking up. She heard a door slide open and looked up to the house. Roger Hayes stepped out onto the deck, a cup of coffee in one hand and a newspaper in the other.

"Hiya, Tori," he said with a wave before sitting down to enjoy the morning.

"Hey, Rog."

"He just take off without you?"

"Apparently so."

She pushed off and swam the leg home.

Braddock was waiting on the dock for her when she arrived. He was sitting on the bench, his elbows on his knees, looking down, a towel draped around his neck.

"You alright?" she asked as she climbed the ladder up to the dock floor.

"Uh, I'm fine," he said, looking up and then tossed her a towel. "Just still waking up, I guess."

Tori wasn't so sure she bought that, but he often demurred when he had something on his mind, preferring to ruminate on it himself. She'd learned not to press. Eventually, if it was important enough, he'd ask her what she thought. "What's on the docket for today?" she said as she dried off.

He exhaled with puffy cheeks. "Paperwork, meet with Boe to go over some budget stuff, meet with the team to see where we're at on various cases, the usual. How about you?"

"I'm going over to the university. We have a department meeting this morning. We're not but two weeks from classes starting so I have some lectures to prepare, plus admin stuff. The paperwork rivals the Bureau."

"Naturally."

"But my schedule is flexible enough for a break," she said. "How about we go to lunch?"

"I'd like that."

They showered and dressed quickly. As she emerged out of the closet, she saw Braddock pull his service weapon out of the nightstand drawer.

"What was that doing in there?"

He usually put it in the top drawer of his dresser in the closet, that he would then lock. She would do the same.

"Oh, um, I just put it in there the other day, I guess."

"I see," she replied with a hint of disapproval. She was not a fan of unlocked guns in the house, period.

"I'll put it back in the locked drawer tonight."

"Better."

While Tori brewed the coffee, Braddock took Boomer outside to do his business. Tori filled his food and water bowls, and the puppy came inside and beelined for them, eating and drinking for a few minutes, his tail wagging as it perpetually seemed to do. After he'd finished with his bowls, Braddock guided him into the kennel and the dog looked back at him as if to say: *That's it?*

"I hate just sticking him back in there," Tori said. "A puppy can take it only so long."

"Quinn will be home in a few hours and then Boom will be running the rest of the day so a little extra kennel time won't hurt him, will it?" Boomer stood in his kennel, staring back at them, his tail wagging.

Quinn would likely come home and then immediately take Boomer back down the road to his cousin's house. Boomer liked to play with their Golden Retriever George. Now, whether George liked the rambunctious Boomer following and jumping all over him was perhaps another story.

Tori poured them full coffee tumblers. She handed one to Braddock, then elevated on her tippy toes and kissed him softly. "I'll see you for lunch."

* * *

Her drive to the university took her ten easy minutes, cutting through Manchester Bay along the way. From her reserved parking spot, a perk as a full-time professor, she strolled casually through the campus and paused at the construction site of the new Riley Auditorium.

The skeleton of the new auditorium was starting to take shape: a rebuild following a bomb attack last year. Fortunately, she and Braddock had uncovered the bomb plot, raced to the campus and were able to get everyone out of the auditorium just before the explosion. The target of the attack, the United States Secretary of Commerce, had survived—and, mercifully, so had all three thousand people in the audience including many of their friends. The only deaths had been those responsible for the attack, she and Braddock had seen to that.

For their efforts and the thousands of lives they saved that day, she, Braddock, and his team of Steak, Eggleston, Reese and Nolan had been awarded the Presidential Medal of Valor. The President of the United States was coming to the campus soon to dedicate the new auditorium and the monument to be erected in memory of the events of that day.

She made her way to her office, which was a ten-foot by ten-foot white cinder block box with a narrow window for some natural light. The office came furnished with a newish L-shaped desk, a floor-to-ceiling bookshelf and an older albeit comfortable dark-brown weathered leather couch that had been left behind by a previous occupant. Tori added two soft visitors' chairs, some artwork for the walls, including a wide panoramic photo of Boston College, her alma mater, and another of the FBI Academy at Quantico, along with several personal photos, mostly of her, Braddock and Quinn, another with Braddock's team when they received their medals of valor and then one with her two best friends from the Bureau, Special Agents Tracy Sheets and Geno Harlow.

She looked around at the office and smiled wryly at how her life had changed in the past three years. A nicely furnished office, not to mention a comfortable home on a lake, were the last things on her mind back then.

Her condo in Manhattan had contained nary a photo or piece of art, the walls blank, boxes of personal effects stacked in corners and closets, not opened in the many years she'd lived in it. And her cubicle at the FBI's New York City Field Office had been much the same. There were no personal effects, beyond the yellow coffee cup Tracy had given her that said: *I am a Ray of Fucking Sunshine*. It was a gag gift that spoke to who she was then: an intense, driven, closed off workaholic who had never dealt with the dual traumas of her identical twin sister's disappearance and presumed death when she was seventeen, followed eighteen months later by her father's death from a heart attack.

Tori had just compartmentalized it, left it all behind, finished college in Boston, joined the FBI and stayed on the East Coast, settling in New York City. She often spoke as if her life began at Boston College.

Tracy was one of the rare few who knew her full life story back then. In giving her the gift of the coffee cup, Tracy had subtly tried to coax her to deal with her past. And as with all other attempts Tracy had made back then, Tori ignored it.

There never seemed to be anything to truly trigger her to do it. It was in the past. It would stay there.

Until it didn't.

The trigger came three years ago.

On the twentieth anniversary of her twin sister Jessie's disappearance, her abductor resurfaced. He took a woman in a near mirror image of the way he'd abducted her sister. And he reached out to Tori, sending her an envelope containing an old newspaper clipping of Jessie's disappearance as invitation to come home. And she knew that invitation meant, in some way, shape or form, an ultimate confrontation with her sister's killer.

It was an invite she could not and would not turn down.

She was going to investigate that abduction and find her sister's killer. In her mind, she was going to put it to rest or die trying.

There was just one person standing in her way.

Will Braddock.

When she arrived at the Shepard County Government Center, he was the man she had to convince to let her into the case. And the minute she saw him, there had been another unexpected jolt. He was tall and ruggedly handsome. He looked good in a tailored suit, in command, with a gravitas she hadn't expected to find. It was a revelation that he was a former NYPD homicide detective, having taken residence up in lake country. That in and of itself provided intrigue. So as determined as she was to work on the case, she couldn't help but feel just a little tickle of attraction.

At first, she pushed that all aside. It was about finding her sister's killer, about finding the man who had so dramatically altered her life. Used to calling the shots, she had definite opinions on how to pursue the case. Braddock wasn't necessarily in agreement. If she was going to tag along on the case it would be his way and on his terms. It was Type A versus Type A. They butted heads at the start.

But then, slowly, the two of them developed a mutual professional respect as they got to know one another. And as she discovered, he'd dealt with his own tragedy, the loss of his wife Meghan Hayes five years earlier to brain cancer, a woman a few years older than Tori that she remembered from Manchester Bay High School. They had that in common. And as the case progressed, she found that he was every bit as committed to finding her sister's killer as she was. That only fueled her attraction to him to the point where it was something she could and would no longer deny.

They solved the case.

They found her sister's killer.

And, in Braddock, she found someone who made her reevaluate her life.

He wanted her.

Lying in a hospital bed all shot up, Braddock had asked her to stay, to take a chance with him.

At first, she resisted, instead going back to New York and the FBI. She told herself she was no good at relationships. She'd never really had one. There had been men certainly. She had no trouble attracting them. But she never kept them around for long. She figured that was what she would go back to. It was the job. Finding abducted children, righting the wrong that she herself had suffered, was what had always sustained her.

But the job wasn't the same after solving Jessie's murder. The ghost of her sister no longer provided the drive that it had. The satisfaction her career had brought her, leading her to be one of the most, if not the most decorated female agent in the Bureau, was no longer enough. For the first time, she not only recognized but truly felt, deep down, the true loneliness and desolation of the life she had led. She didn't want that anymore. There was a desire and need for more and what she wanted most was Braddock. But if a relationship with Braddock was to succeed, she had to do some work first.

She finally took Tracy's advice and got herself some help. And after a few months of therapy and healing, she took a giant leap into the great unknown, resigning from the Bureau and moving back to Manchester Bay to give it a go with Braddock.

It was three years now.

She was back living in her hometown. And despite the fact she had essentially abandoned it for twenty years, it had welcomed her back with open arms. She had reconnected with many of her old friends who still lived here and had made many more new ones. Her life had never been fuller. As she looked at the photos of her and Braddock, along with Quinn, on the shelves, she felt a contentment she could no longer imagine living without. Now, she was a college professor, an occasional part-time investigator, a parent of sorts to Quinn, and there was Braddock, a man she knew loved her deeply, and that she loved in return. Shaking her head, she thought: *I love my life here.*

She opened a folder when her phone buzzed. Tracy Sheets.

"Special Agent Sheets, tell me, how is my goddaughter?"

* * *

Twenty minutes early, and with one last check in his rearview mirror, Braddock slowly drove up to the Halfway Highway Diner. Popular with the locals from Manchester Bay to the south and Holmstrand to the north, the parking lot was well populated on a Monday morning. Pulling in, he drove a slow loop through the U-shaped parking lot as it surrounded the diner, scrutinizing the license plates of each vehicle, checking if anyone was watching or perhaps lying in wait. Backing his truck into a parking slot, he spent a few minutes monitoring the lot checking if anyone pulled in or was watching from the boat dealership situated on the other side of the restaurant to the south.

All these precautions.

He wanted nothing to do with this, with any of this. It was in the past, abandoned, buried, done.

So, why are you here?

It was Julio's words.

"Malik once told me you were a stand-up guy, someone I could trust."

Was he? When he'd thought back to that time, he was far from it. He was in fact responsible for much of the bloodshed eight years ago. Something that had taken him many years to learn to live with.

He gave it another minute, chambered a round and took his time walking into the diner. From the host stand, he let his eyes make a discerning sweep of the restaurant. He didn't get a wave, a nod or glance from anyone.

"Morning, Will," Peggy, one of the regular hosts, greeted him. "How many?"

"Two, Peg." She was one of the few women he ran into that could look him in the eye. It was why regulars referred to her affectionately as Leggy Peggy, a term she had openly embraced. "I'm meeting someone. Can I have the booth in the far back left corner?"

"Sure," she said, grabbing two menus and walking to the last booth. It was near the door to the kitchen as well as an emergency exit. He took his seat, which allowed a view of the entire interior of the seating area. "Coffee?"

"Please."

A half-hour in, it was 8:15 a.m. and Julio still hadn't shown. He gave it a little more time, but Julio did not come through the front door.

Well, you did tell him you weren't coming. Maybe he listened. And Julio did say he might just show up at the office. Perhaps that was what awaited him. He dropped a ten-dollar bill on the table and left.

. . .

He drove to the government center. Nobody was in the waiting area. His office was empty. There were no new messages. Perhaps Julio was bluffing. Or maybe he hadn't yet shown up. Better yet, he'd simply left town after hearing no. That would be the best outcome.

He powered up his computer and went to work. There was a meeting with Boe where they discussed the budget. Neither of them was particularly proficient in the world of Excel spreadsheets, but between interpretations of the collectively bargained wage scale and projected needs, they managed to work through a draft of budget requests, wage increases and staffing needs in ninety minutes. After that he made the rounds to Eggs, Reese and Nolan to get updates on their various investigations.

"Where are we at on that girl who was found strangled in her family's cabin?" he inquired of Eggs. The two of them had worked on the investigation though he'd turned the running of it over to her.

"Nowhere really, boss. I've been talking to some students at the university. There was a big party a few days before she was killed at the cabin. I'm working through people who were there."

Steak stopped in to see everyone. He had two more weeks before he was released back to full duty, which he was keen to do.

"So, you're bored shitless?" Braddock said.

"Completely," he replied. "I never thought I'd say this, but I'm fished out, man."

"Itching to get back out there?"

"You know me. I'm a man of action and intrigue."

"I'll keep that in mind, super cop."

By 11:30 a.m. he had fished a black cherry flavored soda water out of the refrigerator and was back at his desk, absentmindedly clicking through email messages, while Julio, Malik,

Guerero, and other long dormant names and events swirled through his mind.

Tori came strolling in just after 12:00. "Tracy called," she said excitedly.

"Ahh, how are they doing?"

"Good. Talking about making it back out next summer. Baby Kate will be nearly two by then. A little easier to travel with."

"We'd love to have them."

"That's what I told her. As for lunch, I was thinking the food trucks down at the beach. This is their last week. They'll be gone after Labor Day."

"Works for me."

Braddock stood up when his radio buzzed from dispatch. It was Gustafson, one of the senior deputies in the department. "Will, I have a weird one. I'm at a place out deep in the woods northwest of town. It's a hunting cabin and it looks like the O.K. Corral out here."

"How many dead?"

"That's the thing. I've got blood, but no bodies."

"None?" Braddock said.

"Oh this," Tori replied with sudden enthusiastic curiosity, "I gotta see."

FOUR

"UNDER FIRE AND IN A BIG HURRY."

"A ghost crime scene," Tori said, almost gleefully. "How wonderfully... bizarre."

"I'm so pleased you're entertained," Braddock said, a bit more sanguine about matters. "You get to take a look at it, see if it piques your all-important interest and decide if you'll deign to let it interrupt your leisurely summer schedule. Me? I have to do something with it."

"That's why you get paid the big bucks, boss man."

"Big bucks. Good one," Braddock said and then shifted his eyes to her. "Of course, when you're making up your recent absence to me tonight, I'm thinking you should work in a 'boss man.'"

"Hah!" Tori laughed, slapping him on the arm. "I'll see what I can do. So, boss man, where is this mystery murder scene again?"

"We're going northwest of town twelve, thirteen miles. It's a hunting cabin of some kind. It's set back in the woods a good bit. Pretty remote."

Tori looked up the location on the map app on her phone. "Huh, you're right, it's back there a stretch. Barely visible overhead. There are just a few big ponds nearby." She tweezed the satellite closer. "Not many other structures, let alone cabins or homes nearby."

Braddock made a few turns steering his way northwest on ever narrower paved roads to finally find a Shepard County Sheriff's Explorer parked across a gravel driveway entrance, crime scene tape fluttering with the light midday breeze. Right behind them were Eggleston, Reese and Nolan.

"Will, this is a new one on me," Deputy Steve Gustafson said, scratching the back of his head.

"Who called this in?"

"Septic guy. He pumps the system here once annually, always in August, so he just showed up because it was on his schedule today. He turned into the driveway, got about a hundred feet in, saw the cabin was all shot up and had the good sense to stop, back out, and call 911. I took a statement from him and have his contact information if we need to talk to him."

"And what did you find?"

"There are shell casings about halfway down the driveway on both sides. There is a noticeable blood pool in the driveway near the cabin and then you just have to look inside. All kinds of weirdness in there. There are also fresh tire tracks in the soft soil of the driveway. We had those big thunderstorms on Saturday night. It was still moist and damp around here yesterday, given all the shade. Might get tire impressions out of it all."

"Do we know who the owner is?" Braddock asked.

"Lucas Fraser is the listed owner. He lives in Proctor by Duluth. I mean, this is a hunting shack, albeit one with plumbing and electricity, but a hunting shack nonetheless."

Braddock turned to Reese. "Call this Fraser guy and see if he's alive. And if so, then see if he can explain what the heck happened here."

"On it," Reese said. "Come on, Gus," and the two of them walked back to Gustafson's patrol Explorer.

Braddock looked to his crew and gestured for Eggs and Nolan to take the right side. He and Tori took the left. "Let's go slow."

As they deliberately walked the driveway, a one-story cabin came into view ahead in something of a clearing. The large front bay window was shot out, and bullet holes riddled the cabin's wood siding.

"Shell casings here," Tori said, just to the left of the driveway. She stepped ahead. "And then a couple more here." She crouched at the second set of casings and then glanced at a nearby tree. *What was that?* Tori had a small flashlight with her and put the beam on the lower trunk of the tree, a small wood spike jutting out.

"This might be blood here?" Tori said, focusing the flashlight on the discoloration on the tree.

"Could be," Braddock agreed, looking over her shoulder.

"Casings over here too," Eggs said, gesturing with her police radio antenna.

"Look like nine millimeters," Nolan added.

"Two shooters from here," Tori said to Braddock. "And given the appearance of the exterior of the cabin, that's where they were shooting."

Braddock stood with hands on hips, scanning the scene. "Let's move ahead but stay to the side. I see what Gus was talking about. There are some fresh tire treads on the driveway. We might want to get molds of them."

Walking along the left-side of the driveway, Tori crept ahead and caught the reflection of sunlight off more shell casings spread about in the loose sandy gravel of the driveway to the left of the cabin. As she and Braddock approached, there was the area Gustafson had mentioned, a small patch of discoloration in the mixture of gravel and sandy dirt.

"It could be blood," Braddock said, crouched a few feet from the reddish smudges in the dirt.

"And plenty of brass right here too," Tori observed. "Based on these tread marks, a vehicle was parked here."

Braddock nodded.

"The treads seem fresh, and they swing to the right through the grass and then back out the driveway, out toward the county road." There were several shell casings to the left of the blood-stain. "This person was shooting back down the driveway," she said, crouching, miming the act of shooting. "Gun fight."

"Using the vehicle for cover," Braddock added. "If there were two shooters back up the driveway, this shooter had a reasonable field of fire and cover, if the car was here."

"If he used the vehicle for cover, I'm guessing there's one out there somewhere with some holes in it."

"And perhaps a couple of people with holes in them too," he said as he stood up and glanced to the cabin. "Let's get a look inside."

Braddock stepped into the grass to the left of the cabin.

"Braddock," Tori said, reaching for his arm. "What do you make of that?"

There were another set of tire tracks running through the thick grass to the left of the cabin and then around the end of it.

"The grass is matted. Looks fresh too."

"There was a lot going on here," Tori mused, "and we haven't been inside yet."

A rectangular deck ran the length of the back of the cabin, with a crude firepit marked by a circle of rocks thirty feet to the left. Braddock and Tori stepped up onto the deck, between the old black gas grill and aged-wood picnic table. With her gloved right hand, Tori pulled open the screen rear door. Braddock nudged the back door open with his right foot. They both slipped blue covers on their shoes and Braddock followed Tori inside.

They had entered the kitchen area where there was a sink, small counter and wide white refrigerator and a separate freezer. Behind the kitchen there was what looked like a bedroom, then a bathroom and then another bedroom. Further ahead was an open area with a mismatched mix of well-used couches and chairs.

The large front picture window that looked out to the driveway was shot out. Bullet holes punctured the walls and kitchen cabinets. Shards of window glass, sheetrock and paneling lay everywhere and on everything.

"That... looks gruesome," Braddock said as he walked toward the picture window but kept back several feet. There was a blood pool and several droplets on the floor in front of and to the left of the picture window. A large blood splatter marked the wall to the left of the window about three feet up from the floor. Even from ten feet away, he could see that mixed into the blood was other... matter.

"Yet, we don't have a body—"

"But clearly one *was* right there," Tori said. "And dealt with." She nodded to the bedroom. "Come see this."

He walked over to the bedroom door. In the bedroom, by the left bunk bed, there was a small pink suitcase. "I'd say that's for a girl, probably pretty young," Tori said, holding up a small red sleeveless girl's top and then one of the dolls. "Look next door."

In the other bedroom there were two duffel bags, one with men's clothes and the other, women's clothes. They quickly searched each duffel bag but there was no identifying information in either one. "Anything else?" Braddock said.

"In the kitchen there was a large Ziploc bag. Inside were two smaller sandwich bags, one with small round pink tablets and the other with small vials of clear liquid and syringes. I'd suspect it's prescription medication of some kind."

"So, what happened here?" Braddock muttered. He looked at the picture window and the wall to the left. "The attack comes from up the driveway, where we came in. At least two men. And I'd say the blood spot on the wall was at least one of their targets."

Tori agreed. "I'm thinking he was badly wounded such that when the shooters came inside here, they just finished him off. He was resting against that wall, and they shot him in the head. Slug might be in the sheetrock."

"That's one dead body, then," Braddock said. "But we've got shell casings in here, so our man here was firing back. Firing back up the driveway." He edged up to the picture window. "Check this out?"

Tori joined him and looked to their right out the window. "You can't see that other blood spot in the driveway. I don't think he would have an angle on that guy, would he?"

"No," Braddock said. "Our guy here couldn't have fired where that other car was parked. Not from here anyway. He could have from the side door."

"No shell casings over there though."

"Was he friend or foe?"

"I'm thinking friend," Tori said. "So, it was two on two, and they were what? Providing cover for—"

Braddock and Tori looked at each other then headed back out the door, going over to the tracks they had noticed in the grass outside.

"These treads," Tori said. "They're fresh."

"And they were hightailing it," he noted, gesturing to the end of the cabin, the hard turn to the right in the grass that churned up dirt and mud. "As if they were—"

"Under fire and in a big hurry."

They followed the tracks around the house.

"Look at that," Tori said.

The tracks swerved hard left, to the very edge of the driveway, toward where they'd found one grouping of shell casings. A tree was damaged, bark peeled away.

"Is it me or does it look like the driver tried to take out one of the shooters with the car," he said. "Scraped the tree."

"What has me perplexed is the other vehicle at the other blood marking," Tori mused. "Where did *that* shooter end up? Where is *that* vehicle? I mean it sure looks like they were hit too."

Braddock nodded and walked back to examine that blood pool again. It was between there and the cabin. If he looked close enough, there were some sporadic light shoe tread marks coming from the woods. "I wonder."

"What?" Tori said.

He walked to the treeline and peered in for a moment and then saw a freshly fractured tree branch and a half-tread mark, a heel print in a small patch of mud and then, there it was. A glint, a narrow ray of sunlight fighting through the dense tree cover reflecting off brass. "Check this out."

Tori crouched and saw them. Two shell casings. "There was a third shooter?"

"Came through the woods to here. Two come down the driveway and this third man makes a flanking move through the woods to come in from behind."

"Our guy behind the car firing up the driveway—"

"Never saw our third shooter coming. I'm betting he's dead."

"But you know who perhaps isn't," Tori started. "If you found blood back up the driveway by those shell casings, then perhaps he was hit as well, though not as mortally as it looks like the man in the cabin and this man right here probably were. If he made it out alive, he needed treatment somewhere."

Braddock straightened up.

"Nolan!"

"Yeah, boss."

"Start checking area hospitals a couple of hours in every direction. See if any victims showed with unexplained GSWs."

"On it," Nolan said as she pulled out her cell phone.

"Eggs," Braddock called.

"Forensics from the BCA?"

"ASAP."

Braddock looked out and Reese was waving for them. He, Tori and Eggleston made their way to him.

"What do you have?"

"Lucas Fraser on the phone," Reese replied, holding up his cell phone.

"Mr. Fraser," Reese started. "I'm with Chief Detective Braddock from the county and an investigator, Tori Hunter."

"I'm just shocked by what your man just told me," Fraser said. "It's all shot up?"

"Yes, sir," Braddock replied. "Did you know it was being used?"

"Yes. A friend called me late last Friday night and asked me if he could use it. I told him it was just a hunting shack basically, though it has power and water but it's not on a real lake or anything, just a couple of ponds. It wasn't a place to vacation by any stretch."

"Your friend have a name?" Tori asked.

"Hector Ramirez."

Braddock froze.

Hector Ramirez.

Wasn't that the name Julio Gonzalez said he was going by now? "You knew me as Julio Gonzalez, but now I go by Hector Ramirez." *Isn't that what Julio said?*

He looked back at the cabin. There was that massive blood spatter inside on the wall.

"Braddock?"

Would that explain why he didn't show this morning?

"Braddock..."

Is that what happened to him? But if so, who was the other man? Julio never mentioned any other names. Or a woman, or daughter. What was this man's role and who were the at least three other men who attacked the cabin? And where were they now?

"*Braddock!*"

"Uh, what?"

"Are you okay?" Tori asked, touching him on the shoulder. "Hey, what's going on in there?"

"Umm... nothing."

"It was like you blanked out there for a minute. We got this guy on the phone."

"Sorry, no, no. I'm good, just thinking about... what the heck happened out here is all. It's—"

"Weird, I get it." Tori stepped in. "Mr. Fraser, did this Hector tell you why he wanted to use the place?"

"Umm." There was a pause.

"Mr. Fraser?" Tori pressed. "What is it?"

"I've worked with Hector a few years."

"And?"

"He's a good guy, hard worker, reliable, never missed a day of work that I could ever recall, and not a bad dude to grab a beer with either."

"I sense a 'but' there."

"Yeah. Well... I think he has something of a past that he didn't want to talk about."

"Why do you say that?"

"Because, whenever talk of life *before* Superior came up, he'd just talk about something else. I'd ask him about where he was from and he'd just say lots of places, but he'd never get specific."

"He was hiding something."

"Or he just didn't want to talk about it. It was a no-go zone with him. When he called on Friday, he sounded desperate.

Specifically asked to use my hunting cabin by Manchester Bay for a couple of days. It was totally out of the blue. It did have me wondering a bit and I was hesitant to say yes, but he said he really needed it."

"And he didn't tell you why?"

"I asked if everything was alright and he just said, I need to use the cabin. He was insistent. I should have said no."

"He said the cabin by Manchester Bay. Do you own other ones?" Tori asked.

"No. But I do remember he was highly interested in the fact that my cabin was near Manchester Bay for some reason. I figured his interest was because Manchester Bay meant a lake cabin, so I was clear with him that it was a hunting place, not a lake place. I said that on Friday too, it was a hunting cabin. My family has owned and hunted that land for generations, and we've built the cabin up over the years."

"But you don't know why he was so interested in using it?"

"No."

"Do you know if he was married?"

"Yes. Wife, Ana. He has a daughter too. Have you tried to call him?"

Tori and Braddock looked over to Gustafson and Reese. "I've tried," Gustafson said. "Goes right to voicemail. I'll keep trying."

"Mr. Fraser," Braddock asked. "Do you have his wife's phone number?"

"I don't."

"And he lived in Superior, Wisconsin?"

"Yes," Fraser responded. "Or at least I think so. I never went to where he lived. The refinery would have his address information. We worked at the refinery there."

They spoke with Fraser another couple of minutes, confirming the information and then let him go.

A jumble of thoughts swirled through Braddock's mind.

What the heck had happened? And why now, and of all places, here? And what was coming next?

"Confounding... is it... not?"

He turned to Tori. "What?"

"What happened here. It's odd. I mean all the blood yet no bodies. Tire tracks, no vehicles. This Hector guy with a past he wouldn't talk about. Very mysterious."

His mind was racing a million miles an hour suddenly. All he could muster was, "Yeah, you could say that."

"Yeah, it's a weird one, for sure," Tori said, but then offered a sly smile, a twinkle in her eye. "But... an interesting weird one. Now that we have a name, and we know Hector has a wife and daughter that are missing, I think I should jump in. I want to jump in."

Braddock closed his eyes, a sick pit feeling in his stomach. He wasn't sure he wanted Tori so enthused. He knew something she didn't know. There was a very good chance things were going to get worse.

Much worse.

FIVE

"DIAL IT IN HERE."

Braddock checked his watch. 4:42 p.m. He and Tori were leaning against his Tahoe, observing the BCA's forensics officers working while a hundred different thoughts cycled in his mind.

How was he going to handle this?

Would he have to handle this?

Could he just bury it?

Should he?

Was there more to come?

Quinn popped into his mind. He stepped away from Tori, walked across the county road, stepping sideways to avoid a crossing silver sedan, and placed a call to Roger Hayes. Now mostly retired, he and Mary were watching Quinn and his cousins today as they often did in the summer when they were on break from school. However, their watching was pretty loose given the boys' age, growing ability and desire to roam, not to mention the existence of cell phones to track them.

"Afternoon," Roger greeted. "Saw you on your swim this morning. You kind of left Tori in the dust."

"I did?"

Roger guffawed. "Yeah. She got to the dock, and you just bolted. Tori and I shared a good laugh about it."

"I didn't realize that. I'm sure I'll hear about it from her at some point."

"I bet you will. So, what's up? You catch a case?"

"Yeah, and it could be... complicated. Tori is helping."

"And you'll be working it late, I'm sure," Rog said, having received the call so many times it was old hat and came with Braddock as a son-in-law. "We're wide-open tonight. No worries."

"I appreciate it." And he did. They and their son Drew and his wife Andrea helped often. "Can you do me a favor? Keep a good eye on Quinn if you would."

"Uh, sure. Any particular reason?" Roger asked.

Don't freak him out. Give him a reason, a believable reason. "It's just... Boomer. He has the dog with him, and at times he forgets that he does. Quinn wanted the dog, and the deal is he needs to be responsible for him. He can't just go running off without thinking about him. So just have him stay close with him."

"Oh, we like watching the dog too. Boomer is lying at my feet right now, chewing on a new toy Mary bought him." And they did love the dog. Boomer was like another grandkid. They'd be happy to watch the dog and let the boys run wild and free.

"I know, Rog, but Quinn needs to be responsible for him, so don't let him off the hook, if you know what I mean. He should stick around and be responsible for *his* dog."

"Sure," Roger replied breezily. "That we can do. I'll *remind* Quinn of that when we sit down for supper here in a bit. I'm throwing burgers on the grill. Any chance you two could join?"

"Doubtful."

"Well, let us know how it goes."

"Will do."

Roger dropped off. Braddock dialed another number. Steak answered on the second ring. "Where are you?"

"Sitting on my patio, drinking a beer. Perks of not being in the field with you guys."

"I need a favor. And if need be, get Cal to help and one other thing."

"What's that?"

"You can't tell Tori." He explained what he needed from Steak who had several questions he was reluctant to answer beyond saying he needed a favor. "Just trust me on this, I need you to do a little easy watching. I'll compensate you, somehow."

"And she's not aware of any of this?" Steak said. "Are you suspicious of her for some reason."

"No."

"Someone coming after her, or... you?"

"I'm the one asking, what do you think?"

"You then. Why? Who?"

"Just do this for me and keep it between the two of us. When I have a few more minutes, I'll explain it. For now, I just need you to do it."

Steak sighed. "I'm on it. I do hope you know what you're doing though."

"That makes two of us." He dropped the call and took a long cleansing breath. *Do I know what I'm doing?*

"*Braddock!*" Tori hollered from the other side of the road.

"Uh... yeah."

"What's the plan here?" she said, looking at him quizzically.

Act normal. Run it like normal. That's what you should do anyway. Maybe it ends up being nothing. He could allow himself that hope.

"What is with you today?" she said, turning to him, giving him an evaluative look.

"What?"

Tori tilted her head. "You seem distracted. Dial it in here."

She wasn't wrong but he didn't want her digging into why. "I can tell you have something on *your* mind, what?" he asked.

"It's more like I have questions about our ghost scene here."

"Such as?"

"The woman and child."

"What about them?"

"Why not call the police? If they got away from here, why not call us for help, assistance, protection?" Tori pursed her lips. "I don't get that part. She has a young child. If she did get away, then call us for help. Tell us what happened."

"Guilt," Braddock said after a minute, thinking it all through. "Maybe she was in on it too."

"In on what?"

"Whatever it was that went down here. If she calls, then she has to explain it. Her actions suggest she's guilty of... something."

"If she drove that car away, explain trying to take out one of the shooters?"

Braddock took a moment. "I can't. What do you think happened here?"

"I see a scene like this, this shoot-out, I instantly think drugs," Tori said. "I didn't see any evidence of drugs in there, other than that Ziploc bag of tablets and syringes which looked like medication, not illicit drugs. I'm sure the BCA will figure out what that all is, but I don't see this as a drug sale, do you?"

"I foreclose nothing at this point."

"If we assume the woman and the child got in the car behind the cabin, I can interpret the tire marks as suggesting she tried to mow down one of the shooters. If she tried to do that, again, why not call us?"

"Maybe she didn't get away like we think," Braddock replied. "They could have chased her down. The shooters got her somehow. They had a vehicle. Maybe someone gave chase, caught them and they suffered the same fate as everyone else."

"That's... entirely possible," Tori said, resignation in her voice. "That little girl's suitcase, the clothes suggest she was really young, Braddock. How do you kill someone so... innocent? How?"

They had both seen that very thing happen in their careers, but that it always seemed so senseless hadn't stopped them from still asking how or why. "If that happened, it would explain no call but let's not get ahead of ourselves just yet. The reality is, we don't know anything for certain."

"You doubt what we're seeing here? How this went down?"

Braddock shook his head. "No. I think our general read of what happened here is on the money. We just don't know the who or the why or what happened in the aftermath of it all."

"We know Hector."

"We have a name, we think, of a guy with an unknown past if Fraser is to be believed. Beyond that, we don't know anything else... yet."

Tori pondered that for a moment. "We don't."

"Exactly. Let's take another look around here." He started slowly walking down the driveway toward the cabin. "It's weird, but we don't even know when this all went down other than probably sometime last night. They park somewhere along the road back there. Two men come up the driveway, the third makes a flanking move to come in around the back."

"Thick woods," Tori said.

"Navigable, though. Let's assume Hector was inside the cabin. Yet—" he held up two fingers "—there were two vehicles outside the cabin and they're both gone. Let's say the woman and child go out the back door and flee in one vehicle. Who is this *other* person?"

"We don't know who any of these people are," Tori said, turning to him. "Do we?"

We really don't, he thought, although if this Hector was Julio, he knew something of his background. And if it was him, he had a vague idea of the kind of people that were after him and why, but he needed some time to think about all that. "Given where we think the car was located and the location of the shell casings, they were firing back up the driveway, at the two that were approaching. And this person popped off a bunch of rounds."

"It left us with two blood spots. People were wounded. But not so wounded they couldn't get away. Or..."

"Or?"

Tori walked down the driveway, toward the cabin and the area marked off where there was a blood pool. "The third shooter you discovered. He shoots what we'll call Hector's friend here. Does Hector's friend get away? Or."

"Is he done," he said. "What then?"

"The woman and child get away, *we think*," Tori says.

"We don't know that."

"For now, assume they did. But this guy here, he didn't. I think he's dead. The attackers, the two who aren't wounded as far as we know, throw Hector's friend into this car and drive this one and their own away. But this guy here?"

Braddock nodded. "Yeah. He's likely dead. Or."

"Or?"

"Not dead, but they took him away from here to find out what he knew."

"About what?"

He shrugged. "About whatever it is this Hector was mixed up in," Braddock said, his phone buzzing. "Boe." He tapped his screen. "Jeanette, what's up?"

"Get down to the boat launch just north of Fort Ripley."

"Why?"

"Submerged car. Hasn't been in the water long. The water rescue diver says he doesn't see a body inside, but the exterior has a bunch of bullet holes in it. I'm thinking it relates to your crime scene."

SIX

"WE MAY HAVE A BIGGER PROBLEM."

Shepard County wasn't a particularly wide county, but it was a tall one with Manchester Bay set in the middle. To the north of town, it was lakes and forests with limited broad open spaces. South of town lakes and forested areas started to give way to broader stretches of pasture and farms. The hunting cabin crime scene was in the densely wooded far northwest corner of the county. The Fort Ripley boat launch was in the flat open far southwest corner.

Fort Ripley itself was a small town of eighty-four residents that rested between the H-4 and the Mississippi River. The town, which was marked by a gas station, convenience store and bar on the west side of the highway, was situated just north of Camp Ripley, a military base for the Minnesota National Guard.

It took forty minutes for them to cover the distance to the boat launch. Braddock turned right off the highway and then made a quick left onto a road, the waters of the Mississippi intermittently visible through the dense foliage to the right until they reached a clearing where there was a rough gravel parking lot for the boat launch. Braddock parked in the boat launch area, and they walked down to the end of the road where all the emergency vehicles were parked.

What would this lead to?

That was the question uppermost in Braddock's mind. If this was their vehicle, they would be able to trace it and that would give them something.

Was it something he wanted?

"Well, would you look at who is here," Tori said happily.

A familiar face awaited their arrival.

"Frewer, you're back," Tori called to the angular deputy who'd been severely injured a year ago while engaged in a police chase. She and Braddock had pulled him from his over-turned SUV before it exploded in a ball of fire.

"Greetings, Tori," Frewer said, his smile bright beneath his full mustache.

"What do we have?" Braddock asked.

"A few hours ago, an Apache helicopter from Camp Ripley on a training run was making passes over the river. They saw the car just beneath the surface over there on the point. County Water Rescue was called, and they launched. I strolled down here for a look-see." He walked them over to a hill. "See these tracks through the foliage here?"

Braddock and Tori nodded.

"I think whoever dumped it shoved it down the hill here and figured she'd float away, or at least go to the bottom."

The waters of the Mississippi had been elevated all year from the combination of a heavy winter snowfall, a wetter than normal spring and the recent spate of severe weather that had dumped inches of rain across North and Central Minnesota, much of which found its way into the Mississippi as it meandered its way in a wide looping arc through the center of the state to Manchester Bay, where it then started its course to the south. The area they were standing in was low-lying and had briefly flooded in the spring. The river's current was visibly strong, racing by them.

"Frew, it's usually fairly shallow through here, isn't it?" Braddock asked. "They shut the launch down last year for a couple of months because the water was so low."

"You wouldn't know it to see the current and flow right now, but that's right. In a normal summer, six, eight, maybe ten feet through here would be common. The depth is probably closer to fifteen to seventeen feet right now," Frewer said. "You think that car is related to your thing up at that hunting cabin?"

"Could be," Tori said.

Braddock agreed. "Boe told me that the diver who went down for a look reported it was riddled with bullet holes. And that the car hadn't been in the water for long. We know there was at least one if not two other vehicles at that scene last night. This could be one of them."

A large tow truck, with a big winch and thick cabling, rumbled down the road, followed by a flatbed truck from the BCA. The rescue divers came ashore and with the tow truck driver and BCA officer, discussed the options and logistics of pulling the submerged vehicle to shore.

"This is going to take a while," Frewer said under his breath. "Long way from where it is to the shore here."

While the recovery operation was put into motion, Braddock and Tori called Eggleston back at the government center. "This is going to take some time out here to get the car out of the river," Braddock said. "What do you have?"

Eggleston started with Reese.

"Lucas Fraser checks out," Reese said. "He's a third-generation owner of the land, inherited it from his father. He's worked at the refinery in Superior for fifteen years where he is considered a great employee according to his manager. Fraser is married, has two teenaged kids, owns his own home in Proctor, and has no criminal record."

"Solid citizen then," Tori said.

"That's my read," Reese replied. "If you ask me, he reluctantly did a friend a solid and his hunting cabin turned into a target range."

"But why *that* cabin? Why Manchester Bay? Why was this Hector so keen to get here?"

"We might have a reason why," Eggs said. "Fraser had a point."

"Which is?"

"As best as Eggs and I can tell," Nolan added, "prior to four years ago when he emerges in Superior, Hector Ramirez did *not* exist."

"Say what?" Tori said.

"He, and his wife Ana, and daughter Emma, they did not exist," Nolan said. "The social security number he used for employment doesn't match to any Hector Ramirez with Social Security. His wife worked at a memory care facility and her social security number does not match such a name either."

"Are they here illegally?" Braddock pondered.

"That was our first thought," Eggs replied. "However, I think they changed their identities for other reasons which might explain why they wanted to use Fraser's cabin. What Fraser didn't know was that on Friday afternoon, the law showed up at the refinery looking for Hector Ramirez."

"Immigration and Customs?" Tori asked. "Was he fleeing deportation?"

"Not ICE, police. A Superior police detective along with a detective from the NYPD."

"NYPD?" Tori snapped a look at Braddock in surprise. "Odd. Do we know the NYPD detective's name?"

"No, not yet," Eggs answered. "I have the Superior officer's name, and I left him a message. Problem is that he's on vacation up in the Boundary Waters Canoe Area now. He left Sunday morning. As you know, cell coverage up there is generally non-existent. We'll get the name I'm sure, I just don't have it right yet. We're waiting on a call back from Superior PD."

Tori turned to Braddock. "I've been wondering why his wife hasn't called the police. It's either because she's already dead, or could it be that she too is running from something?"

"Assuming she's running," Reese said. "She could have been in on it and skedaddled with the rest of them after the firefight. She's with them, hence no call."

"Nah, if she's alive, she's running," Tori said.

"How can you know?"

"She left both suitcases," Braddock said. "And the medication—if it was medication in those vials."

"That's a... thought," Tori said. "Gives me the kernel of an idea."

"Say I buy all that," Reese said. "That she fled or is still on the run if she got away from this, isn't she better off calling us. Why not call... some form of law enforcement somewhere?"

"Because she fears it for some reason," Braddock said. "Her husband ran from it on Friday. She's running from it now."

"And, what's more," Tori interjected, "if we don't know what their history is beyond four years ago, we don't yet know what their history is with the police. We have no idea what they did or did not do. But the answer isn't in the last four years when their last name was Ramirez. It's before that." She paused for a moment. "This just gets more peculiar by the minute."

* * *

They had cruised out to the cabin in the late afternoon, curious if the scene had been discovered. To their consternation, it had. Even more of a surprise was seeing Braddock. Vooch almost hit him when he stepped into the road and then back. They were lucky not to be stopped and questioned. He imagined the police would be questioning anyone they could.

"Christ, that was close," Vooch said, peering up in the rearview mirror. "He didn't see us, did he?"

"He was looking at his phone, plus he doesn't know you or I anyway," Boo said, watching the reflection of the passenger side mirror. "But all the same, let's not linger."

They didn't linger. Instead, they observed from a healthy distance. When Braddock and Hunter left the scene, they'd followed, at first out of curiosity, then later out of rising concern as they ventured south of Manchester Bay on the H-4. When they saw them turn into the boat launch, Boo groaned. "How did they find this so fast?"

Now, they crouched in the woods on the west side of the river, fighting off the mosquitos while watching the recovery operation.

"This," Vooch muttered, "could be a problem."

"Yeah," Boo replied angrily. "A big one."

* * *

Frewer had made a run to the convenience store in Fort Ripley, a mile to the south, and returned with sodas that he passed out. It was fully dark now and the mosquitos had started attacking them from all angles. Frewer had bug spray and Braddock and Tori sprayed up.

"A shower will be in order," Tori said, spitting out the spray from when she doused her head. "I can't sleep with this stuff on me or... in me. *Ick.*"

Portable lights brightly illuminated the dark roiling waters of the Mississippi, the cables from the crane on the tow truck disappearing beneath the surface. Two divers were pulled up into a sheriff's department boat, took off their masks and gave thumbs up to the tow truck operator.

"Here we go," the operator said as he dropped a gear shift.

The crane groaned to life, the cables slowly grinding in retraction.

A diver had previously explained that the front end of the car had caught on a sandbar and was resting perpendicular to the shoreline they were all standing on. As a result, when the cables began to retract, the rear of the sedan had to be pulled sideways off the sandbar and then would be pulled along the riverbed to the shore. It took fifteen minutes before the back end of the tan sedan began to emerge slowly out of the dark water. Another ten and they had it up the hill and on the road.

Braddock and Tori stepped over to the right to inspect the passenger side of the car.

"There you go," Braddock said, running the beam of his flashlight along the side of the car. There were several bullet holes, concentrated on the rear quarter panel of the tan Chevy Malibu with a Minnesota license plate that he jotted down. "I think this was the car parked by the blood pool to the left of the cabin."

"Agreed," Tori said as she looked in the passenger compartment, scanning with her flashlight. The interior was light gray fabric. The BCA officer and Braddock peered inside as well.

"Huh," Braddock murmured and zeroed his flashlight beam in on the upper back seat. "A big patch of discoloration there. A stain?"

"It could be blood," the BCA officer said, peering closer before taking a photo and then carefully opening the door. "We'll have to take some samples at the lab to see."

"If it's blood, wouldn't the water wash away DNA?" Tori asked.

"Most likely. But if it's only been in there a day or two, maybe we'll get lucky, though I wouldn't hold my breath."

"And we also have a couple of blood patches back at the hunting cabin scene as well, so maybe something to work with there too."

"I'll go run the plate," Frewer said.

The tow truck operator removed the cables from the car, and the flatbed truck called by the BCA went about putting its own cables under the front axle. Ready to pull it up onto the tipped flatbed, that driver hollered, "Stand clear."

The car tilted back, and the winch pulled it up.

Thump! Thump!

"What was that?" Braddock exclaimed. "*Stop! Stop!* That was the trunk, right?"

"I think so," Tori said and turned to the BCA officer who carefully opened the driver's side door and hit the trunk latch.

With his gloved right index finger, Braddock lifted the corner of the trunk hood to reveal two male bodies stuffed inside. "Oh boy."

One male had his back to them, lying almost face down on the trunk floor. He was mostly bald, had a certain width to him and was wearing a dark sport coat and khaki slacks. There were two visible bullet holes in the lower back of the sport coat. The other male looked Hispanic. While also a bit roundish, he was shorter than the other man, with shoulder-length hair and a full thick beard.

The BCA officer took some quick photos. "I'll need to call the medical examiner."

Braddock pulled his cell phone. Eggleston had sent him and Tori a DMV photo of Hector Ramirez. In the photo Ramirez had longish hair swept back and a more neatly trimmed but full beard. His height was listed as five-foot-eight and weight two hundred pounds.

It had been years since Braddock had seen a picture of Julio Gonzalez, who had neither long hair nor a beard back then, but he'd felt a hint of familiarity when he saw Hector's photo. Peering into the trunk, his flashlight on the man's face, he knew that was who he was looking at.

"That's Hector Ramirez," Tori said. "Who is the other man? Can we look quick?"

The BCA officer took a few more photos. "I want to be careful not to disturb too much."

Braddock's phone buzzed. It was Boe. "Jeanette. We have the sedan out. There are two dead bodies in the trunk—"

"We may have a bigger problem."

"Which is?"

"You remember that the Superior cop showed up at the refinery with an NYPD detective? I just got a call from the NYPD."

"Hang one second," Braddock said.

The BCA officer pulled the man's upper torso back so they could glimpse his face. He'd been shot in the head. Yet, despite that, Braddock instantly realized their bigger problem. The body had the pale white pallor of a dead man but the second he saw that big bushy mustache, he knew.

Tori peeked inside and her eyes went wide in recognition. "I've seen him before. That mustache. He's a cop, isn't he?"

"Jeanette," Braddock said. "Let me guess. The NYPD is looking for Detective Ray Lange."

"Uh... yeah, how do you know?"

"Because I'm looking right at him."

SEVEN

"WE EXCHANGED UNPLEASANT WORDS."

The speed run back to Manchester Bay and Boe's house took fifteen minutes. While Braddock drove, Tori did an Internet search on Ray Lange. She was quiet for several minutes, reading and then re-tapping on her phone, murmuring to herself as she often did, but not really saying anything. Usually, he'd let her finish.

"You're killing me here," he said. "What are you finding?"

"A year ago, he was quoted in the *Times* as detective on a murder the Cold Case Squad had solved. So, if I had to guess, he was with the NYPD Cold Case Squad. Maybe you want to call some old contacts and find out what he was up to."

"I suspect we'll find out in very short order what he was investigating and why he was here."

They arrived at Boe's house. She was waiting for them on her front steps. "You're sure it's Lange?" Boe pressed for confirmation as she let them inside the house and led them to the kitchen.

"It's him," Braddock said. "Frewer ran the license plate. The car was rented at the Minneapolis-St. Paul International

Airport to a Ray Lange with a Brooklyn, New York address. That, plus, well, Tori recognized him too. Who from NYPD called?"

"Coleman White, Commander of the Cold Case Squad. You know him?"

"By reputation only. Solid guy. Did he say why Lange was here?"

"Only that Lange and his partner with the Cold Case Squad were working a case in conjunction with Internal Affairs. How was he killed?"

"He had two bullet holes in his lower back, two in his chest and then he was finished off with one to the forehead from what I suspect was close range," Braddock answered.

"Executed."

"Looks like it."

"We think he was our other man at the scene last night," Tori stated. "We think he was firing on whoever was approaching that cabin but didn't see or sense a third man coming up from behind."

"What do you think? Did the shooter know he was a cop?" Boe asked. "A detective with the NYPD?"

"I don't know but one might suspect that was the case," Braddock said. "The killers didn't leave his or Ramirez's body behind. Those bodies were not supposed to be found. They pushed that car into the river and hoped it would go to the bottom and disappear but that tells us one other thing."

"What's that?"

"The shooters weren't local," Tori said.

"Why not?"

"Because if they were, they would have known dumping the car in the river at that particular spot was a bad idea," Braddock said. "The water is too shallow there. The Mississippi River is up this year but most years, that is a shallower stretch of the river. Not a good spot if you're trying to make a car disappear. If it wasn't found this summer, it gets found next year."

"That and it was right next to a military installation where helicopters operate frequently," Tori added.

"And that tells you what?" Boe said.

"Whoever these guys were, they were desperate to dump the bodies quick and get out of Dodge."

"We think one of them might have been wounded as well," Braddock added. "We've been checking, but at least so far no unexplained gunshot wounds showed up at hospitals within a hundred miles. We might have to broaden that search."

"If it was even needed. Maybe they tended to him themselves, or dumped that body too if he was dead," Boe said as she retrieved three cold beers from the refrigerator. Braddock twisted the tops off all of them.

"Did either of you know Lange?" Boe asked.

"I knew him well enough to say hello at the bar or a police function," Braddock said before taking a long swig of the light beer. "I don't ever recall working a case with him."

"Tori?"

"Less so than him," she said, taking a drink of her own. "I worked with a lot of NYPD officers over the years. Lange was assigned to a case I was working on maybe a year before I came back here. He had a fully shaved head but a big wide bushy mustache, so he was a little hard to forget in that sense—easy to recognize him lying there in that trunk."

Boe turned to Braddock. "Is there any reason he'd know you were here? That he could have reached out to you? You were a detective with the NYPD."

"It wasn't a secret where I went when I left New York, but I've been gone a long time now."

"What are you driving at, sheriff?" Tori said.

"Why don't we know Lange is here?" Boe said. "As law

enforcement, you go into someone else's jurisdiction, you call, right? We do, all the time." She looked at Braddock. "It couldn't have gone completely unnoticed in New York that a decorated former NYPD officer was recently awarded the Presidential Medal of Valor. Or that said recipient is my chief detective. Yet, despite all that, the NYPD doesn't call me or you to tell us that they're here investigating. And that's after they extended that courtesy to the police in Superior, but not here."

"There is something a bit ripe about this," Tori said, agreeing with Boe's unstated assertion. "Don't *you* think?" she asked Braddock.

They weren't wrong. He nodded in agreement.

Tori gestured to Boe. "Cold Case and IA is a bit of an odd mix."

"Agreed."

"We need to ask NYPD *what* Lange was working on," Braddock said. "And then you can ask *why* we weren't called."

"We'll be asking them tomorrow afternoon," Boe said. "Two officers are on a flight in the morning to Minneapolis and then are driving up here. I imagine they'll be here by mid-afternoon."

"Who are they sending?" Braddock said warily before taking a drink of his beer.

"The Chief of Internal Affairs, Ira Renko."

"Renko, really," Braddock said, shaking his head.

"You know him?"

"He was a precinct lieutenant in North Manhattan when I left the force. *Ambitious* guy," Braddock said. "If he's the IA chief now, then he's moved several rungs up the ladder since I left."

Boe caught the tone. "What happened?"

"We had an issue between us when he was a lieutenant, and I was a detective. We exchanged unpleasant words."

Tori laughed. "Unpleasant words?"

"Voices were raised."

"Why?" Boe asked.

"Oddly, he was critical of my candor."

"Was he right to be?"

"No. It was his candor that I thought was questionable. Ironic he's now the head of IA."

Tori looked to Boe, and smiled. "Maybe keep them apart."

Boe snorted. "They're coming into my house. They're the ones who can mind their Ps and Qs."

"You said there was another detective?" Braddock inquired.

"A woman, I think she was Lange's partner. Her name..." Boe checked her phone. "Detective Adrienne—"

"Cardellini," Braddock finished.

"Yes."

Braddock closed his eyes. "Seriously."

"Why?"

"She was my last partner."

When they left Boe's the sheriff remained perturbed that the NYPD was operating in her county without her knowledge. Braddock didn't necessarily mind that she had her back up. That could prove useful when the time came.

On the short drive home, he expected Tori would be equally inquisitive about Renko and especially Cardellini, but she'd simply said that tomorrow would be interesting and that they should go home and get a good night's rest so they could meet it head-on. He was relieved that she let it go, but what he didn't realize was that after a long day Tori had something else entirely on her mind.

He showered, brushed his teeth, slid on the gym shorts he often slept in and slipped into bed. He could hear the running water and assumed Tori was doing much the same behind the closed bathroom door. As he was setting the alarm on his phone, the door to the master bathroom slowly creaked open.

She hadn't been doing entirely the same thing in the bathroom.

Tori was leaning with her left hand against the door frame in her extremely short pink silk robe. This was not normal Monday night bedwear.

"Uh, hey there," he said, leaning back against their soft headboard, taking in the beauty of her. Distracted as he was, for this, he could set it all aside.

"Hey, yourself."

Tori's hair fell messily to her shoulders and even from the bed, he caught the slightest whiff of perfume, his favorite of hers that she liked to lightly apply to her pulse points when in the mood.

She stood in the doorway, her eyes locked on his, slowly twirling one end of the pink silky waist tie. He loved this little theatrically seductive side to her. She leaned into it more and more these days.

And that robe. It looked so damn good on her. And she knew it too as she took a slow step toward him, making a show of slowly undoing the waist tie.

"I thought, you know, after a long day you'd—"

"—Be what?" she said, letting the waist tie fall to the sides, the robe drifting open to reveal a tantalizing sliver of her tanned naked body as she ran her fingers through her auburn hair, letting it fall loosely around the soft features of her face. "Tired. Weary. Perhaps exhausted. Forgetful of my promise."

"Um... yeah."

"Hmm," she said when she reached the side of the bed, letting the silk robe slowly descend from her shoulders to the floor, his eyes following it, as her naked body was fully revealed. "Do I look tired to you?"

"No," and he couldn't help but smile.

"And," she said as she pulled the comforter back and then climbed on top of him, "you weren't the only one missing someone the past several days."

"I wasn't?"

"No," she said, gazing down at him as he first slowly caressed her toned thighs, before moving his hands around behind her and then up the taut muscles in her back, his fingers dancing lightly over her silky smooth skin as she leaned down and kissed him, her lips soft to his, lingering, her eyes locked in on his. "I missed you too, *boss man*."

Their half-hour of late-night activity had been a pleasant diversion as had been the fifteen minutes of pillow talk after, until Tori rolled to her side of the bed. In a minute, her back to him, she'd fallen asleep, balled up under the puffy comforter.

A gentle blow of wind rustled the trees outside, sending a fresh cool breeze in under the small gap between the window blinds and window ledge. It was an otherwise perfect night to sleep.

But sleep wouldn't come so easily to Braddock.

Careful not to jostle the bed, he reached for his phone and did a quick Internet search for Dan Guerero. A *New York Times* article with the headline: *NYPD to Reopen Guerero Investigation*, popped up. Braddock didn't look at the *New York Times* much these days.

The article noted that the Cold Case Squad had reopened the murder investigation of NYPD Homicide Detective Dan Guerero, murdered eight years ago by two gunmen in a bodega across the street from his apartment building.

Braddock closed his eyes at the awful memory of Dan's murder. It was a murder that wouldn't have happened but for him.

As he returned to the article, he read that new evidence had recently come to light that had caused the police commissioner to assign the case to NYPD's Cold Case Squad, rather than the detectives who had originally investigated the murder. "The case needs a fresh set of eyes and a new perspective after all these years," the police commissioner had said. "That is what the Cold Case Squad is tasked to do."

Lange was apparently one of the Cold Case detectives and he suspected Cardellini would be another. But Renko was IA— and the article made no mention of Internal Affairs's involvement in the new investigation.

What new evidence?

He was curious about that. Whatever it was, it had led Lange to finding Julio. It had led others to locating Julio as well.

He closed his eyes again.

Eight years.

Regrets? Sure, he had a few.

Mistakes? There had been plenty over the course of his life, on and off the job. That said, as a general rule, he wasn't one to spend a lot of time dwelling on regrets or past mistakes. He took what he could from them and tried not to make the same mistakes going forward. Live and learn.

But to every rule there was an exception.

There was one series of mistakes that had lingered for many years from which he'd not fully moved on. For a time, he'd felt like his head was lying on a tree stump awaiting the axe to fall. He'd left New York City eight years ago and not a moment too soon. And while the events of that period had drifted from memory with time, distance, a new life, Quinn, family, and now Tori, he'd long wondered if it was all truly in the past.

The call from Julio last night jolted those memories back to life. That time eight years ago, all that had and hadn't happened, the things he had and hadn't done, the mistakes he had made, the threats that lingered out there, the murders, the deaths, his role in it all was suddenly coming back to life a thousand miles away from New York City.

Dan Guerero and many others, murdered.

Julio Gonzalez was now dead, murdered.

Ray Lange was now dead, murdered.

Was he next?

Had his day of reckoning finally arrived?

EIGHT

"WHEN THE TIME IS RIGHT, HE'LL COME FIND YOU."

Boo was relieved it was pitch dark when he and Vooch returned. In fact, the sizable houses and villas along the heavily treed resort road were all darkened, people having long gone to sleep for the evening, the cool nighttime air refreshing under the stars.

The cabin they were using was a golf villa and backed up to the fairway of one of the area's resort golf courses. The house itself was a spacious one-story ranch with a walkout basement. Normally they would have spent all their time in the basement, given there was a bar, flat-screen televisions, and a pool table.

Vooch pulled into the middle of the garage and let the door close behind them. Boo grabbed the sacks of groceries, while Vooch retrieved the pizza and they made their way inside to the kitchen to find Stag and Conn waiting, half-empty beers in front of them.

"You get some rest?" Vooch said to Conn.

"He watched a lot of golf, or at least the golfers on the hole the cabin backs up to," Stag said. "For a few hours anyway, later in the day."

Conn was an avid golfer, though with the state of his shoulder, a return to golf was a long way off. "This place sits up on a bit of a bluff but is right on the corner of the dogleg for a short par four. I could watch them hit their drives and then their approaches to the green. That killed a few hours between naps." He took the measure of his two compatriots. "You two look... vexed."

"Because we are," Boo said and summarized the past few hours.

"That's not good," Stag said, suddenly worried. "I picked that spot."

"And I went along with it. Your good buddy wants to have a call."

"Is he pissed?" Stag asked warily.

"I guess we'll find out."

In the immediate aftermath at the hunting cabin the thought had been to take Julio's and Lange's bodies, dump them where they couldn't be found, with the hope that it would eventually kill the investigation. The NYPD and locals would search for the bodies, trace phones, take all those investigative steps but in the end, if they couldn't find Julio, or Lange, or even Julio's wife and daughter, what was there for the detectives to do? The case would dead end. But now, the hunting cabin and the bodies had been found. And thus there were two problems to deal with. Julio's missing wife, and Braddock.

Vooch grabbed beers and opened the pizza box and put the call on speaker.

The voice on the phone came out hot. "It's the Land of Ten Thousand Fucking Lakes and you dump the car in a river, and they find it in less than twenty-four hours. How the fuck did that happen? Who picked that spot?"

"I did," Stag replied.

"Why the hell are you making that call? What would you know about dumping a body?"

"I ordered him to find a spot," Boo said. "And if you'd have seen how the Mississippi was flowing last night, you wouldn't have thought it the wrong place to submerge that car. We saw it go in with the flow and then go under."

"Then how the fuck does it end up found so fast?"

"Best Vooch and I can tell, it got caught on something that hung it up in shallower water. But even then, it was fully submerged. The only way someone sees it is if they go right over it with a boat or—"

"From the air," Vooch added. "An army helicopter flew over us a few times. There's a Minnesota National Guard base nearby. Maybe the chopper saw it. Look, we had to make a call last night."

"It was the wrong one!"

"You don't get to fucking Monday morning quarterback this thing from a thousand miles away," Boo replied, his voice rising, the stress showing. "You weren't fucking here, so fuck you!"

"Remember who you're talking to."

"You might want to do the same, you ungrateful asshole."

Vooch blew out a breath. "Let's all calm down."

The room went quiet for a moment.

"Conn, you there?"

"Yeah."

"How are you doing?"

"I'll live," Conn replied, adjusting his shoulder slightly as he sat down on a stool. "Where does this leave us?"

"Braddock and Julio's wife. Tell me about Braddock's home."

"Secure," Vooch replied. "He has a security system, a very good one. He's on the lake, but his house is not isolated. Neighbors on both sides and the yards are open. Lots of eyeballs to avoid. Braddock also has a dog, a golden lab. It's still a bit of a puppy but it's another issue. To do anything at his house would have to be outside, and even if we did, someone is likely to hear if not see."

"We'd need to get him somewhere away from the house," Boo said. "Maybe use his kid as bait. Take them both out."

"The kid?" Stag said, alarmed.

"If it's him or us, yeah."

"But a kid?"

"That's putting the cart in front of the horse," Conn blurted. "Braddock's a problem but he's coming on the scene *after* the fact. Julio's wife is the bigger concern, if you ask me."

"Any chance the wife could identify any of you?"

"No," Vooch assured. "We all wore masks, gloves, all black clothing."

"At least you all were smart enough to do that."

"Fuck off," Boo retorted. He was the only one of them who could speak freely like that.

"Easy," Vooch murmured.

"Fuck easy and fuck him, Vooch."

"The problem is that whatever Julio knew, we must assume his wife knows as well," Conn continued. "And what Julio knew for sure was Stag, and maybe..."

"Maybe what?"

"You."

"He didn't have me," the voice on the phone replied. "He didn't have my name."

"You're sure?"

"I am sure."

"You really want to bank on that?" Conn insisted. "He sure as shit saw you, more than once. Who's to say he didn't have your name too?"

"He didn't have my name. She doesn't have my name. I know this and you know it too."

"Be that as it may," Boo asserted, "we know where Braddock is. Julio's wife is on the loose. Should we be here, babysitting him, or should we be hunting her?"

"Hunting her, but you don't know where to hunt yet," the

voice replied. "She hasn't returned to Superior. She didn't call the police anywhere so she's not trusting law enforcement, which is good for us. She's on the run but she'll eventually turn to someone for help."

"Family," Boo said. "Or friends."

"That's what I'm thinking. She'll surface. And when she does, I'll get you there. But until she does, stay on Braddock. He needs to keep up his end of the deal."

* * *

Ana pulled to a stop at the stoplight, though her stop was abrupt enough to jostle Emma awake in the back seat, her eyes fluttering open. "Momma?"

"Just a little longer, baby."

The dashboard clock said it was 11:39 p.m. Even at this time of night, there was a flow of traffic to blend into as she motored into the inner part of the city.

She had the burner phone with her. Even now, she checked it from time to time, just in case. Had Julio somehow survived, been alive, he would have called. There was no call.

Her husband was dead.

It had been a long eight-hundred-mile drive thinking about him, about Emma, about what possibly lay ahead for them both.

Emma had been asking for her daddy. It had been all she could do not to break down in tears, only allowing herself a quiet cry while Emma slept last night at the roadside motel.

What was she going to tell her? How was she going to tell her? And what were they going to do? How were they going to live?

They had been on the move for eight years, even going so far as to change their identities before they moved to Superior four years ago and moving every nine months to a year before that. She had pleaded with Julio every time they had to move to go to the police, but he'd insisted he couldn't trust the police, and not just because of what he'd seen, but also because of who he was. Julio had been brought to the United States as a young child by parents who were in the country illegally. In the current political climate, would his immigration status allow him to remain in the United States with Ana and Emma, or would he be deported?

Then there was what happened to Julio's friend Malik and then Detective Guerero, and many others. When Detective Lange showed up in Superior looking for him, Julio said to her, "They found us again. We have to move. Right now. Grab the bag."

She put her foot down.

"I'm not going to do this again. This is home. I'm not running to another new city, settling in a new home, arranging medical care for Emma, hoping you get insurance, getting her into school and then running again. This is no way for us to live."

"I'm sorry."

"Sorry doesn't cut it anymore. We're not leaving everything behind and moving again. If you don't go to the police and tell them what you know, I'm taking Emma and leaving."

"Ana, you know the risks if I go to the police. I name Stagliola and I describe the cop that I've seen, you know what can happen? You saw what happened to Malik, to Detective Guerero. It's not only me at risk, but you are too. They'll kill us all to bury this thing."

"I've been at risk for eight years. I'm not doing it again, and then again, and then again, again. *No!*"

"Then what do we do?"

"Let's do what we should have done back in New Jersey, what we should have done five, six or seven years ago. Let's go see the man Malik said you could trust, Will Braddock. Didn't you tell me he lives in Minnesota now?"

"He does. A couple of hours from here."

"Let's go to him."

They had learned Braddock's name from Malik Muhammed, Julio's good friend back in the day. Living in the same neighborhood, they had bonded over their immigrant status in the melting pot that was New York City and northern New Jersey.

Malik was an operator and quite clever... which was a job requirement if you were a smuggler and mover of stolen property. Not that Julio had ever been involved in that. But Malik was smuggling items through the port where Julio worked, and Julio couldn't help being curious.

When Julio asked about his business, Malik let slip he had "working" relationships with some cops. In return for their protection, he had been a source of information about the pipeline of drug product and people making their way to the United States from Afghanistan, Pakistan and other places in the Middle East. "These cops I talk to are fighting terrorism," Malik had told Julio. "If I can help prevent that, I should and so I do. And they look the other way when I'm just moving certain non-lethal products through the port."

"You have to pay them?"

"No. No cut, nothing like that. I'm surprised they never demanded but they've been straight up with me. As long as I'm non-lethal, they're non-lethal with me."

Malik told Julio about a detective poking around on some thefts of drug shipments from containers that had originated at the docks. And Julio had seen things—things certain people wouldn't have wanted him to see.

Julio had confided in Malik his concerns. His fear that certain people knew he'd seen things that were maybe *connected* to the robberies, and they might not like that he did. "People are dead over this. I didn't go looking for trouble, but I'm thinking it's found me."

"Then it found me too," Malik had replied, relating his thoughts about Dan Guerero and his murder. "We need to be careful but there is another detective I know and trust. His name is Will Braddock."

"Should I go see him?" Julio had asked.

"That's not how it works with Braddock. He's cautious and deliberate. When the time is right, he'll come find you."

Julio waited. A week later, Malik was murdered. Guerero and numerous others had already been murdered. Everyone Julio knew of—who either knew about the robberies and what he'd seen, or was investigating it—was dead, except him. What were the odds of his survival? He couldn't wait for Braddock to come around nor take the time to go find him. Julio's simple thought was get out while they still could. They had been on the run ever since.

After escaping from the hunting cabin, Ana drove her and Emma through the night to just outside Madison, Wisconsin. If there had been one thing Julio had done right through all their sudden moves it was to have a go-bag always at the ready. Thankfully it had been in her purse. The $5,000 cash allowed her to pay for the motel, for food and gas and supplies without leaving any sort of electronic trail.

Later in the day, she got on the road again after having first given Emma her medication. The last dose she had.

The only thing Ana knew for certain was that she wanted to be done running. She wanted to find a place where she could be safe and raise Emma. Julio had promised that at some point in the future they would do exactly that, he just needed time. They had run out of time.

Was that her fault?

She'd pushed him to find Will Braddock. Malik said he could be trusted, yet he turned her husband down. Was that because he didn't want any trouble, or was it because he was part of the trouble as Lange had intimated?

Was Lange right? Had she led Julio right to his death?

She didn't know and she would need time to process all that. And right now, that wasn't what mattered. What mattered now was the little girl in the back seat.

Ana followed the street signs, then breathed a sigh of relief when she drove by the terminal building. It took her another couple of minutes to find a parking space where Josh had instructed her to go. As she looked out the passenger window, she could see the terminal entrance across the parking lot.

The burner phone rang. Cleo.

"I just parked where Josh said I should."

"We saw you and followed for a few blocks," Cleo replied. "We're looping around. Walk up to the corner. We'll pick you up there. We're in a white Mazda CX-90."

Ana got Emma out of her car seat, and they gathered what few things they had. A bit wary of the neighborhood, they walked up to the corner, hearing a train whistle in the distance. At the corner, a small white SUV veered over to them. Cleo got out and rushed to hug her and she immediately broke down.

"Oh, Ana," Cleo said, wrapping her friend in her arms. "We've got you now. We've got you."

NINE

"BIG CITY TYPES."

Tori took a long sip of coffee and let her eyes drift left over to Braddock as he poured himself a tumbler of his own, preparing to leave for work. Boomer ignored them both, chomping away at the fresh food in his bowl.

As nice as last night felt, when they awoke in the morning she sensed unease in Braddock. Usually after a night like last night, he would still linger in those feelings into the morning, even more so than she would. There would be a little light touching and smiling. He might pat her affectionately on the butt or come up behind her, wrap her in his long arms, lean down and gently kiss her neck and compliment her in some small way. On occasion he'd playfully ask if she wanted to go back to bed for round two and on a few weekend occasions when Quinn wasn't home, they had. He almost always did or said something like that, and she loved that. She got a stirring sensation of her own from the look on his face when she opened the bathroom door last night in her slinky little silk robe. It was contrived, but she wanted his reaction, the way he hungered for her as she slowly strode toward him, undoing the robe. As secure as she was about the state of their relationship, she nevertheless drew a certain confidence boost from the affirmation of how he was feeling and how she made him feel. The morning compliment even happened the first time they slept together when she was just trying to slink away before he awoke. She couldn't remember a morning after sex where there wasn't something like that initiated by him.

Until today.

This morning was like it didn't happen.

He'd been up early and instead of going for a swim, he went for a run by himself. Braddock going off by himself, in and of itself, wasn't unusual. They often worked out together in the morning and just as often didn't. Sometimes he wanted to swim, and she wanted to ride her bike or go for a run. It was just that most mornings he would ask, do you want to get up? Do you want to go with?

This morning? There had been none of that, which was why she stood in the kitchen, in a loose T-shirt and yoga pants, as he stood fully dressed in a suit, fumbling silently about the kitchen.

"Everything alright?"

"Yeah," he replied, not glancing at her in response.

"You're fibbing."

"Expert in that regard, are you?"

"I am."

He stopped and exhaled, still not looking at her. "It's just I have a feeling this is going to be a difficult day."

She nodded. It may well be once the NYPD arrived. "I'll be there."

"You don't have to be, you know. It's not your deal."

"Excuse me?"

"You know what I mean. You don't have to do this."

"I choose to. And with Steak out, you need me on this one, especially if it'll be as difficult as you think it will be."

She walked up to him, sliding in between him and the

counter, wrapping her arms around his waist, making him do the same, and looked up to him. "It's not like you've done anything wrong here."

"A cop died in my jurisdiction. A New York cop. I'm going to be in the firing line on this, like it or not. And with Renko?" He exhaled a long, pained breath. "That's a piece of my past coming back on me that I'd just as soon have never again had to deal with."

"If he gets on you, tell him to piss off."

"It's not that easy."

"I kind of think it is, especially when Lange hadn't bothered to check in with the department. Boe is ornery about that. I don't blame her. Do you?"

"No, but that failure to so notify is what has my radar up, especially with Renko. He's a slippery one. This just stirs up stuff and brings people into my life I'd rather not have to deal with."

She stood on her tiptoes and kissed him. "It'll be fine."

He sighed and closed his eyes. He didn't appear to agree even though he said: "I hope so."

"It will be. Now, I demand you give me my morning-after-sex pat on the butt and be on your way."

That finally drew at least a small smile. "Yes, ma'am."

After Braddock left, she sat in a comfy chair, relaxing and gazing out the windows at the lake while sipping her coffee, Boomer resting at her feet. A clatter sounded upstairs. Quinn. Boomer heard him too and popped up and rushed up the steps, looking for his buddy.

Five minutes later, Quinn came down the steps, the puppy in tow.

"What's your plan for the day?"

"The same as always."

"Down to Pete's?"

"That's the plan. And Boomer too. You?"

"Thinking about a bike ride to get going and then some work."

"You want to ride down with Boomer and me?"

She thought for a moment. "Yeah, that would be great."

Tori quickly got dressed in her biking attire, and they rode a mile down the road to his cousin Peter's house, Boomer running happily along, darting in and out of yards and woods, living his best dog life. At Peter's, she spent a few minutes talking to his mom Andrea and then left Quinn and Boomer with her. She plopped in her AirPods, hit her playlist and pedaled off for her ride.

The first tune that came on was "a banger," as Quinn called them these days. "She Sells Sanctuary," The Cult, one of her favorite 80s bands. A good tune to pick up the pace to.

* * *

"Consistent, aren't they?" Vooch murmured.

"In what way?" Boo replied. "The daily routine?"

"Yeah. Braddock exercises every day. She exercises every day; I mean, every day we've ever watched, whether it's a swim with Braddock, a run, or a bike ride. The kid rides down to his grandparents' or cousin's place on his bike every day with the dog, and then home later in the day on the gravel road. Very consistent, very routine."

"And predictable."

As Hunter cycled away, they followed at a distance.

"She has all the exercise gear," Vooch noted, admiring her racing cycle, the yellow riding shoes, the bright riding outfit in various hues of blue and green: helmet, sunglasses, gloves, water bottle, the whole ensemble. Hunter was fully outfitted. She turned sharply right onto County Road 44, cycling north, her legs churning away, riding at a brisk pace on the road's paved shoulder. If she kept to her normal routine when she rode in that direction, she would ride as far as Holmstrand and then turn back.

"She was a competitive triathlete not long ago, back when she was with the Bureau," Boo noted.

"She rides like she still could be one."

* * *

Tori put in a few hours at the university, completing some prep work she had intended to finish yesterday afternoon before getting drawn into the investigation. Checking her watch, it was just past noon. She drove to the government center and walked into the investigations office and immediately saw Braddock.

"Are they here yet?"

"Not yet," he said. "Not long, I don't imagine."

"Quick food truck run? I'll buy."

As they walked down the street, she studied Braddock, the tension of his walk and tautness of his face. His comments about who was coming from the NYPD had told her he had misgivings about them both, but for someone who was even-keeled, even when showing anger, this level of heightened tension was unusual. He wasn't one to sweat things yet on this one, he clearly was.

They stopped at the Greek truck and ordered loaded gyros, Braddock with pork and Tori with lamb, both filled with tomato, lettuce, tzatziki sauce, feta cheese and French fries.

"Mmmm, the tzatziki sauce is so good," Tori said, her mouth full of food. "Makes me want to go to Greece and try this for real in Athens."

Braddock simply nodded as he chewed, as non-communicative as he'd been this morning.

"Anything new from your team this morning?"

"Nothing terribly probative."

"What not terribly probative did they find?"

"There were two tire tread molds taken. One tire tread matched for the Malibu we pulled out of the river. The other tread was for a Bridgestone Ecopia H/L 422 Plus tire, common on a Honda CR-V. Hector Ramirez owned a 2023 silver Honda CR-V, registered in Wisconsin. That was the vehicle that went through the front yard. We have an alert out for that vehicle. We got a preliminary ballistics report. There are shell casings from five different guns, a mix of nine millimeters, .45 autos and .40S&Ws. Now, we didn't find any weapons at the scene, nor did we find any in Lange's car. My guess is by now the guns were all wiped and tossed elsewhere."

"Blood?"

"BCA is working on it. That'll take time. Though it still makes me wonder where our wounded man got care."

"You assume he did," Tori said as they walked along, chewing her gyro. "Like Boe said last night. He might be dead at the bottom of some other body of water. There is no honor among thieves, or killers. We've seen that a time or two."

"We have," Braddock replied before taking a bite of his gyro, the tzatziki sauce smearing on his cheek.

"Hang on. You're a mess," Tori said, stopping, dabbing at his cheek with a napkin. "How about that bag of drugs or probably medication we found?"

"I haven't seen anything on that," he said as they started walking again.

"And the mother and daughter?"

"No sign thus far. Like I said, we have the bulletin out for the Honda CR-V but if she got away, and they didn't catch up to her, she could be a long way away."

"She could," Tori agreed.

"You had a thought on finding them?"

"If she's on the run, she's going to need help. Who do you go to if you need help?"

"Someone I could trust. Family. Friends. There is one problem with that, though. We only can go back four years."

"My guess is after the NYPD shows up today, you'll be able to go back more than four years on their history."

When they arrived back from their quick lunch, Boe's assistant Brenda told them to go into Boe's office. "They're here."

"And?"

"Big city types." That meant big city attitudes.

"We were big city types," Tori said.

"Yeah, but you've both managed to overcome that with time," Brenda replied with a sly smile.

"Ha!" Tori laughed, though Braddock uncharacteristically didn't. "You'll have to forgive the curmudgeon here."

"Need coffee, water, a soda?" Brenda offered. "Perhaps a lobotomy, Will?"

"Let's just get this over with," he muttered and then to Tori said, "Head on in. I'm going to grab something from my office."

Tori pushed into Boe's office. Standing in front of Boe's desk was a man with mostly dark hair and tanned skin. He was a few inches shorter and a few inches wider than Braddock, dressed in a black sport coat, gray slacks and white dress shirt.

"Tori," Boe greeted. "This is NYPD Internal Affairs Chief Ira Renko."

"Chief Renko, Tori Hunter," she said, extending her hand.

"Ahh, the famous retired FBI special agent," he said, offering a toothy grin intended to hide the hint of suspicion in his voice.

"And this is Detective Adrienne Cardellini," Boe said.

"Good to meet you, Special Agent Hunter," Cardellini said, extending her hand, but without the perfunctory smile that

Renko gave her. Detective Cardellini was a few inches taller than her, wearing skinny blue jeans with her cream-colored blouse and sky-blue blazer. She had shoulder-length black wavy hair loose at her shoulders, with dark-brown eyes and a soft pale face. "I've heard so much about you from Chief Renko."

"That's interesting," Tori said, holding the handshake. "I've heard so much about him as well."

Cardellini's eyes looked past her, widening in recognition. *"Will!"*

"Hey, Cardi," he replied, walking in with the investigative file. She opened her arms and offered him a warm embrace that he accepted, closing her eyes, holding the hug.

Huh.

"So, Braddock tells me you two were partners," Tori said.

"Only briefly," Cardellini answered. "Maybe a month, six weeks, something like that, before he moved here. It's been what? Seven, eight years."

"Eight," Braddock said.

"And congratulations on being awarded the Medal of Valor."

"You heard about that?" Braddock said, surprised.

"The retired Chief of Ds was all about it when he stopped in a few weeks ago." The retired NYPD Chief of Detectives was Joe Quinn and a friend of Braddock's. Joe's brother Jim was Braddock's mentor and first partner. Jim died on 9/11. Braddock had made it out of the South Tower. Jim had not. Jim's memory was one of the reasons Braddock later joined the Joint Terrorism Task Force and had named his son Quinn.

Braddock stepped away from Cardellini and extended his hand. "Chief Renko, sir."

"Detective Braddock."

There might have been a firm handshake, but the greeting was not one of warmth between the two of them.

"Chief Renko, Braddock says you two have some history,"

Boe said in a tone that warned she would have her chief detective's back.

"It was years ago. A professional disagreement, but it's water under the bridge," Renko said.

Tori observed the two of them eyeing one another. It might have been years, but she didn't get the sense that either man felt that way.

Braddock's look was of wariness of this man from his past.

Renko's was one of contempt, a look she'd rarely seen Braddock receive in any setting, work or otherwise.

And she could tell Braddock read Renko's expression too, his eyes locked on him, making his own read on the man since their last encounter many years ago. Braddock was not one to back down and Renko, as a chief, of internal affairs no less, would have none of it in him either. Not having wanted to aggravate him more than he already was, she hadn't asked about the specifics of the event that triggered their animosity for one another. Now she wished she would have. This wasn't just a disagreement, there was hostility, particularly on Renko's part. Whatever it was between them, it wasn't just professional, it had been personal.

Better buckle up, Tori.

"If it's water under the bridge, and it should be after all this time, let's deal with the more immediate issue at hand then, shall we?" Boe said.

"Let's," Cardellini said, having observed the stare down herself. "Detective Lange was my partner. He was a good friend of Chief Renko. We'd like to know what happened to him?"

"So would we," Boe replied and waved for everyone to take a seat. "Perhaps we could offer more help if you told us why he was here to begin with?"

"And why would IA and the Cold Case Squad be working a case jointly?" Tori added. "Seems like an odd marriage. No offense, Chief, but in my experience, IA doesn't play well with others in the sandbox."

Renko looked from Boe to Tori. Of the two, he was senior to Cardi in rank and years. "The cold case is a murder eight and a half years ago of NYPD Detective Dan Guerero."

"How was he murdered?" Boe asked.

"Dan was gunned down by two men in a bodega," Braddock replied. "Across the street from his apartment building. Chief Renko, as I recall, led the task force investigation of his murder out of his precinct house."

"I did, which is also why I'm involved now. I know the case, and I'm assisting the Cold Case Squad. I consider it a piece of unfinished business. Especially now, given what happened to Ray."

"I remember this," Tori said, turning to Braddock. "I knew Dan. I worked with him a handful of times." She turned to Renko and Cardellini. "He was a real solid guy."

"Yes, *he* was," Renko said, peering directly at Braddock whose face was placid, staring right back.

And Tori knew Braddock's look, had seen it many times, the one of contemplation and calculation. *What is it with these two?*

"He was a friend of yours," Renko said to Braddock. It wasn't a question.

"Yes, a damn good one," Braddock replied flatly. "We worked homicide and JTTF together. Dan and Monica were good friends of my late wife Meghan and I."

"You were a pallbearer at his funeral, right," Renko noted.

"I was."

Tori let her eyes slide left. She'd never heard Braddock mention Guerero's name or anything about his murder. She'd also gone to Dan Guerero's funeral. Thousands had, forming a long blue ribbon of police officers in uniform as they marched to the cemetery.

If she was remembering the dates right, Guerero's murder

happened around the time Meghan died. A sad time in Braddock's life, made doubly so by Guerero's murder.

"He was killed in the bodega, how?" she asked.

"Guerero was a regular at the bodega, often stopping for coffee in the morning. It was his routine, if you will," Renko said. "He was inside, making a cup of coffee. A man went into the bodega just before Dan. After Dan came inside, that man pulled a mask down over his face and approached the owner at the counter with a gun. Dan must have seen the man pull a gun, because he drew his own weapon. But then, he got smoked by a second man who'd come in the back of the store. Dan never saw him coming. He was shot twice in the back, once in the head. The two men escaped out the back into an alley. Nobody knows where they went from there."

"Chief Renko's task force investigated the case," Cardellini said. "But the shooters were never found or identified. There was no physical evidence beyond shell casings which were 9mm. There was nothing on video surveillance to work from as both men wore masks."

"After a couple of months, the case petered out," Renko said.

"When did his murder become a cold case then?" Boe asked.

"Our unit opened up the case two months ago," Cardellini said.

"Monica Guerero had been pushing the department to reopen the case for years," Renko stated. "So much so that eventually the push came from on high to reopen the investigation. The Cold Case Unit has closed a few high-profile cases in the last year or two, so it was assigned to them to give it a fresh look."

"Were you involved in the original investigation?" Boe asked Braddock.

"No," Braddock replied. He sighed, looking away. "I

followed it as best I could, but I was on leave at the time. Meghan was in the final stages of her fight with brain cancer, so..."

"That's where you were at."

Braddock turned to Cardellini. "Why was Lange here in Manchester Bay?"

"He was pursuing the other dead man you found in the trunk of the car, Hector Ramirez."

"And Ramirez was what?" Tori said.

"Ask Braddock," Renko said.

Tori turned to Braddock, whose eyes narrowed.

"And I would know why?"

"Because he called you on Sunday night," Renko asserted. "At eight thirty-eight p.m. Call lasted three minutes according to Ramirez's cell phone records."

"No. I got a call from a man named Julio Gonzalez," Braddock said.

Tori didn't react, but something wasn't right about Braddock's response. It was how rapidly and... smoothly he responded, as if he'd known the question was coming and he had the answer instantly ready. He wasn't telling the truth, or at least the whole truth.

She glanced over at Renko.

"That used to be Hector's name. He changed it sometime in the last four years," Renko said. "He didn't mention that?"

"No, he failed to do that," Braddock said.

"And you didn't make the connection between the two yesterday? When you knew the cabin was rented by Hector Ramirez. When his body was in that trunk next to Ray Lange."

"I barely remembered Julio Gonzalez to begin with when he called. It's been eight years. He had to remind me who he was."

"Who was... Julio Gonzalez?" Boe said, her eyes narrowing at Braddock. She'd seen what Tori had.

"You need another name first. I had a confidential informant named Malik Muhammed. Malik was a United States citizen, but he was of Afghani descent and had family connections back to Kabul. I developed Malik as a CI during my time on the JTTF. Now, Malik was no angel. He was into dirt of his own, a smuggler and fence, but he was no terrorist and didn't want possible ones screwing up what he had going." He paused and then started pacing around the room. "When Meghan got her... diagnosis, I left the JTTF and went back to Homicide, and I didn't have as much need for Malik. Then, I went on leave. That was for five months. I'd been back to work maybe six weeks when Malik reached out to me and said I should talk to a guy named Julio Gonzalez."

"Why?"

"Said he might have some information I'd be interested in."

"What?"

"He didn't say."

"Really? Come on."

"That's how Malik rolled. He would say, you should go talk to this guy or look at that guy. And sometimes he would say why and sometimes he'd say, you'll understand why once you talk to him."

"Was this Malik reliable?" Tori inquired.

"You remember the case that led to me getting shot by the terrorist in Times Square?"

"That you got your NYPD Medal of Honor for?"

"Yes. Malik put me on to that guy," Braddock said and then looked at Renko. "I trusted Malik, right up until he ended up dead."

"And he ended up dead, when?" Boe said.

"A few weeks before I made the decision to move here. When I heard about Malik, I went to find Julio Gonzalez. If I recall correctly, he was employed as a longshoreman at the Port Newark Shipping Terminal."

"He was," Cardellini confirmed.

"I went to his apartment and there was no answer. I went to the docks and, according to the port's operations manager, Gonzalez hadn't shown for work for two days. I went back to his apartment and had the building super open his unit. His apartment had been ransacked. I also noticed, however, that his clothes were gone, dresser drawers cleaned out, personal effects removed, so it was also possible he'd fled. And that was the last I'd thought about him until Sunday night."

"Did you ever report that to anyone?" Renko asked.

"I reported it to the detectives working Malik's homicide over in Bayonne. I don't believe Malik's murder was ever solved, at least not that I'm aware of."

"How was Malik killed?" Tori asked.

"His throat was cut. He was found in a dumpster in the alley behind his dry cleaners'," Braddock replied.

"And fast-forward eight years and Julio, our Hector, calls you Sunday night," Cardellini says. "What did he want to talk about?"

"He said he wanted to meet. That he had some... things to get off his chest. He asked me to meet him at the Halfway Highway Diner out on the H-4 Monday morning, eight a.m."

"That's it? You didn't want to know what he wanted to talk about?"

"That was the purpose of going to the diner. I figured if he could tell me something about what happened to Malik, I'd be interested. I went to the diner. Julio never showed. And now, I know why."

"And you didn't recognize him in that trunk yesterday?"

"I never met Julio Gonzalez in person. I didn't know what he looked like. I may have pulled a DMV photo eight years ago. My memory is good but it ain't *that* good."

"Braddock, this guy calls you on Sunday night, no shows yesterday morning, and then you see Ray Lange dead in the

trunk with this guy, and you don't put it together?" Renko
said.

"The guy in the trunk was Hector Ramirez, remember? I
didn't know a Hector. I didn't know that this Hector Ramirez
was Julio Gonzalez until ten fucking minutes ago. And Renko?"

"Yeah."

"Fuck you."

"Will," Boe warned.

"I ain't going to take this shit from him again," Braddock
said. "I don't give a shit if he's a chief now. He's a long way from
home."

"What's that mean?" Renko asked.

"That NYPD shield don't mean shit here."

"Is that a threat, Will?"

"A statement of fact."

"Sheriff?"

"Your shield don't mean shit here," Boe retorted. "Chief
or no."

Renko was taken aback. "Perhaps we ought to have another
investigative agency take over."

"Be my guest," Boe replied with a grin, gesturing to her desk
phone. "I believe you would need to speak with the governor.
I've got his number right here. But I'd remind you and Detective
Cardellini that Braddock, and Tori, and four of my other detectives, saved his life a few months back along with the Secretary
of Commerce, several members of the Minnesota Federal
Congressional Delegation and thousands of others. *I'm sure*
he'll take your word over ours. Especially when I explain the
odd circumstances of your arrival."

"Odd?"

"Manchester Bay is thirteen hundred miles from New York
City, Chief Renko. I'm curious as to why an NYPD detective
was here, and *we* didn't know about it?" Boe charged. "He had
Superior police with him on Friday when he went to Ramirez's

place of employment. He doesn't extend us the same courtesy. Why would *that* be? Particularly when my chief detective is a former NYPD detective himself. Explain that, if you would."

"We don't know," Renko replied with a head shake. "Cardi and I knew he was coming up here in pursuit of Hector Ramirez or who Braddock knows as Julio Gonzalez. He and Cardi spoke Sunday evening, after Lange tracked him down again. I can only assume he decided to handle it on his own. But we didn't hear from him after that."

"That's why we called yesterday," Cardellini added. "He hadn't checked in, and his phone was going right to voicemail and cyber couldn't get a location fix on the phone."

"We'd like to see what happened to him," Renko said. "Maybe we might see something you haven't."

Boe sat back in her chair, eyeing Renko and Cardellini. "Fair enough," she said, "Braddock and Tori will take you through it."

TEN

"YOU LOOK VERY UNEASY."

Tori would have preferred to have had a few minutes to speak with Braddock alone, but Cardellini and Renko were riding with them at Braddock's invitation, which seemed counterproductive. From what she'd just observed in Boe's office, Braddock and Renko could barely stand one another. Putting space between them seemed like a better idea. That, and she had questions of her own.

Why didn't he tell her about the call on Sunday night? Why did he seem to know more about this than he was letting on? And might that all have something to do with what the beef really was between him and Renko?

As she replayed the interaction in Boe's office in her mind, she couldn't shake the thought that the impetus for reopening Dan Guerero's murder investigation was about more than the department finally relenting to eight years of pressure applied by his widow. Something more specific had set it off after eight years. *What?* She didn't know but wondered if Braddock did. Might that have been the topic of his phone conversation on Sunday night with Julio? Braddock said that connection wasn't made in the call. She thought that unlikely. So why wouldn't Braddock admit that?

She had all these questions, but this wasn't the time or place for them. And this wouldn't be the first time he'd ever played things close to the vest. And when he did, he usually had a good reason for doing so.

Give him space, Tori. He'll tell you when he's ready.

Braddock drove and Tori sat in the front passenger seat, with Renko sitting behind Braddock and Cardellini behind Tori. Four detectives, everyone with an agenda. The two in the back were assessing the two in the front and vice versa. Interestingly, Tori didn't sense a tight bond between the two in the back seat.

As they drove west out of town, Cardellini tried cutting the tension. "I've never been here, but first quick impression is it's beautiful," she said as Braddock drove past the public beach just west of the government center, half-filled with sunbathers and swimmers, the summer season slowing down. She was looking out to the bay, which was the picture-postcard view that you could purchase in the local gift stores, even if the day was a bit overcast. "The lakes, the forest, beach, boats and all. It's kind of... tranquil."

"It is," Braddock said flatly.

"Must have been a culture shock for a New Yorker such as yourself."

He shrugged. "I'd been here a half-dozen times with Meghan before I moved here. It didn't take long to appreciate the relaxed way of life."

"Where do you live?"

"On the lake you see out there, which is Northern Pine Lake. My house is over on the west side. We'll pass the turn to it on the way to the first crime scene."

"How big is this town? Seemed pretty good sized when we were driving in."

"A whisker over fifty thousand," Tori said. "It's grown a lot the last ten, fifteen years."

"And where do you live, Tori?"

Like she didn't already know. Tori turned and looked back to Cardellini with raised eyebrows. "With Braddock."

"Ahh, I see," Cardellini replied, covering it nicely, following up with: "How long have you two been together?"

Tori turned her glance to Braddock who just peered ahead, his eyes hidden behind his sunglasses. "Depends on which one of us you ask. My answer is three years, living together for two."

"I'd love to see your house. Even if just a drive-by."

"Sure, why not," she replied, drawing a slight questioning glance from Braddock. "Like Braddock said, it's on the way."

Five minutes later, Braddock took a right turn off County 44 and drove in and did a slow pass by the house. "That's it."

"Wow, it's really nice," Cardellini said. "It looks so... new."

"We just put on an addition," Tori replied. "And remodeled some of the interior and re-sided the exterior."

"And you're on the lake too." The deep blue waters were easily visible between the houses to the north and south. "Must be nice to look out to that every day. I can see why you were so eager to leave New York, Will."

"I don't know about eager—"

"But you needed a change," Renko finished with a tinge of disbelief. "Quite the step up."

"Oh, I don't know," Braddock retorted. "Even with the remodel it might not match the value of my old apartment in Manhattan."

"Or my old condo in Lower Manhattan," Tori piped in. "You get more for your dollar here."

As they drove down the road winding around the lake, Cardellini remarked, "Some of these cabins, well, they aren't even—"

"Cabins," Tori finished, nodding. "No, they're not. It's not the lake of my childhood, that's for sure. It's some of the most valuable lakeshore in the state now."

"You grew up here?"

"She did," Braddock said. "Her dad was the sheriff for two decades."

Tori turned back to Cardellini with narrow eyes and a knowing toothless grin. It was a look that said: *Enough with the pretense. You know I grew up here, you know my backstory, you know Braddock and I are living together, and you know we live on the lake, you know all that.* It ended the casual lake talk. However, it highlighted another reason she would have liked to have ridden alone with Braddock. There was an undercurrent of something else to all this, an agenda beyond just Hector Ramirez and Ray Lange and now Dan Guerero's murder.

Fifteen minutes later, Braddock pulled to a stop at the end of the driveway for the hunting cabin, the yellow ribbon blocking the driveway wavering lightly to the late-afternoon zephyr.

"First things first," Braddock said, after they'd gotten out of the Tahoe. "The mosquitoes will eat you alive if you don't spray up on your open skin." He took a can of bug spray and demonstrated how to apply the repellent without getting it in their eyes.

"Do you do this all the time?" Cardellini asked.

"If you want to sit outside at dusk you do," Tori replied, using the back of her hand to rub the repellent on her cheeks and forehead.

While Cardellini and Renko applied the bug spray Braddock explained that Julio had borrowed the hunting cabin from his co-worker and friend Lucas Fraser. "As you'll see, the cabin is nothing special although plenty comfortable if your day was spent deer or bird hunting and your night drinking and playing cards," Braddock said.

"Spoken like you own one," Renko suggested.

"I have friends that do," Braddock retorted.

"Do you hunt?"

"Some. We just got a golden lab. I'm going to have him trained for bird hunting. Now, I have a question for you, Chief."

"What's that?"

"Internal Affairs. Seems an odd choice for you."

"I don't know, I viewed it more as a calling."

"Really?" Braddock replied. "It's a calling to have every cop hate you? Or was it just a way to climb the ladder faster."

"Oh, there might have been a little bit of two birds, one stone to it," Renko replied as he tossed the bug spray back to Braddock. "And, Will, the word you're looking for isn't hate, but fear. And it's only the dirty cops that need to fear me."

"Hmm. I see. Need I fear you, Chief?"

Renko offered a smile, showing his teeth. "As you and Sheriff Boe said, my shield doesn't mean shit here."

"Oh boy," Tori murmured.

"Cock fight," Cardellini muttered and got them back on topic. "Will, is there anything questionable on the cabin owner?"

Braddock stared down Renko while replying: "Not that we see." He turned to her. "Fraser lives two hours east of here. The cabin has been in his family for three generations. Fraser worked with... Hector or... Can we just agree to call him Julio?"

"Yes," Cardellini said.

"Julio called Fraser later Friday night and asked to borrow the cabin for a day or two."

"Did Fraser ask why?" Renko inquired.

"Said he didn't, though he sensed Julio was running from something. From what you and Cardi are telling me, he was right to so suspect." Braddock related what Fraser had told him and Tori about his interactions with Julio. "He was hiding something, but Fraser didn't know what."

"Any thoughts as to what that may be?" Renko asked Braddock.

"Not at the moment."

But he had them, Tori thought, just knowing him as she did. And she sensed that Cardellini and Renko had them too but weren't sharing.

"How did this all go down?" Cardellini asked.

Braddock took out a diagram from his investigative file and set it on the hood of his Tahoe. "Lange gets here to the cabin first, we think, and parks here." Braddock noted the location of the car on the diagram and then gestured to the cabin. "He was parked to the left at a forty-five-degree angle to the house. We know that because of tire tread marks." He pulled out photos and laid them on the hood.

"What time did Ray get here?" Cardellini said.

"We don't know what time he arrived or how long he was here other than he was here before the shooters arrived based upon positioning of the car, and as you'll see, the location of shell casings. Given your timeline of contact with him, this all happened Sunday night."

"Also confirmed given your call with Julio," Renko noted.

"Fair point," Braddock acknowledged. "Next, we think the attackers arrive and park out here on the road and then made their move from here on the cabin."

Tori waved Renko and Cardellini to follow her.

"Two came up the driveway," Tori said, leading them up the center of the dirt driveway. "One was on the left side and one on the right." When they could see the cabin, Tori stopped. "They got to about here and then the shooting started. There were shell casings left and right. On the left here, this man was wounded." She showed Renko and Cardellini photos of the blood. "There was blood on the tree and a small pool here in the dirt." Both of which were still somewhat visible. "Our crime scene investigators with the Bureau of Criminal Apprehension collected samples."

"You can match it if the sample is good," Cardellini mused, examining the photos. "Was it diluted by mud or water?"

"I honestly don't know," Tori replied. "I haven't heard if there was a DNA match. Takes time with the lab backlog."

"I understand lab backlogs."

"As for Lange, we're thinking he and Julio saw these guys coming and were able to fight back. Now, we don't know this for certain, but we strongly suspect Lange was shooting back this direction from the rear of the car," Braddock said, leading them ahead to where they thought the car parked. "There were shell casings concentrated in this area." He handed photos for Cardi and Renko to review.

"Did he ever even get inside the cabin?" Cardellini said.

"We don't know," Braddock said. "If he had the cover of the cabin, I can't understand why he'd have given that up to come out here."

"Unless he went inside unarmed," Renko stated.

"Hmpf. I can see that," Tori said after a minute. "Julio says to Lange you can come in, but only if you're—"

"Unarmed," Braddock finished. "Then the shooters show up and... he makes a dash out here. He got off several rounds, we think, but then he was shot in the back." He pivoted and pointed to the woods. "There was a third man. He came around and through the woods circling behind Lange here. We got a couple of foot impressions. Big guy. Size fourteen shoes. Lange was shot in the back twice from over by the woods there. Then Lange probably goes down or turns and leans against the car and the man approaches, pops him twice in the chest and then finished him off with one to the head from close range."

"And inside the cabin?" Cardellini said.

"Julio was in there, but mortally wounded," Braddock said, letting them follow him to the cabin. He walked them to the splatter of blood on the wall to the left of the picture window. "Julio fired several rounds from in here but was under attack, as you can see. When we found him in the trunk, he had a very large wound in his lower abdomen which we think was bad enough that when the shooters came in here, he probably couldn't defend himself. He was propped up against the wall there. One of the shooters finished him off in the head." Braddock showed them more photos. "We had shell casings all over the place. Here's the preliminary ballistics report." He handed it to Renko.

Cardellini held up the diagram and asked Tori, "What's the other car you have marked on this diagram?"

"We think Julio had his wife, Ana, and his daughter with him. We found two duffel bags, one with women's clothes, and a small pink suitcase with clothes for a little girl," Tori said, showing them more photos. "We think while the shooting was going down, the woman and child escaped out the back of the cabin, got into their own vehicle and fled right up the driveway." Tori took out another photo. "This is a tire tread mold. Tire consistent with one often found on a Honda CR-V. Julio had one registered in the name of Hector Ramirez."

"His wife never called 911?" Renko said.

"No," Tori replied. "We have a bulletin out for the vehicle but nothing so far. We got her cell number, but no answer and we think she dumped it. There has been no sign of her so far."

"Do you find it odd she hasn't called?"

"I do," Tori answered.

"What do you think it means?"

"I could only speculate."

"So, speculate."

"They either caught up with her and finished her and the child off, or the wife is in hiding somewhere, maybe with family, and is trying to figure out what to do."

"But she hasn't trusted law enforcement, has she?"

"Not as far as we know."

"And what is this bag in this photo?" Cardellini asked.

"A bag of medication of some kind, I think," Tori said. "I haven't seen what it is yet. We've been waiting for that."

Tori and Braddock observed as Renko and Cardellini did their own cabin walk through and then around outside.

"They don't trust a word we're saying?" Tori murmured.

"Nope."

"Do you know why?"

"I have thoughts."

"Care to share?"

The screen door opened. It was Renko. "What happened from here?"

"The shooters threw Julio and Lange into the trunk of Lange's car," Braddock said. "And drove to the dump site."

The four of them rode quietly as Braddock drove south on the H-4 to the boat launch. There may not have been verbal conversation but given the amount of time Renko and Cardellini spent on their phones, Tori figured their conversation was in the form of texting one another. It was like watching Quinn and his friends converse. They didn't talk; they texted.

Braddock remained stoic, wearing his sunglasses again despite the quickly setting sun, deep in his own thoughts.

Five minutes from the boat launch, Cardellini finally spoke up. "One question we didn't ask back at the cabin. It's about the one blood pool halfway down the driveway. Do you think medical care would have been required?"

"You sure would think so," Tori said. "Braddock's detectives have checked every hospital within a hundred miles and there were no unexplained gunshot wounds that were treated Sunday night or early Monday morning. We've expanded that search, but so far, nothing."

Cardellini nodded. "Can I ask a different question?"

"Sure."

"How does it fly, the two of you working together like this? Two people living together, investigating together all the time?"

"It's not all the time," Tori said. "I work for the county on an as-needed basis. My fuller-time gig is as a professor at the university."

"And you're needed on this one?"

Tori shrugged. "I kind of volunteered."

"Kind of?"

"It was an odd case, a cabin all shot up with no bodies inside, a mother and daughter fleeing and missing. It piqued my interest as something that wasn't run of the mill. That, and Braddock's lead detective has been out recuperating from the bombing last winter."

"The case where you were awarded the Presidential Medal?"

"Yes."

"Still," Renko muttered. "Wouldn't fly in the NYPD."

"Well," Tori said, turning around. "We're not in New York now, *are we?*"

Braddock turned onto the road that paralleled the Mississippi River and drove past the boat launch and up to the crime scene tape. Between the dense canopy of branches and leaves overhanging the road and the sun setting in the west behind the treeline on the opposite side of the river, it felt almost like nightfall. Braddock grabbed his flashlight.

"There isn't going to be all that much to see here," he said, walking them to the edge of the road and directing the beam of his flashlight down the hillside, following two tire tracks that cut jaggedly down to the waters of the river.

"The water is really flowing," Cardellini said. "Is this normal?"

Braddock shook his head. "No. We had a snowy winter and rainier than average summer with some heavy thunderstorms in the last couple of weeks so it's a lot stronger than usual for this time of year."

"I assume the current is strong."

"I should caveat my comments by noting that I'm not a hydrological expert on the flow characteristics of the Mississippi River."

Cardellini waved him off. "Yeah, yeah. You're not an expert, Will. The river?"

"The current is, I think, much stronger than normal. Whoever pushed the car in likely assumed it would just go right to the bottom. They didn't factor in the current, which is strong enough to have carried the car out about a hundred fifty feet, where it got caught up on a sandbar under the water. Or the fact this area isn't nearly as deep as it looks. In a normal year it's eight to ten feet. Last summer, which was more drought like, maybe three to five feet, bad enough they shut down the boat launch back up the road. If we didn't find the car this summer, we'd have probably found it next."

"Could you see it hung up on the sandbar?"

"Not visually from here. However, Camp Ripley is a Minnesota National Guard base a few miles away. A helicopter on a training flight spotted the car beneath the surface and reported it. That's how we found it. We got it pulled up to shore, opened the trunk and found the two bodies inside."

"Someone drove it down here with those bodies in the trunk," Tori said. "The BCA is processing the vehicle, but I haven't heard if they found anything beyond just the bodies."

"Is this part of the river popular with boaters?" Cardellini asked, crouched, examining the tracks down the sloped embankment to the river. "On the drive down, I didn't get the sense a lot of people live around here."

"That would be right," Braddock agreed. "The surrounding area is the national guard base and farm fields. That said, you saw the boat launch back there, so it sees some traffic."

"In the middle of the night?"

"Very unlikely."

Eggs, Reese and Nolan were waiting for them when they returned. Boe sat in while Braddock made the introductions of his team.

"I've knocked on every door within a mile of the hunting cabin," Reese said. "There are very few people living out that way. It's just a lot of hunting land so I haven't found anyone who saw or heard anything."

Eggs went next. "You've seen the initial forensic report on the shell casings, causes of death and so forth. Cell phone for Ana Ramirez is going right to voicemail and I'm certain it's been dumped. One new piece from the BCA in the last hour is that plastic bag we found with vials and syringes? The drug in the vials is Anakinra."

"Never heard of it," Renko said.

"Neither had I," Eggs replied. "It's for the treatment of systemic juvenile idiopathic arthritis or SJIA." She observed the sea of blank faces. "SJIA is a rare auto-inflammatory disease in children. It leads to fevers, rashes and joint pain. Anakinra is a medication you take for it. It isn't a cure but treats the symptoms. You can get it with a prescription and it's administered daily by injection."

"As for Ana Ramirez," Nolan said. "Using the name Julio Gonzalez, whose middle name was Hector, I was able to find that the two married ten years ago." She held up a copy of an

Ohio marriage license. "After they left New Jersey eight years ago, they first surfaced a year later in Cleveland, Ohio, which is Ana's hometown. Next, I tracked them to Steubenville, Ohio, for about a year and then there was a short stop in Dayton, Ohio where their daughter Emma was born. Then they moved up to Sandusky, Ohio. That's where the trail for Julio and Ana Gonzalez ends and the one for Hector and Ana Ramirez begins."

"You must have known all this," Tori said to Renko and Cardellini, "if Ray Lange tracked him to Superior, and then here."

"It took us some time to pull it all together," Cardellini said hesitantly and then looked to Nolan. "You've done it... in less than a day, Detective."

"Once I had Julio Gonzalez's name it went quick."

"Detective Nolan has a gift for the paper trail," Boe said with pride.

"That she does. Nolan's work leads me to a question," Braddock said, looking from Cardellini and then to Renko. "How is it you came across Julio's or Hector's name to begin with as someone you even needed to talk to about Dan's murder?"

"His name came up through Malik Muhammad," Renko replied, trying to stifle a yawn. "You said earlier you weren't the only cop Malik talked to. He was a CI of Dan Guerero as well. You knew that, right?"

Braddock nodded. He looked as if he was going to say something else but held back.

The room went quiet for a moment, the clock nearing 9:00 p.m. Renko rubbed his face with his hands. Cardellini slouched in the chair and yawned.

It had been a long day.

"What more do you need from my people?" Boe asked.

"I think we'd like to go to our hotel, grab a bite and get some rest. We'll come back tomorrow with any follow-up," Renko said.

"Okay," Boe said. "Let's call it, then. Meet back here in the morning?"

"Yeah, Sheriff, if we could."

Renko and Cardellini gathered their things and left, followed by Nolan, Eggs and Reese. Boe had Braddock and Tori hang behind.

"Thoughts?" Boe said.

"They're not telling the whole story," Tori said, her eyes locked on Braddock's, until he looked away, unwilling to meet her gaze.

Boe grinned. "No, they're not. I wouldn't trust Renko as far as Braddock could throw him. The question is, why? Will, any thoughts?"

"They're holding back."

"Why?"

"My guess is we'll find out the why in the morning," Braddock said as he stood up and checked his watch. "They need rest, we do too."

Tori followed him into the hallway.

"I need to run an errand," Braddock said to Tori as they walked back to his office. "I'll see you at home? I won't be long."

"Uh, yeah, okay."

"Okay," he said, quick-pecking her on the lips, then rushing by her and down the hallway.

* * *

"Here comes Renko and Cardellini," Vooch observed, parked a block east of the government center. "Those legs of hers, my God."

"Licorice legs," Boo said. "They start at her neck. Braddock was fucking her back then. Can't say I blame him."

"That was after her first divorce," Vooch noted.

"And now after her second?"

"I'd say she's out of luck if she was here looking for that. Braddock and Hunter seem very cozy with one another."

"We'll see how Hunter feels about all that soon enough."

The two NYPD detectives descended into their rental car. A moment later, with Renko driving, the two of them passed by, going east, probably to the Marriott down the street.

Vooch gestured to the government center. "Speaking of Hunter, there she is." He snorted. "What does Braddock have that I don't have?"

"Six inches in height, forty fewer pounds, and much better hair. No offense."

"Yeah, like you're Ryan Gosling."

"You hung the curveball. I had to hit it," Boo retorted. "You know, you could always show her your bank account. Women have been known to have a shifting scale when it comes to money and looks. That could tip the scales in your favor."

"Whatever. The more important question is, should we follow her home?"

"I think that house is a little hot now. We don't want to get too close."

They waited another two minutes and Braddock pushed his way through the front door, hustling down the front steps, talking on his cell phone. He got into his pickup truck.

"Follow him?"

Boo thought for a moment. "Yeah, not all the way to the house, but it's on the way back to where we're staying."

Braddock backed out of his parking slot and then turned toward them and took a right turn and headed south.

"That's not the route home, or at least directly home," Vooch said.

Boo pulled out and made a left turn, Braddock's headlights a block and a half ahead of them as he made his way south to Highway 210, a state highway that ran east to west across the middle of the state. Braddock turned right, heading west and drove for nearly two miles before he made a right turn off the highway. Boo signaled his turn and Vooch looked to the right and could see some bright light through the scattered woods, like lights for a field.

They followed Braddock and watched him turn right into a full parking lot. There was a lighted sign for The Outskirts. The lights Vooch had seen through the trees from the highway were for sand volleyball courts behind the bar.

"Do we go inside or wait?" Vooch said.

"Wait," Boo said after a minute. "It's a crowded place. He's probably meeting someone for a beer or something."

* * *

Braddock walked through the double doors to the left of the bar, past the kitchen on the right and then down a narrow set of steps to the basement. He walked down the hallway to the door at the end and knocked.

"Enter."

Inside he found Jones at his desk. On the computer monitor behind the desk, there was a grid of video feeds, the security cameras inside his bar.

When Braddock had first moved to Manchester Bay, The Outskirts was a tough joint, more of a biker crowd that led to a fair share of police calls. Jones, foul-mouthed little degenerate that he often was, had slowly been cleaning up its image over the years. Oddly, he'd found you could have a place that catered to pretty much everyone, the old biker and blue-collar crowd, some of the college crowd and now the more upscale one that had moved into Manchester Bay. He'd started with more security that ran off most of the people looking to cause trouble. He added reasonably priced bar food, big screens everywhere to let people watch games, sand volleyball courts, and started sponsoring teams in every recreational and youth sports league around town.

Jones's rapt attention was on the four big screens on the far wall that had four baseball games on. He was intently following his other business. Minnesota still hadn't legalized sports betting. It left a void for gamblers that Jones filled, running a side hustle as a bookmaker taking bets. Early on when he moved to Minnesota, Braddock turned a blind eye to Jones's side operation in return for information—the kind a cop found hard to come by, but someone like Jones picked up all the time. In addition to useful information, Braddock's terms for looking the other way were: small bets only, no letting anyone get in too deep, and he couldn't use muscle to collect. "Use the muscle to clean up the bar."

Jones had agreed and been good to his word, as had Braddock, and in the process, over time, they'd formed a kind of friendship. Braddock and Tori played in a sand volleyball league at the bar during the summer with other hockey parents and he often stopped by for takeout burgers, and he would bring them home tonight.

Usually, Jones would drop a little nugget on Braddock during one of his visits. But it was rare Braddock would call him for actual help. This had Jones excited. "So, what is it I can do for you?" Jones said, a big shit-eating grin on his face, eager, but then he eyed up Braddock. His friend looked worried, a look of vulnerability he could never remember seeing in Braddock. "Hey, man, what gives?"

"I need a favor," Braddock said, leaning on the desk, looking Jones in the eye. "And not as a cop cashing a chit with you, but as your friend. I need something and I have a feeling I'm going to need it fast."

Jones considered Braddock for a moment and then reached back behind his desk for two drink glasses and a bottle of Buffalo Trace. He poured a splash of bourbon in each. "Well, fuck, Braddock," he said, handing him a glass. "You look very uneasy."

"I am," he said before slamming down the bourbon and pouring himself another. "I've got trouble brewing and it's going to focus on me. That's where you and your Rolodex of outlaws comes in."

Jones sat back, examining the bourbon in his glass. "Dude, how can I help?"

ELEVEN

"POLITICS AND PROMOTIONS."

When Tori arrived home, Andrew Hayes was in their driveway, Quinn pulling his hockey bag out of the rear of the Suburban.

"Hiya, Tori."

"Hey, Drew," she greeted and said hello to Peter as well. "Thanks for dropping him off."

"No worries. You want to grab Boomer?"

Tori opened the rear passenger door and let the puppy out, who immediately jumped up, seeking her attention, licking her hand, his tail wagging. "Hey, buddy." He was just the sweetest, happy dog.

Quinn, Tori and Boomer went inside.

"Have you had dinner?"

"A little something earlier," Quinn said but then grinned. "I could eat again, one of those frozen pizzas from Rafferty's."

Quinn was a growing fourteen-year-old boy who now towered over her by several inches. He was starting to eat them out of house and home. She went to the freezer and pulled out a frozen pizza. She'd be lucky to get more than a slice. He could eat the pizza by himself.

"So, how was your day?" Quinn asked. "You guys still working that case?"

"We are," Tori replied as she set the oven temp. "Nothing new to report though." She looked at Quinn who was smiling at his phone. "What has your rapt attention?"

"Oh nothing," he said.

"What's nothing's name?"

"What makes you think—"

She gave him her Tori look.

"Aubrey. Aubrey Nelson."

"Cute name. Is she the little redhead with the long ponytail who plays hockey?"

"Yeah."

"She's adorable," Tori replied, smiling, and Aubrey was. She'd seen Quinn talking to her, him all tall and she was this little spark plug zooming around the ice. "You two an item?"

"Just... talking."

Tori wasn't one to needle him about girls, much. Aubrey was probably the one he liked right now but she'd snuck a peek or two at his phone and there were plenty of texts from other girls. Quinn was a cute kid, or at least she thought so, unobjective as she was. He was tall, outgoing, popular in his class and he was just a good kid, and these days she felt like she had a little bit to do with that. They talked about hockey, his friends and the impending start of eighth grade. She could hardly believe that he was but a year away from high school. When she pulled the finished pizza out of the oven and started cutting it, she asked him about his father.

"How was your dad while I was gone?"

"What do you mean?"

"Was he normal, good, anything happen while I was gone?"

Quinn took a bite of pizza and shook his head. "Nah, he was good. I think he misses you when you're gone like that though."

"How do you mean?"

"You know," Quinn replied, "how you two will hang and talk all night, watch movies together, drink wine. You're always jibber-jabbering with each other. It reminds me—"

"Of what?"

"I shouldn't say."

"No, what."

"I don't remember that much about my mom. I wish I did, but I don't. I mostly remember her being sick, but even when she was, she and Dad talked and laughed a lot. And I've watched some of the holiday and birthday videos they took. What I noticed was my mom and dad really liked being together."

"They loved each other very much." She constantly had to remind herself that he had taken on his father's powers of observation, even at his young age.

Quinn nodded. "And with you and Dad, I kind of see the same thing. You two like being together. And when you're not around I think he misses it, is all."

"I missed him too. Funny how that happens."

"What do you mean?"

"Just that, three years ago I didn't think I needed anyone. I was by myself and thought I was fine. Of course, I was anything but fine."

"Ah, what is it you say sometimes?"

"That was the Old Tori."

"Exactly."

"What about the Old Tori?" Braddock said as he pushed in the back door.

"Nothing, we were just talking," Tori said as Boomer trotted over to him, smelling the white bag Braddock was carrying.

"You went to The Outskirts?" Tori said. Then asked, suspicious, "Why?"

"I needed to see Jones on something. And grabbed us some late dinner."

The three of them hung around the kitchen island, Quinn eating his pizza, Braddock his burger, Tori her chicken sandwich, talking until the clock tipped just past 11:00 p.m.

"Time for bed," Braddock said to his son. "It's late."

"It's summer."

"Not for long. Say goodnight to Boom."

While Quinn went upstairs, Braddock took Boomer outside to do some business before he got into his spacious crate for the night.

Tori readied herself for bed and was under the comforter, reading her phone, when Braddock climbed in on his side.

Tori turned her body to him. "Is there anything I should know about?"

"About what?" he replied, not looking up from his phone.

"Jones, for example. What do you need from that mouthy little pervert?"

"He's not a pervert," Braddock replied, laughing. He found her disgust with him irrational.

"Deviant then," Tori said. "Degenerate. Reprobate. Miscreant."

"I think 'rascal' might be a fairer term."

"I'll take it under advisement. Why go see him?"

"I asked him if he'd heard anything about our bleeding shooter?"

"And?"

"He hadn't. I conveyed to him the importance of finding that man and he said he'd keep his ear to the ground. He's good at that."

She was not nearly as enamored of Jones as her beau was. Maybe it was the way Jones's eyes took a walk all over her every time she ran into him. That, and the little man was a criminal and a character. She tended to focus on the former and Braddock the latter. That said, she had to admit that the vertically challenged imp had a gift for hearing things that had been helpful from time to time.

"Then tell me this."

"What?" he said warily, his eyes sliding to her.

"Don't *what* me. I will not be *whatted*."

Braddock closed his eyes. "It's been a day. I'm tired and I want to go to bed."

This would not be a long talk. What was the priority?

"What is the deal with you and Renko? I could tell last night when Boe told you he was coming that you weren't happy. Then today? I studied him, his reaction to you. He loathes you. I'm not used to seeing someone, anyone, feel that way about you. And you didn't lock up your contempt either. What the hell happened?"

"If I tell you about it, can I go to sleep then?"

She had other questions, but they would have to wait until morning. "Yeah. What happened?"

Braddock exhaled. "It's a time in my life I just don't like talking about."

"Well, given the circumstances, I think you better."

Braddock looked away for moment, closing his eyes.

Tori turned fully to him, sitting cross-legged now, waiting.

"I left the JTTF when Meghan received her cancer diagnosis. I went back to work as a detective so I could have 'somewhat' more regular hours and be closer to her. My third week back, I got detailed over to the 44th Precinct."

"Renko's precinct."

"Yes. I was added to an undercover investigation that four other detectives had been working. There had been a series of street muggings in Tudor City over the late fall and winter months."

"Colder weather, fewer pedestrians."

"Right. So the detail had an idea of the two assholes they

were looking for. They had theft and assault priors, had been seen in the area and matched the general description we had. The men on the detail had been watching these men for some time, and they didn't want stale faces around, lest they become familiar. I was brought in as a fresh face."

"And while you were there, they finally made their move?" Tori said.

"It's a Tuesday night. It's late February, and chilly. I'm in a hoodie, leather jacket, stocking cap, jeans, hiking boots, standing still, uncomfortable, cold. I'm watching a woman in her early thirties with a white-collar professional look to her walking down the other side of the street. She's got a bag of groceries in one hand, her purse around her shoulder, talking on her phone, oblivious to the danger. I've seen her make this walk a couple of nights in a row now and so have these two skells we're watching."

"Your Spidey-senses started tingling."

"Oh yeah. You could just see how she could be a mark. And on this night, I know one guy is in a gap between two buildings just like me and the other is further up the street, waiting in a car parked near the intersection. She walks by the first man, and that night he slips out of his gap and starts following her. I peek around the corner, and I see the guy in the car get out and he starts walking ahead of her towards the street corner."

"They're running a front and follow on her?" Tori said.

Braddock nodded. "I radio exactly that to two detectives named Haller and Orlin. They're Renko's guys. They've been on this detail for weeks and their annoyance with it all had been palpable. They're positioned down the street from me, in gaps between buildings. And the patrol unit ahead has been alerted as well." He took a moment, closing his eyes, thinking back. "I think this is going down, Tor, so I start to follow on the opposite side of the street but I'm way back, and Haller and Orlin are up ahead of me. I see the first man turn the corner, then about ten seconds later the woman does and I'm thinking, it's a dark side street, tight, poorly lit."

"That's when they're going to hit her."

"Yes, and I radio they're going to box her in around that corner. And then I hear the woman scream." Braddock shook his head. "I saw it coming but still didn't react quickly enough."

"It's a tough call."

He nodded. "I start sprinting, but I'm over a half-block back, though Haller and Orlin are ahead of me. There's street traffic I have to cut through. I get around that corner and find the woman sprawled out on the sidewalk, the grocery bag contents scattered all over. They'd taken her purse. She said the men and the two chasing them—"

"Orlin and Haller," Tori said.

"Yes, those two had chased the muggers down an alley on the next block."

"What happened next?"

Braddock exhaled. "The patrol unit arrives. I leave her with them and run after the other two. And as I'm running—" Braddock tapped his left ear "—I can hear in my earbud that Olin and Haller have one of them. I can hear a struggle taking place, the smack of punches, groans, swearing."

"They're beating on the guy."

"I think so, but I don't see it happen."

Tori shrugged. "You know, on a certain level—"

"Yeah, I get it." Braddock nodded. "They've both been after these guys for months, standing outside, freezing and they were exacting a little street justice in an alley, but—" he grimaced "—it didn't go unseen."

"Oh boy," Tori murmured, knowing where this was heading.

"The mugger they caught is African American. Haller and Orlin are white. Residents in the apartment buildings on either side of the alley hear the ruckus and their heads are sticking out the windows, watching. Some are videoing."

"Not good."

"I finally get to the alley. The asshole is lying on his stomach, hands cuffed behind his back, but Olin has his knee on the man's throat. I look at the suspect's beaten face, the blood, a tooth on the ground. I ordered Olin to get off the guy."

"Did he?"

"He tells me to fuck off." Braddock reached with his arm. "I yank him off the guy and throw him to the side. Haller steps to me, but I'm a lot bigger and he thinks better of it." He shook his head. "It was not a good scene. You know the job."

"I do."

"You have those..." he struggled for the words, "those situations where you just know it's—"

"Bad."

"Yeah. And I'm in the middle of it. Though at least someone was still videoing when I intervened. That saved me or... at least should have."

"I assume this is where Renko comes in?" Tori asked.

Braddock nodded.

"Olin and Haller are his guys, right?"

"They are, but you'd have never known it," Braddock replied, shaking his head angrily.

"How so?"

"Fast-forward a month, the video footage goes public of what looks to be Olin and Haller beating this guy to an absolute pulp before I get there. Now, it's dark and even enhanced, you see shadows of arms flying but Haller and Olin are saying the guy was fighting back, he wouldn't go down, they had to get physical to subdue him. A not completely implausible argument."

"But you know otherwise."

Braddock exhaled. "Do I really?"

Tori thought for a moment, and then her eyebrows raised. "You didn't see it."

"I just heard the altercation in my earbud. I didn't hear them say we're going to tune this guy up. I didn't hear them say anything racist. I just heard the fighting."

"And Renko's role in all this? It wasn't to protect his guys?"

Braddock laughed. "No. NYPD wants to nail these guys before the inevitable lawsuits and public outcry but to do it, they need a police witness to say these guys are out of line."

"You. You were the one who was there but who looks okay on video at least."

"Both Internal Affairs and Renko came down on me to go along. I told him, I told the IA detectives, I didn't see them beat the suspect. But Renko—not necessarily IA, *but Renko*—wants me to, quote, 'play ball.'"

"To lie," Tori said, slack-jawed.

"That's what I said," Braddock replied, still shocked about it years later. "I refused. I said it would have to play hard. I could testify to what I saw when I arrived on the scene. I tell Renko and IA they'll have to make that work but in their eyes that's not enough."

"And what about what you heard?"

"What did I hear?" Braddock replied, holding his hands out, shrugging. "I'm running to the scene, it's garbled, but I hear fighting. It could be those two beating him. It could be him resisting them. It could be and probably was some of both. I can't testify to anything definitively."

"But Renko and IA pressed."

"He and IA tried the old, One Police Plaza wanted this one to go down right and there would be something in it for me. And I might need that given my personal situation."

"Meghan."

"Yeah."

Tori shook her head in disgust. "Now I hate the guy."

"He's leveraging me with Meghan, *with her cancer*." He shook his head. "I was not in the mood for it and that's when things started getting tense."

"You wouldn't play ball."

"I was no rat. I had not laid a finger on the suspect and wasn't present when he was beaten and wasn't accused of being so. Had I been, I'd have stopped it, as evidenced by me pulling Orlin off in the first place, and Renko and IA knew that. Think what you want of a cop who holds up the blue wall, but it's hard to have a career if you're a rat. I told the IA cop, if I do that, I end up in his spot, an IA puke spending his time tearing down other cops. No thanks."

"Oh, I bet that went over well."

Braddock laughed wearily. "No. And after that, I went back at Renko, on him not having my back and pushing me to lie about his guys. And then I said: And what happens when I tell his precinct house, he's throwing his guys under the bus."

"Oh boy."

"He didn't like that. He started blaming me, the most senior on the detail for what Olin and Haller did, that I was every bit as at fault and maybe this needed to play *that way*."

"Screw you to make you—"

"Screw Olin and Haller."

"It was you or them."

"Yeah. Now, those two did that to themselves but I wasn't going to be the one to seal their fate, especially when I didn't see it. I mean in my head I was playing out the trial and how I'd end up the discredited witness on the stand caught in a lie. Then I'd be the dirty cop. And I put that to Renko. 'Did you ever think about that?' And then I added: 'asshole.' And then he's up, jabbing me in the chest, who the fuck do I think I'm talking to, playing rank on me, barking that I represented the reason people didn't trust police. I was the problem. We were nose to nose."

"You and a lieutenant?"

"At that time..." He shook his head. "I didn't care about his rank. Honest to God, Tori, I wanted him to throw a punch. I was so angry with the world."

"Meghan."

"Yeah. I mean here's this asshole trying to provoke me to take a swing at him. He was trying to compromise me *that* way. And it damn near worked. The IA detectives stepped in, or I do think we'd have come to blows. Who knows how that plays out? I mean, Renko is a big enough guy who can handle himself but..." He shook his head. "I wouldn't have cared."

"He's a lieutenant," Tori cautioned. "You could have gotten into serious trouble."

"Yeah, but standing there, I had more, far more, in the way of commendations. He was the political climber. I was the better cop."

"Why have it so bad for you? I don't get that."

"Politics and promotions. Renko got the One Police Plaza offer before I did. Get someone to testify against these guys, we'll run them out of the department, and we'll—"

She saw it. "Bump you up. You cost him a promotion."

"Maybe," Braddock said. "Here he is a decade later a chief, so things seemed to work out for him."

"Chief of Internal Affairs though. Kind of ironic."

"That's one way to put it," Braddock said as he punched his pillow and pulled up the comforter.

"Hold on. I have some other questions."

"They can wait," he replied curtly.

"But..."

"It's late, Tor, and I'm exhausted." He pecked her on the cheek, rolled away, turned off his light, and lay with his back to her. The question-and-answer session was over.

Tori rolled onto her back and in the quiet of their bedroom, closed her eyes.

He had explained the origins of his strained relationship with Renko, but they hadn't discussed the other elephant in the room.

Dan Guerero.

She had questions.

Many, in fact, the most unsettling of which was why Braddock wasn't telling her everything.

He was holding back. Why?

TWELVE

"WATCH, LISTEN AND THINK."

The drive into the government center was quiet. In fact, Braddock had uttered barely a word the entire morning. Boe's assistant Brenda waved them down upon arrival. "Sheriff Boe wants you to go into Conference Room B," Brenda said and then lowered her voice. "Those New Yorkers, and then Back-strom and Wilson are in there too." Backstrom was George Backstrom, the Shepard County Attorney. Wilson was Ann Wilson, his chief prosecutor.

"Why are *they* here?" Tori said.

"I don't know," Brenda replied. "Boe wasn't happy that they were. She wasn't pissed at Backstrom and Wilson, but at the New Yorkers. Voices were raised earlier in the boss's office. Something is up."

"Sounds... ominous," Tori muttered to Braddock. "Don't you think?"

Braddock didn't respond. Instead, he started toward the conference room.

Conference Room B was their mid-sized room that sat eight. Braddock opened the door and Tori walked inside. Renko and Cardellini were seated in chairs on the opposite side of the table. On the far end was Backstrom and Wilson. Boe sat opposite Cardellini. There were two open chairs. Braddock took a seat on the end, and Tori one opposite Renko. Tori sat down and read the room.

Brenda wasn't wrong.

The five of them had not been engaging in friendly chit-chat while waiting for her and Braddock to arrive. There was palpable tension in the room, akin to what she'd felt when the four of them were riding together yesterday. Given what Brenda told them, there was a pre-meeting that didn't include the two of them. The question was, over what?

An Airpot with coffee sat on a tray in the middle of the conference table. Tori grabbed a cup and depressed the plunger, filling her cup, and decided to break the ice. "As much as I like George and Ann, why are they here?" she asked, and then took a sip of her coffee.

"I didn't invite them in," Boe said. "And they didn't invite themselves in either."

"And to be honest, *former* Special Agent Hunter, I don't think you should be in here," Renko asserted.

"Is that so?"

If they didn't want her in the room, this was about Braddock. She glanced to her left. Braddock didn't respond, instead sitting in the black leather chair, his eyes zeroed in on Renko and Cardellini. She knew the look. It was how he looked before they would question a suspect, running all the scenarios and questions through his mind. Except in this case, she was thinking he was the one about to be questioned.

"You're compromised."

"By?"

"Your relationship with Braddock."

"Hmm, I see. Well, given what I know about you, Chief Renko, and *your* history with Braddock, I don't see myself being any more compromised than you," she retorted. "So, if it's all the same, I plan on staying. Unless—" she turned to Braddock "—you want me to go."

"Sheriff," Renko stated. "She should not—"

"Braddock's call," Boe blurted.

"I want her to hear whatever it is you have to say," Braddock said calmly. "Get on with it." He sat forward in his chair and reached for a coffee cup of his own.

"We have some questions, and we'd like answers," Renko started.

"About yesterday?" Braddock said.

"Not necessarily."

"Then what?"

"The murders of Ray Lange and Julio Gonzalez, the tie of those murders to Dan Guerero's eight years ago and how the common thread through all of it is—you."

"Me?" Braddock replied flatly. "Really."

"Seriously?" Tori blurted, stunned. One look at Renko and she saw the eager intention in his eyes. It was a look of relish. He was chomping at the bit on this. She let her gaze shift to Cardellini. Her expression was more neutral. Was it the ying to her partner's yang? Tori turned to Boe, Backstrom and Wilson. "And you guys are onboard with this?"

"Chief Renko and Detective Cardellini have raised some questions, Tori," Backstrom said evenly. "I've heard enough that I want to hear what Will has to say about all of this."

"About all of what, George?"

"I'll extend them the courtesy of letting them ask their questions."

After a rough start, Backstrom and Braddock, while not friends per se, had developed a mutually respectful working relationship. In Braddock's eyes, Backstrom was more politician than prosecutor. He was the face of the county attorney's office, liked the glad-handing and schmoozing of local businesspeople come election and fundraising time, but was not a prototypical courtroom brawler. That he left for Ann Wilson.

Ann Wilson was not a politician. She was a prosecutor. Tori had spent her career working with top-notch federal prosecutors and Wilson was every bit as good as them. Ann and Braddock had a very good relationship. Ann and her husband had been to their house for dinner and the Wilsons had reciprocated. They weren't just work colleagues; they were good friends. Wilson's eyes met Tori's. Her look said to Tori, this was serious.

Tori turned to Braddock. "Out in the hall for a minute."

"I'm fine."

She glared.

Braddock sighed, gave her a nod and stood up.

"Give us a minute," she said as they stepped into the hallway. One look around and she saw Eggs, Reese and Nolan looking anxiously in their direction.

"What is it?" Braddock started.

Her immediate thought was he should have an attorney. "I should call Deirdre." Deirdre Brown was a college classmate of Tori's and a former Assistant United States Attorney who was now in private practice in Minneapolis. While she handled mostly white-collar crime these days, she more than knew her way around criminal charges.

Braddock shook his head. "I don't need her."

Tori wasn't so sure about that, given some of her own wonderings the past couple of days. Braddock had been behaving oddly. He had lied about the phone call from Julio, and he was holding information back. That he held things back until he was ready to talk about them was nothing new. He'd do it to Boe, and from time to time, from his investigative team, but rarely, if ever, from her. Yet, he was doing that now too.

"I can tell Ann's worried. You can see the angst in Boe's

face. I looked at Renko and he's frothing at the mouth like a rabid dog."

"I see it too."

"And you're not concerned?"

"I'm extremely concerned, but that's why I want to hear this."

"Fine but put this off until Deirdre gets here. They're teeing you up for something—"

"I suspect so," he said, shaking his head. "But I'm not going to say anything that can hurt me."

"Are there things that can hurt you?"

"All depends on the context."

"What the hell does that mean?"

He looked her in the eye, determined. She wasn't sure what to make of it. "I know who I'm dealing with here. I need to hear this and you need to trust what you know—about me."

"How can I if I don't know what this is about? Do you know what this is about? Is this about Dan Guerero?"

"Dan's a piece of it."

"A piece? What the hell is this all about? How can I trust you if I don't know that? How can I trust you if you won't tell me or let me in?"

"You just... do. I need to let this play out."

She walked away from him, hands on hips. "And I can't talk you out of this?"

He shook his head, firm in his determination. And she knew, when he made a decision, it was made.

"I'm flying blind here. I can't defend if I don't know."

"Watch, listen *and think*. That's what I need you to do. I'll take care of myself."

His cryptic responses were not comforting. Renko and Cardellini were targeting Braddock for something from his past for which she had no knowledge. There were things he hadn't told her about, which both worried and angered her. And even now, he wouldn't tell her what this was really about. He was playing a dangerous game, and he was playing it against everyone in the room, including her.

"Come on," he said. They went back inside and sat down.

Braddock turned to Renko and Cardellini. "Let's get on with it then."

Tori took a sip of her coffee, feeling the tremor of nervousness in the fingers of her hand as she raised the cup to her lips. Braddock seemed calm. The questions swirled in her mind. *Did he know this was coming?* Given what he'd told her, he knew a play was being made on him, yet she sensed he'd expected it. *Did he know what this was all about? Was he ready for it? If he was, should that make her feel worse or better?*

"On Sunday," Cardellini said, leaning forward on her elbows, her hands clasped, closing the distance between her and Braddock, "Will, you had a phone call with Hector Ramirez. Or, as we've agreed, Julio Gonzalez."

"I spoke with Julio Gonzalez. I also told you—"

"Yeah, yeah, yeah," Renko said dismissively, "that he identified himself as Julio Gonzalez and not Hector Ramirez."

"That's right."

"I don't buy for a second that Julio didn't tell you he had changed his name to Hector Ramirez."

Tori hadn't bought that either when Braddock said it the first time. It was a question she had meant to ask last night but after he told the story about Renko, he'd cut off any more questions and at that point, the last thing she wanted to do was accuse him of lying.

Braddock scoffed and took a drink of coffee but didn't otherwise reply.

"So, I don't buy that," Renko continued. "What did you do after the phone call?"

"On Sunday I played golf at Northern Pines Golf Club, the Steamboat Course. I teed off at ten past two. Played eighteen holes with three friends. After, we had beers and burgers on the patio. I left for home around eight thirty and I know that because I noted the time of the dashboard clock. As I was pulling out of the parking lot I got a call from Tori. She was at the airport in Pittsburgh. After the call from Tori, a few minutes later I got the call from Julio. As you'll see from my phone record, I didn't answer the first time the call came through. I didn't recognize the number. I answered it the second time."

"Why answer it then?" Renko inquired.

"The job. I get calls from other jurisdictions, and I recognized the 715-area code as being for Wisconsin. I answered the second call."

"What did you talk about?"

"I told you that already."

"Do it for Backstrom and Wilson."

"Julio said he wanted to meet. He wanted to talk about some things he knew. I assumed about Malik Muhammed." Braddock explained his past confidential informant relationship with Malik. "As I said yesterday, I figured if he could tell me something about what happened to Malik, I'd be interested. I told you, first thing on Monday morning I went to the diner. Julio never showed. And now, we know why."

"And he never said anything about Dan Guerero? About Dan Guerero's murder?"

"No."

"Okay, we'll get back to that. What time did you get home on Sunday?"

"Just before nine p.m. It was dark. And I spent the night *at home*."

"Can anyone verify that?" Renko said. "How about you, Tori?"

"We don't know each other well enough for you to call me Tori. That's Agent Hunter to you."

"I asked a question, *Agent* Hunter."

"Braddock was home when I got home around two a.m. I had been out of town at a conference for work."

Renko looked to Braddock. "Do you have a security system for the house?"

"Yes."

"Was it on when you got home?"

"Yes."

"You turned it off. Did you reset it at some point that night?"

"No."

"Why not?"

"Tori was coming home late from out of town."

"And where was your son?"

"An overnight at a friend's house. It had been scheduled for several days."

"You got home around nine p.m. Agent Hunter got home around two a.m. so we have a five-hour window," Renko said, holding up all the fingers on his left hand for emphasis. "The shoot-out occurred at a cabin that is ten point four miles from your house, a thirteen-minute drive according to my map app. What do you make of that, Detective Braddock?"

Braddock took a drink of his coffee. "Continue."

"I'd like an answer to my question?"

"Ask a specific question then."

"Can anyone verify that you remained at home from nine p.m. until Agent Hunter arrived home at two a.m.?"

"No."

Tori pushed up out of her chair. "Excuse me. I'll be right back." She stepped out of the conference room and found Eggleston and Reese in the hallway.

"Tori, what the hell is going on?" Eggs said worriedly.

"Not sure yet."

"They're questioning the boss?"

"Yeah."

"About?"

"We're getting there," Tori said. "Hand me your notebook." She took Eggleston's notebook and wrote down two names and then went into her phone and found their cell phone numbers. "Here's what I need you to do." She explained to Eggleston and Reese. "I don't care whatever else you're doing, do this right now. Tell them I sent you."

"We're on it," Eggs said.

Tori stepped back into the conference room.

"Look, Renko—"

"That's Chief Renko."

Braddock snorted a laugh. "You're looking to play a game here, Renko," he said before taking a drink of his coffee. "I don't play games, but I'll tell you what I see here. Dan Guerero's murder investigation has new life. Perhaps Monica, to her credit, never gave up on it or, more likely, it's something else that you've not yet disclosed. And I find Internal Affairs's involvement curious. Now, you can say you're in the case because you originally investigated Dan's murder, but that's only part of the story. The other reason IA is investigating the case is that while the department doesn't want to say it, it thinks cops were responsible for Dan's murder."

"We do suspect police officer involvement in Detective Guerero's murder," Cardellini said. "Several officers, in fact."

"How do you get there?" Boe said.

Cardellini steepled her fingers under her chin, taking a moment, collecting her thoughts. "Six months ago, Monica Guerero's mother passed away. She lived in an apartment building a few blocks north of the Guereros and Dan was close to her. He checked on her many times a week. Monica was cleaning out her mother's apartment, which included a basement storage locker. Buried in the back of the locker was an old Nike shoebox containing two steno pads. There were no markings or labels on the box to indicate the contents. They were

Detective Guerero's notebooks, the pages full of notations in his cryptic penmanship. The notes were about an investigation he was working on."

"What case?" Tori asked.

"An old one of Braddock's. Well, not *that* old of a case. It was the Espinosa warehouse shooting." Cardellini eyed Braddock. "I assume you remember that case."

Braddock nodded.

"And that case was what?" Boe inquired.

"Let Braddock explain it."

Braddock took a moment, sipped his coffee, looking away in thought. "It was September almost nine years ago now, if I recall right. I got the call to the Espinosa Furniture Warehouse that there was a robbery homicide. When I arrived on the scene, there were six dead bodies, all lying on the warehouse floor relatively close to one another. One was the owner, Rafael Espinosa. There was his warehouse manager, and a warehouse employee named Alejandro Mercado. Plus three known gang members. The bodies weren't discovered until morning when the first employee showed up to work, so we never had a fix on a time of the shooting other than likely between midnight and two a.m. based on liver temp of the decedents."

"And Espinosa Furniture?"

"For years they'd had one rundown retail location in the Bronx and were struggling just to keep the business afloat. Then, in a four-year span before the shooting, they had moved to a new location, opened two more retail locations and bought the warehouse."

"Where did the money come from?" Boe asked.

"Drugs," Tori blurted. "Well, I assume that is where you're going."

Braddock nodded. "Gangs needed their drug supply from somewhere. Heroin and cocaine got into the country somehow.

For at least one gang, it appeared to be coming in through that warehouse."

"And your theory of the case was an inside job, right?" Cardellini said.

"It *was* an inside job," Braddock said. "There was no evidence of any forced entry. The surveillance cameras were down, shut off by Rafael Espinosa himself, who I'm sure didn't want a video record of the deal going down. The night of the shooting there was a delivery of twenty-six pieces of furniture to the warehouse. Five sectional couches were missing from the delivery. They were just gone. Based on what I was seeing after a couple of days, my theory was someone on the inside knew the drugs came in the couches. The gang members came to take delivery, but the shooters got the drop on them. They never had a chance. All three had guns, but they never pulled them. The killers dropped everyone inside, mowed them down."

"Which told you what?"

"Someone on the inside with Espinosa Furniture helped the shooters get in. I think it was likely the warehouse manager. We found fifty grand in cash in a paper sack in a closet in his apartment."

"Your investigative file indicated you thought the robbery was rival gangs fighting over product and turf."

"That's correct."

"What other leads did you pursue then?" Renko asked.

"There wasn't much else to go on. There were no witnesses. From a forensic standpoint, we had shell casings, but there were no ballistic matches. No prints. No surveillance footage. I had tracked the delivery truck over to the Port Newark Terminal. The furniture had been in a cargo container that had arrived on a ship from—I want to say, Morocco."

"That's it?"

"That's as far as I got," Braddock said. "Like you noted, the warehouse manager was dead. It was an inside job. I didn't have a lead or name to go on from there. I made some inquiries with narcotics detectives and while word of the robbery was on the street, they couldn't point me in any useful direction."

"Any history of the warehouse manager working with or being related to anyone in a gang?"

"No, not that I recall," Braddock said. "That didn't mean there wasn't, but if it existed, I didn't find it. Things petered out from there and then... I went on leave."

"But that wasn't the end of the investigation of the warehouse robbery and murders, was it?" Cardellini pressed. "Dan Guerero took a look, didn't he?"

Braddock nodded. "He did. Alejandro Mercado, the murdered warehouseman, was Dan's nephew, the son of his wife Monica's sister. It was personal for him."

"And did you know that during the course of your investigation?"

"I did."

"Yet, you hadn't done much with the investigation," Renko asserted.

"I did what there was to be done."

"Did you and Detective Guerero discuss your investigation?"

"He came to see me. I walked him through what I had found. He asked if I minded if he poked around on it some more since Mercado was family."

"And your reaction to that was?"

"Well, it was Dan. He came to see me about it, and it involved his family, and he said he wanted to poke around a bit. And work? For me at that point, work was not my focus. Meghan was..." He paused. "By the time Dan came around, it was in February, we were getting pretty late in her battle. She didn't have long at that point."

"Let's talk about your wife and your financial situation at that time," Renko said.

That was an odd and cruel segue, Tori thought.

"My... financial situation," Braddock replied, his brow furrowed. "What about it?"

"You were a detective first grade. When you left the NYPD, your annual salary was $87,250. That doesn't go very far in Manhattan, yet you were living in a three-bedroom apartment with thirty-five hundred square feet with all the bells and whistles, the furniture, the art," Renko asserted.

How would he have known that? Tori wondered. She let her eyes slide left to Braddock whose eyes had shifted to Cardellini. *Is that how?*

"It had a hefty mortgage payment, especially on a cop's pay."

Braddock turned back to Renko. "Meghan and I purchased the apartment on both of our incomes."

"But hers was quite a bit more at the time, was it not?"

"She made a good salary but that pretty much ended when she had to leave the company."

"They cut her off, right."

"Yes."

"No paid leave? No disability payments?"

"No disability plan. It was called Meghan Hayes Designs, but she was only a fifteen percent owner of the business. She had another partner and then a group of investors. They were starting to do well and were getting some good press. Meghan and her partner were optimistic about where they were headed but they weren't there yet. Then she got her diagnosis, and when that became public the business lost all its value."

"It collapsed, did it not?"

"They sold it for what they could. Meghan got a piece, but it certainly wasn't worth what it was. Hard to make a go of Meghan Hayes Designs without Meghan Hayes designing clothes."

"And you got what?"

"A little under a hundred grand after the bills, the investors and her partner, and the lawyers were all paid."

"I would have thought it would have been more," Renko opined. "I bet *you* thought it would be more."

"I don't know that I thought anything about that. It was her business, not mine. I had zero role in it. And given her condition, what she got for it wasn't my biggest concern."

"Really?" Renko said. "Call me a skeptic."

Braddock snorted his disgust.

Tori thought it would have been more as well. Braddock had told her they got paid for her chunk of the business and she'd assumed it had been for more, though she realized she had never really asked about the details. She didn't like prying about that time in his life. And as for his finances, she'd seen some of his financial records and while he wasn't wealthy by any means, he looked comfortable.

"And life insurance?"

"We had $250,000 for Meghan. We should have had more on her given where her income was likely heading, but... we hadn't gotten around to it and then she got sick. And she had about a $100,000 in her IRA."

"So, with her passing, you were going to have what?"

Braddock shook his head. "You do the math."

"Back of the napkin math is $450,000 give or take, plus what you were earning. You had no other assets of your own, right?"

"The apartment."

"Had it appreciated significantly in value at the time?"

"Just the opposite," Braddock said, shaking his head. "We bought it just before the Great Recession where the real estate market then crashed. It was back to maybe even when Meghan died. There was no great windfall when I sold it."

"Anything from your family? Your parents were long deceased, correct?"

"My parents were not wealthy people. They lived on small pensions and Social Security. All they had left when they died was their house and what was in it. After my mom died, I sold that and used the proceeds for part of the down payment on our apartment."

"And you were, what? Thirty-eight at the time of Meghan's death."

"What's your point?"

"That while you and Meghan had planned for a certain future, your finances upon her illness couldn't support your Manhattan lifestyle. With your wife's passing, you lost your future meal ticket."

Braddock glared at Renko.

"Meal ticket?" Boe said, stunned.

"You're such a fucking dick," Tori muttered, shaking her head.

"That *was* crass," Renko said unapologetically. "The point remains; a detective's pay takes little steps up the ladder each year. You two had expected a lot more future income from Meghan. You had spent like it."

"Are you here to give me a financial evaluation?"

"I've found over the years that people don't like to compromise their lifestyle once they've gotten it to a certain level. You had a five-year-old son to take care of, a lifestyle to maintain and while you had what you had as a result of your wife's death, it's hard to make that math work long-term in Manhattan in that apartment, or even Brooklyn these days, for that matter. You might have had to go to Queens, the Bronx, or Jersey even."

"I was born and raised in Uniondale, asshat."

"What does any of this have to do with Ray Lange or Dan Guerero?" Tori interrupted. "Or are you just here to pick at the scab of Meghan's death?"

"It relates back to Dan Guerero's notebook," Renko said. "Dan started poking around on the murders at the warehouse.

As Braddock noted, it was drug related and from Dan's notes, he seemed to confirm it. Word on the street was the drugs stolen were worth quite a lot."

"What's a lot?"

"Street value of twenty-five to thirty million dollars," Renko replied. "At least, according to Dan's notes and Braddock's source, Malik Muhammed."

Braddock chuckled. "Malik wasn't just *my* source. Dan worked for the JTTF too. We both used Malik. And we weren't the only ones. Malik was open for business."

"And Julio Gonzalez as well?"

"Maybe he was a source for Dan," Braddock said. "As I've said, I never met him in person. The first time I ever spoke to him was Sunday night."

Renko shook his head. "Did you ever speak to Malik on the warehouse robbery?"

"Not that I recall," Braddock said.

"Why not?"

"I used Malik for his Afghan connections when I was with the JTTF investigating and preventing terrorism. Not homicide."

"But the JTTF work did include drugs, didn't it?" Renko pressed. "I seem to recall hearing of a drug network that ran from Afghanistan, through Northern Africa and to the States."

"There was. I wouldn't be surprised if there still is, though our pulling out of Afghanistan may make that a lot harder now."

"But you didn't connect that here? You said earlier drugs were involved in the Espinosa Warehouse shootings, did you not?"

"I did. But no, I didn't make the connection."

"In fact, from my review of your work on the Espinosa Warehouse murders, you didn't do much of anything after you found the money in the warehouse manager's apartment, did you?"

Braddock shook his head and took a drink of coffee.

"Am I wrong?"

"Are you here to give me a performance review nine years after the fact?"

"You dogged the fucking case."

"Fuck you." Braddock shook his head. "Typical IA puke. Those who can't investigate, investigate those who can. IA is perfect for you."

Renko ignored the barb. "You went on leave at the end of October. In February, Dan Guerero came to see you and then a few weeks later, he was murdered."

"In a robbery, at a bodega," Braddock said.

"Or was it because he was poking around in the warehouse robbery?"

Braddock shook his head. "If that was what it was about wouldn't *your* investigation have uncovered that, Renko?" He let the question hang in the air for a moment. "You concluded, did you not, that Dan was in the wrong place at the wrong time. Or did you dog your fucking case?"

"I didn't have the benefit of Detective Guerero's notebooks," Renko said. "Now we have them. Now we know he spoke with Malik Muhammed. And then there was this note of his discussion with Muhammed. Dan wrote: 'Braddock didn't come to Malik on warehouse. Odd.'" Renko slid over a photo, it was a picture of the notepad page. "How do you read his comment?"

"I don't know that I can. And you're only providing me one page of his notes so any comment I'd have would be out of context with the whole."

"I read it as you didn't avail yourself of an obvious source of information."

Braddock shrugged. "Did Malik tell him anything?"

"A notation to look at the docks and the name Julio Gonzalez."

"That's it?" Braddock said.

"Not long after that Dan was murdered."

"And this relates to me how?"

"It relates because Monica Guerero told us she asked you to dig into Dan's murder a few months later, after you'd returned to work, didn't she?" Cardellini said.

Braddock didn't respond right away.

"Come on, Will, I know you looked into it," Cardellini pressed. "I know. I know because I saw Monica leave your apartment building one day. I know because I saw your notes on your desk at home. I know because Monica told me a month ago that she asked you to do it, and you did."

Braddock reluctantly nodded. "She did ask that."

Tori froze in place. Braddock had never said a word about Monica Guerero asking him to dig into Dan's murder and certainly nothing since all this started. *Why? Why not tell her about that? Why withhold that?*

"Funny, you never did me the courtesy Dan Guerero did you," Renko noted.

"When?" Cardellini pressed. "When did she ask you to investigate?"

"It was late May. I'd only been back to work a short time when she came to see me."

"And what did you do once she asked?"

"I was very reluctant to do so."

"Why?"

"Dan's shooting was high profile. There was the task force that Renko led that investigated the case, and I already had some bad history with him. A lot more feathers to be ruffled than Dan looking into my non-high-profile case."

"Yet you did investigate, did you not?"

Braddock took a moment. "I said yesterday, I followed the investigation."

"You did more than follow it."

Braddock took a moment before responding, leaning forward, resting his elbows on the table, his eyes fixed on a spot on the wall just above the heads of Renko and Cardellini.

Tori knew the look. Braddock wasn't pausing to find an answer. He was... strategizing, as if he was thinking a few steps ahead. *Was that a good or bad thing? Why did he need to think that way?*

Braddock's eyes blinked and then fixed on Renko and Cardellini. "I reviewed your investigative file. The task force, led by you, Renko, concluded wrong place, wrong time. I checked out the bodega and talked to the owner about that day. Monica told me Dan had spoken with a confidential source named Malik. I knew that had to be our Malik Muhammed."

"And did you talk to him?" Renko said.

Braddock nodded. "I met up with him and he told me what he had told Dan, and that you noted a few minutes ago, that I should look up Julio Gonzalez and that some shit was going down at the Port Newark Terminal, and he had an eye for it."

"And did you look him up?"

"Belatedly, unfortunately."

"What do you mean 'belatedly' and 'unfortunately'?"

"I spoke with Malik, but I didn't get to Julio Gonzalez right away," Braddock replied. "I had been back from leave for a short time. I had case work. I was trying to figure out the logistics of my schedule and looking after Quinn. Frankly, I wasn't eager to do much of anything."

"You had a lot going on. A lot of worries," Renko said. "Financial, about your son, about the widow of a supposed friend of yours asking you to look into his murder."

"Supposed friend?" Braddock replied, shaking his head. "That's what you're going with? That Dan was my alleged friend. Only you, Renko, have alleged friends."

"What conclusions did *you* draw from your look at Dan Guerero's murder? What did you see or find that I didn't?"

"I never got very far."

"Why not?"

"Because Malik pointed me to Julio Gonzalez, but I hadn't yet tracked him down when I got a call that Malik had been murdered. At that point, I immediately went looking for Julio Gonzalez. First at his apartment and then at the docks. He was nowhere to be found."

"Which said what to you?"

"It was one of three things. One, Julio was dead like Malik, just that his body hadn't yet turned up. Two, Julio killed Malik and then skipped town. Three, Julio just skipped town."

"And you did what with this?"

"As I said to you yesterday, I informed the investigators in New Jersey looking into Malik's death of my discussions with him and that he gave me Julio Gonzalez's name but that I could not find Julio."

"And did you do anything else after that?"

There was a knock at the door. Tori and Braddock turned around to see Eggleston, who stepped into the room and handed Tori a folded note and a nod, whispering, "It's solid. Does that help?"

Tori quickly read the note. "We'll see," she replied quietly, and Eggleston backed out of the room.

Braddock gave her a look. "What?"

"In a minute," Tori whispered.

"Something you'd like to share, Special Agent Hunter?" Cardellini asked.

"Why don't the two of you just continue with whatever it is you want to call this," Tori replied while she eyed up Braddock. Renko and Cardellini's purpose was coming into focus for her. What she didn't yet have a read on is what Braddock was after, though she could tell he seemed to know much of what Renko and Cardellini did.

"I'd asked Detective Braddock if he did anything after he

learned Malik Muhammed had been murdered and he couldn't find Julio Gonzalez. I mean, I'd assume for a detective of his abilities, that would have raised some red flags."

"It would have, had I stayed," Braddock replied, sitting back in his chair, crossing his legs. This was more comfortable turf for him. "I decided to move to Manchester Bay at the strong encouragement of my father-in-law. My son had been off with his grandparents for a few weeks for a vacation with family in Michigan. My father-in-law brought Quinn home from the vacation. Roger told me he'd been giving my situation thought and strongly urged me to move here to be with family. He pointedly said he didn't think I'd make it on my own."

"And you accepted that?"

Braddock sighed, shaking his head. "I was... not in a good place. It was going to be a struggle." He paused. "I was a single father of a five-year-old boy, and it was already proving difficult with the job. Rog made me an offer to move here. Cal Lund, Sheriff Boe's predecessor, offered me a job as his chief detective. It was a chance at a fresh start with family there to help. I made the move."

"The timing of your move is curious though."

"I'm not following," Braddock said.

Tori didn't buy that Braddock wasn't following. He knew exactly where this was going. What was it he said to her? *Watch, listen and think.* She'd been watching, listening and *thinking*, particularly about one aspect of the case.

"Since yesterday, I did a little reading on the reopening of Dan Guerero's murder," Tori said. "It was an article buried in the *New York Times* from a few months back. The article reported on the Cold Case Squad reopening the investigation based on some new evidence. You know what wasn't mentioned? Internal Affairs. Yet here we are. The Cold Case Unit is just the public face of this." She paused for a second. "You'd like to close an old case, I'm sure, but that isn't all. You're involved, Chief Renko, because, as Braddock said earlier, the NYPD thinks cops were responsible for this robbery and murder at the warehouse, Dan Guerero's murder, as well as the murders of Malik Muhammad, Julio Gonzalez and Ray Lange. You're after rogue cops. That's why you're here."

"Or former cops," Cardellini murmured.

"Cut the bullshit," Tori said. "We've been at this all day. Get to what you're really after."

Renko stood up and went over to the whiteboard. He started by writing "Braddock" in the middle of the board with a large circle around his name. "Here's what happened," Renko started.

"The Espinosa Warehouse robbery couldn't have been assigned a better detective. Will Braddock, detective first grade, commendations, medals for bravery, a lengthy record of closing cases. A detective of significant accomplishment. Yet the investigation of the robbery and murder of six souls was less than vigorously pursued. You found cash in the apartment of the warehouse manager, who had conveniently been shot in the robbery. So, the investigation was essentially ended with the conclusion it was an inside job. Not long after that you conveniently went on leave."

"Conveniently," Boe murmured.

"His wife was dying," Tori interjected angrily. "Have some compassion, asshole."

Renko plowed ahead, undeterred. "The timing can't be ignored." He wrote "Warehouse Robbery" to the right of Braddock and drew a circle, the lines intersecting with Braddock's circle and Tori saw what he was going to do.

"You go on leave, the warehouse investigation dies, and all is quiet until some months later when Dan Guerero comes to see you about the case. He contacts your old source for information. Malik in turn provides him a lead in Julio Gonzalez—and but a few weeks later Guerero is shot dead in a bodega he went to on a daily basis." Renko wrote "Guerero" on the board and circled it, the outline of the circles intersecting with the one for Braddock, the Venn diagram forming.

"And you're saying cops did that?" Tori retorted. "That certainly wasn't your conclusion at the time."

"No. But that's what we're thinking now."

"Why?"

"I'll get there. First, Monica Guerero came to you, Braddock. She prevailed upon *you* because you were her husband's good friend, and he was looking into the murder of her nephew because *you* didn't get it done on that case. She called you out, did she not?"

"What of it?"

"So, you had to look into his case. And hell, she gave you a lead. She told you about Malik Muhammed, right?" Renko wrote "Malik" on the board and circled his name, again intersecting with Braddock's. "And you said you went to see him."

"I did."

"Any evidence of that?"

"Like what?"

"Notes. Witnesses. Anything like that?"

"I don't know about you, but in my experience there typically aren't witnesses when you talk to a confidential informant. They don't stay confidential that way."

"But he gave you the name Julio Gonzalez, right?"

"Asked and answered."

"But you didn't go see him."

"As I said, not right then and there."

"No," Renko accused. "You took your time, and then Malik —" Renko tapped his name on the whiteboard "—ends up murdered after you went to see him. Just like Dan Guerero was murdered after he came to see you. Just like Julio Gonzalez died as he came to Manchester Bay to contact you." Renko turned to Boe. "You want to know why Ray Lange didn't call you in advance, Sheriff Boe. Because everyone who reaches out to Braddock ends up dead! It all revolves around *him*."

Tori held up the note in her hand. "I have two witnesses, neighbors Leslie and Joe, next door neighbors to Braddock and I who recall seeing him come home around nine p.m. Sunday night. They were sitting at their fire pit in their yard down by the lake with a clear view of the house. They were still sitting out there when I got home at two a.m. I spoke with them when I got home. They invited me over to the fire. They saw Braddock come home. They never saw him leave and then return."

Renko waved her off. "Agent Hunter, I thought you'd be smarter. I'm just assuming your boyfriend is far too shrewd to be the one to pull the trigger. I mean, I can tell today that you didn't know about any of this. He's lied to everybody about this, including you."

It was her turn to glare at Renko. The prick wasn't wrong though.

"No, no, no. He didn't do it alone all those years ago. He's not doing it alone now, though he's doing it behind *your* back."

He was making her out to be a fool. She shook her head, not sure who she was angrier at, Renko or now Braddock.

"These are not one-man jobs. Killing Guerero took at least two, if not three men, we have footage of that. You both noted, and Cardellini and I agree, there were likely three men involved in the shooting Sunday night. You didn't have to be there, Braddock. You just had to tell them where to go in *your* county after Julio told you where he was." Renko turned to Backstrom and Wilson. "I don't think he's pulled the trigger on any of these murders. It was his job to tie the warehouse murders up in a quick little bow. He did. It was his job to warn others about Dan Guerero's interest. He did. It was his job to set up Malik Muhammed. He did. It was his job Sunday night to set up Gonzalez and Ray Lange. And. He. Did."

"I didn't know where Gonzalez was. I didn't ask him. I was going to meet him, remember?" Braddock stated.

Renko was unbothered. "If that's even true, all you did Monday morning is make like you were going to meet him. Sure, you went to the restaurant, had a cup of coffee, waited an hour, all to make it look right. But we both know you got off that call Sunday night with the man you know as Julio and made another call. By the time you went to that restaurant Monday morning for your 'meeting,' Gonzalez and Lange had been underwater for hours. The evidence, what happened, all says Gonzalez told you where he was, and you relayed that information to your co-conspirators, and they did what needed doing."

"Which are who?" Braddock said calmly. "Check my calls."

"Oh, I have," Renko replied. "That's how I know you talked to Julio. But I'd be selling you short, if I thought you were using your own cell phone for any of this. Gonzalez calls you Sunday night. You're what? Ten minutes from home. All you have to do is get home and make the call on another phone. Clearly, the killers were already here to begin with given what happened Sunday night. So, there are the murders and then I look at how you're living here. The big house on one of Minnesota's most expensive lakes."

"The house was a gift," Braddock said. "From Roger Hayes to get me to move here."

"Yeah, yeah, because you were 'so distraught' over the loss of your wife."

Braddock shoved his chair back and bolted up. He was no longer calm.

"No!" Tori said, grabbing his arm. "No, no, no. He wants that," she cautioned, stepping between Braddock and Renko, who was still sitting, grinning up at him. "He's goading you," she whispered. "Just like years ago."

Braddock backed away. To Renko, she said, "I'd be careful if I were you."

"Or what, Special Agent Hunter," Renko replied flippantly. "He'll have me killed."

"I should bring Roger Hayes in here," Braddock said as he sat back down in his chair. "He'd eat you alive."

"He'd learn who his son-in-law really is."

Tori turned and stepped at Renko, this time Braddock grabbing her arm.

"Bring him in," Renko continued. "I'm sure what he's going to tell me is the house was a gift. It makes for a good way to live a lake lifestyle. It also makes for a good way to hide all that money. I mean, add it up. You have the big remodel and addition completed in the last year. That must have cost three, maybe four hundred grand?"

"Been doing some research, have you?" Braddock retorted.

"You're living kind of large with the house, you've got the new eighty-thousand-dollar Silverado pickup truck. There's the new surf boat for the lake and the new boat lift to go with it. New, new, new."

"The boat was used," Braddock replied.

Renko laughed. "It still cost over a hundred grand at Manchester Bay Marine. And the vacations you've taken. Costa Rica, Marco Island, all pretty good on a chief detective's pay for a rural county in Minnesota."

"Yeah, I add nothing," Tori retorted.

"Tori has more money than me," Braddock added.

"More legitimate money, anyway," Renko said. "But we haven't seen any evidence she's spending it any differently than she ever has."

Tori was flabbergasted. "You've been looking into *my* finances?" She was being pulled into whatever story it was Renko and Cardellini were weaving.

"We just can't help but note all the big spending for a county detective. Unless, of course, money is no object."

"I live nicely, not lavishly."

"Looked pretty lavish to me yesterday," Cardellini noted. "At least it did to this Queens girl."

"That explains a lot," Tori said snippily.

Boe chuckled.

"Just so I'm following," Ann Wilson interjected, "you two are alleging that Will Braddock, a highly decorated law enforcement officer, most recently the recipient of the Presidential Medal of Valor, is part of a vast criminal conspiracy with other cops or former cops involving murders, drugs and money. And you have what actual evidence of this beyond your Venn diagram?" Wilson said. "Because from where I'm sitting, I don't see it."

"How can't you?" Renko said and went to the whiteboard. "Espinosa Warehouse. Dan Guerero investigating the case you dogged, Braddock."

"Fuck you!" Braddock railed, his composure leaking. "Meghan was dying."

"That certainly provides an excuse. And cover."

"You're such a fucking piece of shit."

"Then what about Malik then, Will?" Cardellini said. "Monica comes to you, asking you to look into Dan's murder. Telling you he spoke to Malik."

"And you don't want anyone looking into any of this," Renko said, gesturing at Braddock. "And you can't have anyone talking about this. You need to shut it down. You get Malik, but miss Julio when he goes on the run, changes his name to Hector Ramirez and moves around to stay hidden until we, and you, finally found him."

"I found him?" Braddock replied, shaking his head. "He drove here."

"So much the better," Renko retorted. "He still thought he could trust you, apparently. A fool's errand."

"There is a trend here, Will," Cardellini said. "And after Malik is murdered, you rather abruptly left for Minnesota. It wasn't, I'm moving in six months. It wasn't a planned, transitional, logical or methodical move. You were here one day and gone the next, as if you had to get away. Fast."

Braddock shook his head, closing his eyes. "You're a fucker," he growled at Renko and then to Cardellini. "You should know better, Cardi."

"Should I? I can't deny what I'm seeing here. And I know what I saw back then in your apartment. It didn't make sense to me then. It makes sense now. You have to know how this looks and it's not good. Get ahead of it. Let me help you."

"Help me?" Braddock chortled. "Really?"

"I want to," Cardellini said.

"I know how you're making it look, Cardi. Don't let Renko take away what you know."

"If what you allege is true, why would Julio Gonzalez call Braddock then on Sunday night?" Tori said. "Why would he trust Braddock?"

"Because Malik had," Renko said. "Because Julio knew cops were involved in whatever this was. He thought he'd go to the one NYPD cop still alive that Malik trusted. Little did he know that he walked himself, and Ray Lange, right into a trap of Braddock's making." He wrote "Lange" on the board and a circle and then stepped at Braddock. "It all comes back to you!"

"It's a really nice doodle," Braddock snarked.

"A Venn diagram doesn't make a case," Wilson said. "Do you have any direct evidence?"

"The phone call, that he admits took place on Sunday."

"That's your word against his. Do you have a recording of it?"

"No."

"So, you have no idea what they actually discussed."

"I think it's rather apparent."

"I don't and even if I did, I don't charge cases on what's rather apparent," Wilson retorted "Do you have any physical evidence? This other phone, or this money you speak of, for example. Do you have any evidence that Braddock has some other bank account?"

"I know one way to expedite finding it. Get us a search warrant for his house."

"You ain't got enough for one," Tori snorted.

"Not your call."

"No, it's mine," Wilson said. "And she's right, you don't have it."

Renko gestured to the board, tapping with the marker. "It's all right there."

"I won't deny how what you have on the board looks, but at this point it's nothing more than a story, well-conceived and told," Wilson stated. "But it's not evidence, it's conjecture. If that is all you have for an affidavit in support of a search warrant, you do not have probable cause sufficient for the warrant."

"Are you both defense attorneys now?"

"No, but I know what Braddock's would say in court, and I know what the judge would tell me," Wilson said. "Innuendo and supposition might fly on Page Six in New York, but it doesn't cut it for a search warrant here, or anywhere."

"You think I'm involved in this?" Braddock said. "If I were, the clusterfuck of Sunday never happens."

"How so?" Boe said.

"I explained this to these two yesterday. Anyone from around here who has any knowledge of the Mississippi River would know that it runs very shallow in that stretch where that car was dumped. There are hundreds of bodies of water in this county alone that are much deeper and much better to dump a car, a body, anything. And on top of that, if I was involved in this, do you think I'd do anything here! In my own county?"

"Why not, if you could get rid of Julio Gonzalez, kill him, bury or dump his body, so that nobody knows whatever it was he knew," Renko said. "Your crew fucked up. Ray Lange showed up and he put up a fight."

"Again, innuendo and supposition," Wilson said.

"How do you live with yourself, Will?" Cardellini said. "Mixed up in all this."

"And how do you, knowing me as you do, think I could do something like this?" Braddock replied. "Come on, Cardi. You think I could do this? *Really?*"

"What galls me is how you used your wife's death as cover to do all this," Renko asserted. "That tells me what kind of man you are right there."

Braddock's head snapped to Renko and Tori saw it. The look and there was nobody between the two of them and Braddock was out of his chair again. Renko was standing right there.

"Maybe we *should* bring your father-in-law in," Renko asserted, jabbing Braddock in the chest. "Then he can see you for the traitorous, cold-blooded, murdering son-of-a-bitch son in law you really are!"

"Oh God," Tori murmured.

Braddock batted Renko's right hand and shoved him hard, propelling him backward against the whiteboard. Renko pushed himself from the wall and took a step at Braddock, clenching his fist.

It was a mistake.

Braddock's quick right hook caught Renko in the jaw, buckling his legs, sending him sprawling to the left. As he crumpled to the floor, Braddock pounced, hammering him with another right from on high.

"Will, no!" Boe yelled.

Tori grabbed at his left arm. "Stop. *Stop!*"

Renko, stunned, pushed himself up. Braddock unloaded another right, landing it on the bridge of his nose with sickening cracking sound and squirt of blood.

"Reese!" Boe yelled out the door. "Get in here!"

"Stop!" Cardellini yelled.

Renko got to his feet and bull rushed Braddock, driving him back into the conference table and then rolled left into the wall. He tried to get his right arm free, but Braddock pinned it against his own body with his left arm while driving another right, catching Renko just above the eye, stunning him again as he dropped to his right knee.

Tori and Cardellini jumped in, Tori grabbing Braddock's left arm, Cardellini trying to drag Renko free, but Braddock was in a rage now, throwing another right, battering Renko.

Reese and a deputy burst into the room. They grabbed Braddock off Renko, pinning him up against the wall, each with an arm. Renko crumpled to his knees, his face a bloody mess. Two more deputies arrived.

Tori looked up at Braddock, breathing heavily, a fury in his eyes she'd never seen.

"Get him out of here," Boe said to Reese and the deputy. "Put him in my office." To Braddock, she said, "And you will go!"

Braddock let out a sigh and then nodded. The deputies and Reese stayed between Braddock and Renko as they escorted him out.

"He's going to need to go to the ER," Boe said.

"I'm fucking pressing charges on that asshole," Renko said, spitting blood to the floor.

"Feel free," Wilson said. "But I'm not charging it."

"What!" Cardellini yelled. "Take one look at him."

"I saw the whole thing, Detective," Backstrom said. "Chief Renko, someone who should know better, provoked him, again and again verbally and then he battered him. And after Braddock pushed him away, he charged him."

"But, but... look at him."

"It was a fair fight between two men who know how to handle themselves. Renko chose poorly."

"I'll be dealing with Braddock," Boe said. "I know you all might do things a little different in New York, but Chief Renko was out of line, and he paid the price for it. Commander White and I will be discussing this, I assure you."

"You tried to provoke that reaction," Backstrom said to Renko and then Cardellini. "If all you have on Braddock is what you've presented in here, we're done."

A deputy helped a wobbly Renko to his feet.

"Deputy, please escort Chief Renko and Detective Cardellini to their vehicle and lead them over to the ER at County and see that he is treated immediately due to being a law enforcement officer injured in the line of duty," Boe ordered.

"Yes, ma'am."

Tori fell in behind Boe as she charged down the hallway toward her office. She looked back at Wilson and Backstrom, who were following.

A deputy stood outside the sheriff's office and opened the door. They found Braddock sitting on the couch, his elbows on his thighs, a bottle of water in his hand. Tori decided to hang back and lean against the wall.

"What the hell was that!" Boe barked after the door closed. "You beat the hell out of him. He's a chief with the NYPD, for Christ's sake."

"I ain't apologizing."

Boe stood with her hands on her hips. "I think you broke his nose."

"I certainly hope so."

"This ain't funny, Will," Backstrom barked. "What the heck are you mixed up in?"

"Not a damn thing, George."

"I'd really like to believe that," Ann Wilson said, her arms folded, her eyes piercing. "I'd like to continue to believe that. But you are not out of the woods, my friend. Right now, they've got nothing but a story but it's believable. Are you going to tell me all that was a coincidence? What is it you like to say about coincidences, Will?"

"No such thing."

"Then what did I just see?"

"A theory, unsupported by evidence."

"Tell you what, they get one piece of hard evidence on you, a gun—a disposable phone, a bank record, a witness—the game changes *significantly*. Clearly, they think you are a part of something far larger, that has been going on for a long time: drugs, money, murder."

"They're not done digging on you, my friend," Backstrom added. "And especially after that... beatdown. What the hell were you thinking?"

"I was thinking of beating the shit out of a piece of shit, George." Braddock took a drink of water. "I guess we best solve our case then."

"You'll be doing no such thing," Boe asserted.

"Excuse me."

"You're suspended."

"Jeanette, look I know it got a little out of hand."

"*Out of hand!* You just sent an NYPD Chief to the hospital. Don't for a minute think the fact I defended you means in any way I found that acceptable from someone who has been my most-valued person. You're done. Suspended. Gun and badge on the desk."

"Look..."

"Now!" Boe bellowed loud enough for anyone outside the office to hear.

Braddock sat back on the couch for a moment, peering around the room, seeing the disappointment, if not shock, on everyone's faces. He offered a slight nod, then slowly pushed himself up from the couch and placed his gun and badge on her desk with his bloody right hand. He grabbed his suitcoat and threw it over his shoulder and walked out, following Tori who'd opened the door and left ahead of him, walking toward his office.

"Tor—"

"Not a word," Tori said and led him to his office and closed the door. She stood close to him, her hands on her hips. "You're lying to me. You're lying to them. What I'm wondering is if you're lying to yourself too."

"Tori, I'm—"

"I'm talking!" she said in a clipped whisper. "You lied about that call on Sunday night. Julio Gonzalez told you his name was Hector Ramirez, no way he didn't. I was looking right at you when you answered that question, and you lied. You haven't told me about Dan Guerero, his murder, that his wife asked you to look into that case. And I don't buy for a second, *a second*, that Julio didn't mention that Sunday night."

"Tori—"

"We're not married but we're not boyfriend-girlfriend either. Do you understand me? Whatever is going on with this shit from your past, is need-to-know information *for me*. Renko was out of line. He deserved a beating, but only if he's full of shit and right now, I don't know who to believe. So let me tell you something. What Renko and Cardellini put on the white-board in there has me questioning who I'm living with."

"Let me—"

"Who are you? Seriously? I mean they're dragging me into this, looking at my finances, what I've been doing. They've been looking at you, and not just since Sunday."

"Tor—"

"And that beating? That was about more than what they're alleging. You unloaded on him because of Meghan. You have some unresolved issues there. And Cardellini?" She paused for a moment, staring him in the eye. "We haven't even gotten to that yet, and when and where *it* happened."

Braddock closed his eyes.

"Do not come home right now. Don't! I'm going to give you a couple of hours to go have a beer, take a drive, a walk, whatever, to get your thoughts together and you better have all the answers because you're in a heap of trouble and I have to decide if I even want to stay."

"Tori."

"Not a word. Not a one right now."

Tori turned around and walked out of the office, closing the door with a loud *kathump!*

Braddock leaned back against the front of his desk and closed his eyes. "Good work there, Ace," he muttered to himself and slowly pulled on his suitcoat. That said, he'd learned a few things.

He pulled out his cell phone and placed a call.

"What's up?"

"A lot of not good," Braddock said.

"So, I've heard," Steak replied.

"Already?"

"I was getting updates from Eggs and Reese. You bludgeoned the IA prick. I'm good with that. Just wish I could have been there to see it."

"I'm suspended. Boe is *really* pissed."

"You know, my friend, that might not be the worst thing right now."

Braddock snorted. It wasn't. In fact, it was part of what he was angling for. "Tori is on her way home. She's mad. *Really* mad. Like leave me mad."

"Leave you? For what, beating on the IA prick?"

"I haven't told you everything on this, not by a long shot, but I haven't told her anything. I've left her completely in the dark."

"*That*, my friend, was a very bad idea."

His phone buzzed. A text. Jones: *We need to talk.*

"I have to go. Jones might have something."

"Alright. You go. I'll watch. And if she comes out of the house with luggage, I'll let you know."

* * *

Hunter came hustling down the steps of the government center and beelined to her Audi SUV.

Vooch's phone buzzed. "Yeah," he answered as Hunter backed out of her parking space and drove speedily away.

"You and Conn get Braddock," Boo ordered. "Stag and I will take Hunter."

THIRTEEN

"WIPEOUT."

Dan Guerero.

Tori hadn't thought of him in years. He wasn't someone who had made that kind of impression on her longer-term life. That is until now.

The funeral was on a late, gray, cool winter day. She'd huddled in her wool topcoat as she observed the pallbearers, a mix of police officers in their dress uniforms and men in civilian clothes, lift the casket of Dan Guerero from the rear of the hearse and then slowly up the steps and into the cathedral. She remembered, could picture in her mind, that she had gone to the service with Geno Harlow, Tracy Sheets and other fellow agents from the New York Field Office. They had all worked with Guerero at one time or another and while they were not close, she'd considered him a friend, certainly a well-respected law enforcement colleague.

The funeral service itself had been solemn yet moving, a tribute to an officer's career, his sacrifice and his faith. She remembered seeing Monica Guerero holding the hand of her daughter as they had walked down the center aisle of the cathedral, following the casket after the funeral service.

Braddock had been a pallbearer yet when she thought back on it, she couldn't picture him as one of the men in full-dress uniform, white gloves, carrying the casket down the center aisle of St. Patrick's Cathedral. She'd noticed those men certainly but hadn't focused on them. Nor could she picture him at the cemetery, as they laid Dan to rest. It was difficult to do that in a crowd of thousands, especially when thinking back eight years.

Had a man responsible for his death been one to lay him to rest?

When she pulled into the garage Tori realized she'd been so engrossed, thinking back to the funeral, that she'd driven home in a brain fog. She had no recall of her travel home, as if she'd traversed the route from Manchester Bay to their home in an autopilot-like trance, thinking back to that day.

She went inside, deactivated the security system and stood in the kitchen, peering about her home. A home that just a few short years ago seemed like something so far out of reach. The sense of place with comfortable couches and chairs, the fireplace, the warmth, the photos on the bookshelves and walls, their small family, love, a happy life.

Now she was questioning who she had built it with and what it was built upon.

Should she be?

She couldn't believe Braddock to be the man described today. It would go against everything she ever thought she knew of and about him. Yet the portrait Renko painted was damning. The rage Braddock had exhibited in beating him was something she had never seen before. And then there was Cardellini. And Meghan.

For ten minutes, she manically paced around the main level of the house, alternately folding her arms across her chest, running her fingers nervously through her hair, rubbing her face and eyes.

Was Braddock the man she'd thought he was or was he a

murderer? Was their life in this house, on the lake, their relationship, all built on a series of lies? Was the comfortable lifestyle paid for with blood money?

How was it possible she'd been that wrong about him?

Or was she?

If she'd driven home in a daze, now in the quiet of the house she was spiraling. She needed to get out of the house.

Ten minutes later she was on her bike and pedaling hard, in her bright-yellow jumpsuit and matching bike shoes, Bruce Springsteen blaring in her ears.

As she settled into her cadence, she let the music play, just wanting to clear her head. She was angry, rightfully so, she thought. But rarely did such fury allow for clear thinking, so rather than contemplating the day, she rode hard, pushing herself, letting the sweat build. She focused on the winding county road that roughly followed the western shoreline of Northern Pine Lake.

She made her way around the north end of the lake and over the Channel Bridge, past the Channel Stop Bar and Restaurant, then the Northern Pines Resort on the right before she went up and over the vehicle and pedestrian bridge that arched high over the H-4. Once over the bridge she turned left and cycled two miles north into Holmstrand and down the main street parking her bike at the Chocolate Moose ice-cream shop.

The Moose was not a usual stop for her. Ice cream defeated the purpose of exercise. Today, she didn't care. Inside, she walked around aimlessly for a bit mindlessly perusing the hundreds of boxes of candy on the shelves, while the server made cones for a group of six. The group fully served, she stepped to the white refrigerator case and evaluated her thirty-two ice-cream options, ultimately settling on a big scoop of cookie dough in a waffle cone, along with a bottle of water. She sat on the park bench out front, slowly ate her cone and scrolled through Instagram and TikTok, and in general took in what was left of the early evening light while she calmed her mind.

A half-hour later, her cone finished, she checked her watch and the sky. It was that time of year when the sun seemed to set ten minutes earlier every day. She knew that wasn't the case, but it just seemed that way. Better hustle, she thought as she set off for the return leg, pedaling south and her more settled mind turned back to Braddock.

How did he end up in this situation?

Braddock was a smart man. He was as canny and intuitive an investigator as she had ever run across, which made what she had seen the last two days even more confounding.

Or was it?

She had conflicting thoughts running through her mind—what she'd seen but also, what Braddock had said to her before today all started. "I need to let this play out," and, "I need you to watch, listen and think."

Let this play out?

What did that mean?

For starters, that meant he knew something was coming and it was coming at him. He'd never said a thing about Dan Guerero. She'd heard Malik's name once or twice over the years as a confidential source, but it was always in the context of the work he did for the JTTF and the stories he told about that. Braddock had never said he was dead.

But why did he have to let it play out?

She chewed on that thought for a minute as the familiar signature drums of the Mighty Max Weinberg started "Born to Run." She'd recalled reading somewhere that "Born to Run" was the greatest rock song ever. She wasn't sure she agreed with that, but it was certainly in the discussion for top ten or twenty. The beat of the song increased the pace of her cycling.

Braddock knew this was coming. Why else say it needed to play out. He likely didn't anticipate everything that had happened, but he knew something was coming at him. And in letting it play out, they had shown him their case, maybe not every little nit and nat, but certainly the overall theory. As Wilson and Boe said, they didn't have it, not enough for a search warrant though she thought Wilson's warning on point. If they did get one solid piece, they'd get the search warrant.

Was there something in the house Braddock had to be worried about? Did Braddock want it to play out because he wanted to defend himself because he was innocent? Or guilty?

And what are you going to do about all this?

She thought about that as she pedaled on the bridge over the H-4.

* * *

Boo and Stag had followed from a distance along County Road 44, passing by her, parking at the Northern Pines Resort and watching her cycle by and then parking along the street in Holmstrand opposite the ice-cream shop. It was still light out though the sun was close to falling behind the treelined horizon to the west. His phone buzzed, a text from Conn. *Braddock is on his way to the Outskirts.*

He texted back: *Now is the time.*

* * *

As he drove, Braddock replayed the day in his mind. Since Sunday night he'd tried to block the thought of Dan out of his mind, what had happened to him, and especially his part in that. Now, out of necessity, he had let it all back in.

Espinosa Warehouse. Alejandro Mercado. Monica. His talk with Dan about it all, even all these years later, was still clear as a bell in his mind, as it was when he'd first moved to Minnesota, trying to get himself straightened out.

It started with a call from Dan. He was stopping by and would be there in twenty minutes.

"We can talk now," Braddock remembered saying.

"I need to see you, face to face."

A half-hour later Braddock was opening the door. "Dan, good to see you."

"Will, you too," Dan Guerero greeted, extending his hand which Braddock took before Dan brought him in for a warm embrace. "How are you doing, man?" he said quietly.

Braddock looked right down the hallway toward the bedroom. "I'm okay."

"And Meghan?"

He shook his head. "She's been able to speak a little bit today. You want to go in? I know she'd like to see you."

"In a bit. Look, there's something I wanted to tell you."

"What's that?"

"The Espinosa Warehouse."

"What about it?"

"Listen," Dan said, pausing before looking him right in the eye. "Your mind has been elsewhere, and—" he looked down the hallway to the bedroom "—understandably so. But Alejandro was my family. I need to know what happened to him. Monica wants to know. Her sister wants to know, and I think there's more to what happened there than you found."

"O-kay," he replied haltingly, surprised.

"I wanted to tell you I'm going to dig into it to see if that's the case. I'll be doing it on the side, but I'm doing it."

"I... see."

"We're good friends. We've worked together for years, and I feel shitty about it, but I wanted you to hear from me directly, not from someone else." He wasn't asking for permission; he was telling him what was going to happen.

Braddock sighed and looked away.

"Tell me I'm wrong, man," Dan pressed. "Straight up. Tell

me there is nothing else to find. You look me in the eye and tell me that's the case, I'll walk away."

Braddock looked down at the floor, then shook his head. He knew he hadn't worked the case hard, that he'd taken the easy win without digging more, even when his instincts said there might be more, even knowing Dan's nephew was the victim. "I'm sorry."

"It's alright, man. I understand," Dan said, patting Braddock on the shoulder. "Look, if I do find something, I'll come to you first and we'll figure out what to do with it? Fair?"

"Yeah," Braddock said, nodding. "Yeah, that's more than fair."

"Okay." Dan looked down the hallway toward the bedroom, then leaned in. "How long does she have?"

"A few weeks, month at the outside. We're not at hospice yet but it's getting close."

"I'm so sorry, man," Dan said softly. "So sorry. Take me in to see her?"

Braddock looked up and nodded. "I think she'd like that. But just so you're prepared. She's... pretty... frail. You're almost not going to recognize her."

"I hear you," Dan said and threw his arm around his shoulder. "Lead the way in, bud."

Braddock led Dan down the hallway to the master bedroom. Lying in a hospital bed looking out the window was Meghan. She turned to them. "Dan! Hi," she greeted in a raspy voice, holding her hand out to him. "Come over here."

"Hey, Meg."

That was the last time he saw Dan, he thought as he parked. A few weeks later he was dead. It was only later that he realized how responsible he'd been for that.

While not in any mood to laugh, he had to, at least a bit, as he surveyed The Outskirts parking lot. It was Wednesday, just after 6:00 p.m. and nearly September, a typically slower time of late summer leading into school and yet Jones's front parking lot was nearly full. He was just printing money these days with his operation—most of it legit. As he walked toward the front, the enthusiastic sounds of volleyball players and music emanated from the back.

"Busy night?" he said to Colette, one of the hostesses when he walked inside.

"What night isn't these days," she replied with a bright toothy smile.

"And Napoleon?"

Colette laughed. "In his office. He told me to send you down."

Braddock made his way through the kitchen doors and checked his phone, a text from Steak: *She just went for a luggage free bike ride.*

That was a relief. She often used exercise to clear her mind and that's what he wanted her to do, *think.*

He walked down the steps and to the end of the basement hallway. The door was open, and he walked in.

"Close that," Jones said.

Braddock closed the door.

"You remember when you and I first chatted about my side hustle. What you told me I couldn't do?"

Braddock nodded. "I'd let you continue as long as you shared information and didn't use any serious muscle to collect. Threats, implied or otherwise were fine, but—"

"Don't hurt anybody," Jones finished. "So, I don't do that. I'm not a fucking bank. I don't extend fucking credit. I don't let anyone get into me for any real amount of money. You place a bet you have to have the cash."

"Hell, Jonesy, from the looks of your parking lot as of late, I don't know why you still make book. It's a Wednesday night in late summer and the lot's full. You're killing it."

"Ha, fuckin' right, I am!" Jones laughed. "I've been fucking killing it for five years. I don't need to do it. I do it because I love the fucking action, watching all these flat screens, keeping the tally. Am I winning or losing? I'd be bored shitless without it. But—" Jones held up a finger "—your rules for me were also wise. I am far more careful about who I take action from. I don't need some dicknose douche canoe coming in here, losing and then blowing everything up on me."

"Not that I don't love your colorful dissertation here, Jonesy, but what do you have?"

Jones eyed him for a moment. Braddock usually liked the back and forth. "You're really jammed up here, aren't you?"

"You could say that."

"I made some calls. Let me preface this by saying not everyone who does what I do is quite so careful. Some do use certain forms of physical persuasion to get their bills paid."

"I well imagine."

"I know a couple of fellas who are willing to extend credit and the risk that comes with that, i.e., collection activities. But what I'm about to tell you, it can't come back on them, or me, because if it does..."

"You're doing me a serious solid. I need to do it back."

"That's what friends do and as much as it pains you to admit it, we're actually friends."

"The point, Jonesy?"

"There's a guy who keeps a little black book like mine that had a doctor into him for fifteen grand, plus the juice which had run long enough that the fucking tab was twenty grand. My 'colleague' had been hounding the doctor and threatened that the next time he came to collect, it wouldn't be pleasant. And I know that is not an idle threat, not with this guy, and this doc fucking knew it too. That warning was conveyed late Saturday night at a watering hole far less reputable than mine down St. Cloud way. The doc said then that he didn't have the money. He was doing all he could to get it, but he needed more time. Apparently, he has one ex-wife, one soon-to-be ex-wife, kids and is a fuckin' gambling addict."

Braddock understood. "That's a bad trifecta."

"Fucking right it is. I'd never extend credit to a guy like that. Even when you win, you lose. But this guy? This was not the first time he'd been delinquent."

"And you're going to tell me then he wasn't delinquent," Braddock said.

Jones smiled. "Monday night, two days after he didn't have it, the fuckin' doc showed up with twenty grand *cash* in nice crisp one hundred dollar bills, and settled his tab. My guy says the doc takes off-the-books medical cases to cover his debts. It's not well known in St. Cloud, but his name floats around down in the Twin Cities if you need some medical care that is better not reported. He only takes cash, and he doesn't work cheap."

"The doctor's name?"

"Julian Vance." Jones handed him a slip of paper with Vance's address. "I looked him up. He's with St. Cloud Physicians Group, working out of the Division Street Clinic. The clinic is the two-story middle of an L-shaped strip mall."

Braddock examined the name on the slip of paper.

"What do you think?"

"I think he's worth a check. I owe you?"

"Bon and I want a rematch."

"Done," Braddock said, holding up the slip of paper. "Thanks, man."

"I got you," Jonesy replied. "Hey, you need a pizza or something? I'm buying?"

"You know, that would be good. Could you throw in the cheesy breadsticks with that? Tori loves those."

Jones, ever perceptive, inquired, "You're in the fucking doghouse with her, aren't ya?"

"One might say."

* * *

Conn pulled up to the portico over the rear building entrance of K-Advance, a boxy, dingy one-story office building across the road and just to the south of The Outskirts. Vooch jumped on the roof of the SUV, up onto the portico and then hoisted himself up onto the flat roof.

The rooftop air conditioner ducts were set back ten feet but ran parallel to the building's north wall. There was a four-foot-wide dip in the housing that sat at just the right level for Vooch, both as cover and as a flat surface. It left him with a good angle and wide view down into The Outskirts parking lot and front entryway.

* * *

"There you go, my man," the pizza chef said as he closed the top on the pizza box.

Braddock left a twenty-dollar bill on the counter.

"It's free, dude."

"Your time isn't. Have a beer or two on me."

"My man."

Braddock carried the pizza toward the front door and checked his watch. 7:50 p.m. It had been just a bit over two hours. Hopefully a peace offering of pizza would give him a chance to apologize.

* * *

Vooch had the crosshairs aligned on the front entrance of The Outskirts and a clean field of fire between there and Braddock's pickup truck. The sun was well down behind the trees. It would be fully dark in ten to fifteen minutes. Dusk and the large airducts concealed his presence. Through the scope he could see the two hostesses in tight white T-shirts at the host stand.

He caught a glimpse of someone inside, walking toward the host stand. He was in a suit, carrying a cardboard pizza box.

Braddock.

He stopped at the hostess stand.

Vooch exhaled a breath.

Come on. Just two more steps.

* * *

"Who is your friend here?" Braddock asked Colette.

"This is Mandy," Colette replied and turned to Mandy. "You started when, a week ago?"

"Yes," Mandy answered. "I'm a student at the university."

"What year?"

"Senior."

"What are you studying?"

"Business. Marketing and Communications."

"What did you get?" Colette asked, gesturing to the pizza.

"Canadian bacon and pineapple."

"That's for Tori then."

Braddock nodded and checked his watch. 7:55 p.m. "I best get home with this."

"Braddock!"

He turned back.

"The cheesy bread," the cook called out, rushing toward him, carrying a bag.

Boom!

The shot hit just to left of the hostess stand.

Boom!

"Get down! Get down!" Braddock yelled, dropping the pizza.

Boom!

He rushed at Colette and Mandy.

Boom!

He tackled both girls to the floor inside the bar.

Boom! Boom!

Terrified patrons screamed, running for the back of the bar, others ducked down under tables.

"Call 911! Call 911!" Braddock yelled.

The shooting stopped.

He crawled as near as he dared to the entryway and peered outside.

"It came from across the road! Across the road!" yelled a man in blue jeans and a black T-shirt hiding behind a pickup truck.

"Just stay down."

"I called 911!" Jones yelled, coming into the restaurant, a shotgun in his hands. "What the fuck?"

"Put that thing away," Braddock said of the shotgun.

"It ain't for me, it's for you."

"That isn't going to do me much good, Jonesy."

"Why?"

"That was a sniper rifle." He looked to Colette and Mandy. They were terrified but unharmed.

"Mr. Braddock," Colette pointed. "Your shirt."

For the first time he felt it and looked down. On the right side of his rib cage, his shirt was moist. He ripped open the buttons on the shirt and then felt it for the first time, the burning sensation. He lifted up his undershirt.

A waitress with clean towels came running. She beelined

for him and immediately pressed a towel to the wound as it oozed blood.

"Dude. Are you okay?" Jones said.

Braddock grimaced, hearing sirens in the distance.

Tori.

"My phone. Where's my phone?"

* * *

Vooch pulled away from the ducts, turned and ran to the back of the building, the gun strapped over his shoulder. He jumped down onto the roof of the SUV and jumped inside. "*Go! Go! Go!*"

Conn hit the gas, drove straight ahead a hundred feet and turned right on the gravel road.

"Get out of here."

"Did you get him?"

"I don't know. Just get out of here."

* * *

I need you to watch, listen and think.

What had she seen that jumped out to her?

The whole Venn diagram was concerning but what bothered her more was the money. And what she thought about that was they knew about Braddock's finances, about her own finances, and they knew all that *before* they had come to Manchester Bay. They were looking at all of that before Julio Gonzalez and Ray Lange ever showed up.

That meant that even if the Sunday night shoot-out had not happened, they were still investigating him. Was it just based on what was in the notepads Monica Guerero found or was there something else?

Think.

Or, in wanting Renko and Cardellini to show their hand, was that about more than just knowing what their case was? Was Braddock looking for something else? And would that be to exculpate him or could she spin that more positively? Was he looking for something about Guerero's investigation?

Still, why not tell her about it? Why withhold it? That didn't make sense to her, unless... he had a good reason for doing so. *What was the reason?*

As she pumped her legs, the Northern Pine Resort was coming up on the left, and she glanced to the parking lot and noticed a Ford Explorer, parked facing the road, two men in the front seats. It had a flat dullish gray color.

Her phone rang. She looked at her Apple Watch. It was Braddock.

She wasn't answering him here.

* * *

"Answer, dammit!"

She didn't pick up. Braddock switched to their location sharing app. Thankfully, Quinn was still at his grandparents'. Tori was up on the north end of the lake on County 44 just past Channel Bridge. She was still on her bike ride.

He tried her again. Answer. *Answer!*

She didn't.

He called Steak.

"Yo. What's up?"

"I've been shot."

"What!"

"Somebody tried to snipe me. I'm okay, grazed. Tori's not answering her phone. She's up on 44, north end of the lake."

"You're thinking?"

"Go. Now!"

* * *

Boo, his eyes behind his sunglasses, the brim of his baseball hat pulled down low, watched as Hunter cycled by at a rapid pace, her legs pumping, and her body leaned forward, looking like a racer. She looked sleek and efficient, her ponytail the only thing whipping about. He turned out of the parking lot, made his way around the roundabout and followed.

He checked his rearview mirror. It was clear behind him. He saw Hunter up ahead, on the right shoulder. She was up, out of the saddle, halfway up a modest incline in the road.

* * *

Tori pedaled up the rise. It wasn't steep but there was enough slope that she pushed up out of the saddle halfway up the incline to keep her momentum going. And doing so always led to a little extra good burn in her thighs.

As she reached the top her phone buzzed again. Braddock.

He was persistent.

* * *

Boo started up the incline, Hunter a quarter mile ahead just about to the top. He knew this stretch of road and that the road started back down and then veered sharply to the left.

As Hunter disappeared over the top, he accelerated.

* * *

Tori started down the hill, coasting, gaining some speed. She had to be mindful here, the drop-off to the ditch to the right was steep and deep.

Her phone buzzed again. Really persistent. She glanced at her watch. Now it was Steak. *What does he want? Something was up*. She answered.

"Steak?"

"I'm coming to you, right now!" Steak said.

"Why do you need to come to me?" she said as she started turning with the road to the left at the bottom of the hill. "What happened?"

"Somebody tried to snipe Braddock at The Outskirts."

"What!"

"Shit's going down. Where are you?"

"I'm on 44. Just coming down the hill past the Channel Bridge."

Without the music blasting in her earpods, she heard a sudden rumble behind her.

She glanced back.

* * *

Boo depressed the accelerator, roaring down the hill, a hundred yards and closing on Hunter as she started the turn left. He gradually angled to his right, the right front side crossing the white edge line onto the shoulder.

Hunter glanced back.

* * *

Plain gray Ford Explorer. It was right on her.

She jerked the bike hard right. Too late.

The SUV grazed the back of the rear tire, launching her. She careened out of control down the embankment. The front wheel hit the mud and water pool on the bottom, stopping the bike instantly. She sailed over the handlebars, flipping over, landing back first on the other side of the ditch and then rolling back down to the bottom of the ditch, stopping just short of the mud and water.

She lay still, her back searing in pain and she could feel blood oozing in various places. But she could feel. That was good.

Could she move?

Very slowly, she reached to push up with her right arm to sit. "Oooh. Wipeout." She looked at her bike, lying at the bottom of the ditch fifteen feet away, mangled.

"Tori! Tori!" Steak's voice called in her ears. "*Tori!*"

"I'm... okay, I think," she replied, breathing hard, reaching for her phone on her right hip. Somehow it had survived the crash and tumble.

"What? What happened?"

"Ah," she started, still shaking the cobwebs. "Gray... SUV." Her mind cleared. "It was a gray SUV, a Ford Explorer, I think." Suddenly she looked up the embankment. Was it still there? "It ran me off the road. If it's still going, it's coming your way."

"I'm coming! I'm coming!" Steak called.

She heard the siren. Her right knee was bleeding, and she had a long road rash-like scrape on the outside of her left thigh. She checked the back of her arms, and her left elbow was all chewed up. Her body ached, especially her left wrist, but she could move and slowly stood up. "Ow." With the sound of the siren getting closer, she carefully climbed up the embankment.

When she reached the top, Steak was a quarter-mile away. He pulled up and made a U-turn, his wheels squealing on the road.

"Are you alright!" he called as he leaped out of the truck cab and raced around the front.

"Do I look alright!" she replied, angry again.

"No. Well, yes. Certainly, better than the alternative."

"Did you see the SUV?"

"No. I didn't pass anyone. They must have turned off."

Steak shuffled down the severe bank of the ditch and retrieved her bike. "Let's get you to the hospital."

"And Braddock."

"He's already on the way there."

FOURTEEN

"HE'S NO JOKE."

"She's alive," Vooch said when Boo stepped inside the rental house. "We heard it on the scanner."

"Fuck," Boo growled, disgusted. "Just at the last second, she saw us and veered right. I clipped her rear tire and sent her flying down into the ditch. I saw her tumbling, but I didn't dare stick around. You?"

Vooch shook his head. "I hit him but not good enough. Had him dead center and he turned when I fired. I moved with him as he scrambled inside but I missed him."

"Shit."

"I'm a good shot but I'm not a sniper."

"And the getaway?"

"We got out of there right quick," Vooch said. "No issues there."

Conn agreed. "Rearview mirror was clear the whole way. No description of our vehicle on the scanner. There is of yours though. Gray Explorer, though no license plate was given. Gray Explorers are a dime a dozen in these parts, but we need to rid ourselves of it. Conn and I have a good place to get rid of it. Not far from here."

"Let's get then," Boo said.

They packed their gear and clothing and anything else they'd brought into the back of Vooch's rental Suburban. They wiped down the house and were gone within fifteen minutes. The police were on the lookout for gray Explorers. If law enforcement saw one, they were pulling it over.

"Where are we going?" Boo said as he drove the Explorer, following Conn.

"This lake here," Vooch suggested, holding up his phone, displaying a map. "We drove it this morning. No cabins or structures anywhere. The road on the east side is gravel and runs close to it." He switched screens. "This is the Minnesota DNR website depth chart for it. See how at that point in the road the depth goes from zero to twenty then to thirty feet quickly. I'm thinking that's the spot."

"We thought that Sunday."

"Let's not be wrong this time."

They followed Conn as he led them through a series of turns that kept them moving east, northeast. They were on the gravel road, winding its way through low lying wetlands and then thick forested areas until the road veered gradually left and up a slight rise.

"Stop here."

Boo pulled to a stop. To the left there was a thick run of trees except for a twenty-or-so-foot opening.

Vooch led him into the trees and the edge of the embankment. They peered down to the water.

"This is the spot?"

"Yes," Vooch said. "I figure we push it in from here and we wait until she's under. To be sure this time."

Boo turned off the headlights, powered down the windows and turned the Explorer into the tall grass, and drove through the gap in the trees to the edge, then stopped, leaving it in neutral. He,

Vooch and Stag pushed it over the edge and watched as it rolled rapidly down the steep bank and splashed into the lake and then, as it filled with water, it disappeared beneath the surface. They all took out flashlights and focused the light beam on the water.

"You see anything?" Boo said, slowing running the light beam over the surface twenty feet below.

Vooch scanned the surface, the ripples in the water dissipating. "Nah, I think we're good."

They drove another couple of minutes and found another small pond. They tossed the sniper rifle into the water. It was 9:30 p.m. Vooch was driving, Conn riding with him in front, though he was turned around, talking with Stag. Boo sat in the back and thought of the last four days, if not eight years.

Braddock.

There was much concern when he was assigned to the Espinosa Warehouse investigation. He was considered a serious threat, a decorated detective with a spotless record and service with the Joint Terrorism Task Force. And in his JTTF work, he had developed sources at the docks and in the tri-state area of New York, New Jersey and Connecticut.

Vooch though had a good read on the Braddock at that point in time. "He's just punching the clock?"

"Says who?" Boo remembered asking.

"Says people I know. His wife is dying from brain cancer. His heart isn't in the job. He's perfect for us."

Vooch's insight had been on the mark.

To their relief, Braddock did not pursue the Espinosa Warehouse investigation with his customary zeal. The fifty grand planted in the warehouse manager's apartment convinced Braddock he was the inside man. It was a completely reasonable conclusion based on the evidence at hand, though if someone were to dig deeper, there was more there. That had not been the only place they had robbed but with Espinosa, they had dodged a bullet, and they shut it down. Three heists and the money obtained was enough.

What they hadn't realized at the time was that the warehouseman they killed was Dan Guerero's nephew. For that reason, Dan Guerero was even more dangerous than Braddock. He was as well regarded as a detective, had also worked in narcotics and, unlike Braddock, was motivated at the time.

They followed Guerero around twenty-four-seven, especially at night when he was off shift. He repeatedly met up with Malik Muhammed. Conn broke off and started keeping an eye on Muhammed, while Vooch and Boo kept their eye on Guerero. He started poking around the docks and zeroed in on Julio Gonzalez and then Stag.

Stag had told them Gonzalez could be a problem after Guerero questioned him.

"He's seen and noticed some things that he shouldn't have. And then Guerero pressed me hard. He's no joke. He's got a hard-on for this and he's putting things together."

Guerero was working it like a regular case.

He was a real threat.

Guerero went to the bodega every day, sometimes twice. It was on a quieter street, had two ways in and out, and an unmonitored alley. It was just a matter of doing it and they did.

After, they hunted for his notebooks and anything else he had compiled but there was nothing in his desk at work, his vehicle, his precinct locker or even his apartment. Nevertheless, they thought taking out Guerero would end it.

It didn't.

Several months later Braddock started snooping around his own Espinosa Warehouse case and then Guerero's murder. He wasn't bird dogging it with Guerero's intensity, and it didn't appear he was working from Guerero's missing notes and files, but he was poking around, plowing some of the same ground Guerero had.

Malik Muhammed was a frequent Braddock source, and they knew there was a connection between Muhammed and Gonzalez. They took care of Muhammed and planned to do the same with Gonzalez, but he disappeared before they could. While they hunted for him, they took a different, indirect approach with Braddock than they had with Guerero. Braddock's abrupt move to Minnesota ended things.

That left Julio Gonzalez. They kept searching for him for several years. He was a troubling loose thread hanging out there and they had nearly gotten to him a few times, until the trail went ice cold. They suspected Julio had changed his identity. With the passing of the years and the fading of memories, the urgency of the search waned.

Dirty work had been required to get the money and even more to protect it, so they kept the circle tight on their small group of five. They were very careful with the money, careful not to flash too much of it. There were new vehicles, but nothing out of the ordinary. A fully loaded Chevy was fine, but a fully loaded BMW or Mercedes was not. There were new condos but nothing too plush, just comfortable in Brooklyn and Queens, not Manhattan. Nothing anyone would notice or question.

In the ensuing years the money had more than doubled. They were all itching to start accessing it more fully when Monica Guerero found her dead husband's investigative notebooks and files. She went to the police commissioner. Knowing she would go to the media and the city council if he didn't act on this discovery, the commissioner assigned the case to the Cold Case Squad.

All those years of pressure she'd applied finally paid off when she had evidence to go with it.

It had been eight years, yet it was a serious threat. And there were two loose ends from the old case. Julio Gonzalez and Will Braddock.

They knew where Braddock was. Boo and Vooch had traveled to Minnesota to check on him. Braddock seemed content with his life, working his job, living on the lake, and raising his son. New York City and his past seemed to be the furthest thing from his mind. And then there was the complicating factor of Tori Hunter, a name that still resonated in New York City with the FBI.

Nevertheless, it was only a matter of time before the investigation was re-visited upon Braddock. How would he react to that? What might he do? Was that a risk they could bear, or did they remove it before it ever came? Before they got far down that path, Braddock and Hunter were awarded the Presidential Medal of Valor. At that point, the risk wasn't viewed as being worth the reward. Especially if they could find Julio Gonzalez.

Their search for him ramped up but Cardellini and Lange were searching for him as well and found him first, living in Superior, Wisconsin as Hector Ramirez. They followed Lange, who anticipated Gonzalez's next move. Manchester Bay. He was going to see Braddock.

They got Gonzalez and Lange, but now they'd missed Braddock and Hunter.

What would that mean going forward?

And Braddock and Hunter weren't their only problem now. Gonzalez had a widow, and she was still out there. She might try to run and hide but what if she didn't?

It felt like the more they tried to eliminate their risks; they multiplied instead. It had Boo thinking he might have to start attacking their problems from a different angle.

FIFTEEN

"THAT WAS THE EPIPHANY."

As Steak drove her to the hospital, he asked: "You think anything is broken?"

"No, well, maybe my wrist," she groaned, slowly flexing her left hand and wrist. "I feel like I just went ten rounds."

"And you lost," Steak said.

"Thanks, pal."

"I'm here to brighten your day."

"Then brighten it."

"You and Braddock are alive."

She turned to him. "Not that I'm not appreciative, but do you care to tell me why you were able to get to me so quickly? I know where you live and it's not really that close to where I was."

"I'd prefer Braddock tell you why," he replied.

"Do you know what's going on with him?"

Steak took a moment. "Something is up. And I can tell you're hella pissed at him."

"Yeah, well," she replied. "Shouldn't I be?"

"On Monday he called me and asked me to keep an eye on

the house while you guys were gone. Basically, he wanted me to watch until you or he got home."

"And were you to be armed?"

"Yes."

"And what were you supposed to look out for?"

"Anyone overly interested in your home. Anyone who tried to get in."

"He tell you why?"

"You know how cryptic he can be."

"I've seen it firsthand the last two days. What did he tell you?"

"Only that some troubles from his past were coming back on him. Tor—" Steak paused, trying to find the right words. "He sounded... spooked."

"Spooked?"

"And he doesn't spook. From what I gathered from listening between the lines, was that there are people after him and he doesn't know who they are."

"Does he know why?"

"I think he does but he hasn't really been any clearer on that with me than he was with you and everyone else today. He's holding that really tight for some reason. Just don't assume it's for a bad one."

Steak had called ahead saying he was bringing in an injured law enforcement officer. That got Tori into an examination room immediately. Her wrist X-ray was negative. The doctor diagnosed a bad sprain. "It got jammed good," she said, "probably when you put your arm out to brace your fall." She put a brace on her left wrist and told her to ice it repeatedly and if pain lingered to see an orthopedist. The rest was cuts and bruises. The nurse repaired the easiest of the wounds, leaving the road rash on her left thigh for last. As the nurse was finishing up, Braddock stepped into her exam area, wearing a large blue The Outskirts T-shirt.

He was moving gingerly himself.

"Let me see," Tori said.

Braddock gingerly pulled up his shirt. His right rib cage was bandaged. "Fifteen stitches for the wound."

"Hurt?"

"I'll live. You, my gosh—" He looked over her battered and bruised body. He let out a sad breath.

"I'll live too," she said. The nurse finished the bandaging and gave her instructions for wound care, particularly the one on the side of her left thigh. "Keep that one very clean," the nurse instructed. "That one could infect if you're not careful the next couple of days. No exercising, for example."

"Don't worry."

"I do," the nurse said, looking from Tori and then to Braddock. "I worry for both of you." Word of the night's events had traveled fast.

She limped out of her treatment area with Braddock. Steak, Boe, along with Cardellini and Renko were waiting for them.

"Why are you two here?" Tori said.

"I'm the last person in the world who should give him a chance, but I'm here to give him a last one to come clean," Renko said, though he kept a wide berth between himself and Braddock. "Before he gets himself killed. Before he gets you killed."

"You are a piece of trash, Renko," Tori replied. "He's lucky to be alive."

"Oh, I agree because he's a risk now, a *vulnerability* to be eliminated," Renko asserted. "To whomever he's in this with, he's a liability. They know it's only a matter of time before he breaks. Braddock, you should try and save yourself. Save her. Save your son."

"The only thing that broke today was you, bitch," Braddock said as he put his arm around Tori and walked by Renko. "Other than that, I've got nothing to say to you." He walked by

Cardellini. "I'd get away from him, Cardi, before you can't wash the stink off."

"I think you're the one with the stench, Braddock," Renko said.

"Go nurse *your* wounds, asshole."

Braddock walked through the automatic doors, Tori with him, Steak and Boe right behind. Once out of earshot, Boe stopped them.

"What the hell is going on?" she asked Braddock. "Who is after you?" She turned to Tori. "Do you know what's going on?"

"No," Tori said. "I'm as in the dark as you."

Boe held her gaze on Tori for a moment, evaluating. "I believe you are." She pivoted to Braddock. "I have questions."

Braddock nodded, but held up a hand. "I have answers, but Tori and I need to talk first."

"You know that's not how this works."

"Tonight, it's how it works."

"Will?"

"Or arrest me, Jeanette," he said, leading Tori away. "Or fire me."

"I'm not going to fire you."

"Then give me tonight. We'll talk in the morning."

It was after 11:00 p.m. when Steak drove them home to find a rattled Quinn along with a worried Roger awaiting them. Quinn could see that his father was moving slowly. Then he got a look at Tori, all banged up, brace on her wrist. "What happened to you?"

"It's alright, buddy," Tori said, offering him a pained grin as Steak retrieved her twisted bike from the back of his truck. "I just wiped out on my bike, is all."

Quinn was smart and had seen enough of the pressures of

their jobs to know a fib when he heard it. He wasn't buying that was all there was to it.

"Quinn, there's nothing for you to worry about," his father said.

"That's a load of crap, Dad. You were shot at. Tori's injured."

Tori almost smiled, proud of how Quinn was not settling for the deflections his father, or she, were serving up.

"No, Quinn," she said. "We're here, we're alive, but you're right, not everything is okay." She looked at Braddock, and said pointedly, "And even I don't really know what's going on."

That raised Quinn's eyebrows.

"I'm going to go upstairs and clean up. Why don't you practice telling me the truth by starting with your son, and maybe by the time you get to me, you'll have your story straight."

She walked up the steps, Steak handing her a beer before whispering, "Pretty tough on him there, especially in front of Quinn."

"You're probably right," she said, stopping to look back and see Braddock with his hands on Quinn's shoulders. "But he has some explaining to do."

"He does. But whatever it is that's going on, he's going to need your help."

Tori carefully cleaned up with a washcloth, not wanting to fully shower lest she have to do all the bandages over again.

After washing, she stood in front of the long mirror in the bathroom in her bra and underwear, drinking her beer, examining the damage. She was a bit of a mess.

Knock! Knock!

She turned to see Braddock sticking his head around the corner. "Need any help?"

"No. Just loose clothes." She waved for him to come in. "Let me see yours again."

Braddock stepped into the bathroom and pulled up his shirt. Tori carefully pulled back the bandage. There was a long diagonal run of stitches on his right side. "What happened?"

He told her what he recalled. "Shooter was up on the roof of that building across the road. We have the brass. They'll run ballistics but nobody saw the shooter or the getaway. They slipped away in all the chaos."

"So," she said as she reapplied his bandage. "Why is someone shooting at you and running me off the road?"

His phone buzzed, a timer going off. "That's for the pizza. Grab another beer and meet me in the workroom in the basement."

"The... basement?"

"The answers are down there. I'll explain what the hell is going on, all of it, *if* you truly want to know."

Eight years ago

Braddock parked the car, took a quick look around before getting out, and then walked in the front door of the Thai food restaurant. He went to the counter, examined the menu on the wall and placed his order and then paid.

"Be ready in about a half-hour," the counter attendant said. "Just long enough for you to go have a chat," he said, handing him a tall plastic glass he could fill at the pop machine.

He filled his soda, then stepped through a door and took an immediate left and quickly climbed a narrow set of steps up to the second floor and then pushed through another door and took another set of steps that led to the roof. Once on the roof he turned right and climbed over the short walls dividing the buildings until he reached the dry cleaners'.

A man in a dark hoodie leaned against a brick wall, awaiting his arrival.

Malik slid back his hood, a Styrofoam cup in his hand, the end of the tea string dangling from under the white plastic lid. Braddock took a sip from the straw of his soda. "You have to be warm in that hoodie." It was Malik's basic form of dress. It could be ninety-five degrees in the middle of a brutal July and Malik would have a hooded sweatshirt on.

"What have you found?" Malik asked before taking a quick sip of his tea.

"Enough. I suspect I'm nearly as far as Dan was," Braddock said.

"Then you know it's in your house."

Braddock nodded. "I think so."

"You know who?"

"No. Well, scratch that. I have a theory but that's not enough. I need another way in. You said before that Dan was interested in some goings-on down at the Port Newark Terminal."

"He was," Malik replied, nodding.

"And you said you had a contact down there. I need to talk to him."

"That would be my friend Julio Gonzalez."

"Can you make an introduction? *Will* you make an introduction?"

Malik paused. "I don't know, man."

"What do you mean you don't know."

"This shit has gotten very real and gotten people killed. Are you sure you want to keep poking your nose into it? This guy, Julio, I sent Dan his way. And now Dan is dead."

Braddock nodded. "I have no interest in suffering the same fate, but I need to find out who was responsible. I owe Dan that. I owe his wife that."

"But at what price, dude. Think of your kid."

"I am. I'm being careful."

"Uh huh."

Malik took a slow sip of his tea and then nodded. "Julio is spooked too. He saw things he shouldn't have and told Dan about them. Dan was killed not but a few days after he talked with Julio. I don't want him ending up like Dan. I don't want to end up like Dan."

"Me neither. People need to stop dying because of this."

"People were watching Guerero. They could be watching you, my friend."

"I've been watching my back. We've been careful. That's why we're up here. Being careful is how you've survived doing what you're doing for so long. I can find Julio one way or another. Better if it's through you."

Malik reached inside his pocket and pulled out a slip of paper. "His address. It's not far from here. Phone number too."

"Describe him."

Malik gave him a general description. Braddock examined the address on the slip of paper. "Tell Julio to keep his head down, do his job, and act normal and give him my description."

"And you'll reach out to him when?"

"Being... deliberate here, is the play. I'll come talk to him when the time is right."

Braddock shook his head, thinking back to that night. How he played it with Julio was just another of his many mistakes back then.

"Time to stop making them," he murmured to himself, hearing Tori coming down the steps.

Having dressed in baggy gray cotton sweats, and a dark-blue loose, long-sleeved T-shirt, her hair up in a bun, Tori did as he suggested and grabbed another Corona, this time with a lime shoved in the bottle, and gingerly made her way to the basement.

The workroom was an area for storage with full shelves of boxes and tubs. There was their gun safe, and a large work-bench with a tall pegboard containing tools and then the rectangular worktable in the middle that Braddock had cleared off. A long fluorescent light hung on short chains over the table. Another was alight over the workbench. Braddock's open laptop sat on the worktable.

It was time for some answers.

"You're angry with me," he said without preamble.

"Oh," she started with an almost angry laugh, shaking her head, looking to the ceiling. "I'm beyond angry. How you haven't told me—"

"I had my reasons. And when you hear me out, and you *will* hear me out, you'll understand why. You may not agree, in fact, knowing you, you won't, but I think at least you'll understand."

"If I truly want to know?"

He looked her in the eye. "It's like Malik said to me years ago. This shit has gotten a lot of people killed."

"And your role in all of it?"

"The patsy." He took a drink of his beer and then closed his eyes for a moment. "I *have* lied about certain things. Yes, Julio Gonzalez did tell me his name was changed to Hector Ramirez and yes, he specifically wanted to talk about Dan Guerero's murder. It is also the case that I originally told Julio I wasn't going to show up at the restaurant, because I didn't want to touch this with a ten-foot pole. Then I lied awake all night and changed my mind and went because I did want to know what he might have known about Dan's murder. But I had nothing, *nothing*, to do with his murder or any of these murders or robberies."

"Then why was someone trying to shoot you? Why was someone trying to run me off the road?"

"I'm not dirty. You have to know that."

"Do I?"

"*I'M NOT!*" He slammed the table and immediately crumpled, grabbing his right rib cage.

She folded her arms. "Volume doesn't convince me."

"You are the one person in the world who has to trust me."

"Then earn it," she replied tartly. "I'd like the truth, for once."

He exhaled a breath. "I'm not dirty but I was a... catalyst because I ended up in the middle of something when I wasn't doing my job well. And that started a chain reaction of events that led to Dan's murder. All these years later, that led to Sunday night at that cabin. I can tell you what I do know, and what I suspect, but my question is, are you sure you want me to? Do you want to know all of it? Because if we pursue this..." His voice drifted off. "Pursuit of this is pure risk. And if we do this, we can't do it from here and we may have to cross some lines we otherwise wouldn't ever cross."

"I know," she replied, knowing what that implied. "And... I want to know. I need to know."

"You're sure."

"What choice do we have! NYPD is coming after you. And someone else is shooting at you, and now they're after me. I mean, how long until they go after Quinn? We can't just sit here and hope it all goes away. Hope is not a strategy."

"Then are you with me? Because you didn't seem to be with me earlier."

"Because you've been lying! To me, to Boe, to your team. Because while Renko and Cardellini didn't have any hard evidence, you can't ignore what they put on the table. So, damn right, I've got questions. Do you have any answers? Because if you're not going to tell me what's going on, I'm gone, Will. I'm...

gone. Now, you said the answers were down here. Where are they?"

Braddock turned and stepped over to the workbench and picked up the electric screwdriver. Mounted on the wall over the back of the workbench was a brown pegboard filled with hooks that held various tools. He used the electric screwdriver to undo five screws for the bottom middle three-by-four-foot section.

He pulled the middle section loose and set it on the floor next to the workbench. Behind the pegboard was a rectangular piece of sheetrock that he pried loose with a flat-head screwdriver. He pulled it away to reveal a hidden compartment. From the compartment he pulled out a cardboard box.

"Aren't you just full of surprises. How long has that been there?"

"I built it after I moved in just for this purpose," he said, gesturing at the box, taking the top off. "I never wanted to have to open it up, *ever*."

"And this is what?"

"My 'Just in Case' file." He took out two brown expandable files. "These are my copies of the investigative files for the Espinosa Warehouse and Dan Guerero murder investigations. I made copies of both along with what I developed on my own, things *not* in the official files of either case. My notebooks and impressions. Things Cardi was referencing she saw in my apartment back in New York City." He took out and handed her a yellow envelope. "Open it."

"What is it?"

"The reason I haven't told you or anyone else anything."

Tori opened the flap and pulled out an eight-by-eleven color photo. It was of a more youthful, clean-shaven Braddock with not a touch of gray, walking with a much younger Quinn. Given the skyline in the background, it was in Manhattan. She could make out the distinctive spire for the Chrysler Building in background. On the back was a message written in block letters: GUERERO CASE. BACK OFF OR YOUR SON WILL NOT HAVE A FATHER.

Tori's hand went to her mouth. "My God. When was this?"

"I'm pretty sure the picture was taken the day *before* Roger and Mary flew to New York to pick up Quinn to take him to Michigan for the first time with his cousins." He walked around the table and looked over her shoulder. "Our apartment was on East 77th Street a few blocks from the East River. I was walking Quinn into John Jay Park. He liked that playground there. This was about four months after Meghan had passed. This was our little going away day. We went to the park and then to a local diner that he liked because of the banana splits they made. The envelope had been slid under the front door of my apartment sometime two days *before* Roger returned with Quinn."

Tori closed her eyes. "Back off or..." Her voice drifted off. "This has been hanging over your head—"

"For a long time. I guess I should feel lucky. At least I got a warning," Braddock observed. "Dan didn't. But had they killed me after having killed Dan—"

"That would have brought too much heat, too many questions," Tori finished. "Dan looking into your case and—"

"Me looking into his. I get this picture, this warning, and then Roger offers me the chance to move here."

"The move wasn't just about how you were struggling in the aftermath of Meghan's passing."

"I *was* struggling, badly, I was, but..." He let out a long exhale. "You're right, the move here wasn't just about that."

"Still, it was good timing. Or as they said today, convenient timing."

Braddock nodded. "I hoped that whoever was warning me off would see that I took the hint." He took a long drink of his beer, wiping his mouth with the back of his hand. He sighed and closed his eyes. "I'm not proud of running from it, Tori. I just... didn't see that I had a choice. I made my peace with that and for eight years, all was quiet. Until Sunday night."

"And you were hedging and lying, bobbing and weaving, because you didn't want to bring attention from whoever sent you that picture."

"A lot of good that did, given tonight," Braddock said angrily, shaking his head. "When I found out Renko and Cardi were coming, my strategy evolved."

"Strategy?" Tori replied skeptically. "You've had a strategy?"

Braddock nodded. "A rope a dope, more or less."

"Was going off on Renko like Conor McGregor part of the strategy?"

"Not until about halfway through today when he was thundering away at me," Braddock said and then offered a sly grin. "I feel no remorse for it. And I wanted to antagonize him. I wanted to piss him off as much as he was doing the same to me."

"Why?"

"We'll get to that."

Tori took a moment. "You told me to watch, listen and think. And this had to play out."

He nodded.

"And this *is* dirty cops." It wasn't a question.

"Always has been."

"Which is..." Tori understood now, "why you had Steak watching the house."

"Right." Braddock nodded. "Although planting something here isn't the only way to get to me. Like Ann said, if Renko or Cardi find some bank account with my name on it or some piece of evidence planted somewhere else, I could be in a world of hurt."

"Did you think that before today?"

"Not nearly as much as I do now but that's why I wanted to

let it play out. I knew if I pushed the right buttons with Renko, he'd play his whole hand."

"He did at that, I think."

"What tonight showed is that I'm caught in the vise between the official investigation and who is responsible for this shit and both sides want to pin everything on me. That said, I don't think it's necessarily two distinct things. It's all one in the same?"

"All one in the same?" Tori replied, momentarily confused and then not. "Do you know who is behind this?"

"I had an *epiphany*, in more of an 'I wonder' kind of way, about someone years ago. I never pursued it because, one, I wasn't sure how to do it, and two, I moved here."

"Who?"

"I want to see if you see it." He opened up the Espinosa Warehouse file and grimaced, shaking his head in disgust. "There is one true thing you heard today. This was not my finest work."

They each spent some time looking through the Espinosa file, which was a combination of statements, notes, photos and forensic reports.

Braddock took a long drink from his beer. "When I first investigated that case, I reached the conclusion I was supposed to reach. Inside job. I had it two days into the investigation. The warehouse manager had all that cash in his apartment. Plus, I had no other real leads and—"

"No motivation to probe further," Tori said.

"Yep." Braddock nodded in agreement. "But I should have dug deeper because it was just a little too neat and easy. And I knew Monica and Dan's nephew was one of the victims. That should have pushed me to dig more but... I just didn't have it in me. I shouldn't have even been on the job. Not doing that anyway. I should have taken the day shift driving the commissioner or something."

"Then Dan showed up."

"He stopped by a few weeks before Meghan died."

"And he wanted your blessing to look into the warehouse murders."

"Blessing?" Braddock replied with a snort. "Dan didn't ask permission; he told me he was going to do it. I'd done lazy work. We both knew it, but he didn't crucify me for it. He said if he found something, he'd bring it to me first."

"To protect you?"

"He was going to let me save face. But he never got the chance to come back." He began pacing around the room. "That was the last time I saw him. A couple weeks later he was murdered at that bodega and then I'm at his funeral."

"As was I," Tori said. "As were a couple thousand."

Braddock closed his eyes. "I was a pallbearer, Tor."

"And then what? A week later—"

"Meghan died." He took a long drink of his beer.

They stood in silence for a minute or two while Braddock fought back his watered eyes. "Fuck."

"Renko used all that today, to provoke you. And it... worked."

Braddock turned to her. "I knew he would."

Tori paused. "You knew?"

"Fast forward two months after Meghan's passing, I went back to work. After a month or so, Monica asked me to stop by. And that's when I got sucked into this."

"Tell me about that talk," Tori said.

"It was tougher than the one with Dan, I'll tell you that."

* * *

Monica opened the door.

"How are you doing? Are you hanging in there?" he asked, giving her an embrace, which she returned.

"Probably about as well as you are, Will," she replied.

Dan had been dead two months. Meghan one week less.

They sat down in the living room and talked about their kids for a few minutes and how they were coping. Then the conversation drifted to Braddock returning to work. "You asked me to stop by," he said. "And when you did, I sensed there was a purpose behind it."

Monica nodded. "I want to talk about Dan."

"What about?"

"Do you really believe he was murdered because he was in the wrong place at the wrong time?"

Braddock took a moment. "That's the official company line."

"You believe that?"

"I don't know what to believe anymore."

"He was investigating Alejandro's murder, Will. My sister's child." She paused. "And he was talking to that old source you two had."

"Malik?"

"That's him. He knew some things and I know Dan had the scent of something. I'd seen the look many times when he was on the hunt. But this time, it was something that involved cops."

"He said that?"

Monica nodded. "He said he had to be careful. He was going to talk to you about it. Did he?"

"About cops? No. He came to see me. Told me he was going to take another look at the warehouse case, but that's the last time we talked. He didn't say anything about cops, or dirty cops, then. Did he know who?"

"Like I said, he was onto something."

"I see," Braddock said. "If Dan was looking into this, did he have notes, a file, something he was keeping?"

Monica exhaled. "He did, but I've looked and looked and looked, but I can't find them."

"I see."

"You need to pick up the trail. He died investigating your case. I've lost two people I love because of it. I want to know why. I want to know who is responsible and I want them to pay."

"Monica, I can't—"

"You owe me. You owe Dan." She leaned forward and looked him in the eye, "And you owe yourself."

* * *

Braddock took a long drink of his beer. He closed his eyes and slowly shook his head. "I let her down every bit as much as I did Dan, Tor."

"She put it to you pretty hard," Tori said in a soft voice.

"Yeah, if Monica was anything she was direct." He leaned over the worktable, looking down. "Kind of like you were with me earlier tonight in front of Quinn," he replied. "Thing is, she was right then, and you were right tonight."

"Did you start digging into Dan's case?"

"I decided to review mine first," Braddock said. "I didn't think reviewing my own work would raise suspicion, though in retrospect it probably did."

Tori spread the crime scene photos from the warehouse on the table, along with a diagram of the warehouse, and examined the collection in totality. "You know what I see in these pictures?"

"Tell me."

"The gang guys were armed to the teeth, automatic weapons shouldered, handguns stuffed in the front of their jeans. Yet none of them appeared to get so much as a hand on their gun."

"And what does that tell you?" He prodded.

"If it was gang rivals that got the drop on these guys, they'd have drawn their weapons, they would have fought back or at least tried. They didn't even fight."

"Which is one thing I missed in the original investigation, but I saw it the second time through. And it got me thinking. Who comes in and these guys don't draw?"

"Hmpf," Tori snorted and looked him in the eye. "Cops. And they come in yelling, *Police!* They flash their badges and have their guns up. Nobody wants a firefight with cops. They all put their hands up. As does Espinosa and his two employees. They were basically defenseless." She smiled, seeing it. "How many to pull this off, do you think?"

"Ballistics had casings from three different guns."

"Yes, but as I read the report, the three gang members are killed with different guns, but Espinosa and his guys are killed with—"

"The same gun."

"They kill the gang members first, boom, boom, boom," Tori said, gesturing with her beer before taking a quick sip. "And then they turn on Espinosa and his guys and one of them takes them out one by one, boom, boom, boom. Because you can't leave living witnesses. They killed three, what's—"

"Three more," Braddock finished. "The prison sentence is the same whether it's three or six. When I went back all those months later, that's what I saw. I had that, and then Malik told me about murmurs on the street about two other drug robberies before Espinosa. One was at a warehouse in North Bergen on the Jersey side that had happened two months before the Espinosa Warehouse."

"Did you look into that robbery?"

Braddock nodded. "I spoke with an employee of the warehouse who survived it. He had a criminal record, had been in the drug game at one time. He was a guy who'd seen a thing or two. He told me there were three men. When they came in, they *seemed* like soldiers."

"Soldiers?"

"It was planned, efficient, orderly. They knew exactly what they were after, and where to find it, which in that case, was in barrels. They took what they wanted, tied up the workers and left."

"Drugs?"

"Yes, heroin and cocaine based on what the employee saw them pull out of the barrel. And guess where the container they raided had come from—"

"The Port Newark Terminal."

"Ding, ding," Braddock replied. "Nobody died in that one, but guess what that was a robbery of?"

"A different gang's drug product."

Braddock tapped his nose.

"And Espinosa Warehouse was the one gang coming back at the other that stole theirs."

"Or so one might be led to think. And there was actually a third robbery I found which might have been yet another completely different gang's drug product. During the time I was out on leave, and while Dan was investigating, Malik said there was a sit-down after Espinosa between reps from several rival gangs and drug crews, a clearing of the air because they had all been hit but word was they didn't think they were being hit by each other. They *all* suspected someone else."

"Cops?"

"That was the suspicion. What they knew for sure was that the three robberies all occurred after deliveries of ship containers picked up at the Port Newark Terminal."

"And did Dan know all this?"

Braddock nodded. "According to Malik, he did. I really started to get the sense of the thing, probably like Dan did. That's when I then went back and looked at what happened to him."

"But you didn't go to Renko like Dan came to you?"

"I couldn't figure how to go to a superior and tell him I wanted to review *his* work. Especially after the quality of my own original work."

"So, you did what?"

"I finagled my way into a look at the investigative file. I made a copy of what I could."

"That could have gotten you fired."

"Ahh, you put a couple Franklins in a guy's pocket, he goes for a long cup of coffee in the middle of the night and there's no record of my visit." He opened the file on Guerero's case, laying it out. "It's been eight years, but I know this front to back. I want your take on it."

He cleaned up the pizza tray, paper plates and empty bottles while she reviewed the file. She started with the crime scene photos. Dan Guerero lying face down in an aisle, shot in the back of his head, his own service weapon lying near his right hand. Then she examined the photos for the store.

Bodegas—what many people would think of as small convenience stores—were a staple of street corners in New York City. The bodega had a front and rear entrance, though the owner stated that while the rear entrance was unlocked during normal business hours, it didn't generally get much usage. The owner said the apartment tenants on the five floors above would sometimes come in the back way.

She thought of her many trips to such stores, there having been one just down the street from her condo in Manhattan. Not one to keep a full fridge back then, she visited the bodega several times a week. She knew the owners and employees well enough to converse with them and they with her as a regular. When Braddock came back with a fresh beer for her, she asked: "Renko and Cardellini said there was surveillance footage of Guerero's murder."

Braddock reached inside the box and pulled out a square

white envelope. He slipped the disk out and put it into a portable drive for his laptop. He pressed play.

The footage was black and white from a camera angle over the register counter that looked out over the interior of the bodega. The time was 7:22 a.m. A minute later a man with a full bushy beard wearing sunglasses and dressed in black gloves, black jacket, turtleneck, and stocking cap walked into the store and started perusing the small newspaper and magazine rack near the checkout counter, his back to the camera.

A minute later Dan Guerero came in the front entrance and waved to the man behind the counter on his way to the coffee counter. Dan began making a coffee in a tall cup, snapping a small paper sugar wrapper while he waited. His back was to the register counter.

The man who had come inside glanced at Guerero and then pulled down on his stocking cap to make it a mask. He spun to the register counter and pulled a gun. The owner slowly put his hands up.

Guerero glanced back over his right shoulder at the register counter as the owner's hands rose. He reached down with his right hand and pulled his gun and dropped below the height of the shelves and stepped slowly toward the register area. She could see that he was calling the man out.

The man with the gun at the counter slowly started raising his hands as Guerero took another deliberate step, his gun aimed.

A second man stepped around the corner behind Guerero, his gun up.

He was dressed in all black and wearing a mask.

The man fired immediately, and repeatedly, hitting Guerero in the back, one of which hit him in the back of the head.

Guerero collapsed to the floor, his gun falling from his hands.

The two men ran out of the back of the bodega and out of view. The owner immediately grabbed his phone and rushed out from behind the counter to check on Guerero, but he was dead.

"He never saw that guy come in the back," Tori said.

Braddock nodded. "What's wrong with this picture when you look at it?"

Tori ran the video back and watched it unfold again.

"What do you see?"

"It's more what I'm thinking. Who robs a bodega?" Tori said.

Braddock nodded. "I mean, even eight years ago just about everyone was paying with credit, right? How much cash would have really been in the store?"

"A couple thousand maybe."

"On that day, $1,000 was in the register first thing in the morning, $1,027 and change when they hit the store," Braddock said. "An additional $7,000 cash if you included the safe in the little back office. Eight grand and change total."

"That's worth killing over?" she said and shook her head. "Life sentence for that? Killing a cop for that? And they didn't even take the money."

"I maybe get the holdup for a quick buck but that's a solo tweaker guy getting in and out when the store is empty. But what happened to Dan? That was a hit." Braddock shook his head. "That first man in the store waited until Dan was there before he pulled his gun. They hit him in a spot they knew he would be. A place they had no doubt reconnoitered. They knew the layout, that the owner wouldn't be much to deal with, that there was a front and a back entrance and a narrow alley out the back with no camera coverage of any kind. It was a place to kill him and make it look like something else completely."

"Okay, but if you and I conclude this, why didn't... Renko," Tori said, her eyes wide. "Ooooh."

"That was the epiphany," Braddock said. "I don't know how you look at that video, and think about what could have actually been stolen that day, and just conclude—"

"Wrong place. Wrong time," Tori said. "Okay, you see that. What did you think at the time?"

"At first, cover-up. I thought one possibility was Renko went up the chain with his findings, and they told him to bury it because the department didn't want it coming out that cops were killing other cops. Or—"

"He buried it on his own, because he needed to," Tori said.

"Renko had complete control of that investigation but how he handled the case didn't add up to me."

"When did you come to this realization?"

"About two weeks before I got the picture and note."

"What did you do?"

"Well." He took a long drink of his beer and then grabbed an old barstool to sit down. "I went back to see Malik. I wanted to know more about the situation at the docks."

"And Malik pointed you to Julio Gonzalez?"

Braddock nodded. "He reluctantly said I should go see Julio. He said I needed to be careful. He'd sent Dan in Julio's direction and Dan was murdered. That's when I got some cold feet. I've got Renko's investigation and the odd way it was handled. I've potentially got dirty cops killing cops. There's millions of dollars in play. They killed Dan. Why wouldn't they kill me too? So, I was thinking about how far I wanted to pursue this, who I could go to with it, and—" he grimaced and looked down "—I got distracted."

"Cardellini."

Braddock just shook his head.

As much as she wanted to know more about that, now wasn't the time. They had bigger problems. "You and Cardellini were sleeping together." It wasn't a question, though she did have one that she needed answered now. "Was it *after* Meghan died, at least?"

Braddock nodded. "Yes."

"Did you eventually seek out Julio?"

"I told the truth on that. I was too late. When I got the call Malik was murdered, I immediately went looking for Julio. He wasn't at work. His apartment was *trashed*. I wasn't certain if he'd been killed, or he had fled. The place was ransacked but most of his and his wife's clothes were gone as were a lot of personal kinds of effects. I kind of figured he'd got away. Then, when I went home that night—"

"You found the picture."

Braddock nodded and took another long drink. "That was a long, long night, Tor. I didn't sleep for two days. I got paranoid, called in sick to work, was never more than five feet from my gun. Then Roger brought Quinn back. Quinn went to bed, and he and I sat down and had a drink, and he said: You're not going to make it on your own. You need help. You're moving to Minnesota. And while I didn't agree on the spot, I knew I was moving. It was my way out of all this. I resigned a few days later. I had no idea who was after me, but I wanted word out I was leaving. I wanted whoever was after me to know I'd gotten the message."

"That may have been, but now the NYPD is coming after you, they think you're a dirty cop. And dirty cops are coming after you because they think you're a... threat."

Braddock offered a grin, of menace. "They didn't get me tonight, or you. I plan to make them regret that but to get them, it may require getting every bit as dirty."

"Then let's get dirty together, shall we," Tori said.

"You're with me."

"I'm still angry but... I'm starting to understand. You said you had a strategy. Is your strategy evolving into a plan?"

"Part of it was to get suspended," Braddock replied. "I

decided to go after Renko if I got the chance because I didn't want to give Boe a choice. She had to do it. I had to be put on ice."

Tori saw it and scoffed a laugh. "Because if you're suspended, if you're on the bench—"

"I can disappear and go off the grid. I haven't been able to see them coming. I figured if I went under, they wouldn't see me coming. But I underestimated something."

"What?"

"I thought they'd try to hit me, but I didn't think they'd do it two hours after Renko and Cardi tried to railroad me. That was awfully quick, don't you think?"

Tori looked at him intently. "Renko..."

"My name isn't the only one that spans eight years here, is it?"

"Say it was him—the investigation today was to dirty you up. And then if they killed you—"

"They could just point the finger at me. Say that my part-ners took me out before I took them out. Renko feeds that to Monica, the department, and the media. Then they'd spend weeks digging into me. It wouldn't matter that they couldn't find any connections, names, dirty money, any of it. As long as they could point at me, that I was the dirty one eliminated before I talked, the case would eventually—"

"Die," Tori said.

"Exactly."

"Why come after me?" Tori said.

"I could have brought you in on it—told you everything. They were worried you would come after them after they killed me."

"And I would have."

"Right, so why leave a motivated party out there?"

"Renko," Tori replied after a moment, thinking it through. "Huh. Now, I have some questions for him."

"Oh, so do I," Braddock said. "But we need proof first. I don't have it—yet."

"What's the first move?"

"Leaning on some friends for help."

"Steak?"

"And Boe if I can cool her down."

Tori nodded. "Why were you meeting up with Jones?"

"He gave me a lead on an off-the-books doctor down in St. Cloud with a gambling problem."

"Our mystery blood pool from Sunday night."

Braddock nodded. "The other person we need to find is Julio Gonzalez's wife, if she's still alive. If she is, we need to find her before they do. Whatever Julio knew, I'm betting she did too."

"That one is mine," Tori said. She took out her cell phone, scrolled through her contacts, tapped the screen and put it on speaker.

"It's well after one a.m.," Braddock warned.

"It's even later in Brooklyn," Tori said and then she heard a sleepy raspy voice answer her phone. "Tori? Girl, it's... late. Like really, really, late."

"So late it's almost really, really, early."

"Is everything alright?"

"Some people tried to kill Braddock and me tonight. We need to get them before they get us."

That got FBI Special Agent Tracy Sheets' attention. "Okay... umm... that's... holy... shit. Give me a second." They could hear that she was getting out of bed and then the creak of a door opening and then closing. "What the heck happened?"

"Braddock was shot but is standing right here."

"Sorry about the hour, Tracy," Braddock greeted.

"Are you okay?" Tracy said, the tired raspy voice gone. "Shot?"

"Someone tried to sniper me, but I got lucky. Just grazed me in the ribs."

"Sniper? *Sniper!*" She was fully awake now. "Man, you two sure know how to find trouble. What the hell is going on?"

"It's a long story. Tori was biking and someone ran her off the road and down into a ditch. Our girl here is really banged up."

"Tori, you alright?"

"Yeah," Tori added. "I've got bandages all over the place, I'm sore as can be, but nothing broken. Trace, we need some under the radar help, and we need it fast, like fifteen minutes ago."

"Tell me what you need." They could hear her tapping away on a keyboard, having moved to her home office.

Tori began, "For starters..."

SIXTEEN

"AN ARMY OF SIX."

Tori had climbed into bed first, lying on her aching back, her eyes transfixed on the slowly spinning ceiling fan. It had been a day.

Braddock had a blanket in his hand and grabbed a pillow.

"No," she said. "No."

"You still seem pretty mad."

She was. There were things they still had to talk about. But she'd not truly understood the predicament he was in until the last few hours. Did she agree with how he'd handled it? No, he should have told her. But, having seen the photo of him and Quinn all those years ago and the threat attached to it, she understood he'd had his reasons.

"Yeah, some." She sighed and turned her head to him and patted his side of the bed. "But I'm not so mad that I want that. It's going to be hard enough to get comfortable as it is. It'll be even more uncomfortable if I have the bed to myself. Sleep here, please."

He nodded, climbed into bed and turned off the light. They both lay still for a minute, only the light whirring sound of the ceiling fan puncturing the silence.

"Are we okay?"

She took a moment. "We can have our secrets we keep to ourselves, but lies—"

"We can't have." He tenderly reached for her left hand which she let him take, their fingers lightly interlocking. "I'm sorry."

"That's all I need for now."

It seemed just when she'd fallen into a deep sleep that she felt the mattress rising, Braddock heaving his long body out of bed. She heard the shower running, then the low rumble of his voice on the phone in the bathroom, before hearing the bathroom door open again. Her eyes fluttered open to see that it was 5:47 a.m. She'd slept at best four hours.

"I'm going to go down, start the coffee, and make a few more calls," he said.

"I'll get up," she said, stretching, albeit very deliberately. "Make the coffee extra strong, huh?"

"You can count on it."

She got up, carefully showered, redid most of her bandages and then took a long look at the outside of her left thigh. "Ow, ow, ow," she yelped as she lightly touched the wound, following the care instructions and very gently rebandaging it and then wrapping her thigh in an Ace bandage to keep everything in place. One look in the mirror told her she was going to look pretty beat-up for a few days. Everything hurt, even pulling on a bra elicited a groan.

As she made her way slowly down the steps, she peered out the windows and saw Braddock standing out on the dock, coffee cup in hand, looking out to the lake.

In the kitchen, she noticed the two slabs of bacon thawing on the kitchen counter, along with a carton of eggs and two bags of hash browns. She poured herself a big cup of coffee, adding flavored creamer. She wrapped her left wrist in an ice pack and took four ibuprofen. Then she exited via the sliding glass door and walked down the yard and onto the dock.

The morning was overcast, the lake calm. There were three boats out a couple of hundred yards, fishing the drop off for walleyes.

"Sore?" he asked.

"Only everywhere. You?"

"Ribs are the worst. It hurts to turn and take in air, but we better heal fast."

"We usually do."

Braddock nodded and took a drink of his coffee, then looked back out to the lake. "I love this place. I love my life here." He turned to her. "And you."

"Right back at you," she replied, closing her eyes, taking in a fresh breath of morning air. "I love my life here too." She turned to Braddock. He leaned down and kissed her, very softly. "We can't let them take it away from us."

"And we're not going to," he replied.

"How come all the food is laid out on the counter inside. Are you feeding an army?"

"An army of six."

"Six? Who?"

"You, me, Boe, Steak, and the Mannions."

The Mannions? Tori wondered for a second. "You called Kyle?"

"He talked to Boe last night and then texted me asking if he and Eddie could help. That's who I was talking to in the bathroom."

"You sure you want to mix them up in all this?"

"That's what I asked Kyle, and he didn't blink for a second. He said anything you and I need. I could think of a few needs. They'll all be here by seven."

"We better get cooking then."

"We have a little time," Braddock said, turning to look back out to the lake, tenderly wrapping his right arm around her. "I just want to enjoy this a bit longer."

Kyle and Eddie arrived at the same time as Steak. Eddie, like Steak, was one of Tori's oldest childhood friends. He moved in for a hug.

"Easy," Tori begged. "I ache all over."

The good-natured Eddie embraced her tenderly. "I can feel all the bandaging. Man, you took yourself a spill. Does it hurt to even move?"

"Yeah," she said with a wan smile. "But it's not anything that won't heal."

Kyle grabbed the coffee pot and was pouring coffee while Steak and Eddie checked out Braddock's wound when Boe came in the back door. Tori could tell she was still peeved at Braddock and then confused when she saw Kyle and Eddie.

"What are you two doing here?" Boe asked, accepting a coffee cup from Tori.

"Offering assistance to our good friends," Kyle said. "Because we both owe them our lives. And—" noticing Boe's miffed look "—so do you. Or have you forgotten that little explosion over at the university."

"I have not."

"Then for Pete's sake, cut him some slack."

Boe turned to Tori. "Did he tell you everything?"

"Yes."

"And?"

"I ain't going anywhere."

Boe thought for a second. "I still need to know what's going on. Even if I can't tell others, knowing helps me *lie* more effectively. And I have a sneaking suspicion you're going to be needing me to do that."

"That's fair," Braddock said. "Let's grab some breakfast and we'll explain it."

While they ate Braddock gave them the CliffsNotes version of what he'd run through with Tori last night. He handed around the photo that had been left in his apartment with the message written on the back.

"You're going after these guys?" Eddie said.

"We've already started working on some of it," Tori said.

Boe, her eyes glued to the picture still in her hands, started, "What do you need from me?"

"First, to let me investigate the case without having to report anything to you," Braddock replied. "I need to cut Eggs, Reese and Nolan out of it. NYPD is looped into our investigation. Anything we find, they know about, *if* I report it. If I don't, they won't."

Boe grimaced, not loving that idea.

"NYPD can't be trusted," Tori noted. "Not right now."

"I get that."

"Second, if we do need something from Eggs, Nolan or Reese, they're doing it for us, and it doesn't go into the investigation unless I want it to."

Boe sighed. "Okay, but you have to let me know what you're doing. Just so someone knows where you are and what you're up to."

"I can do that. And I need you to let me use Steak," Braddock noted. "He's not officially back but I need him to have a badge and a gun for a thing."

Steak turned to Braddock. "The St. Cloud doctor?"

Braddock nodded.

"Done. But how about finding Julio Gonzalez's wife?" Steak said. "She must know something, if she's alive."

"I'm working on it," Tori said.

"How?" Boe asked.

"I have friends too."

Everyone knew that meant Bureau friends.

"And if we find her," Braddock turned to Kyle and Eddie, "that's where you guys come in."

"The plane is yours," Kyle said. "For as long as you need it. Eddie will take care of it."

"Transportation Secretary Edward Mannion at your beck and call, my good man," Eddie said with a big grin. "The jet is ready. Just say when."

"If you find her, you need to let me know," Boe said.

"Jeanette, if we do that—"

"You misunderstand. If you find her, you may need law enforcement assistance wherever that is. And they're going to need to understand what is going on. I'll see to it that they do. And..." She reached inside her purse. "You might need these." She slid his badge and gun to him.

Braddock peered at them for a moment and nodded. "Officially, for now, keep me suspended. I want the message in the office and on the street to be I'm sidelined, and Tori and I are going to take some time away. And to everyone here at the table, you need to be careful. Whoever is behind all this has shown no reluctance to kill anyone in their way or anyone trying to expose who they are. They've gone this far. There is no limit to what they'll do."

SEVENTEEN

"REMEMBER YOUR GEOGRAPHY."

Everyone, save the erstwhile deputy, parked in their driveway had left after breakfast. The deputy, not to mention two men from Kyle's Mannion Companies security team, followed Tori and Braddock to Roger and Mary's where they checked in on Quinn. Braddock hugged his son, told him things would be okay but for the time being, he would have some people watching after him, and his aunt and uncle and grandparents.

"Is this about what happened last night?"

"Yes. I have a problem I need to solve, and Tori is going to help me solve it. And she and I? We're pretty good at that sort of thing, aren't we?"

"How long will it take you?"

It was a good question. "Hard to say. My sense of it now, for reasons I can't explain to you, is that I think this is going to move pretty fast. And Tori and I might need to travel some to solve it. But I promise you, it'll all work out. I promise. That's the best answer I've got. But Tori and I, we need to go to work, okay?"

"Okay."

With that, Braddock gave his son a last hug, turned around

and hustled off with Steak. Tori stood with Quinn while he watched his father drive away.

Braddock had soft-pedaled last night's events to Quinn in an attempt not to worry him. Yet, Tori glanced to her right and knew that message wasn't bought. He had been through an attack once with Tori when someone shot at and tried running them off the road. It had both scared, and matured Quinn beyond his fourteen years. He had seen things most fourteen-year-olds would never see. His naivete regarding what his father, and his father's girlfriend, did for a living was long gone.

"Why? Why are these people coming after you and Dad?"

She took a moment to think about her answer. "It's about some things that happened a long time ago, back when you and your dad lived in New York City."

"Did Dad do something wrong?"

"No, not really," she replied.

"What does 'not really' mean?"

"Let me just say this. People threatened that if he didn't stop investigating something, bad things could happen to him, *and you*. This happened not long after your mom died. To protect you, and him, your dad moved here and left what he was investigating behind. But now, that case has come back to life. And despite your dad's efforts to avoid it, we're caught up in it."

"What people?"

"We're going to find out."

"Are they going to keep coming after Dad and you?"

Tori paused for a second and then turned to him and looked him right in the eye, making sure she said it in a way he would understand. "Buddy, not if we hunt them down first. Understand my meaning?"

"I do."

Tori left Quinn with Roger and Mary and drove home.

Given the events of the past couple of days, neither she nor Braddock for that matter, had dug into any of the information from Eggs, Reese and particularly Nolan, who had been pulling together the residency history and pattern of Julio and Ana Gonzalez. And the interesting thing was, as Tori continued to read, the file continued to update. Nolan was going beyond their joint residency, she was pulling together Ana's entire life, prior to their marriage, prior to when they even met.

They had met in Newark, New Jersey, or at least that's where their historical paths merged on paper before marrying in Cleveland, Ohio. Ana was born in Cleveland and spent much of her childhood there, save for a four-year period during her high school years where she lived in Toledo, Ohio before returning to Cleveland for another three years and then moving to Newark, New Jersey. Nolan had Ana's entire life detailed in the system, along with her family members and schooling history. There was even a reference to a citation for minor consumption when in high school.

Reviewing Ana's history, Tori had a thought. She grabbed her laptop, a small stack of sticky notes and went to the loft over the garage.

Braddock liked maps and atlases and had a globe on a stand in their family room where she found him from time to time just spinning it around, studying the map of the world. Sometimes she would find him on his computer, looking at Google Maps satellites of cities, finding where stadiums and arenas and famous landmarks were. It was mindless entertainment for him. When they were decorating the loft over the garage, the south wall had windows on each end but a wide windowless blank space in the middle.

"What should we put there?" she had said.

"I know just the thing," Braddock said.

He ordered a massive United States map. She had been skeptical of his idea, until she'd seen it up on the wall and framed. It looked great. It was a discussion piece if they came up there with friends. Even Quinn and his buddies thought it was cool and would study it, pointing out all the places they wanted to go and visit.

Tori opened her laptop and the residency history of Julio and Ana Gonzalez.

* * *

St. Cloud was an hour south of Manchester Bay and served as the county seat for Stearns County where Steak's cousin Mark was a sheriff's detective.

They were parked behind Mark awaiting Dr. Julian Vance's exit from the clinic for the day.

"I shake my head at this doctor," Braddock mused. "Four kids, child support, maintenance, gambling debts, and a brand-new Mercedes S-Class sedan."

"Some people just can't manage money," Steak said.

"Really makes you want to entrust your health to this douche."

"You assume one has something to do with the other. He could be a great physician."

Braddock snorted in disgust.

"What? You don't read *TMZ*?"

"No."

"I bet Tori does. Funny shit there. Anyway, there are lots of professional athletes and celebrities who are amazing at their profession and total idiots in their private lives. Yet, we still cheer them."

"Stop defending him," Braddock retorted. "I'm not in the fucking mood, man."

"What? Did you get shot or something?"

That made Braddock laugh and then wince. "Just shut the fuck up."

"You know," Steak replied with a wry grin, "I've been meaning to tell you that you say 'fuck' a lot."

"Don't make me shoot you."

"Check it out." Steak nodded at the clinic.

A brown-haired man, tie loose at the neck, putting on a pair of Ray-Ban sunglasses, exited the clinic and strolled toward the Mercedes, using a key fob to unlock it.

"That's him," Braddock said.

"Cuz, that's our guy," Steak called into the radio.

"On it. I'll bring him to you."

* * *

Tori folded her arms and leaned back against the ping-pong table, examining the map and the collection of orange and yellow sticky notes. The orange ones were for where Ana lived as a child, teen and before she met her husband and were all in Ohio in the towns of Cleveland and Toledo. The small yellow sticky notes reflected all the places Julio and Ana lived together: Newark and Jersey City, New Jersey. After the murder of Malik Muhammed, they left New Jersey and moved back to Cleveland, then Steubenville, followed by Dayton and then Sandusky before they changed their identifies and snuck up to Superior, Wisconsin.

The employment pattern was consistent, Julio working in manufacturing of some kind and Ana in a retirement or assisted living facility, both places where the employer would have you fill out the employment application, the I-9 and background check forms, but probably wouldn't follow up too much on the employment references as the positions were so hard to fill. And while they had not yet had the chance to ask, Tori couldn't help but suspect that they were moving to avoid the investigation or the cops who did the robberies, and maybe both. It would explain the sudden fleeing of Superior when Lange showed up last Friday at the refinery to find Julio.

They were scared. Turns out they had been right to be.

Her phone buzzed. Tracy.

"It took some doing and serious favor cashing that I might need your help paying off."

"Done. Whatever you need, I'm paying."

"That's TBD. There are still some issues with it, but I just emailed you a report of all prescriptions of Anakinra that have been filled across the country since Sunday. I know the disease is not all that common, but there are three hundred and forty million people in this country. The list isn't short."

Tori opened her email, and the report. "Tracy, there are no names."

"That's one of the issues. You're trying to operate under the radar without a subpoena."

"HIPAA privacy, I presume."

"I can use a law enforcement exception and get names on a specific prescription if you can identify a claim or claims that need a closer look. I can tell you there is no prescription for Emma Ramirez or Gonzalez or Ana Ramirez, or Ana Gonzalez or even Ana Martinez, her maiden name. That means she either has enough to get through, is going without, or figured out a way to fill under another name."

"No way she goes without." Tori turned back to the map. "Talk something through with me."

"Shoot."

"You're a wife whose husband is dead. You're a mother, with a young daughter and on the run from people who want to kill you for what you know. What do you do?"

"Call the police."

"But they haven't."

"They could be dead."

"Assume they're alive."

"Do what I've done before. Move, establish a new identity, and hope they don't find me this time."

"Except," Tori said, "I wonder if that's what she really wants."

"Why?"

"Because of what they did when Lange showed up. Instead of doing what you just said, moving, new identity, they instead drove from Superior up to Manchester Bay. There was only one reason for her husband to do that."

Tracy got it. "To talk to Braddock."

"Right. I think it's possible she said to her husband: I'm done running. So, instead, they finally came to Braddock for help."

"But Braddock never spoke with him."

"Yeah, well, Braddock would tell you now, he screwed that up," Tori said. "But still, she can't want to keep running. She wants it to be over. What do you do?"

"You go to people you trust, family."

"That would be my first thought," Tori said as she stepped closer to the map. "Though wouldn't you assume if you were her, that we, the NYPD and whoever else is after her would check with and question her family? And, I think in our case, while we are researching her residential and familial history, the NYPD is using their weight to have checks made with family and thus far, zip."

"Where is home?"

"Ohio originally, mainly Cleveland, and I know inquiries are being made there. Her father died a few years back but there is an older sister and cousins and so forth in the Cleveland area. Plus, she and Julio moved around Ohio, I presume to stay close to her family."

"You know what might explain that?"

"What?"

"As you said, her father died within the last few years."

"You're thinking she stayed relatively close so she could see her dad."

"It's plausible. He died when they were living in Sandusky. But then after he passed away, they left for Superior to put some distance between themselves and Ohio hoping that would throw the pursuers off. That, and it was then that they changed their identity from Gonzalez to Ramirez. Now, maybe that's because they were found, or sensed they were going to be found, and moved, or just decided to change their names so they had a better chance to settle somewhere."

Tori's phone beeped. It was a message from Nolan, from her personal cell. The text read: *CM-U. Translation: Call me – Urgent.*

"Tracy, I'll call you right back."

She switched and called Nolan. "Urgent?"

"Detroit PD found a car registered to Hector Ramirez. It was parked along a street in Detroit, across the street from a joint Greyhound Bus and Amtrak Train Terminal."

"When did that come in?"

"Ten minutes ago, *from* NYPD. Now, how long they knew before we knew? Couldn't tell you. What I can tell you is that Detroit Police and the NYPD are making inquiries of both Greyhound and Amtrak to see where Ana and Emma went. The car has been parked there at least a couple of days. Parking cop kept ticketing it until they noticed the bullet holes and then did a little more checking. I thought you'd want to know, not that I'm talking to you because... I'm not."

"Copy that."

"Does Detroit mean anything?"

"Let me think on it," Tori replied. It did mean something.

She called Tracy back. "The Ramirez's car was found abandoned in Detroit."

"Where?"

"Parked at a joint bus and train station."

"So, she got on a Greyhound or an Amtrak from Detroit. We can check that."

"I suppose... so."

"Or not," Tracy replied, sensing her friend's hesitation at the thought. "What?"

"Detroit is interesting."

"Why? Because you're a Lions fan?"

"No, I'm definitely not a Lions fan. I bleed Vikings purple." She turned back to the map, looking at Detroit. There was no history of her or her husband living in Detroit but there was in, "Holy..."

"Holy what? Moley?"

"No."

"What then?"

"Holy Toledo."

"Toledo. Why Holy Toledo."

"Toledo. Ohio, Tracy," Tori said, and she went back to the file with Ana Ramirez's familial history. "Tracy, Ana lived in Toledo for four years when she was in high school."

"So?"

"Remember your geography. Toledo is fifty miles south of—"

"Detroit. Does she have any family in Toledo now?"

"No, but you spend four years someplace during your high school years you make a friend or two, don't you? Maybe a couple you stay in contact with? Especially given all the time that you've lived in other parts of that state. How many prescriptions were in Toledo?"

* * *

Braddock and Steak had taken a rear booth at a bar ten minutes and several miles away from the clinic. They each had a club soda and a bowl of peanuts in front of them when Mark led a worried Julian Vance to them. Mark let Vance slide into the booth and then took a seat next to him, blocking him in.

"What is this about?" Vance said nervously, peering around the bar. "The detective said it would be in my interests to come and speak with you. Why?"

"You know why," Braddock said as he cracked open a peanut. "Because very early last Monday morning you treated a man with a gunshot wound and perhaps other injuries," he said, not looking at the doctor as he popped the extracted peanut in his mouth and then reached for another one to break open. "You treated him at the clinic. Once you were done, they paid you cash, at least twenty thousand dollars in nice fresh one-hundred-dollar bills." He popped another peanut in his mouth and brushed his hands clean and finally looked Vance in the eye. "How am I doing so far?"

"I... I... I don't know—"

"*Pleeeease*, Doc," Steak quipped and turned to Braddock. "Supposedly smart people can be such terrible actors."

Mark laid out four photos from a surveillance camera for the jewelry store next to the clinic that monitored the back alley. Just after 2:00 a.m. Monday morning, the doctor pulled up and parked behind the building. Not but a minute or two later, from off camera to the right, three men came stumbling across the rear parking lot. One man bent over, holding his left arm, the other two helping him walk. They all wore black clothing, including black ski masks. An identification would not be possible, at least from the video footage. "As the detectives were saying."

Vance looked at the photos and shook his head. "You are detectives from where, exactly?"

"That's need-to-know information," Braddock said. "And right now, you don't need to know, Doc. Just like the Minnesota Board of Medical Practice doesn't need to know about your illicit nocturnal medical activities."

"That is assuming," Steak added, "you tell us all we want to know about your Monday morning patient."

Vance exhaled and sat back, closing his eyes. "Dammit."

"Fess up, Doc," Mark said. "Who were they?"

"I honestly don't know," Vance replied.

"Come on," Steak pressed.

"I don't know their names. Heck, they wore masks the whole time so I can't even tell you what they looked like."

"Walk me through what you do know," Braddock said, leaning forward. "How did they get ahold of you?"

"I got the call just after one a.m."

"From?"

"One of them because I recognized the voice when he showed up."

"Phone number."

Vance pulled it up on his phone and turned it around. Steak took a photo.

"Probably a burner but I'll get it run anyway," Steak said and started on a text to Boe.

"And they arrived about an hour later?" Braddock led.

Vance nodded. "There were three of them initially. I said before I did anything, there was the subject of my fee."

"Which was?"

"Twenty-five thousand. The big one whipped it out from a duffel bag just like that," the doctor said with a finger snap. "I probably should have said more. I mean, where were they going to go at that point? That might have been pushing my luck."

"You seem to do that a lot, Doc," Mark interjected.

"Yeah, whatever," Vance replied.

"And they paid it?"

"Half at the start. The other half after I'd finished. I put the first half in a safe and the big guy left, leaving the other two behind. The injured guy had a gunshot wound in the upper left shoulder. I removed the bullet, sterilized the wound, stitched and bandaged him up. If you were to find him—" the doctor pointed to his upper left shoulder, closer to the shoulder joint "—he'll have a fifty-cent-piece-sized wound right here. And to the right of it, he'll have two round moles."

"Did you take an X-ray of the clavicle?"

"Yes, the break was clean for which he was lucky. If I had to guess, he broke it from a fall, not getting shot. As for the X-ray itself, they took it, along with anything that had blood on it. The one guy helped me wipe everything down. They weren't taking any chances."

"You ever see their faces? Anything like that?"

"No. They had those masks on, the ones that cover the mouth. All I could see were eyes. They both had dark eyebrows. I guess I saw that."

"The patient. Was he short? Tall? What?"

"I'm six feet tall, and he was an inch or two shorter than me. Medium build albeit with a bit of middle-aged girth around the waist."

"And the other guys?"

"One was my height, maybe an inch or two taller. Thinner, lanky. The last guy who arrived but then left right away was a big man, wide shoulders, thick, big round head. He left but the lanky guy stayed."

"Was he injured?"

"No. But he watched me like a hawk. I started wondering if he was going to shoot me when I finished."

"Doc," Braddock said, casually waving a peanut, "I'm half surprised they didn't. Was it just the two of them most of the time then?"

"Yeah, though the taller guy kept taking calls."

"Did you see what they were driving?"

"No. And when they left, I didn't watch after they went out the door. I stayed inside and waited for the clinic day to start."

"Can you tell me anything else about the tall guy?"

The doctor thought for a moment and then his eyes brightened. "He had a birthmark."

"Birthmark?"

"A port-wine stain really. Both guys were wearing black gloves the whole time, but the tall guy pushed up his sleeves and took the glove off his left hand once to answer the phone and I noticed it, some red discoloration. A port-wine stain, on his left hand, running up his wrist and arm. It had been treated, lasered to lighten the color but you don't really get fully rid of it, you just make it less glaringly noticeable."

Braddock nodded, thinking. They were disguised the whole time. "Tell me about their voices."

Vance sat back for a moment. "You know, they didn't say much. Their voices were a bit muffled with the masks, but I think they had East Coast like accents. The guy I was patching up said 'fuck' a couple of times and I thought I was watching an episode of *The Sopranos*."

"What da fuhk," Steak mimicked.

"Not a good impression, but yeah, something like that."

Braddock and Steak questioned him for another ten minutes. "Here's the deal," Mark stated. "No more after-hours doctoring. I find out you are offering services like this again, losing your medical license will be the least of your concerns. Are we clear?"

"We are."

"And, if my friends here require your further assistance, it will be provided post haste."

"Understood, Detective."

Mark slid out of the booth and Vance hustled away. When he slid back in, he asked: "Helpful?"

Steak turned to Braddock. "Port-wine stain. You know anyone with one of those from your NYPD days?"

"No," Braddock said. "But now I've got something to ask

around about." His phone buzzed. "It's Tori." He answered. "What's up?"

"We need to jump on a plane."

"To where?"

"Toledo. I think I have a line on Ana and Emma but we gotta hustle."

"Why?"

"NYPD has it too."

EIGHTEEN

"THAT'S NOT THE QUESTION YOU SHOULD BE ASKING."

In the afternoon sun, Vooch and Boo sat in the front seat of their black rental Tahoe on West Baltimore Avenue, a half-block south from the entrance to the joint Greyhound and Amtrak Train Terminal in Detroit. For the time being, Stag and Conn were holed up at a hotel by the airport.

Boo surveyed the general area. To their left was an open-air parking lot for the terminal. The lot was framed by an apartment building to the south, a parking ramp to the west and another apartment building to the northwest that had a series of businesses occupying the first floor. Directly north was a White Castle fast food restaurant. To the east were train tracks.

"Where did the wife leave the car?" Vooch said.

"Next street over, West Milwaukee Avenue. She parked but didn't plug the meter. The meter maid—"

"Parking enforcement officer."

"Whatever. They wrote a ticket, then another, and then came back again and noticed the damage to the car, the bullet holes, and called it in. That brought the real police out. They towed the car, logged it and then the bulletin hit."

"They find anything else?"

Boo shook his head. "Not that I've heard but then again, how hard are they going to try. They assumed she either got on a bus or a train. The car was parked there for a couple of days, so... *If* she did get on a train or bus, she's most likely gotten to wherever she was going."

"*If?*" Vooch said, turning to him. "You doubt that? You don't think she got on a bus or a train?"

"Why here?" Boo said. "If she drove here from Minnesota, she could have stopped and jumped on a bus or a train in Duluth, Minneapolis, St. Paul, Madison, Milwaukee, Rockford, Chicago, any number of places between here and Minnesota. She could have driven west and done the same thing, Fargo, Bismarck or south to Des Moines. You get the idea. So why Detroit?"

"It dawned on her to get as far away as possible and she settled on Detroit."

"Or, given her history of living in Ohio for much of her life, she did it with a specific intent." Boo drove ahead, took a left turn and then a quick right onto West Milwaukee Avenue and parked. He eyed up the bus station and where the car had been parked about a hundred feet ahead, just short of the intersection with Woodward Avenue. "I want to take a walk around."

The two of them strolled along the sidewalk, past where the car was parked and then another hundred feet to the corner.

To their left across the street was a parking ramp. Straight ahead through the intersection was the apartment building but to the northwest, on the corner, was a bar. They made their way to the bar, which had a small run of outdoor tables along the sidewalk, two of which were occupied. The tables were serviced via the bar's front door.

Vooch looked up over the front door, noticing the small black glass ball hanging down. He nodded to Boo.

"Let's go inside and have a drink," Boo directed.

. . .

The interior of the bar was dark, dark wood and stools, little in the way of light. A good place for a private conversation. The two of them sat down toward the far end where there were several empty stools. They observed as the bartender spoke with two servers, giving orders. He saw the two of them and made his way down to them.

"Are you the bartender or manager?"

"Both. What can I get you?"

"Tap beers," Vooch said, and then held up his right hand with two one-hundred-dollar bills looped through his fingers. "And a look at your surveillance system. Particularly the camera over the front door from a few nights ago."

"And if you find what you're looking for?"

"I got two more of these for you."

The bartender took a quick look around and then said, "Follow me."

A half-hour later they were walking out the front door of the bar, $400 lighter, as they walked across the street. Boo called Conn. "Julio's wife didn't get on a bus or a train. She was picked up late Tuesday night by someone driving a white crossover SUV. I've got what I think is an Ohio license plate. I'm texting you a picture of it."

"I'm on it."

"We're on our way to you."

* * *

Tori looked up from her computer for a moment and gazed around the interior of the nicely appointed private jet. It occurred to her, not for the first time in her life, that you find out who your good friends are when your back is up against the wall.

Tracy had dropped everything at work to help. She was calling in favors left and right.

Eff'n Jones, lascivious little lech that he was, stuck his neck out and found them the after-hours doctor.

When Kyle and Eddie said they'd do anything to help, they meant anything. Kyle arranged for additional private security for Quinn and Braddock's family. When Tori called about the plane, Eddie's only question was: "Where? I need to file the flight plan?"

"Toledo."

"I love Toledo. Just get to the airport."

The only condition was Eddie was coming along. It was his plane and, "You might need me in a pinch. We have a restaurant in Toledo, and I have connections there."

And then there was Boe, making calls to the police in Toledo, but only after she had a couple of old friends from the Marshal's Service make calls on her behalf to the chief of the Toledo Police, putting in a good word and asking for a discretionary favor. Braddock had the call with Boe on speaker.

"Art Long is the detective's name. He will be waiting for you at the drug store," Boe said.

"And they're keeping it on the down-low?"

"Long and his chief know the score, what's going on, what's happened to you, and the cloud you're under. They get it and they're playing ball."

"Anything from NYPD on their end about the car?"

"It's my understanding from Nolan and Eggs that they're still pursuing the bus and train lead," Boe replied. "You know, if this Toledo gambit pans out, we'll have to figure out how to finesse this with them."

"Let's find and talk to her first. Then we'll worry about how or what we communicate with them."

"Good luck."

Done with the call, Braddock undid his seat belt and quickly stood up.

Bang!

"Ow!"

"Watch your head there, big guy," Tori said, chortling a little laugh.

"First time flying private, Will?" Eddie Mannion asked sardonically, relaxing in his seat, sipping on a club soda.

"Yeah," he replied as he rubbed the back of his head. "The extra leg room is nice though maybe on your next one you could get one with a tad more head room, you know, for your taller guests."

"Duly noted," Eddie replied, still chuckling.

Braddock turned to Tori, who was tapping away on her laptop as if the whole thing was old hat, and for her, it was. She'd taken plenty of small jets while with the Bureau, though none quite as comfortable as this one.

Braddock sat down across from her. "You've got more?"

"Maybe."

Tori explained that she and Tracy worked through the prescriptions for Anakinra, and they sifted down to a specific prescription filled in Toledo.

"The car was abandoned sometime on Tuesday night. There were two new prescriptions filled by pharmacies in Toledo yesterday, Wednesday. And in the notes field for one of them, there was a notation that the prescription was called in from a pharmacy in—"

"Superior."

"Yes," Tori replied. "It's for an Emily Collins. That could be Emma. There is a Toledo address for the prescription but it's—"

"Fake."

"Yes."

"Your theory is she drives to the bus and train station in Detroit, dumps the car and is picked up by a friend she had from the years she lived in Toledo. And dumping the car where she did was meant to deceive everyone into looking for her on a bus or train when in reality she basically stayed right there, albeit fifty miles south."

"That *is* what I'm thinking," Tori replied. "I mean, if the idea was to take the train or the bus to disappear, she could have done that a lot quicker in Minneapolis, Madison, Milwaukee, Chicago and she didn't. Instead, she drives all the way to Detroit. She has history in Ohio. She sought out help from someone."

"Who is Emily Collins?"

"I'm thinking if the Anakinra prescription was called in from Superior, Ana somehow convinced the pharmacist there to transfer it under an alias. The pharmacy in Superior wasn't Walgreens or CVS and neither was the one in Toledo, a Cuyahoga Pharmacy. They're independent drug stores, which tend to be places with loyal owners or managers who do things for their faithful customers."

Braddock smiled. "The pharmacist knows Ana's friend."

"You don't look the other way or finagle things for people you don't have some regard for. You do something like this for someone who has gone to that drug store for a very long time."

He noticed an additional small backpack sitting at her feet. "What's in the backpack?"

"Something that might help grease the skids if we do in fact find them here."

* * *

By the time Boo and Vooch got back to the airport hotel, Conn had an identification for the license plate.

"The car is registered to a Joshua Liriano of East Toledo. Nevada Street. His wife is named Cleo, a graduate of Waite High School, Class of 2008, same as one Ana Martinez, once known as Ana Gonzalez and now Ana Ramirez. Cleo lived on the same block as Ana when they were both in high school."

"How long to Toledo from here?" Vooch said

"An hour give or take," Stag said. "It's right down I-75."

Boo looked to the corner and the two large duffel bags. "Bring all that."

After an hour's drive, they turned onto Nevada Street and searched for the Liriano house. As Boo drove, Vooch checked house numbers.

"Three up on the left, I think. The white one with the covered porch along the front."

Boo slowed to a crawl as they rolled by Cleo Liriano's white aged two-story clapboard house set mid-block amongst a series of similar two-story homes, some single-family houses, others based on the exterior stairways constructed along the outside of the houses, converted to duplexes. It was a working-class street, the Toledo Refinery mere blocks away.

It was early evening, the east-west running street still basking in the evening sun, kids and adults out and about creating a pulse of activity, though the Liriano house was quiet.

"Let's give the alleyway a look," Vooch suggested.

Access to the alley was a bit unique as the entrance was reached before the end of the block. Boo swung into the narrow alleyway, clearly built long before everyone started driving bulky SUVs. "I wouldn't want to have to race out of here, that's for sure," Boo said as he negotiated the hairpin turn.

The Liriano house came up on the left. A man was out on a small back deck standing over a gas grill, flipping over what looked to be hamburgers with a spatula in his right hand, a bottle of beer in his left. The man looked up briefly as they approached the detached garage and then disappeared behind it. By the time they had passed, he had turned his attention back to the grill.

"I didn't see any indication she was there," Conn said. "Though I didn't see anything that says she wasn't."

"We'll come back once it's dark," Vooch suggested. "And take another look."

* * *

Eddie had a black Tahoe waiting for them at the Eugene F. Kranz Toledo Express Airport. "I'm dining with friends. Call me if you need anything."

Braddock immediately drove them away.

"I've never been to Toledo," Braddock said as they drove east on I-90 from the airport, which was out in the countryside to the west. "You?"

"Once, early on in my career with the Bureau. I was here for a couple of weeks on an investigation. We were working with the Behavioral Analysis Unit."

"You ever get out and look around?"

"Not much beyond our downtown hotel. What I do remember is Toledo was a working-class Rust Belt city. It reminded me a little of St. Paul. You know, older buildings and businesses, figuring out how to reinvent itself into a modern twenty-first century city."

"And how was it doing on that?"

"Okay, I thought, from what I did see. There were still some rusted-out and abandoned buildings and factories and such back then, but there were also a few nice restaurants and bar districts downtown, classic buildings that were remodeled on the inside but kept their old unique exterior character. The hotel we were at had a rooftop bar on like the twelfth floor with a scenic view that overlooked the river."

"Which river?"

"Maumee. It cuts right through the city."

Following the map instructions, Braddock drove them into

East Toledo and pulled into the parking lot for Cuyahoga Pharmacy. The driver's side door for a silver Ford Explorer swung open and a stout barrel-chested man stepped out, dressed in a black sport coat and cream golf shirt, service weapon visible on his left hip.

"I know his name is Art Long," Tori said. "But maybe he should be Art Wide."

"Ha!" Braddock said as they observed the man shaped like a fire hydrant approach them, holding up his identification and then greeting and amiably shaking hands.

"From what my chief says in talking to your sheriff, it sounds like you two have had quite the twenty-four hours," Long said.

Tori noticed his ears, the skin bumpy like cauliflower. "You were a wrestler?"

"Yes, ma'am," Long replied with a prideful grin. "All the way through college. Still help coach the high school when I can." Long looked at his watch, it was nearly 9:00 p.m. "You got here not a moment too soon. Store closes in five minutes. Show me what you have."

Tori showed Detective Long the claim report, explaining it. "We know the prescription is bogus. We need an address, license plate, something to work with to find the woman and her daughter. Not only do we need to speak with them, but we're not the only ones trying to find them and we're the friendlies."

"I get it," Long said and turned to the drug store. "George Lingren owns this place. He's also a pharmacist. Been around a good long time. His pops started this place way back in the day."

Long led them inside and to the right to the pharmacy counter where a tall man in light-blue scrubs handed a small white bag to a customer.

"Art, hello," Lingren greeted.

"Evening, George, I need a few minutes, as do these folks."

"Come on back then," Lingren said, waving them into his

cramped office that wasn't much more than filing cabinets, an old metal desk and bookshelf on which it appeared the books had not been touched in years. Tori took the one guest chair in front of the desk, Long stood behind her, and Braddock stood by the door.

"George, this is Will Braddock, Chief Detective for Shepard County in Minnesota. This lady is Tori Hunter. She's a retired FBI special agent who now works with Shepard County. They have some questions for you and we're assisting them."

"Where is Shepard County?" Lingren asked.

"Middle of the state," Braddock replied. "Lakes country."

"What is this all about?"

"We're looking for someone. They filled a prescription here."

"How do you know that?" Lingren asked.

Tori pulled out the claim report, stood up and walked around the desk and set it in front of him. "This one right here for Anakinra. It was actually transferred from a pharmacy in Superior, Wisconsin, and filled here yesterday. But... the address is fake. The name is fake."

"How did you even get this?"

"That's not the question you should be asking," Tori said.

"Illegal prescriptions," Braddock observed in a low voice, shaking his head. "That could be a real problem for you. For your business here. What else illegal might be going on—"

"Whoa, hey, hey, Art, hold on here—"

"Or," Tori said, leaning toward Lingren, "this was a favor for a friend because they're in some danger. And we know they're in danger. If you help us, we can help that friend, and they can help us find the people who are after them. See all these scratches on my face, there are more on my body." She gestured to Braddock. "He was shot at last night, thankfully only grazed. By the same people after the person you're protecting."

"George," Long said. "Don't jam yourself up here. You took this prescription from Superior and issued it in a fake name and address. They need to find this woman. Help them help her and you."

Lingren sat back in his chair for a moment, thinking it through. He sat back up and turned his chair to his computer. "Cleo Collins, well, Cleo Liriano now. I've known her since she was a little girl. Cleo claimed her friend and daughter were trying to get away from an abusive spouse, but her daughter needed her medication." He tapped at his keyboard and then slid the mouse and maneuvered. He grabbed a pen and wrote down an address. "That's Cleo's address. Nevada Avenue. Not too far from here."

* * *

Boo turned right onto Nevada Avenue this time, coming in for a look from the east. It looked a bit different with the dark of night setting in. The street was long and dimly lit, the white light from the few streetlamps that existed having trouble piercing the dense overhanging tree canopies. The street was quiet now, perhaps only a third of the houses having their front porch lights on. Boo made a slow pass of the house on their right.

"Porch light is off, but it doesn't help there is a streetlight right in front," Vooch said as they eased by.

There didn't appear to be any lights on in the front of the house, though through the small square windows crossing the top of the front door, light emanated from what looked to be the back of the house.

"Let's check the alley again," Conn said.

This time they came in from the west end of the alley. The alley was a mixture of loose dirt and gravel with an uneven light grass strip down the middle. It was narrow, tree branches hanging so low it looked as if they'd brush the top of the Tahoe.

Boo stopped and turned off the headlights and let his eyes adjust to the darkness. With the detached garages hugging the alleyway it was like being in a narrow tunnel. There was a light at the entry to the alley behind them and one at the far end. It left enough ambient light that with his eyes adjusted, he could drive without the headlights and just crept along.

"Two up on the right. Lights on in the back," Vooch said.

Boo slowed, catching a glimpse of the rear of the house. The lights were on, the curtains open and he was able to see into the kitchen and eating area. There were three people sitting at a table, a man and two women. The man put a beer to his lips before standing up in a way that said he was going for another.

Vooch had a small pair of binoculars, also eyeing up the back of the house. They started passing the detached garage and slowed to a crawl, inching forward. The back of the house was divided by a door. To the left was one double window. That was the kitchen, a white refrigerator and upper kitchen cabinets visible through the window. To the right there appeared to be an eating area. A man stood while two women were sitting at the table.

"Easy," Vooch murmured, eyeing up the women and the photo on his phone. "I'm pretty sure that's her. The one on the right."

"I agree," Conn said. "That's her."

"The guns are in the back," Stag declared.

Vooch shook his head. "I love how you just think you can give orders."

"I'm not giving orders. But now you know where she is. I figured—"

"If you had figured a little more carefully eight years ago, we wouldn't be creeping down this alley trying to figure how to snip a dangling thread," Boo said pointedly.

"You wouldn't be if you'd have done it right the other night."

"Really, Stag?" Conn murmured, shaking his head. "Shut your pie hole."

Boo let his eyes drift up to the rearview mirror. Stag was one of those guys who always had to get in the last word, even when it was in his best interest to stay silent.

He drove ahead, turned right, and then right again onto the street, and pulled to the curb six houses east of the Liriano house. The street was up a slight incline from west to east. From their perch they looked down upon the front approach to the house. With the illumination of the streetlight and the tree-free front yard, going in the front door was not the optimal approach tonight.

Boo turned around to Vooch. "Options?"

Vooch leaned over. "If we go tonight, it would have to be you and me from the back. Drive in, jump out, go in hot and do it, fast."

"We could get stuck in that alley."

"Too many eyes to come in the front, even at night. The back is tight but there is lots of cover for the approach and for after. Nobody would be able to see shit back there."

Boo looked into the back seat. Stag was of no use for this. Conn would have been, though with his arm in a sling, he wasn't going in and he might not even be able to drive if a quick getaway was needed. "It's two on three, four if you count the kid. We don't know what the man is capable of. You can assume he has a gun in the house."

"So."

"It's Thursday night," Boo said. "The Lirianos work. Tomorrow, they go to work, which leaves Julio's wife and kid alone at the house."

"You assume."

"At most, Cleo Liriano stays home. We can handle both women."

"In the daylight?" Vooch replied skeptically. "I don't know about that. Pretty loud."

"We don't have to shoot them."

"Suppose not."

"If we wait for daylight, it's two-on-three but one is a kid, a five-year-old girl. In and out, these two pull up behind and we get the hell out of here. Drop the vehicle not far away, get back up to the airport and we're in the air before anyone really knows what happened."

"Maybe," Vooch replied as the rearview mirror suddenly blazed with blue and red flashing light. "What the..."

Boo checked his side mirror as a police patrol unit with the flashing lights sped by, followed by another unit, and then two other vehicles. They all pulled to a stop in front of the Liriano house.

Vooch and Boo shared a look.

A thickish man waited on the sidewalk as a tall man and slight woman got out of a black Tahoe and were walking toward him. The tall man and short woman walked into the illumination of the streetlight.

"That's Braddock and Hunter," Vooch said. "How? How!"

"They followed the breadcrumbs too."

"Now what?" Stag asked.

* * *

"Cleo Collins," Tori said with an air of whimsy, a smile creasing her lips. "Should have known."

"Known what?"

"When Ana Martinez was eighteen years old and a senior in high school, she was cited for minor alcohol consumption along with her friend."

"Cleo."

"Girls gotta stick together. Cleo is her BFF, through thick and thin, so when she needed help, that's who she called."

"If you don't have family or can't go to them, then it's friends. Just like us."

"Exactly. Nolan had Cleo, the minor consumption, in her research on Ana Gonzalez." Tori shook her head, smiling. "Nolan. That girl just knows how to find stuff. You know, you're going to lose her to some other bigger law enforcement agency."

"And if that's what Nolan wants, I'll do anything to help her."

Braddock pulled to the curb behind Detective Long and the patrol units. Long was out quickly and walked to the patrol unit and leaned down to instruct the uniformed officer and then led Tori and Braddock up the short sidewalk to the house, his police radio to his ear.

"Is there a problem?" Tori asked. In the far distance she heard sirens. Something was up.

"Shooting a few miles east of here. Multiple units are responding."

Long knocked on the front door.

It took a few seconds, but then they heard footsteps and then the porch light flipped on. A man opened the door. "Can I help you?"

Long held up his badge. "Detective Long, Toledo Police. These folks are police from Minnesota."

Tori glanced at Braddock, who nodded. He too saw Liriano's flinch at the word Minnesota.

"Are you Joshua Liriano?" Long said.

"Uh, yes. Has something happened, Detective?"

"We're here to speak with your friend Ana."

"There's nobody here by that name."

"You're a bad fibber, Mr. Liriano," Braddock asserted but with a friendly grin. "I could tell by your reaction when you heard we were from Minnesota. I'm Detective Will Braddock.

I'm Chief Detective for Shepard County. We need to speak with Ana. We know she's here."

"Do you have a warrant?"

"Well, now, Mr. Liriano, I can certainly get one," Long replied with eyebrows raised. "And until I do, we'll all sit here and wait. Or you can let these people help Ana."

"It's okay, Josh," a thin woman with long black hair said, appearing behind him. It was Ana. "Let them in."

Everyone crowded into the dining area in the back of the house. Ana sat back down next to Cleo, the two of them holding hands. Braddock took a chair at the end of the table.

"So, you're Will Braddock?" Ana said derisively.

"Yes, ma'am." He showed her his identification. "Tori is a retired FBI special agent who works with our department. We've been looking for you since Monday."

"My husband asked for your help. You turned him down."

Braddock nodded. "I did. I shouldn't have because the same people who came after him, and you, and your daughter, have also come after Tori and me."

"Momma?"

They all turned around. A young girl with her hair in pigtails, dressed in pajamas, was looking at them.

"Emma, honey, you're supposed to be in bed," Ana admonished.

"Who are all these people?"

Tori crouched to a knee. "Are you Emma?"

The little girl nodded.

"Hi. I'm Tori."

"Are you police?" She pointed to the gun on Tori's hip.

"Yes. I'm an investigator. My specialty is finding missing children, though you're not missing, sweetheart, but I also sometimes find dolls and return them to their owners." Tori grabbed her backpack, unzipped it and pulled out three dolls they had found at the cabin. "I believe these are yours."

Emma nodded eagerly. Tori handed her the dolls and Emma happily hugged them.

"You can take those up to your bed, honey," Ana said.

"Can I have some juice, too?"

Ana sighed. "Sure," and began to stand up.

"That's okay, you stay, Ana," Tori said, reaching for Emma's hand. "I can get it for her. In the fridge?"

"Yes," Cleo said. "Glasses are to the right of the sink."

* * *

"You got them ready?" Boo asked Vooch, who was now in the back passenger seat.

"Yeah," Vooch said, an AR-15 perched in his left hand, another resting against the seat between him and Stag. "Just say when."

Boo had made a long multiple block loop around the area to mask their approach and was now turning left into the west end of the alley. After the turn was made and he had the Tahoe centered he motored ahead slowly, the Liriano house up on the right. After they passed the neighbor's garage, they were able to see into the back of the house. Several people had crowded into the same dining area.

"I see Braddock, he's sitting next to the woman," Vooch said. "Plus, two other cops and Liriano."

"And Hunter?" Boo said as they slowly drove behind the Lirianos' garage. When they came out on the other side, they'd have a full view of the back of the house.

* * *

Tori led Emma by the hand into the kitchen and opened the refrigerator. There was a bottle of apple juice and orange juice on the top shelf. "Apple or orange?"

"Apple," Emma replied immediately.

"Well, okay, then."

Tori took the bottle, turned to the counter and reached up for a glass. As she poured the juice, she glanced out the window and then looked again.

What was that?

She leaned forward.

Long saw her reaction. "What is it?"

"I'm not sure," she replied, instinctively flipping back her blazer and putting her hand on the gun. "Something in the alley... An SUV, with its lights off," she said, moving to the back door.

* * *

"They saw us," Conn yelped.

"We're blown. We gotta go! Now! Go! Go! Go!"

Boo hit the gas and roared ahead, starting the left turn to exit the alley.

"Ah shit!"

Another truck came from the left and he suddenly jerked the wheel back hard right, the left back-end crashing into the front fender of the truck.

* * *

Tori burst out the back door, Braddock right behind, and rushed to the corner of the neighbors' garage.

They heard the crash.

At the corner of the garage, Tori looked up the alley to see the SUV had collided with another vehicle.

She stepped into the alley and moved ahead cautiously, sliding to the left side, gun up.

It was so dark.

She couldn't make out the background but could hear the engine revving for the black SUV that was trying to pull away.

* * *

"Get loose! Get loose!" Conn yelled.

Boo hit the gas, feeling the wheels spin, but they weren't moving, tangled up with the other truck. "Reverse! Reverse!" Stag yelled.

Vooch looked back and saw movement, someone darting across the alley. "They're coming."

"I can't get it loose. I can't get it loose," Boo exclaimed.

"Shit!" Vooch growled and turned in his seat.

* * *

Tori edged ahead and then she saw movement. A man in the back seat was turning.

"Braddock?"

"Tori, gun!"

Boom! Boom! Boom! Boom! Boom! Boom!

* * *

"Go! Go!" Conn yelled.

Boo threw it in reverse again, gunning the accelerator, the engine roaring. "Come on, come on."

Boom! Boom! Boom!

Boo felt the fender get loose.

"Go!" Stag yelled. "Now!"

* * *

Tori heard the screech of the two vehicles and peered around the corner of the garage. The SUV pulled away to the right, to Nevada Avenue. She looked back and Braddock saw it too. "Come on!"

They ran back to the house. Long was standing at the house's back door.

"Long, come on! Come on! Dark SUV north in the alley! It's coming out on the street. Come on!" Braddock yelled as he and Tori ran between the houses.

Long came charging out the front door as Braddock and Tori ran through the front yard, but Long's car was jammed in between cars. Their Tahoe was not. "We'll take mine!" Braddock yelled and then to Long. "You got a radio?"

"Yeah, yeah, yeah," he said as he went to his car.

Braddock and Tori got into the Tahoe and Braddock whipped it around in time to see taillights a couple of blocks ahead turn right. "Come on!"

Long rushed to the Tahoe, jumping in the back. "What was that? A Tahoe like this one?"

"Yeah, accept ours isn't dragging a bumper," Tori said.

"Dispatch, 10 William 25 in pursuit of shooters from Nevada Avenue shooting," Long reported. "They are in a black SUV, possibly Chevy Tahoe, damaged left side and rear bumper. They are now going east on..." He had to wait for the street sign. "Starr Avenue. East on Starr Avenue."

"Copy, 10 William 25."

Braddock zoomed ahead. "Oh, yeah. It's them. They're weaving through traffic like maniacs," he said as they went through an intersection on a red light.

* * *

Boo looked into the rearview mirror. "Is there anyone back there?"

"No, I don't think so," Stag said.

"I'm not so sure about that," Vooch said. "There's a dark SUV back there weaving through traffic. No police lights, but they're coming. It could be Braddock and Hunter. They pulled up in a black SUV."

Boo peered ahead and at the dashboard map. "How far back?"

"Not that far. And... I see flashing lights further back of them," Vooch said. "And this thing is all banged up. We gotta get out of sight."

"Straight ahead, Boo. Coming right at us," Conn called. "They know what they're looking for. They see us and—"

"We have to make a move!" Vooch blurted.

Boo looked at his dashboard map. Up to the right was Pearson Metropark. It looked to be a city park with woods and trails. Through the intersection, he veered to the right and took the entrance into the park.

* * *

"They turned right," Tori said, gesturing. "Is that a park of some kind?"

"Yes," Long said. "Dispatch, 10 William 25. The black Tahoe has veered into the Pearson Metropark." To Tori and Braddock. "The park is mostly trails, though there are areas with tennis and pickle ball courts, playgrounds. It's mostly a pedestrian park."

"Do you know it?"

"Not all that well," Long said.

"I'm guessing neither do they. I'm going in," Braddock said, gunning it as he turned into the park, flipping on his bright lights.

"They're going to kill their lights in here," Tori said.

"I think I caught a glimpse of them," Braddock said. "I saw a flash of taillights ahead."

* * *

Boo ripped around a curve. "Where do I go?"

"This road just loops back southwest and out of the park. If they're coming, they'll be there."

They passed a sign for pickle ball courts, which were on the right, then a playground. He saw a sign for ballfields to the left and he took it.

"That's just a path!" Conn bellowed.

"I know."

Boo roared ahead, no headlights, relying on natural moonlight.

* * *

"He turned left!" Braddock said.

"Onto what?" Tori questioned

"That's a path," Long answered. "At least, I think."

"No turning back now." Braddock turned left, the back end of the Tahoe flying wildly.

* * *

"We still have a tail," Vooch yelled. "I can see headlights. They're still on us!"

"Vooch! Light 'em up."

* * *

Braddock followed the path as it weaved toward softball fields.

They all called out intermittent flashes of taillights. But no headlights.

Ping!

"What was that?"

Ping! Ping! Ping!

"They're firing."

Braddock skidded to an abrupt stop, ducking down, looking Tori in the eye, breathing hard.

"Long?"

"I'm okay." He raised the radio. "Dispatch, 10 William 25, shots fired in the park! Shots fired in the park!" Long reported. "They are armed and will fire."

The shooting stopped.

Braddock and Tori both slowly rose, peering just over the edge of the dashboard.

"Now where are they?" Braddock muttered.

* * *

"Go! Go!" Vooch said. "They stopped."

Boo drove past the ballfields and then saw in the distance through the trees flashing lights, driving rapidly west, but away from them. Another patrol unit. There would be more. Soon the park would be crawling with police. Then he saw a gravel path branching off left toward a solitary light and what looked like a barn. He turned hard left, throwing everyone to the right.

"What the fuck!" Stag yelled.

"The maintenance facility," he said as he raced ahead through an opening in the fence, between two maintenance barns and out a driveway that led back to Starr Avenue.

* * *

"They're moving again," Tori observed. "I saw the taillights."

"Me too," Braddock said, and he hit the gas and zoomed ahead.

Long's radio belched: "10 William 25, park exits are blocked. More units en route."

"Copy," Long said.

"But I'm not sure that's right based on the map," Tori said. "Heck, I'm not sure where we are."

Braddock saw a flash of red in the distance to the left and jammed the brakes.

"What?" Tori said.

He turned hard left. "I think they turned here." He zoomed ahead on the narrow gravel jutted road toward a light and then a fenced area, catching the flash of a sign: Maintenance. He drove through the opening in the fence and then left between two corrugated shed structures. As he emerged from between the two long sheds he looked to the right. Out on the road, passing under a streetlight, a black SUV, no lights on, rear bumper loose.

"Dispatch, be advised the shooters are back on Starr Avenue," Long reported. "They have escaped the park via the maintenance area. They're driving east."

Braddock turned right onto Starr, but having had to stop when fired upon, they were further behind.

* * *

"They're coming again!" Vooch said, peering back.

Conn looked at the dashboard map and then ahead where the road curved to the right before reaching a T-intersection. "Boo, turn left at the T ahead, and then I have an idea."

Boo hardly braked as he turned hard left and approached a railroad crossing.

* * *

"I lost sight of them," Braddock said.

"Me too," Tori said as they reached a T in the road. She and Long both glanced right and saw flashing police lights in the distance to what she thought was the south.

"They had to go left," Tori said.

Braddock turned left, zoomed over the train tracks and hit the gas, seeing another set of police lights flashing in the distance, coming at them. Another set was behind them, closing. He glanced right and there was a third set coming from the east on a road.

But the road ahead was clear other than the police unit with flashing lights coming at them.

"Where did they go?"

The flashing police lights ahead stopped and then turned to block the road. It was an Explorer that said, Toledo Police.

"What the hell?" Braddock said as he slowed to a stop.

The other unit came up on them from behind, stopping fifty feet back of them. The doors on both sides opened but the officers had their guns up.

"Hands up where we can see them!" a voice boomed over a speaker.

"Oh, for Pete's sake," Tori said, raising her hands, as did Braddock.

Braddock laughed in resignation. "We're in a black Tahoe."

"You can't make it up," Tori moaned.

"It never occurred to me to tell them we were driving the same damn thing the shooters were," Long said. "Fuck."

An officer came up slowly on the passenger side. In the side mirror Tori could see he had his gun up. Long let his right arm drift out the window, the police radio in his hand, the volume up so the officer could hear it as he approached.

Ten feet short, the officer stopped. "Who are you?"

"10 William 25," Long said.

"Ah shit. Art is that you?"

"Yeah."

"Well shit, put your hands down."

"The question is, where the hell did those guys go?" Braddock said, looking back.

* * *

Boo had turned left and driven in the narrow rail bed between the treeline along their left and the train tracks to their right. The uneven gravel and rock of the railbed made for a rough and bumpy ride, but there was no longer anybody behind them. The flashing police lights were now far off in the distance, visible across the open field, blocking the road they had been on less than a minute earlier.

"Good call," Boo said to Conn.

Conn nodded. "We're not out of the woods yet."

They drove along the train tracks that made a straight run to the northwest. They crossed underneath two bridge overpasses and within ten minutes, they had come upon a railyard, exited it and were on city side streets approaching I-280.

"I think we're in the clear now," Vooch muttered. "We have to be a good four to five miles from that turn."

"Now what?" Stag said.

"We're clear so let's not drive like a bat out of hell," Vooch said to Boo. "Just drive normalish."

"Fair point, though the whole back of the driver's side is banged up. We're still noticeable," Boo said, easing back on the gas but still sneaking a peak at the rearview mirror before he made the turn onto an entrance ramp for the Interstate.

When they passed over the state line into Michigan ten

minutes later and the rearview mirror was clear, the immediate tension amongst them eased considerably.

Conn exhaled. "That was close."

"Yeah, but it tells us something else," Boo said. "Braddock and Hunter were there. They're not on the sidelines anymore."

NINETEEN

"TALK ABOUT SETTING MYSELF UP."

The confusion cleared up within five minutes with the Toledo officers, Braddock, Tori and Long tried to figure out where they lost the other Tahoe. Then Tori saw it after they turned around and followed the route the chase had been on.

The train tracks.

"What do you want to bet they went that way," she said, gesturing west on the train bed.

Braddock pulled to a stop. The three of them got out and instantly saw, in the heavy gravel and rock of the trail bed, skid marks on the south side of the tracks, as if the vehicle had swerved and fishtailed before straightening out. "That's what they did." He looked to Long. "What do you think?"

Long nodded in agreement and called it in. But within ten minutes it was clear the trail had gone cold. "It's five miles to a railyard area and my guess is they got there and drove off. And from there they could go anywhere. We have a bulletin out for a black Tahoe, damaged on the driver's side. That's gone out to all law enforcement in Ohio and southern Michigan, so we'll just have to see."

. . .

Thirty minutes later they were pulling up at the Lucas County Sheriff's Department. Ana and Emma had been relocated to the Sherriff's Office for their safety. Josh and Cleo were protected as well with patrol units stationed in front and behind their house.

Long led them to an elevator. "We've got them situated for the night anyway." Off the elevator, he led them down several hallways into the bowels of the sheriff's department building to a door where a Lucas County Sheriff's Deputy and Toledo patrol officer were standing watch. The door opened into a windowless breakroom that had two small couches arranged around a small television and then an area with two round tables with chairs. There was a small kitchenette with a refrigerator and microwave.

Ana sat on one of the couches while Emma slept with her head on her mother's lap, her left arm wrapped around one of the dolls Tori had returned to her. Emma's eyes opened momentarily to see Tori. The little girl looked exhausted, and Tori could only imagine the trauma of the week for her. No child that age should have to live through what she'd lived through, and it wasn't over yet.

Tori caught Ana's eye and nodded to a table on the other side of the room. Ana carefully stood up, put a small couch pillow under Emma's head, letting her sleep on the small sofa. She joined them at the small table on the other side of the room. A pot of coffee had been brewed. Long grabbed the pot and white Styrofoam cups.

"The police haven't found them, have they?" Ana asked.

"I'm sorry, but no," Braddock said, shaking his head.

"They'll just keep coming after us," Ana said, looking at Emma sleeping on the couch. "I thought we'd be safe with Cleo and Josh, at least for a little while."

"I understand why you and your husband ran," Braddock

said. "I understand why you didn't call the police after you fled that cabin on Sunday night. I understand it."

"How?"

"I just... do," Braddock said. "Ana, I'm not your enemy."

"I'm not so sure you're my friend. Detective Lange said to my husband you might not be any kind of a friend."

"I'm sorry to hear that he said that. I knew Ray from when I was a detective with the NYPD, and I've come to understand why he might have believed that, but he was wrong."

"Julio asked for your help. You said no."

"And I'll regret it for the rest of my life."

"Why? Why say no?"

"Let's talk about what you know, and I'll tell you what I know and maybe you'll understand why I did what I did. For now, let me just say that I wanted to avoid getting mixed up in all this but now, I'm mixed up in it. We both are."

"They tried killing us last night," Tori said, explaining what happened to her and Braddock, both displaying their wounds and injuries.

"They've killed a lot of people," Braddock continued. "And you're right, they may come back at you, and at us, if we don't find them first."

"Why are they after you?"

"For similar reasons they were after your husband," Braddock said, and he quickly explained the history of the case, his involvement in it and the cloud of suspicion that hung over him.

"You're a... suspect?" Ana asked, glancing to Detective Long.

"I think what they went through last night and then tonight ought to disabuse you of that notion. Tonight, they saved your life."

"And last night," Braddock said, "they made a big mistake."

Ana sat back. "What?"

"They missed," Tori said darkly.

"It's them or us now," Braddock added. "We're going after them."

"Who are they?"

"Dirty cops," Braddock said flatly. "Or, at this point, I suspect former NYPD cops." He paused for a moment, taking a sip of coffee, wanting to get this part right. "Julio told me on Sunday night he couldn't trust the NYPD, so I take from that, he thought cops were after you and it wasn't just to question you but to silence you."

"Yes."

"Ana, we need to know what you and Julio knew."

Ana thought for a moment, her hands nervously clasping her Styrofoam coffee cup. "Back when we lived in New Jersey, Julio worked as a longshoreman at the port. It was a good job. He had good pay, good insurance and retirement benefits. I was working as a nurse at a children's hospital. I really liked that."

Tori nodded along. "You two were on your way."

"Julio worked nights back then, as did I," Ana continued. "That way, we'd have time together. Julio worked there for a few years and had a good sense of how things operated. He was observant about things like that, and he had a good eye for what you would call oddities. And you know, down on the docks, you'd see some shit."

"I can only imagine," Tori agreed.

"Julio said that on the night shifts there would be a dock foreman there if a decision needed to be made but rarely upper-level management types. The suits he'd call them, though I don't know that they dressed that way. But Julio started to notice that the terminal operations manager was hanging around here and there at night. You just didn't see someone like that all that often when you were on the night shift. And what Julio noticed after a couple of times was that when he showed up, it was for a brief time when a specific shipping company's ship would come in and the manager seemed interested in certain containers coming off the ship. He'd be there, watch the container be loaded onto a trailer and then would talk to some others, get into a car with them and then he would be gone."

"Something out of the ordinary was going on," Braddock said. "An oddity, if you will."

"Maybe not quite at first. At first, he thought the manager was working with the police on something."

"Why?"

"Because the man this manager was speaking with looked like a cop to Julio."

"And who was this terminal operations manager?" Tori asked.

"Carmine—"

"Stagliola," Braddock finished, his eyes wide. "It was Carmine Stagliola?"

"Yes." Ana nodded. "That was the name."

Braddock sat back, slack-jawed, shaking his head in disbelief. "Son of a bitch. Talk about setting myself up."

"You know him?" Tori asked.

"I spoke with him once. We'll get to all that." To Ana he said: "Keep going because Stagliola is *not* a cop. But Julio thought the man Stagliola was talking to or working with was a cop?"

"Yes."

"And what did you say?"

"Don't get involved. Don't let anyone think you know what's going on." She shook her head in exasperation. "But Julio being Julio..."

"He got involved," Tori said.

"Moth, flame," Ana said, shaking her head, speaking of her husband who, Tori had to remind herself, had died a mere four days ago. "I know he talked to Malik about it because Malik was an operator. Malik had stuff going on down on the docks."

"He did," Braddock said. "I worked for the Joint Terrorism

Task Force for some years. Malik would feed us information and in trade, we'd look the other way on his shenanigans."

"What was Malik?" Long inquired.

"Among other things, a trafficker in ill-gotten goods."

"A fence?"

"He called himself a broker but, yeah, he was a fence," Braddock said. "A well connected one."

"Julio talked with Malik about it and then not long after that, with this other detective."

"Dan Guerero?"

"Yeah, that's when he started poking around and Julio told the detective about what he saw on the docks, with Stagliola and this other man. But from what I gathered this Guerero said there wasn't a police operation at the docks at that time."

"It was something else."

"Yes. And then one night when Julio arrived for his shift, he saw Detective Guerero and Stagliola and from what Julio could tell, it looked like Guerero was questioning Stagliola intensely, whatever that meant. He said the detective had him 'cornered.'"

"Cornered?" Tori said.

"I could see that," Braddock said with a nod. "One of Dan's nicknames was Eclipse because if he got tight with you, he blocked out all the light. He could put someone in a corner, and they would have nowhere to go. It was one of his interrogation techniques. But then a few days later—"

"Julio told me that the detective was shot and killed in Manhattan. He didn't think the timing was coincidental. After that, Julio kept his head down and I heard nothing about it for a few months until he said there was another detective showing interest in what Guerero had been looking into." Ana turned to look at Braddock. "Malik told Julio that Detective Will Braddock would be coming to find him. That you were someone he could trust." Ana snorted her disgust. "But you didn't come and find him. And then Malik was murdered."

"And Julio figured if he hung around, he was next," Tori said.

"Yes." Then she turned back to Braddock. "Sunday night wasn't the first time you let Julio down."

Braddock took a moment. Fair or not, the assertion stung. "That investigation that I was doing, was on my own time. It was not... sanctioned by the department, so I was working it when I could," he explained. "But when I was told Malik had been murdered, I immediately came looking for Julio, at your apartment and at his work, which is when I spoke with Stagliola because I was trying to track Julio down and he told me he hadn't shown up for work for a few days. And..." He sat back, shaking his head in anger, mad at himself. "I have realized something just now that I didn't at the time."

"What?"

"Braddock, you dumbass. Why didn't you see it?"

"See what?" Tori said.

"Did your husband know Stagliola at all?" he asked Ana.

"No, I don't think so."

"Did Stagliola ever speak with him, indicate he knew him in any way, shape or form?"

"Not that Julio ever said."

"Ana, Stagliola knew of your husband right when I asked about him. He didn't even have to look him up." He sat back, looking at the ceiling. "Why would the terminal operations manager, someone many, many, rungs above a longshoreman on the organizational chart, just know those things about a regular old night dock worker?" Braddock stood up and paced around. "Why? Because he wanted to know what I knew, because whoever he's working with was looking for Julio," he said, a tinge of regret in his voice. "Ana, you and Julio were right to have left. I went back to your apartment after I'd gone to the docks. The building supe let me in. Someone had gotten into your apartment before I did. It was ransacked."

"And then *he* was warned off the case," Tori said of Braddock.

"Warned off?"

Tori took out the photo and slid it to Ana. She looked at the photo and then flipped it over and read the message they had left for him. "How old is your son now?"

"Just turned fourteen. They were watching me too. It was why I originally told your husband I didn't want to meet on Sunday. I didn't want to put my son at risk. It was..." He paused. "But one of many mistakes I've made the past week. I'm just so very sorry."

Ana studied the photo and looked back to Emma. "I get protecting your children."

"What happened Sunday night at the cabin?" Tori said.

"After Julio tried to call Braddock and it didn't go so good, we were at the cabin when Lange showed up. Julio was leery of speaking with him, but I told him he needed to." She gestured to Braddock. "When Julio came home on Friday saying we had to go, I said this was it. I'm not running again. He needed to just tell someone what he knew so that's why we drove to Manchester Bay. Because Malik told him he could trust you."

"I'm sorry."

"I understand now why you did what you did," Ana said. "But at the time, we had to do something, so Julio let Lange in. They started talking, and Lange said what he said about you. I was looking out the window and I saw them coming."

"Who?" Tori said.

"We couldn't tell, or identify them," Ana replied. "That's when Julio mentioned this Stagliola guy's name to Lange."

"And nobody else? No other names?" Braddock pressed. "He didn't know any cop names?"

"No," Ana said. "He described two other men though. I'll never forget this, but Julio said one man showed up in a plain silver sedan about a half-dozen times, always wearing a dark suit, barrel-chested, had a big round head, black hair slicked back."

Braddock glanced over at Tori, and he could see she was thinking the same thing. "You said there was another man?"

"Julio only saw him a couple of times. Big fella as well, shaved head, burly, thick. Thing was, Lange seemed to recognize the descriptions of *both* men."

"You're sure about that?"

"Yeah. I mean he said he thought he knew who they might be."

"He didn't say a name?"

"No but Lange was... surprised by it."

"Ana, what happened next?" Tori said.

"Julio and Lange thought they saw two men coming up the driveway. And they started firing. Julio shot back."

"Why did Lange go outside?" Braddock asked.

"He'd left his gun in the car. He made a show of it for us before we let him in the cabin."

Tori turned to Braddock. "That explains that part of it." She looked back to Ana. "You got away. How?"

Ana took a moment. "Our car was parked behind the cabin. Julio told me to take Emma and go. He was shot at that point, bleeding, could barely... stand. I didn't want to go, but..." Her lip started trembling and she looked back to Emma.

Tori slid a little closer. "I'm so sorry."

"I got Emma into the car and—" she sat upright "—I drove right at them, like I was a crazy woman or something."

"We thought you did," Tori said. "We saw the tire tracks. The damage to the tree."

"I saw one man, briefly in my headlights. He was dressed all in black, wearing a mask. He shot at us. The car had bullet holes in it. From there, I drove for a while down toward the Twin Cities, trying to think what to do when I finally called Cleo and

Josh. They said to come to them, and we'd figure something out. I drove to Detroit, and they picked us up."

"What is it these guys are protecting?" Long asked.

"Money. A lot of it," Braddock said, going through the robberies. "They took down millions of dollars in drugs and sold it. And with this renewed interest in what happened to Dan Guerero, it's all at risk so they're trying to cut off anyone who might know anything about it and make me, or my corpse, take the fall for all of it."

"Ana," Tori said. "Julio described the man talking with Stagliola and the other man with the shaved head, the big guy. If Julio had been shown photos, do you think he would have been able to identify both men?"

"Yes. He described these men to Lange. And he did it well enough that Lange seemed to recognize them. And..." Her voice drifted off for a second.

"And?" Tori prodded.

"One time when we ran, he said he saw the big man from the docks, the one with the shaved head. We were in Sandusky then. We packed up and moved again. It was after that we changed our names. Because this man had almost found us."

"And the other times you moved?"

"Local police had showed up and questioned Julio, asking odd questions, whether he was from New York or New Jersey. When that would happen, we'd just move again."

"These men. Would Julio have described these men to Detective Guerero, you think?"

"I assume so."

"How did Julio learn about Malik's death?"

"Someone down on the docks told him they'd heard he'd been killed, had his throat cut. He clocked out, came home and said we had to leave right then and there. He figured Malik might have been forced to give him up. These men would be coming after us. We packed in a half-hour. We went to the bank, withdrew all our money and drove west. We've been on the run ever since. And now we're on the run again." Ana looked over to Emma. "I don't know where we can go or what we're going to do."

"Where do you want to go?" Tori asked.

"I want someplace where Emma and I can just live, where I can have a job, she could go to school, and I wouldn't have to worry about all this anymore. I just want a normal life."

"You were a nurse before all this running. What kind?"

"I worked at a children's hospital."

"Did you like it?"

"Very much."

The four of them sat quietly for a moment. Braddock turned to Tori. "Any other questions you can think of right now?"

"No. Maybe we sleep on it and see if we have some follow-up in the morning."

He turned back to Ana. "For the time being, we need to hide you and Emma until we can end this," Braddock said.

"Hide us? Where?"

"Here tonight. After tonight, you let us worry about that," Tori said. She and Braddock stepped out into the hallway.

"So where do we hide them?" Braddock asked.

"I'm going to call Eddie. Tell him we need the next favor," Tori replied. "Then I'm going to call Tracy and see what she can dig up on Carmine Stagliola."

"Barrel-chested guy with a dark suit and slicked-back black hair," Braddock said. "Who does that remind you of?"

"That fucker Renko. But—"

"It's still not proof."

* * *

Boo took a seat in the back of the small jet, a few seats away from the others. Just after takeoff, the phone rang.

"What happened?"

The voice was urgent, demanding as ever.

Boo rolled his eyes.

Renko was always on edge. Though to be fair, he now had good reason to be.

Boo explained the night, what the plan had been and how it didn't pan out when Hunter spotted them and that they had to get away from Toledo.

"There was no shot?"

"No. We had to get out of there."

Renko was quiet for a moment. "And Braddock was there, in Toledo. Along with Hunter."

"And it would appear the Toledo police were working *with* them."

"Missing him the other night was costly, Boo. I could have put this thing to rest with him gone. He's not gone. That's a problem."

"Hmpf," Boo snorted. In his mind, he wasn't sure it was *his* problem.

Renko heard the snort. "You disagree?"

"It was a mistake to make him such a focus of your investigation all along. He's a smart, resourceful, and innocent man."

Renko's turn to snort.

"You disagree?"

"We wouldn't even be in this spot if you had disposed of those bodies Sunday night."

"Easy to second-guess, sitting well above the fray. I don't see you getting your hands dirty."

There was a sigh on the other end. "Boo, I can still control this thing on my end, but we have a problem that could be made easier. You know what I'm saying?"

Boo understood the implication of what Renko was saying. "I understand. And I'll take care of it."

Renko hung up and Boo reclined back in his chair at the back of the plane, peering out the window.

All five of them had grown up within a twelve-block radius of one another in Port Richmond on Staten Island. When they were in their early twenties, they all were frequent drinking buddies at Lou's Pub—as were many young Port Richmond adults. Renko and Stag had grown up on the same block. Renko and Boo, who'd grown up eight blocks away, had gone to the police academy together and were patrol officers, until Renko moved into homicide and Boo into narcotics work.

Stag, as had many other denizens of Lou's, worked at the port. Later, Vooch, and Conn came along, cops, younger neighborhood guys but they ended up in narcotics and gravitated to Boo. For a three-year stretch the five of them, single, or at least not yet married, often drank with one another at Lou's and bowled in a league, the team sponsored by Lou's. Then, as is often the case, as their twenties gave way to their thirties and attempts at marriage and families were made, they all drifted apart, until fifteen years later.

It might not have all happened were it not for marital strife. Boo, Vooch and Conn all worked narcotics, and such work was not always compatible with a happy domestic home life. There were odd hours, nights, weekends, stakeouts, undercover work and the stress that entailed. It led to drinking, and, in the cases of Boo and Vooch, carousing and then getting caught by their spouses. They both divorced. A cop's pay for a tough job didn't go that far to begin with, especially in New York City. Add in child and marital support payments, it covered even less. When Conn's marriage hit the rocks nine years ago, misery loved company, that made it all three of them.

"It's hard to live anywhere around here when you have to pay for one and a half places," Conn said.

"Try paying for two, sometimes three," Vooch said. "Hell, I'm working private security on top of the job."

"Me too," Boo said. "And we've all had our pensions halved, have we not?" He lowered his voice with his two friends. "We're not without an option."

All three of them had gotten wind of a newer drug pipeline coming from Afghanistan, through North Africa, across the Atlantic on container ships from the Port of Tanger Med in Morocco to the Newark Terminal. Gangs and drug crews they knew and watched were using it to supply themselves. The three of them had it cold. Typically, such knowledge was shared with the powers that be and the work would then start and something like this could have gotten them all a promotion.

"What if we kept this one to ourselves?" Boo had suggested and the other two knew what that meant. "I mean at this point, what's a promotion really worth?"

A few more rounds of beers, and further discussions of their personal financial situations, all led them to truly consider it and think about what they needed to do to pull it off.

"It means getting dirty," Conn said.

"I've been getting dirty my whole career, and to what end," Boo replied. "Maybe for once, I should get paid for it. We all should."

"We have the pipeline and some of the details, but if we're going to do this with the least possible risk, we need eyes and ears at the port," Vooch said. "We need to know when the ship arrives, when the container comes off, so we can set-up on it. And you know who can do that for us?"

"Stag."

"We're going to need him and if we're going to get him, you know that means Renko because he'll tell him about it and if we didn't cut him in—"

"He'd probably hang us all," Conn finished. "Boo, we need him on board."

"Given where he's at, I don't think he'd risk it. He's climbing the ladder."

"That may be, but if we have Renko, and we pull this off, we'd have an inside source in case someone started poking around. You gotta talk to him and cut him in."

To Boo's surprise, Renko wasn't completely allergic to the "hypothetical" he put to him, subject to certain conditions. "All Stag and I hypothetically need to do is tag the container, the truck and where it's going."

"That's right. We'll take it from there."

The argument had been over the share.

Renko insisted on an equal one for himself and Stag.

Vooch and Conn bucked at that thought.

"We do all the dirty work, take all the real risk and they take an equal cut?" Vooch railed. "I said cut them in, but this? Greedy fuckers."

"I find it distasteful as well but a fifth is better than nothing at all," Boo replied. "Do we want the payday? If we do, this is how it has to play."

The first two jobs had gone off without a hitch. Having observed prior deliveries, they knew that once the drugs were delivered there was a several-hour interlude before the gangs would show up to take delivery. They used that window, getting inside at each location and taking the drugs upon or just after delivery. By the time the gangs showed up, the drugs were gone and the people in the warehouse were tied up, tape over their mouths. That was the plan on the third one, the Espinosa Warehouse. That one was a big one, primed to double their haul.

The three of them were in the warehouse hidden, the surveillance system down. Then it all changed in an instant. This gang had gotten wise and were there when the container was backed up to the warehouse.

They could have let it all go, slid out the side door and

walked. But then one of them spotted Conn and there was no choice.

"Police!" Boo bellowed and the three of them came out, guns up.

Six sets of hands went up in the air.

Boo fired first, took out the first gang man, Vooch and Conn didn't hesitate and each took one. Boo spun to his left, the owner, the manager and a warehouseman, eyes wide, arms all still in the air.

They had just committed three murders. There was no choice for them to make. It just had to be done. Boo did it.

Boom! Boom! Boom!

They had now committed six murders in a matter of less than thirty seconds.

That was the last job.

They had ducked Braddock's investigation but then Guerero started poking around and was getting close. That had been another murder. Killing one of their own rang a very loud bell. Renko got control of the investigation, deflecting it away from Boo and company and slowly denying the case of oxygen.

That seemed to end things, until Braddock of all people started poking around months later.

He was plowing the same territory as Guerero and was on the right path. That had necessitated the killing of Malik Muhammed, and Julio Gonzalez, though they missed the latter by a half-hour. Ringing the loud bell again by killing Braddock would have increased the heat exponentially, Renko said, so they warned him first. His almost instant move to Minnesota told them he'd heeded the warning. Not that they hadn't kept a loose watch on him over the years. They always knew where Braddock was and what he was up to.

The only loose thread was Julio Gonzalez. They'd kept up a search for him and had nearly caught up to him in Cleveland, Steubenville and then Sandusky. But then the trail on him went cold, they had no leads, and they suspected he'd taken on a new identity. Boo counseled Renko that they let it go. "He's not come back. He's not spoken to the police. He's fleeing. It's been four years now. The trail has gone cold. If we stay quiet, maybe he'll stay quiet."

That left the money. They had all remained careful, particularly about the money and especially with all the dust-up with Guerero and then later Braddock. Any flash of money at that point could have drawn attention. So, they kept living their lives, working until they could retire with their pensions, just as anyone in their positions would have been expected to do. When they retired, they started to allow themselves discreet tastes of it through their security business. They did do some legitimate security work and that allowed them to earn, but then also papered other non-existent jobs that allowed them to access the money.

The question was becoming when would they be able to really experience it all? It had been eight years. They were all in their mid-fifties now.

Hadn't enough time passed? They were thinking it had.

Then Monica Guerero found her husband's notebooks and files. The case was reopened and assigned to the Cold Case Squad. But in the eight years since all had happened, Renko had become particularly adroit in the art of departmental politics. He managed to get Internal Affairs a role in the case, in part because the Guerero murder investigation had been his back in the day, and in part because there was strong suspicion of the involvement of cops in Guerero's murder, based upon the cryptic notes in his notebooks, what he'd been investigating at the Espinosa Warehouse and Braddock's name featuring prominently. If there were dirty cops or even ex-cops, Internal Affairs needed involvement in the case.

Renko wanted to deal with Braddock before the investigation got to him. Boo, Vooch and Conn went to Minnesota and

Manchester Bay to scout him. They came back to Renko with a hard no.

"He got our message. He moved a thousand miles away," Boo reported after the scouting trip. "He's raising his kid, and he's got Tori Hunter, an ex-Bureau agent as a live-in girlfriend. New York and the Dan Guerero case is the furthest thing from his mind. You don't go poking that bear."

"So, what's your other cliché here? Let sleeping dogs lie."

"Braddock is an apex predator. And he ain't afraid of killing someone," Boo counseled. "He's done plenty of that. And he was just awarded the Presidential Medal of Valor. Kill someone with that profile and you're going to draw a lot of unwanted attention. Braddock did exactly, *exactly*, what we wanted."

"You act as if that was the result of a negotiation," Renko asserted. "We didn't do to him what we did to Guerero back then because we had another option. We may not now."

"We're not doing it. Not right now. If circumstances change, we'll talk."

Circumstances changed two weeks later when Lange and Cardellini found Julio, living as Hector Ramirez in Superior. Renko got wind of it and tried to get Boo and the others there first, but Lange beat them all to Ramirez in Superior. And then Ramirez didn't run away to another city as he had before. Instead, he made for Manchester Bay.

"Looks to me like he's running to Braddock for help," Renko said. They knew Julio could hurt them. He could give them Stag and from there, it would be possible to get them all, whether Stag said a word or not.

Boo remained reluctant to go after Braddock but when Lange went to that cabin, they had no choice. They got Julio and Lange, but then the wife and child got away. And then not even twenty-four hours later, Lange's and Gonzalez's bodies were found, by Braddock no less.

"You think Braddock's going to leave us alone now?" Renko

railed. "If this thing goes the way I see it going, Braddock will have to speak to it because right now NYPD views him as a person of interest if not a suspect. That's where it's going after Lange. Right at Braddock. He will not be left with a choice. And if he has no choice, then neither do we."

"Or we could let our previous threat speak for itself. Or let me leave him a reminder."

"Don't you get it, Boo? He's not going to have a choice. He is going to try and find us as a matter of his own survival, so kill him before he does. You said it yourself; he's an apex predator. Only one way to stop one of those."

They'd tried and failed and now, he was coming for them.

Vooch pushed himself up out of his seat and went to the small galley area and poured himself a drink then made his way to the back, taking the seat in front of Boo, facing him.

He took a sip of his drink, peeked back to the front to make sure Conn and Stag were still asleep before whispering, "Renko?"

Boo simply shook his head. "I ran it down for him."

"And?"

"He thinks we have a problem."

Vooch looked to the front of the plane and Conn and Stag. "Well, we do."

"It's bigger than even Renko realizes."

TWENTY

"LET IT RIP."

Tori and Braddock slept for four hours and were up not long after sunrise.

"Everything ready?" Tori asked Long.

"We're set with the van and the decoys, just in case."

Tori and Braddock entered the small breakroom. Ana and Emma were eating a breakfast that had been brought in for them.

"What happens now?" Ana asked.

"You're going to catch a plane," Tori replied.

"Plane? What plane? To where?"

"You'll see when we get to the airport. I think you'll welcome where you're going."

A half-hour later, and after a shell game with three groups of black police vans, Ana, Emma, Braddock, Tori and Long arrived at the small Toledo airport in a black police surveillance van. Waiting on the tarmac for them was Eddie Mannion. He had the wealthy jet-setting business-look going: RayBan sunglasses, weathered jeans, a cream button-down collared shirt along with blue plaid sport coat and brown loafers, no socks.

"These are my passengers?" Eddie asked with a big smile. "Welcome to Air Mannion!"

Tori introduced Ana and Emma to Eddie.

"I'm glad to meet you both."

"This is your plane?" Emma asked shyly, hanging on to her mother's leg.

"Sure is, Emma," Eddie said, crouching to get eye to eye with her. "It's how Tori and Braddock got here."

"Ana," Tori started. "Eddie is one of my oldest and dearest friends. I've known him since I was Emma's age."

Eddie smiled and pulled out his phone. "She ain't lying." He showed them a picture of them arm in arm, wearing their costumes for a school play when they were in middle school. "That's Tori and me. *Peter Pan* was the play. I was a Lost Boy, and she was Tinker Bell."

"You were Tinker Bell?" Braddock said, smiling. "*This* I have to see."

"Oh my God, you still have that photo!" Tori said in amazement and took her own look at the photo. "You need to send me that."

"Done," he said and winked at Emma. "She and I, we're old friends."

"Ana, I trust Eddie, and his brother Kyle, with my life. You can trust him."

"And we're going to... your house?"

"My brother and I own a vacation house in San Diego on Coronado Island," Eddie said breezily. "It's warm there. We have a house and a pool. The ocean is only a block away. My wife is going to join us. It will allow you to just relax a couple thousand miles from here while Braddock and Tori figure this all out."

Ana looked at the plane, Tori, and then Braddock, but with a wry smile this time. "You're sure you're not a dirty cop?"

Braddock smiled. "No. Eddie and his older brother Kyle do

well. They own several companies, but they're based in Manchester Bay and we're just incredibly fortunate they're our friends."

"And they'd do this for you?"

"Heck," Eddie said. "Tori said she'd trust me with her life. My brother and I owe them ours. So let us look after *you* for now."

"For how long?"

"Until we finish this," Braddock said coldly. "One way or another, it's ending."

Ana looked down to her daughter. "You want to go get on the plane?"

Emma nodded eagerly.

"I like it!" Eddie said and reached for Emma's hand, and she let him take it. Eddie walked Ana and Emma to the steps and the pilot welcomed them aboard. Braddock turned to Tori. "If we hustle, we can make New York City by nightfall."

* * *

"Cardi! Your large Cold Brew is up," Luann the barista called out.

"Thanks, Lu."

"Sure thing, Detective. See you back tomorrow?"

"If it's a day ending in y, you will."

Cardellini grabbed her large coffee and departed for her meeting, one that had her nerves tingling, and not necessarily in a good way. It would involve her boss, Cold Case Squad Commander Coleman White, and other detectives for their squad, and Chief Renko, and likely a detective or two from Internal Affairs.

And things with Renko were frosty.

After confronting Braddock and Hunter at the Emergency

Room on Wednesday night, the two of them had their own confrontation in the parking lot at the hotel.

"You were quiet at the ER," Renko charged.

She kept on walking.

"You didn't have my back there. You didn't have it today," Renko barked. "You haven't had it period, Detective!"

She kept on walking.

"I'm talking to you!"

Cardi spun around. "Maybe you and I don't see things the same, Chief. You ever think about that?"

"Excuse me?" Renko had replied in a tone suggesting he viewed her as his subordinate, answerable to him. "I'd heard you had a reputation for a sharp tongue, Cardi."

"No, I have a reputation for not kissing ass and calling it as I see it. So, here's what I saw today, Chief. *You* picked that fight," Cardi charged. "You were out of line. And yeah, so was Braddock, but you instigated it, and he was only too happy to oblige. And you got your ass handed to you."

"Someone had to stand up for Ray and Guerero."

"Oh, that's what that was?" She let the comment hang in the air for a moment, suspecting there was more to it than that. It was clear to her that Renko and Braddock had some history, something in the past between the two of them. "It seemed... more personal to me."

"Dead cops are personal to me."

Cardi smirked.

"What? They aren't to you?"

She ignored the barb and instead said, "You know, what I'm not sure of is if you wanted to intentionally provoke him today, or did it just happen. Either way, it was wrong. *Sir*." She started walking away.

"Whose side are you on here?"

She stopped again, looking back. "I'm on the side of finding out who killed Dan Guerero, Ray Lange and everyone else, full stop."

"Braddock was responsible."

"He might be."

"Might?"

"We haven't proven it. And thanks to today, and him getting shot tonight, it's not like the Shepard County Sheriff's Department is going to help us."

She and Renko had departed Manchester Bay very early yesterday morning with barely a word uttered between them as she took on driving duties to the airport. At the Minneapolis-St. Paul International Airport, they went in opposite directions upon arrival. On the flight, Renko sat at the front of the cabin, and she sat in the far back. By the time she'd reached baggage claim at LaGuardia, Renko was gone, not that she'd minded.

When she arrived at work, she was greeted by her own boss, Cold Case Squad Commander Coleman White in the hallway outside his office. The two of them had conversed privately last night about the trip to Minnesota, and how things had gotten a bit adversarial with Renko. White had heard from Renko as well. What her commander wanted her to do left her feeling uneasy.

"Renko *is* a chief. He and I are already not seeing eye to eye."

"Cardi, don't back down. Be you."

"Do you think I did in Minnesota?"

"I put you in a tough spot. I didn't appreciate the degree to which Renko would assert himself into the case. We're going to get this back under control."

"Is this going to put you in a bad spot?"

"You let me worry about me," White said with confidence,

which suggested he knew exactly where he stood. "I have you covered on this. Let it rip."

He opened the door into the conference room. Inside was Renko, two of his investigators and two other investigators with the Cold Case Squad who had assisted her and Lange on the investigation up to this point.

Cardi evaluated Renko, now two days post-fight. Renko's nose was swollen, his left eye still noticeably blackened, though it looked as if he'd applied some makeup to it to make it less glaring. There were two visible cuts over his right eye, somewhat obscured by his thick eyebrows, and his bottom lip was a bit swollen, though less so than yesterday. It was a rough look despite his otherwise wearing stylish dark-rimmed glasses, a sharp dark wool black suit with a purple tie and pocket square and his as always well-coiffed hair.

"So, tell me where the case is at?" White demanded. "Where do we stand with this thing? On the Guerero case, on Lange's murder? On all of it?"

"It's Braddock, it's always been Braddock," Renko asserted.

"If it's him, why then did someone try to pick him off, and his girlfriend, a highly thought of former FBI special agent?" White retorted. "Explain that to me."

"His co-conspirators tried silencing him before he folded."

"Didn't seem like he was going to fold to me," Cardi said.

"Look, Cole. Braddock didn't do it alone, he might not have even been the one to pull it all together, but he's one of them," Renko insisted. "We have to stay on that. He's our one link to it all."

"You buy that, Cardi?" White asked.

"Braddock is a part of this, there's no denying that, but I'm not as convinced of his guilt."

"A part of it? Seriously, Cardi?" Renko prodded. "Braddock is everywhere in this case, *everywhere*. He's knee-deep in all of it. And you know it. Why can't you see that?"

"We're talking about a man with a record of valor that far exceeds anyone sitting in here."

That quieted the room for a moment.

"You think his record makes him innocent?" White said.

"No, sir. Good cops can turn bad. But it also makes me ask questions because with all due respect, Chief, this is all a lot less black and white than you say," Cardi asserted. "I get the circumstantial case. I get the idea his name is everywhere on this. His name appears in Guerero's notes. There's the phone call and then a few hours later Ray and Gonzalez being killed. It's all a problem for Braddock given the timing and that it happened in his backyard. But that's all we have, odd timing and his proximity to it. No actual proof of wrongdoing. And yes, I think Braddock and Hunter being targeted the other night ought to have us asking some questions about our theory of the case. Our minds should remain open."

"I think the others know that we're onto him. They tried to silence him before we broke him."

"Broke him or broke you," Cardi snapped back.

"That's a cheap shot, Detective," Renko barked. "I notice you don't seem any the worse for wear. I didn't see you defending your partner."

"You're not my partner."

"*Right,* Detective. Your partner was Ray Lange and he's dead. And you're defending the man responsible."

"I don't know that he's responsible. We don't have the proof. What I do know is you provoked him with, among other things, the memory of his late wife, and you should have thought the better of it."

"Watch yourself, Cardi," Renko warned.

"And you watch yourself, Chief," White warned back. "You're in my house talking to my detective."

"She's insubordinate."

"And I would have thought a chief would have comported

himself more responsibly," White replied, folding his arms. "The Chief of Internal Affairs getting into a physical altercation with a suspect? Imagine the headline if that happened here? It still could happen if Braddock, Hunter or the sheriff out there decide to drop dime on you."

Renko turned his look from Cardi back to White and exhaled. "Point taken. One I've had to... reflect on the last day or so. But look, Cole, we all agree this case is about dirty cops, do we not?"

"We do."

"And even Cardi concedes that Braddock is a key person of interest in this case, do you not?" he asked her.

"I do."

"If he is involved, it's with other cops he knows, worked with, that he had relationships with, either through his time at the Academy, in uniform, as a homicide detective or when he was with the JTTF. We need to go deep on those people. This is about dirty cops, it's what we do."

"And solving old murders others were unable to is what we do, Chief. Which is why my unit was assigned the case and not yours, and not to you because you couldn't solve it the first time with your task force out of the 44th."

"Now hold on—"

"Is *that* not true?"

"Now listen, Cole. I could take this up the chain—"

"I've discussed this up the chain. It's my unit's case and that supersedes your rank. IA is attached here and your knowledge of the original Guerero investigation has served a purpose, but it is my view that what transpired in Manchester Bay tells me you've elbowed your way to a larger role than I'm comfortable allowing. And that is over."

"Meaning?"

"This is my unit's case; my people run it, not you. You still want in on the case and to have a role, you and your detectives here best get comfortable with *that* concept. And that means you're going to be answering to me and Cardi, as lead on this, not the other way around."

Renko sat back for a moment, contemplating what White had said before nodding slowly in resignation. "Your case, Cole. I think we all want the same thing here. Don't shut us out."

"Not my intent so long as we all understand our roles. Do we, Chief?"

"We do."

That ended the meeting. White had Cardi hold back for a moment.

"You think that settles it?" Cardi said.

"Hmm," White said with a wry smile. "I don't know. He rolled over there at the end."

"Maybe acknowledging reality?"

White shook his head. "Or stepping back and thinking about his next move. He'll have one. He didn't get where he is now by just falling in line. We need to make progress on this case somehow, or we'll be riding second fiddle too. I need you to dig in and tell me how we're going to do that, and I will help."

"You're going to jump back in the trenches?"

"For Ray, yeah," White said. "As much as I don't want to agree with him, I don't see how Braddock's not a suspect, Cardi. Smoke, fire." He thought for a moment. "Set aside all the bluster, and all the arguing, and the fight between them, is Renko wrong about Braddock?"

Cardi filed out of White's office and made her way down the hall toward her cubicle when her left elbow was grabbed, and she was dragged into an interrogation room.

Renko.

He slammed the door closed. "What was that shit?"

"What?"

"Those were cheap shots, Cardi. Just because Braddock bent you over a few times doesn't mean you do it to someone like me."

"Wh-wh... Excuse me?" she replied, stunned. She'd had plenty of offensive comments hurled in her direction on the job, but this was another level. True or not.

"What, you don't think I didn't pick up on that?"

"You are way out of line." White was right, Renko had another move in mind.

"Am I? I did my homework on you, and Braddock," Renko declared. "After you volunteered that he was looking into Dan Guerero's murder just before Braddock left for Minnesota eight years ago, I thought it was interesting you knew that, knew what he was doing in his off hours. So, I did a little digging of my own. His wife had passed a few months before, brain cancer, such a terrible way to go and I bet he hadn't been laid in a long time because of it. And then there you were, all lonely, your divorce, or at least your *first* divorce, in process. I wondered about whether the two of you—" an evil grin parted his lips "—consummated your partnership."

Smack!

The slap was quick, with force.

Renko reached for his jaw, massaging it. "I'll take that as confirmation."

"Tori Hunter was right. You are such a dick."

"You're playing with fire here, Cardi. You might want to start working with me, not against me."

"I'm not going to be your IA stoolie."

"You're soft on Braddock. I'm thinking it's because of your time making sheet music with him. He must have really, really, done it for you."

Her fists balled up tight on her hips. The next strike might not be just a slap. She'd give him a shiner on his right eye to match the one on his left. "You want to question my objectivity because I slept with him eight years ago? You want to go to White with it? Or go somewhere else, go right ahead. However, I'm not the only one with a history with Braddock. I did my homework too. You tried to squeeze him years ago for a promotion."

Renko stepped back. "I have no idea what you're talking about."

"*Oh, yes you do.* Heard about it from my father. He said you tried to get Braddock to lie on a police brutality investigation that the higher-ups wanted to go a certain way. It was dirty pool, and he wouldn't do it no matter what you threw at him, including his sick wife. He didn't give in. He didn't throw fellow officers under the bus without proof. He was—" she smiled wickedly "—all man, not a pussy. You? He made you his bitch the other day because of it."

"Hmpf."

"I bet he called you far worse than I just did when you tried to bend *him* over. Knowing him, he told you to go fuck yourself. And I could tell, I saw it in Minnesota when you were thundering away at him, that that has infuriated you ever since. That he had the balls to hold his ground. One can't help but wonder if this case is your opportunity to punish him for that. Maybe that's why you're so eager to pin this all on him." She smirked, folding her arms, shaking her head at him. "Tell you what, Chief. Lick all your various physical and mental wounds, maybe ice that shiner a little more. But I tell you what, you try to fuck me on this, I'll fuck you back."

She turned to leave, opening the door.

"Braddock's guilty, you know," Renko asserted, still massaging his jaw from the slap.

"And I'll say the same thing I've been saying all along. Prove it."

* * *

The plane landed at Morristown airport, west of Newark.

"Renko wants to chat tonight, and he wants a plan," Boo said. "We need to go somewhere and talk about what that's going to be."

"How about the office?" Stag suggested.

"Makes sense," Conn said, slipping the sling off his left arm. "I don't want anyone in the building to see me using this thing. Too many possible questions."

"What about your shoulder?" Stag asked.

"I still have the brace on underneath my shirt. It makes it hard to move but at least nobody can see that."

"You look pretty normal to me."

"Let's go. I'll drive," Boo said, sharing a glance with Vooch.

He could have taken several routes to their Jersey office. He chose a more backroads trek with less traffic, fewer homes and businesses and more green scenery, one they were all familiar with.

"Boo, when is the last time you played golf?" Stag asked as they passed a golf club. Stag played and carried a low handicap. Boo played regularly but was not as low a handicapper.

"With all this shit going on, it's been what? Six weeks," he said, turning to Stag and then looking up into the rearview mirror at Vooch. "I'd like to get this shit over with so I could go back to playing, you know."

"I hear that. I—"

In a flash, Vooch dropped the rope around Stag's neck and yanked back, pulling his neck and head hard against the headrest.

"Ahrg... Ahrg..."

Stag frantically kicked the dashboard, fighting.

"Ahrg... Ahrg..."

Boo turned left onto a dirt road. Vooch kept the noose tight, the rope wrapped around his gloved hands, Stag reaching for it with his hands, contorting his body, his legs flailing.

"I'm having... trouble," Vooch yelped.

Conn pulled his gun. "Pull over."

"No, don't shoot him."

Boo pulled to the side, parked, reached over and with both his hands pressed down on Stag's legs.

"Ahrg... You... Fucks..." Stag swung at Boo, his left glancing off his nose.

Boo pulled his right arm back and punched Stag in the jaw.

"Again!" Conn exclaimed. "Again!"

Thwack! Thwack! Thwack!

Stag's hands and arms fell away with the third punch to his temple. Vooch leaned back, pulling on the rope, grunting. Conn and Boo peered around outside, making sure nobody was coming or had seen anything.

"Clear?" Boo said.

"I think we're clear," Conn replied, still looking about the treed area surrounding the dirt road.

Vooch held the rope for another minute, the white nylon fibers digging deep into the skin of Stag's neck.

"Okay, ease up," Boo said and Vooch let the rope fall away, though he kept hold of its ends just in case.

Boo pulled a rubber glove onto his right hand and then checked Stag's neck for a pulse. "Nah, he gone."

Vooch sat back, breathing heavily, using the back of his hand to wipe the sweat away from his brow. "Now what?"

"Well," Boo said, putting the SUV in gear, "the beauty of the Jersey swamplands is there is no end to the number of places to dump a body. And this body is *not* going to be found."

TWENTY-ONE

"CONFESSION IS GOOD FOR THE SOUL."

Eight Years Ago

As he lay on his back, awake though his eyes were closed, his body long since satiated and fully relaxed, he could hear it over the low hum of the air conditioner. The familiar murmur of early morning Manhattan. There was the rumble of the traffic, the bellowing call of a distant police siren reverberating in the concrete canyons of the buildings, an occasional abrupt honk of a car horn, no doubt followed by ill-mannered and exasperated hand gestures back and forth, the New York way of saying: good morning.

Then he heard another sound, that of the light tap of slow deliberate steps on the wood floor, and his eyes fluttered open.

"Good morning, Will," she greeted with a gleaming smile.

Cardi.

She paused at the bedroom door, her black hair loose and messy, down well past her shoulders. She was wearing his long loose white T-shirt, and nothing else. The way she stood, the sunlight directly behind her, provided him with a full-length silhouette of her slender, inviting body as she leaned casually against the doorway holding two cups of coffee.

"You do like your coffee in the morning."

"I do though I'll need a latte or something later," Cardi said. "You know, a quality commercial coffee. You should get some for your kitchen."

As if to allow him as long a look as possible, she sauntered slowly into the room, across the front of the bed to his side, before sitting down and leaning in, kissing him, her soft lips tender on his and he felt that jolt again, like an electric current running through his body. The past several days had made him feel at least a little alive again.

He sat up and took the cup she was offering, sipping it and feeling the heat of the coffee rouse him. He reached for his wristwatch on the nightstand, it was 6:05 a.m. Their shifts started at 8:00. "You don't have much time if you need to go home and change."

"I have a fresh change of clothes in my car," she said. "If you don't mind me changing here."

"I don't," he replied, though he knew he should. The question, *What are you doing?* had run through his mind more than once in the past ten days. Sleeping with your detective partner, no matter how desirable, was a recipe for disaster. They were violating several departmental rules. And then there was the fact that Meghan had been gone only a few months.

"You were... energetic last night," he said, taking another drink of the coffee.

"Well, I had some extra energy to burn off," she said with a smile, leaning in and kissing him again. "I've missed you the past few nights. Where have you been?"

"Oh, just, uh... dealing with some personal matters is all," which was both true and a lie all at the same time.

Cardi took a sip of her coffee and glanced over at the nightstand, picking up the picture of Braddock and Quinn. "When does your son come back?"

"Two days," he replied, and sat up more.

It was time to nip this in the bud.

"Look, Cardi. When he does get back, you and I, we need to—"

"Stop."

"Yes." He nodded. "And it's not just because of him. We're partners. We work with other detectives. They're going to get wise to this, if they haven't already. Or somebody is going to see us."

Cardi shrugged. "And then maybe we're not partners anymore."

"Look, with where I'm at right now that's just not—"

"Hey," she replied, putting a soft finger to his lips. "I'm not much better right now either. My divorce isn't close to final. This—"

"Isn't serious?"

"I was going to say, feels really good." She let out a light sigh and smiled. "Let's just... not talk about all that right now."

"But—"

"Shhh," she hushed him, taking the coffee cup out of his hand and setting it on the nightstand along with hers, before pulling back the sheet and throwing her right leg over his naked body to straddle him, her thin fingers lightly running across his muscled chest.

"We should really get ready for work," he said, though his body was responding differently.

She sat straight up, but her eyes locked on his as she crossed her arms and made a slow tantalizing show of raising the T-shirt up and over her breasts, letting the morning light reveal her lean fully naked body. She closed her eyes and arched her back and began to slowly move her hips but now with an arousing purpose, taking his hands and guiding one to her soft left breast and the other to her right hip. "Mmm. You were saying?"

"Something about... work."

"Hmm. That. Well." Cardi leaned forward, her lips slowly parting to meet his, raising her hips just slightly to allow her right hand to slide down and reach for him, whispering, "Are you sure, are you really sure, you want to get ready for work just yet?"

Contemplating lunch, he feigned interest in the report on his desk, because what he was looking into while off the clock weighed more heavily on his mind.

"Braddock!" their aide Connie yelled out.

"Yeah."

"Line four!"

He picked up the call. "Detective Braddock."

"Will, Harry Schuler, over here in Bayonne."

"What's up, Harry?"

"I'm at a murder scene behind Kahn Dry-Cleaning. Do you know the place?"

"I do," Braddock said, suddenly sitting up.

"Will, I'm sorry, it's Malik Muhammed. We just found his body in a dumpster out back of the store."

He closed his eyes. This was not good. "Harry, I'm on my way over there."

Cardi came into the squad room, cracking open a can of Diet Coke, just as he was pulling on his suit coat. "We get a call?"

"No, but I have to go take care of something. Cover for me, will you?"

"Uh, sure."

He started walking but she grabbed his arm, stopping him, eyeing up his expression. "What happened?"

"It's a... personal thing with an old friend. I need to go take care of it."

The drive from his northern Manhattan precinct out to Bayonne took over a half-hour in midday traffic. A patrol officer let him under the yellow crime scene tape. Harry Schuler met him and walked him over to the dumpster. He peered inside, and saw Malik's lifeless body, which crime scene officers were still taking photos of. Schuler let him get close enough to see what had happened, the deep gash across the front of Malik's neck.

"It's like they tried to cut his head off, Will."

"Harry, how long has he been in there, you think?"

"Doc will have to tell us but given the amount of garbage that has been tossed on top of him, I'm thinking a couple of days," Schuler said. "You know, at least among us local police, Malik was known to peddle information. Cutting his throat like that is suggestive of sending a message."

"You'll talk no more."

"Have you spoken with him recently?"

Braddock shrugged. "I'd speak to him from time to time. I have for years."

"Anything recent?"

"You know, just some drug talk that isn't necessarily applicable to homicide, which is what I'm working these days. Did you find anything on him?"

Schuler shook his head. "No wallet, no phone, nothing. I just happened to recognize him because I took the call. I knew you would chat with him from time to time when you were with the Task Force, you and Danny Guerero. Any thoughts on who I should look at?"

Braddock contemplated his location. Malik lived in an apartment not but a few blocks away. And not that he could see it from there, but the Port Newark Container Terminals weren't far to the west, a place with which he was familiar and conducted a fair amount of business. "Who to look at? No. But, Malik worked in... 'logistics.'"

"Yeah, for stolen shit."

"True," Braddock replied with a nod. "Not that this is mind blowing insight, Harry, but his was a dangerous occupation and while he had a well calibrated antennae for trouble, I suspect he crossed the wrong person somewhere along the way and just didn't see them coming. If you find anything, you'll let me know?"

"Sure."

The question foremost in his mind became: Had that wrong person noticed what he'd been spending his time on? Malik's murder had his own paranoia meter in the red zone as he pulled to a stop in front of the apartment building.

Strategically, he had been less than forthcoming with Schuler. He had spoken to Malik three nights ago to have him reach out to Julio Gonzalez to arrange a meet. Given what had happened to Guerero, he didn't want to meet with Julio publicly where prying eyes could see them. But Malik wasn't answering his phone for the past few days, and he'd been unable to find him when checking his usual haunts. He'd intended to go out looking for him again last night when Cardi called, wanting to see him.

Now, he knew why he'd been unable to find him.

What about Julio? Though he'd wanted to keep it on the down-low, there wasn't time for that now. Malik had given him Julio's apartment address, but there was no response to his repeated ringing of the apartment. He drove to the port terminal he knew Julio worked at. He spoke with the terminal operations manager, Carmine

Stagliola, who told him Julio hadn't shown for his shift for two days.

"I hope you find him. Let me know if you do," Stagliola said. "This is very unusual for him. It has me concerned."

Not good.

Braddock went back to Julio's apartment building in Jersey City. He tracked down the building superintendent, flashed his badge and made the point that there was urgency to his request.

"You have a search warrant?"

"No."

"You're a New York City cop, you're in Jersey."

"I hadn't noticed," Braddock replied sarcastically. "I'm not looking to search the place. If I want to do that, I'll get the warrant. I just want to make sure you don't have a dead body up there. A quick in and out is all I need."

"Dead body?"

"Yeah."

The super let him into the unit.

"Oh boy," the super murmured.

The apartment had been ransacked, every drawer pulled out, cabinet door opened, and piece of furniture turned over.

"When is the last time you saw him?"

"I saw him and his wife—"

"Wife? He has a wife?"

"Yes, I *saw them* earlier in the week, maybe Monday."

He took another more thorough look through the apartment and one thing he didn't see in all the mess and rubble was much clothing, either men's or women's. And then as he looked further around, he didn't see any suitcases or duffel bags either. In the bathroom, much of it had been cleaned out.

"Do they have a vehicle?"

"Yes," the super said. "It's a white sedan. A Toyota Camry, I think."

"Do they park on the street?"

"Usually."

Braddock took a walk up and down the street but didn't see a white Camry anywhere. *Had they managed to get away?*

"What should I do?" the super asked.

"Call Detective Schuler with the Bayonne Police," Braddock said, handing him a card. "Detective Schuler will call me."

Braddock drove with the easy pace of early evening Manhattan traffic. The casual draping of his left hand over the steering wheel belied his rotating scan of the traffic surrounding him.

Was anyone following?

He had been cautious and deliberate, contemplating whether to move forward each step of the way with what Monica had asked him to do. At first, he was doing it out of a sense of obligation. Now, the obligation had given way to his own sense that answers were needed. But that didn't come without a price. As the days had gone by and he learned a bit more and then a little bit more, his sense of intrigue was turning to dismay and the larger question of assessing his own responsibility for the carnage that had been wrought.

Especially after today.

This was all getting closer to him.

He parked a half-block west of his apartment. Warily, he lifted his fatigued body up out of his car and pulled on his suit coat.

Given the day's events he needed to keep his head on a swivel while he figured out what to do. As he strode along the sidewalk, he discreetly peered about the street, using reflections in windows and vehicle side mirrors until he reached the steps to his building. As he trudged up to the front door his phone beeped.

Text message.

Cardi.

My place tonight? I have better coffee.

This was another problem he had to deal with. Yet, he also needed to talk to somebody about what he was dealing with. Cardi might be as good a person as anyone to discuss it with.

He made his way to the second floor and fumbled with his keys for a moment before he slid the key into the deadbolt and opened his apartment door. On the floor just inside the door on the wood floor was a blank 10 x 13 manila clasp envelope. Given the day, he hesitated to pick it up. Instead, using his car key, he flipped the envelope over. Both sides were blank.

He closed the door, went to the kitchen and from a drawer pulled out a pair of white rubber gloves and then picked up the envelope and placed it on a clean cutting board on the kitchen counter. He snapped open his pocketknife and with the tip of the blade, carefully flipped up the clasps and then used the tip to flip open the flap, then used the blade tip again to press the top side of the envelope up to peek inside.

It was a photo.

"Hey."

With his gloved right hand, he slid out an eight-by-eleven-inch color picture. The picture was of him and Quinn, the two of them walking hand in hand at the park a few blocks away. Based on the clothes they were both wearing, it was a photo from a few weeks ago, the night before Quinn left with his grandparents for Michigan.

"Hey."

He flipped the photo over.

"Hey... Hey... Hey!"

* * *

Braddock snapped out of it. "What?"

"Where did you go?" Tori said from the passenger seat.

"What do you mean?"

"I said 'Hey' about four times before you finally reacted, she said as she arched her back and gingerly stretched her arms. "You were lost in thought. What about?"

"What do you think?"

Tori nodded knowingly. "Last night, this week, eight years ago?"

He snorted a wry laugh. "Just now, eight years ago. I was thinking about *that* day, you know."

"The picture?"

"Yeah."

Tori nodded and took a drink from her water bottle. "How far away from New York City are we?"

"Four hours, give or take."

They drove for a few minutes in relative quiet, soft rock music playing on the radio.

Tori let out a long breath. "There is something we need to talk about."

Just by the tone, he knew what was coming.

"Cardellini," Tori said. "We need to talk about it."

Braddock grimaced, looking away. "I don't even know *how* to talk about it."

"Confession is good for the soul."

"How do I talk about this," he started and then looked to her, "and have you still have any faith in me?"

"By having some in me, Braddock. Something you've been struggling with this week."

Ouch. It was a painful yet fair admonishment.

He took a moment, peering out at the lush green Pennsylvania farm fields as they motored east on I-80. This was something he had never spoken of, to anyone. He'd never wanted to go back to that time, to any of it. And while he'd speak of Meghan from time to time with Tori, he rarely spoke of the end for her and never the aftermath, other than when Roger pushed him to come to Minnesota.

"Just... tell me about it," Tori prodded.

He let out a nervous sigh. "I went back to work two months after Meghan died. I wasn't sure I was ready for it: the job, but just being at home, at the apartment, especially when Quinn wasn't there..." His voice drifted away. "I had to do... something. The job was all I had."

She just waited.

"There was no cure for glioblastoma, no miracle was coming. I knew for over two years that Meghan was going to die, it was just a matter of... when. She and I tried to explain it to Quinn as best we could when she couldn't get out of bed anymore. In a way, at the end I..." He felt his eyes moisten, his nose runny. "In the end I welcomed death when it came for her, she was suffering so. She fought and fought *and fought* for every second she could have with Quinn."

"And you."

"With me," he replied, like a man who thought he wasn't worthy of it. "I'm guilty of a lot in that stretch of time, but the worst of it was what I did with Cardi."

"How did it happen?"

"We shouldn't have been partnered to begin with. Someone didn't think that one through."

"Why?"

"I was a new widower. She was in the middle of a divorce. Neither of us was in a good place mentally. And then Monica Guerero came to see me and laid it on me about Dan. I know this sounds self-pitying but that really weighed on me, especially once I started seeing what I should have seen before. Then Roger and Mary came to New York City for a few days and took Quinn to Michigan with them for the first time on what has become their annual three-week summer trip. I think they thought it would be good for me to have that time to get my shit together and figure some things out." He shook his head in disgust. "That ain't exactly what happened."

"What did happen?"

"You know what happened."

"I want to hear it."

"Come on," he said. "I... please, no."

"You need to talk about it."

He wasn't so sure he agreed with her on that point, but they had four hours of driving in front of them, and she wasn't going to let him off the hook.

"Come on," she prodded.

He sighed. "With Quinn gone, I worked my day shift with her, then nights I was poking around on my old case and what happened to Dan. I was starting to get some traction on it, had spoken with Malik and he said he had a contact for me down on the docks."

"Julio."

"Yes. One day, we got done with our shift and my plan was to head out for the night to keep going when Cardi said she could really use a drink and asked if I wanted to join." He paused for a second. "You know, I should have said no."

Tori nodded, knowing what was coming. "You went."

"I went. I had one, then two and started to relax."

"As did she, I'm sure."

"Yeah. And then she started to get a little flirty and touchy and..."

"You did too."

"I didn't stop her, Tor. And then after a few more drinks she just threw it out there. Your place or mine." He shook his head. "It was wrong. It was so, so, wrong."

Listening to him, Tori was beginning to understand why he had lived so quietly, not dating, just working and being a dad after his move to Minnesota.

Guilt.

And it was clear to her that this was the first time someone had made him talk about it. "God, Tori. What was I doing? I was cheating on—"

"No," she said vehemently. "No, you weren't. You were not cheating."

"But—"

"You didn't cheat, Braddock," she said. "Meghan was dead."

"Only a few months."

"You said it yourself. Glioblastoma was a death sentence. You watched Meghan die day by day, piece by piece for over two years. And for most of that time, you and Meghan couldn't be intimate."

He shook his head.

"It had probably been a couple of years since you..."

"Yeah."

Tori was surprised to a degree as to how little jealousy she felt about this. Maybe that was because she'd never felt any jealousy toward Meghan. She had been the love of his life. That was a part of Braddock's life, and she always knew he'd carry some of that with him and if she was going to be with him, she had to be good with that. She'd just tried to find her own space in his life and had. "Braddock, a... *semi*-attractive woman made a pass at you and you... were human."

"It was wrong."

"It might not have been wise, sleeping with your partner, but it wasn't... wrong. I'm certainly not going to judge you for it."

He turned to her, surprised. "But—"

"I'm standing in for Meghan on this one and I understand. You just wanted to feel something again. Who wouldn't after what you'd been through?"

"What about what Meghan went through?"

"And you were there, every step of the way. And that's not

just me saying it, that's Roger and Mary, and Drew and Andrea, all telling me about it."

"They have?"

"Yes, in part so I knew, and in part so I knew you and how committed you were to Meghan. So that I knew you were a good man."

"I don't know if I was then. I've tried to be one since."

"You were, and you have. Will, you were alive. And you were hurting, and alone, and felt guilt about Dan, and Quinn was gone, and she caught you at just that time," Tori reasoned. "Now, it wasn't just a one-night thing, was it?"

"No," Braddock replied, ashamed, no matter what Tori said. "We carried it on for ten days, two weeks, some nights her place, some nights mine, the home I'd shared with Meghan."

He sat in silence, just breathing. Tori just waited.

"The last night we were together was the night before I found that envelope in my apartment. I got that envelope, and two days later Roger showed up with Quinn, took one look at me and could see that I was a mess. It wasn't a discussion. He simply said: 'You and Quinn are moving to Minnesota.' I wasn't about to fight it, not having just gotten that picture, not given what I was doing, and the risk I was running. I needed out and Roger threw me a lifeline."

"And Cardellini?"

"I told her I was moving here and that ended it."

"And how did it end?"

"What do you mean?"

"How did she take it when you told her?"

"She was surprised I was moving. I had never said anything about that because it truly happened *that* fast. But I think she got it," he said and then looked to her. "However—"

"There's that little part where she saw that you were digging into the Dan Guerero case, that she saw the notes in your apartment on your desk," Tori said.

"Hmm."

"Renko isn't the only one besides you who goes back eight years on this. She does too."

"I suppose she does."

"Did you ever talk about it with her?"

"No. I never spoke of that to anyone."

"You sure?"

"I was *thinking* of talking about it with her. I needed to talk to someone about it but after that picture, no way. I wasn't exposing anyone else to that. I didn't ever want to expose you, Boe, Steak, anyone to it because just about everyone whose touched it is dead."

"But she saw that you were doing it."

"I didn't know that at the time," Braddock said and shook his head. "As I think back there was this one night, we went drinking and... I got really drunk. I was in such a bad way, Meghan, the Guerero thing, Cardi, all of it. We went back to my place that night and after we... well... I pretty much passed out. If I had to guess, that was the night she must have been poking around my desk because I think otherwise, I would have noticed."

"The question is was that just idle curiosity, a woman poking around the apartment of her paramour, getting to know him, or—"

"Was she part of all this."

"Did she have a key to your apartment?"

"No," he said. "No, no, no. You're thinking the picture, the warning?"

"Someone got into your building. She could have found a backup key or something, had a copy made, then snuck in and stuffed the envelope under your door. It's possible. You have to consider it."

Braddock crinkled his nose.

"I'm just saying."

He exhaled a breath. Not an impossibility but he just didn't think she would have done something like that, knowing her background, who she was as a cop. He chewed on his bottom lip for a minute.

"What are you thinking about?"

"If we're going to bring this thing home and bring it home the right way, we're going to need someone we can trust that's tied into the current investigation. We need to know what they know, *and don't know*."

"I'm not sure who we can trust. You got any ideas?"

"There's..." he cringed before blurting, "Cardi."

He caught the snap of Tori's head turn out of his peripheral vision and could just feel her piercing look, as if she was lasering him with X-ray vision.

"I'd prefer," she started slowly, "that you refer to her as Detective Cardellini."

"Uh, okay."

"I said I wouldn't judge *you* on it, and I won't. I won't hold it over your head, I'll never joke about it, I never want to even speak of it again. But that doesn't mean I'm good with *her* on that. That she's *Cardi* to me."

"Understood," Braddock replied. "But still—"

"But still," Tori said with a sigh, "you raise an important question. Can we trust her?"

TWENTY-TWO

"WE NEVER LEAVE FINGERPRINTS."

Tori glanced to her left when the lights of Manhattan first became visible in the distance. She saw that Braddock allowed himself a small smile.

"Home sweet home?" Tori said.

He scoffed. "This isn't home, not anymore, but it still grabs me a bit, you know."

"I do." Her phone rang. "Ah, Tracy."

Braddock listened as Tori said, "Uh huh... Uh huh... Interesting..." several times as he heard the rapid cadence of Tracy's voice though he couldn't make out the words. "I'll tell him," Tori replied. "Thanks, for everything, Trace. Over and above... Love you too, girl."

"Tell me what?" he asked after she'd hung up.

"Good luck. She's sending me an email," Tori said and patiently watched her phone and then tapped the screen when it came in. "Okay. Let me see here... Carmine Stagliola, aged fifty-five. Twenty-five years at the port. He retired four years ago. He is drawing two pensions, first for his union work and then later on the management side. Total $8,925 a month. Also has an IRA with a little over $200,000 in it and three bank accounts that have just under $40,000 in them. Address for a three-bedroom house over on Staten Island, not far from where he grew up. Drives a Chevy Traverse, three years old. Divorced and is paying maintenance to his ex-wife of $2,500 a month and will for another five years. One child, a daughter, married, who lives in Sunrise, Florida."

"After taxes that doesn't leave much."

"I thought that interesting as well," Tori said. "Math is not impossible, but tight with that pension, yet he seems to make it work without what appears to be any current employment that Tracy could find. It requires further investigation but it's what Tracy could get us right now. We have Stagliola's name, we know how it registered with Lange. I'm eager to put his name in play and let someone beside you go under the spotlight. We just have to figure out how to do it," she said as Braddock drove around the wide loop for the Lincoln Tunnel.

"I haven't driven the Lincoln Tunnel in a long time," Braddock noted with anticipation as they swung around the turn on the highway leading beneath the Hudson River that would bring them into the west side of Manhattan. "In fact, not since..."

"Since?"

"The day Malik was murdered," he answered, shaking his head. "The little things that make it go full circle, I guess." Braddock sighed as they went underground. "So, these friends of yours?"

"Oliver and Connie."

"Former special agents?"

Tori nodded. "Mentors. They're maybe ten, fifteen years older than me. Tracy and I both looked up to Connie. She was this little woman, a couple of inches shorter than me even, that was one tough cookie. Oliver is tall like you, though thinner through the body. He comes off very mild-mannered, almost professorial. He looks like a man that wears cardigan sweaters and smokes a pipe, though in reality he's a bourbon and cigar guy."

"My kind of guy."

"They were great agents who were great to young agents. I mean, you would just hang around their desks. They'd talk and you'd learn. They're just a wonderfully interesting couple."

"They sound a little like us."

"A bit, I suppose," Tori said. "You didn't seem so mild-mannered when you pummeled Renko."

Braddock smiled, an evil grin. "I was provoked."

"Renko fucked around and—"

"Found out," Braddock finished. "But back to your friends. You're sure it's alright with them if we stay with them? They know what's going on? I hate painting a target on anyone."

"I talked to Connie while you snoozed earlier today. I told her everything. They are fully aware, and they not only offered, but insisted we stay," Tori said.

Wanting to stay off the grid, they didn't want to stay at a hotel and have their names registered. And while they thought about staying with Tracy and Sam over in Brooklyn, if it was found out they were in New York City, the first place people would look for them would be there. They were already asking Tracy for enough. Connie and Oliver Reid were an under the radar choice nobody would think of.

"And they both dabble in some private security work and have a lot of law enforcement contacts. They could be helpful."

Braddock cringed. "I just worry about involving anyone else in this. They don't even know me."

"They know me."

They exited the tunnel and made their way north to West 47th Street and found a parking spot.

"Tori!" Connie yelled from the front door of the apartment, Oliver standing behind her. When they got inside and settled, the four of them relaxed in the living room. Connie poured Tori a glass of white wine and then sat down next to her on the sofa. Oliver opened a fresh bottle of Blanton's, pouring himself and Braddock a bourbon over a large ice cube. "I bet you could use one of these, Will," Oliver said, handing the drink to Braddock.

"Oliver, I could use several of these."

"I'm eager to oblige." Oliver and Braddock took the soft chairs on opposite ends of the sofa.

"Now, Tori told us a little about what is going on," Connie said eagerly, peering to Braddock. "But tell us everything from your side of things."

Braddock grimaced.

"It's alright, Will," Oliver said before taking a sip of bourbon. "We're aware of what is going on, we're curious and you never know, we might have an insight or two."

"Tell them," Tori prodded.

Braddock spent the better part of an hour and a couple more bourbons laying it out. "We have a couple of things. One is Carmine Stagliola and his work at the port. We need to go deep on him but I'm not sure how much we can accomplish on our own. I'd love to convince someone in the NYPD to go to work on him but I'm not sure anyone would listen to me without more and without me being able to truly prove that I've got nothing to do with any of it."

"And, we have the man with the port-wine stain," Tori added. "Which isn't much to go on, but it's what we got. That and descriptions of men who might have been cops who were down at the docks the same nights Stagliola was interested in certain shipping containers."

"Any idea who those men were?" Connie asked.

Tori hedged, not wanting to put Renko's name in play without more. "No, not yet."

Connie looked over at her husband, who nodded. Tori caught the look, something she'd seen between the two of them before. "What have you two been up to?'

"We did some researching and calling of our own," Connie said.

"Connie!" Tori objected. "I told you how dangerous this has been. It's one thing to offer us the guest room but—"

"It wasn't direct, Tori," Connie said with a dismissive wave. "Oli called someone, then I called someone, who then called someone else, who went and had a drink with someone tonight," Connie said, a twinkle in her eye. "Who called me about an hour before you arrived."

"Tori," Oli counseled, a sly smile, his left leg over his right, casually twirling his drink. "We never leave fingerprints."

Oliver and Connie knew something, and they were eager to share.

"What? What did you hear?" Tori asked, intrigued, moving closer to Connie.

"There was a meeting today that involved the Cold Case Squad and IA leadership and detectives. It was in Coleman White's office. The Guerero investigation is being handled as a cold case as you know. IA is there in support, although that part isn't public."

"Renko weaseled his way into it," Braddock muttered.

"Probably," Oliver agreed. "He's a very political animal. A man who has eyes on another step or two up the ladder."

"Anyway," Connie continued. "The good news for you is, IA and the Cold Case Squad are not necessarily on the same page. As you said, Will, IA is looking hard at you. Renko pushed that narrative, but Commander White and Detective Cardellini with the Cold Case Squad weren't necessarily of the same mind. She said they needed proof and had yet to find it. The two of them, Renko and Cardellini, went at it and it got a little personal, not only in that meeting but also in a side meeting the two of them had after. There is tension there, perhaps useful tension."

"You don't say," Braddock said before taking another drink of bourbon, his eyes sliding to Tori who met his glance.

"My sense of it is Cardellini isn't convinced of your guilt, but she also didn't exculpate you," Connie continued. "In part, because they don't yet have anyone else to look at. At least not a name."

"But now, from what you tell us, they could," Oli said. "Perhaps Detective Cardellini would be interested in something like that."

Tori looked at Braddock. "Your insight on Cardellini is interesting. The question Braddock and I have is whether we could trust her."

* * *

"Boss, you sure you don't want us to hang for one more?"

"No," Renko replied, checking his watch, 12:10 a.m. "I'm good," he replied to his two detectives, his eyes casually drifting to the short brunette with her hair up wearing the lower cut summer dress at the other end of the bar. His two detectives saw his eye shift, the shared smile between Renko and the woman and understood what was next. "We'll see you Monday, Chief."

The two detectives left and Renko picked up his drink and walked to the other end of the bar and took a seat. "I was starting to think you weren't going to make it."

"Well, it was a little late for a text, Ira," Rita replied. "I was about to go to bed when you reached out." She paused for a moment. "But I'm glad you did. And it's a Friday night. A good night to go out, even if it was a little late."

"Ah, it's not that late, my dear, when you don't have to go to work in the morning. The night is still young."

They had matched on Hinge a few months back and had had some enjoyable casual moments together. She had recently ended a long-term relationship and was looking for companionship. He was divorced long ago and not looking for any sort of commitment beyond a good time. So far it was working for them both. "What happened to you?"

"Duty called," he replied, turning to her, moving in close. "You should see the other guy."

"Looks like it got a little rough," Rita replied.

"Just a little," he replied as he slid his hand along her thigh. Which she playfully batted away.

"Not so fast. You got me here late on a Friday night. I'd like another glass of very nice wine first."

"Of course," Renko said and gestured to the bartender.

The two of them did have another drink, talking and flirting for another hour as the bar continued to thin out such that the bartender slid by to mention it would be closing time soon.

"Shall we?" he asked.

"We shall," Rita replied. "Your place or mine?" They both lived within ten minutes of the pub.

"How about yours tonight?"

"You just want me to make you breakfast in the morning."

"Well," Renko replied. "A man can hope."

The two of them walked out of the back of the pub and into a narrow alley. "I'm parked down here," he said as they walked along, her left arm hooked around his right, her three-inch heels leveling her up a bit height wise with him.

They reached his car, and he escorted her to the passenger side and opened the door for her, then closed it after she'd sat down. He walked around the front of the car and then got into the driver's side and started the car.

"Ira?" Rita asked as he fastened his seat belt.

"What?"

"Who is that?"

Renko looked up. "A... friend of mine," he replied as he powered down the window. "What are you doing here?"

TWENTY-THREE
"YOU'RE SAYING YOU TRUST ME NOW?"

Cardi opened the door to the coffee shop and stepped to the counter. "Morning, Lu."

"Morning, Cardi. I got your coffee for you right here."

She was surprised. "Lu, you sure? I didn't call ahead or anything. Are you just anticipating my arrival these days? Am I that predictable, even on a Saturday?"

"Your friend ordered it and paid," Lu explained.

"My... friend?"

"She's waiting for you. She has the back booth around the corner, wearing a Yankees hat. She said to send you back when you got here."

"And she came in when?"

"A few minutes ago."

"Huh." Cardi took her coffee and a wary sip as she slowly walked to the last high-backed booth. Who the heck was this friend?

Then she saw her.

"Well, this is an interesting start to the day."

"That's to be determined," Tori said.

Cardi took a seat and a slow deliberate drink of her coffee, eyeing up the woman across from her and also peering about for any prying eyes or ears. Hunter had picked a reasonably good spot. The booth provided cover and isolation, and the one immediately behind her was empty. "What the heck are you doing here? Is Will here?"

"He's lurking about," Tori said before taking a drink of her coffee and then, while picking away a piece of her croissant, announced, "We found Ana Gonzalez."

Cardi's eyes widened. "Really? Where?"

"Of all places, Toledo."

"Hmpf," Cardi replied, taking another drink. "She and her husband had a history of living in Ohio. When she dropped the car in Detroit, I figured she went to someone in Ohio she knew she could trust for help. Where is she now?"

"Safe."

Cardi pressed. "Where?"

"Uh, uh." Tori shook her head. "We're not trusting anyone beyond a select few with that information."

After a moment of thought Cardi said, "Well, you're here. You must want something, though I am curious about one thing."

"Which is?"

Cardi smiled. "Why you're here and not Will."

Tori looked up from her croissant. "Why do you think, Detective?" she said, before biting down on a flaky piece.

"Will thinks he could trust me. But you?" Cardi stared Tori down. "You, Special Agent Hunter, are not so sure. The question is, is that because I'm NYPD or because I bedded him once upon a time."

"Both," Tori said. "I'm curious if you're sleeping with him was personal, or professional?" Tori eyed Cardi. "A little mix of business and pleasure. The true definition of undercover operation."

"Any other clichés you want to throw in there?"

"Fishing off the corporate pier? Dipping your pen in the company ink?"

"Aren't you guilty of that?"

"One hundred percent. I'm not judging the act itself. I'm questioning your motive in doing so in this particular instance."

"Interesting way of asking, Special Agent Hunter."

"I'm not a special agent anymore."

"Then how am I to refer to you. As Tori?"

"We'll see. Answer my question."

Cardi shrugged. "I'm sure you're referencing the fact I had seen his notes about Dan Guerero's murder, back then. One night when I stayed at his place I woke up and started looking around his apartment."

"Snooping?"

"Like you wouldn't have. What woman doesn't. I was interested about him."

"Because you had long-term interest?"

Cardi shook her head. "Nah, I didn't really think that was happening. I was just... nosy is all. I saw his notes on his desk, saw what he was doing and was mildly curious at the time, but I didn't report it, nor did I ask him about it. Perhaps I should have. But I'll fully admit I remembered seeing that when we started investigating the Guerero case a few months back and Will's name started popping up in a lot of ways and places, especially in Dan Guerero's notes. As for sleeping with him? I wanted to do that for the same reason you did."

"He was mourning Meghan," Tori pressed. "She'd been dead only a few months."

"You say that like I forced him to take me to bed at gunpoint or something. I made the first move, but I didn't have to force him to do anything. He was a very willing and fully engaged participant."

"It didn't feel wrong to you?"

Cardi shrugged. "He had reservations. He probably felt

some guilt. As for me? It was about the sex. I wanted to feel good, to be desired. Sometimes you just... need that, you know. And he was a six-foot-four good-looking guy who was also, I thought at the time, a good guy. And it felt nice to be with a good guy for a little bit after I was with not such a good guy."

"Your divorce. You're going through your second as I understand it," Tori said cattily.

"It's done. My marital track record is a disaster, but that's not what this is about. And from a relationship standpoint, tell me you weren't having some doubts about Will earlier in the week," Cardi said. "I saw your reaction when *we* were questioning him. He hadn't told you anything about the past on this thing, had he?"

"No," Tori replied, shaking her head. "No, and he and I have had it out over it, but I understand better now why he did what he did."

"And what is it exactly that you know that I don't?" Cardi said.

"I'm not ready to share that just yet."

"Hmpf," Cardi scoffed, before taking a drink of her coffee and then leaned forward, quieter. "Why are you here? It's not to talk about my marital foibles or whether Will got me off."

Tori leaned in herself. "I've got two things for you. A name and a description. We'll see how this goes and then I might have a little more for you."

"What's the name?"

"Carmine Stagliola."

"And he is who?"

"I don't know exactly what he's doing now, but eight years ago he was a Port of Newark terminal operations manager."

"Where Julio Gonzalez worked."

"And according to Julio's wife..." Tori recited what Ana had told them and what she knew from Tracy, without divulging Tracy's involvement. "I think there is the odd behavior on the docks and that there is a bit of a math problem there. Stagliola is worth a look. Now, I have others who could dig on that, but I'm curious to see what you find, or if you even want to find anything."

"That's not much to go on. His name, that he was maybe dealing with cops eight years ago and his income seems a little too tight."

"That name is why people were after Julio, why they thought he needed to be taken out. That's the name he gave Lange. That's the name Ana gave us. And if you want confirmation of that, you can call Detective Art Long in Toledo. And he'll also tell you that whoever is behind all this was in Toledo. We got to Ana in the nick of time. Heck, we almost caught them then and there."

"What!" Cardi said, truly shocked. "You did? How do I not know this already?"

Tori explained the chase and why Cardi didn't yet know about it. "We just lost them. I mean, they got away by about ten or fifteen seconds, literally." Tori shook her head. "We could have had them. Call Long, he'll tell you all about it. He was with us every step of the way."

Cardi reluctantly nodded. "Stagliola. Art Long. Got it. You said two things though."

"We're looking for someone with a port-wine stain on his lower left arm, wrist and hand," Tori said and quickly explained how they knew that. "The doctor recognized it for what it was. It was probably lasered to reduce how noticeable it is, but you can't erase it completely. This guy wasn't the one who was shot, but he was with the man who was."

"You're assuming this port-wine stain guy was an NYPD cop. He could have been a Newark cop, some sheriff's cop, Port Authority cop, Bayonne cop, you know what I'm saying. It's a bit of a needle in a haystack."

"Maybe not if you look in the right haystack. Braddock

thinks at least one or two of the cops could be ex-narcotics offi-cers. They learned of a drug pipeline drug crews and gangs were using that was coming through the Port. Stagliola was the guy who could tell them when the ships—"

"Came in," Cardi finished, understanding the thought. "These ex-cops got onto the drugs coming in. They went to Stagliola because he could identify the container and what its final destination was. He's the spotter, so to speak, but then it's the others who did the rest."

Tori nodded. "Maybe that narrows the search, especially when you add in Stagliola's name. We're going to dig into that on our own as well. Braddock doesn't know anybody like that but there's what? Thirty-five thousand police officers with the NYPD alone. But we're thinking, make a few calls, six degrees of Kevin Bacon being what it is, someone knows someone."

"And Braddock still has friends in the NYPD."

"As do I," Tori said. "If you're looking, and we're looking, maybe we find this person."

Cardi's phone buzzed. "Excuse me for a second." She answered. "Yeah..." Her eyes went wide, and she looked up at Tori, stunned.

Tori mouthed: *What?*

"And this was where?" Cardi said. "Yeah, I know that bar. You said the car was in the alley?... Uh, huh... And it was just found this morning, but they'd been dead for a few hours? ... Okay. Yeah, on my way." She hung up and stared at her phone for a moment in shock.

"What happened?" Tori asked softly.

She looked up to Tori and stared her down for a moment.

"What?" Tori said. "What is it?"

"Tell me you don't know," Cardi said through gritted teeth. "Tell me, Tori!"

"Tell you... what?" Tori said, confused. "What? What!"

Cardi took a moment, evaluating Tori's reaction, her confusion. Was she acting or was it genuine? "You don't know anything about it?"

"About what? I would know about what?" Tori replied, now eyeing her back. "What happened?"

"Ira Renko and a woman were found shot and killed an hour ago in Renko's car in an alley behind the Flatbush Pub."

Tori's eyes closed. "Oh no. No, no, no."

"When did you and Braddock get into town?"

It was Tori's turn to be thrown off.

"Tori? *When?*"

"Uh... last night, around ten p.m. We drove here from Toledo."

"Can anybody verify that?"

"Yes. Yes. We're staying with some friends of mine. I don't want to involve them if I don't have to, but if I do, I will. We got there about ten p.m. and sat up for a few hours talking and went to bed sometime after midnight."

"And they'll verify that?"

"Yes, without question."

"Can you and Braddock account for all your time since you've gotten here?"

Tori furrowed her brow. "Yeah. We didn't—"

Cardi shook her head. "Tori, this thing is about to go nuclear. Lange was killed last Sunday night in Minnesota. Now Renko, the Chief of Internal Affairs. And you and Braddock are here, in New York. There was the fight the other day between Will and Renko. And the fact that we strongly suspect this is dirty cops responsible for these murders. You do the math. The powers that be are going to think the 'others' Renko has repeatedly alluded to have acted. And with Will here, that'll be too much to ignore." Cardi started sliding out of the booth. "Me even being seen with you right now could be a problem. Keep out of sight until I can see where this is going."

"Take this," Tori said, handing her a slip of paper.

"And this is?"

"Detective Art Long's phone number and a way to reach us."

"You're saying you trust me now?"

"I think we're going to need to trust each other."

Cardi was a jumble as she zoomed over the Brooklyn Bridge from Manhattan into Brooklyn, exiting onto Flatbush Avenue and driving southeast through traffic and stoplights for two miles until she saw the collection of patrol units and flashing lights.

Hunter surprising her as she did at the coffee shop was a jolt to start the day. And she offered up information that should be helpful. Cardi hadn't heard the name Carmine Stagliola before. Guerero's notes of his investigation were cryptic, perhaps intentionally so if he was digging into dirty cops. In fact, per her recall, the only full names she remembered were Malik Muhammed, Julio Gonzalez and Braddock. Carmine or Stagliola were nowhere in those notes, at least she didn't think so, though something about the name was resonating with her for some reason. Nor, when she thought about it, was there a description of a man with a port-wine or birthmark-like stain on his left arm or hand.

Hunter and Braddock telling her to look at narcotics officers made some sense. There were plenty of notations about narcotics in Guerero's notes. In a sense she had interpreted those notations as being about drugs themselves but perhaps they related to the "who" as much as the "what."

Her thoughts went back to Renko, and Braddock.

Renko was certain Braddock was involved in all this. Now Braddock was here in New York City, and Renko was dead.

Did that make Braddock seem more guilty or less?

Braddock and Hunter had found Ana Gonzalez and said she was now safe, but did she really know that? *Was Tori Hunter feeding her a line of crap? Was Braddock?*

In her mind it would all run counter to everything she knew of them both and of what their careers reflected. That had always made her dubious of the suspicion of Braddock, no matter what the circumstantial evidence had shown. This was especially true after the attempt on his life in Manchester Bay.

And what about this man with a port-wine stain or birthmark on his left forearm, wrist and hand? *Who was that? How could they find him?*

There were a lot of questions she suddenly had and then there was one more.

Would she be the one to continue to pursue them?

* * *

Tori watched Cardi run out the front of the coffee shop. She waited two minutes, keeping a wary eye on anyone else walking into or out of the coffee shop. Tori pulled her ballcap down low over her face, slid her sunglasses back on, carrying her tall coffee high to her face and walked out the front door, down the steps and turned right and jogged south for a block to the black Tahoe and climbed into the passenger seat.

Braddock took one look at her face. "It went bad?"

"It went fine until she got a call. Renko was shot and killed sometime last night. He and a woman that was with him. Cardellini's on her way to the crime scene now."

"What? Where?"

"In the alley behind the Flatbush Pub in Brooklyn. Do you know it?"

Braddock nodded. "Yeah, I know it. It's a Brooklyn bar. It's not a cop bar per se but they go there." He shook his head in disgust. "Dammit. They're cleaning up. They know we have

Ana." He pulled into traffic and pounded the steering wheel. "I should have seen this coming. You know what this means?"

"Stagliola is probably dead too," Tori said.

"Was she going to look into him?"

"I think she was but with this, who knows. She said we need to stay out of sight because if the powers that be learn you're here, they'll be coming for you. They'll dragnet the city."

"The heck with that, I'm checking this out."

* * *

Cardi parked along Flatbush Avenue and clipped her shield to her blazer.

The Flatbush Pub took its name from its location in Flatbush, a neighborhood in the borough of Brooklyn. She knew Renko's condo wasn't far from the bar.

The pub itself was something of a revived dive located on a street corner but there was a narrow walkway between the pub and the next building to the north that led back into a wider alley. Based on the location of the crime scene tape and all the people milling about, the walkway was cordoned off, as was the whole block, from the looks of it. She parked, walked across Flatbush Avenue and then caught the eye of White.

"Cardi," White greeted just past the crime scene tape. "Come on."

"A lot of suits milling about, sir," she said as they walked the narrow walkway to the back alley.

"On the order of the commissioner, our investigation is being folded into the Major Case Squad investigation of this shooting."

"This shooting has to be a part of what we're looking into on the Guerero case."

White nodded. "I agree but now, it's out of my hands. We have a dead detective and a dead chief in five days. We're still in it but with all that's happened, the commissioner is turning to the MCS. They're probably going to want to sit down with you and me, go over what we have. We're still in, we're a part of it, but I'm not calling the shots now."

Cardi nodded, understanding her role would be greatly reduced, if not eliminated. That was unless she could bring something to the table.

Standing in the alley, the bar was to her right. As she looked left to the north, forensic officers were processing a black Cadillac sedan, taking photos and placing small yellow number tents next to pieces of evidence. On the opposite side of the alley was a large apartment construction project, six stories tall. The outside shell of the building was complete though it was clear construction continued inside.

"How did this all go down?"

"Renko was here late last night according to the two bartenders who worked until close. They both knew him. He's something of a regular. The bartender said he was here at first with two other cops he recognized. Around midnight, the two cops with him left and he made his way to the other end of the bar and sat down with a woman, our other victim. The bartenders said it appeared that Renko knew her well. Renko and the woman, named Rita Hanratty, left just before closing time at two a.m., so late, via the back door of the bar. Renko was parked all the way down there." White gestured to the car at the north end of the alley. "The bartender said they had a pretty decent crowd in the bar until twelve thirty, one a.m., so Renko probably had to park that far down to find a spot."

White led her down to the vehicle. Inside the car were the bodies of Renko in the driver's seat and the woman in the passenger seat. Cardi let out a long breath. "Oh, man."

She had no love for Renko, misogynistic asshole that he'd been to her. Whether she agreed with how he went about performing the job was irrelevant. He was a fellow officer who'd been murdered. But in her mind, she just didn't think Braddock had anything to do with it.

Who did? Hunter had given her a name. Was he responsible? Or the port-wine stain guy?

She took a step toward the vehicle to get the full picture.

"Renko three times, her just the once in the head," White said.

Cardi stepped around to the front of the car. "And nobody heard anything?"

"The apartment building is unoccupied. The pub was mostly empty at that point, though the bartenders say the back door is thick and music was playing inside. Bartenders didn't hear anything, and this alley would confine the sound. And if they used a suppressor, even less likely it would have been heard."

She looked around the area and then back to the positioning of the bodies in the car. They had been shot from the front as evidenced by the bullet holes through the windshield. The driver's side door was open and being printed, but the door's window was down. The passenger side door window was still up. Renko's service weapon was still secured in his duty holster. Shards of glass were as visible as the splatters of blood within the interior. She walked ahead of the car thirty feet then stopped. There was a deep tunnel-like entryway that led into the apartment building. White walked up to her. "What are you seeing?"

Cardi led White down the alley and away from everyone else, wanting some privacy.

"Cole, the shots are from the front, right through the windshield, but the driver's side window is down."

"It was a warm night," White replied, looking back at the car. "Even at two a.m. It's still summer. At that time of night, it was probably still in the low to mid-seventies and humid."

"That's what air conditioning is for," Cardi said. "What if

he lowered the window because someone was coming. And who do you lower the window for?"

White grimaced. "Someone you know. Someone either he or she knew."

"I'll do you one better. Renko's gun is still holstered. He didn't sense danger."

"It could be someone she knew. We don't know anything about her."

"Given recent events, do we really think it's about her?" Cardi said. "The window is down on Renko's side. That man approaches, but I'm betting he's not the shooter."

"He's the distraction."

"The second man is hiding in that entryway right there. He waits until his partner has Renko engaged and distracted enough that he can come right at them. It's thirty feet to the car. Renko and the woman are right there, surprised, trapped in the car, nowhere to go. It's a kill box. It's over in an instant and in this alley, nobody... hears... a... thing."

* * *

Braddock drove up upon the plethora of squad cars, lights flashing.

"There's suits everywhere, Braddock," Tori said nervously. "Cardellini might be right, this might be pushing it."

"I just want a little look," he said. "I bet I already know what happened."

He swung wide around the block, parking on the next street over and a block north, well away from the scene. Tori had her Yankees hat and sunglasses. He pulled on his own Yankees hat that Quinn had given him last Christmas. He slid on aviator shades and was dressed casually in jeans and a navy-blue long-sleeved shirt that he'd pulled up to just below his elbows. They both grabbed their coffee cups and walked south, crossing the street and then turning right to see the crime scene tape up and two uniformed officers standing at the end of an alley.

The morning was sultry, the sky a hazy gray blue, the streets filled with their characteristic Brooklyn buzz and hum.

"It is so different being here," Tori mused as they walked along. "The constant sound. Like it's a heartbeat."

"I find it amusing you miss it so. You practically want a hot dog already."

"I'm more of a pretzel gal. I've always been amazed at how much you don't, this last week notwithstanding."

He smiled. "You're right, I don't miss it that much."

"Why?"

"I'm a proud New Yorker. But now—" he threw his arm gently around her, in part to cover their approach and in part in affection "—I live on a lake. The air is fresh and clean. I have you, Quinn, family. Life is very good."

There was a crowd that had gathered at the end of the alley, looking back down at the detectives and crime scene officers surrounding the Cadillac. They stopped and used the crowd to hide their presence. As they peered down the alley, they could see Cardi. "Who is that she's with?" Tori murmured.

"I think that's Coleman White. But I see two other guys further down that alley. They're Major Case Squad detectives. Serious guys. This is going to be all hands on deck, I think."

"Cold Case is being usurped," Tori said. "Cardi may be out."

"Unless we get her back in." He eyed up the alley, the car, able to get a sense of what happened. And then he caught Cardi's eye. She looked right at him and then Tori, who leaned in. Braddock nodded. Cardi nodded almost imperceptibly back. "Okay, I've seen enough."

They got into the Tahoe and started back toward Manhattan.

"What did you get from that?"

"Confirmation."

"Of Renko?"

Braddock nodded. "He manipulated that investigation of Dan's murder. I told you I suspected it then, and I know it now. I know it. He wasn't on this to finish it. He was on it to monitor it, to keep his guys one step ahead, whether it was on Julio, or me, or then in Toledo, but that all failed."

"And now?"

"After Toledo, his guys are cleaning up and they decided *he* was a liability. And as you said, you can bet your bottom dollar, Stagliola is dead too."

"Dammit," Tori groaned. "This is confirmation that the cop Julio saw Stagliola talking to down on the docks, big head, slicked back hair, was in fact—"

"Renko," Braddock finished.

A phone rang in Braddock's pocket. "That didn't take long." He answered. "Cardi."

"Dammit, Will, what did you learn?" Cardi asked.

"Stagliola is probably dead too."

Cardi sighed. "I was worried you were going to say that."

"This case might have been moldering around for eight years, Cardi, but it's moving fast now."

"Hell, Will," Cardi chuckled. "I'm being shown the door. It'll be the Major Case Squad's show now."

"This thing will be over before they get caught up on what is truly going on. You want to bring this thing home, start with Stagliola, and any connection between him and..." He paused, thinking it through.

"And?"

"And Renko."

"Hold on. You want me to investigate Renko?"

"No, encourage the MCS to do that," Braddock replied. "Carmine Stagliola is not on their radar and is not a cop. If you're being shown the door, nobody will care if you're looking into Stagliola. But I'm telling you, there's a connection between Stagliola and Renko. Find it."

"What are you doing?"

"We'll work on finding the ex-cop with a port-wine stain. But to do that I need to see someone, and I'm not sure she'd see me without a call from you first."

TWENTY-FOUR

"THAT'S MY EXCUSE, BUT THAT'S NO EXCUSE."

Boo and Vooch occupied the quiet back corner booth, eating their barbeque sandwiches, tall beers in front them, the U.S. Open tennis matches playing on the big screens over the bar. They looked up when Conn came in, stopping at the bar to grab a beer of his own. As he walked back to the table, they both noticed him grimacing.

"What happened?" Vooch asked. "You aggravate it?"

"A bit. As I was driving over here, this asshole cut me off. I had to slam the brakes, and I rammed it right into the seat belt."

"Ahh."

"It was like a knife was jammed in there," he said, sitting back in the booth, taking out a bottle of ibuprofen, stuffing four in his mouth and then washing it down with the beer. "Fuck me that hurt."

A waitress stopped by and he placed a lunch order.

"No problems with the salvage yard?"

He laughed. "Those guys spend their day looking the other way," Conn replied, having dumped the vehicle they used last night on Renko as well as Stag's Chevy Traverse. Then he tossed the guns and silencers from last night, along with the burner phone they pulled from Renko's pocket into a river. "You guys hearing anything?"

Vooch wiped his mouth. "No actually, I haven't heard from anyone." He turned to Boo. "You?"

"A few people texted. Renko had many friends and was politically connected. He was in line for another step up the ladder if he wanted to take it. The chief of IA gunned down is going to stir up the department." He wiped his mouth. "MCS is taking over the investigation, but it'll be all hands on deck."

"Everyone will be after us."

"Ah shit," Conn murmured.

"I'm not surprised."

Vooch looked to Boo. "Time to go on vacation?"

When they talked of vacation time, that was the euphemism for their escape plan.

Boo took a long drink of beer. "You two could go at any time and you might want to think about it. You don't have documented history with Renko, or Stag, for that matter, once people start looking for him."

"What about you?"

"Renko, Stag and I do have history."

"We all have history together," Vooch said.

"Yours is far more distant and attenuated. Mine is not. I could see someone coming my way and if I abruptly can't be found, that could raise a question, not just for me but you as well because if they start looking for me, then they'll come looking for you two."

"Give it a few days?"

Boo nodded. "Tomorrow night there's a gathering at Lou's for Renko. You know, like for anyone from the old neighborhood, right. We all need to be there, be seen by everyone, pay our respects and be angry. Plus, if we're there we might get a feel for where things are at, investigation wise. People always talk. MCS, Cold Case, IA, will all be there." He thought for a moment. "That said, today make sure you're ready to go at a moment's notice if need be. We need to be ready. Get a go-bag and have it at home." He checked his watch.

"Check in with each other every four hours," Vooch suggested. "Stay in touch."

"Will do," Conn agreed. "And ears to the ground. People always talk."

Boo nodded. "We meet back right here tonight."

* * *

Braddock parked and he and Tori walked along the street.

"Is this the bodega?"

"Yeah," Braddock replied and ducked to the right into a narrow alley and to the bodega's back door. "The shooter came in the back through that door. And they both fled into this alley-way. From here nobody really knows where they went but I'm betting there was a vehicle waiting at the other end of the alley down there to the south. It's a forty- or fifty-yard run. Takes, what? Seven or eight seconds at most from the back door to a waiting vehicle. In that amount of time?"

"Nobody sees anything."

"Right. And then come look at this." Braddock led Tori back to the street. "The third floor in that apartment building on the corner. That is Dan and Monica's apartment. So, you know how the first man comes into the store just ahead of Dan?"

"Yeah."

"Well, I'm thinking the shooter was standing in this alley, right in this spot, with reasonable cover, watching and waiting for Dan to come out. Then he calls his partner who goes inside and plays stick-up at the counter, drawing Dan's attention while this guy goes in that back door, comes in from behind and kills him."

Tori took it all in. "Hard to believe Renko wouldn't have

made a similar conclusion. Except, of course, if you're burying it."

"Which he was. But remember the context of everyone other than Renko. To everyone else at the time, it did look like a random act of violence."

"You think this man with the birthmark was the stick-up man or shooter?"

"Or driver," Braddock said. "I'm thinking three men. The third being the wheel man."

He led Tori across the street to the apartment building, walked up the front steps and hit the buzzer for Apartment 3A.

"Yes?" the voice answered.

"Monica. It's Will."

The door buzzed after a second and Braddock pulled the door open.

"I'm amazed she still lives here," Tori whispered as they walked up the steps. "I could barely go back to Minnesota, let alone stay after what happened to Jessie and then my dad."

Braddock stopped on the landing, leaning in. "I don't think she's ever given up on solving Dan's murder. Living here, seeing that bodega every day, never lets her forget. It's a daily reminder. And I'm a reminder of what *didn't* happen." They walked up to the third floor and knocked on the door. They heard the chain and deadbolt flip, and the door opened.

"Will," Monica acknowledged coldly after a moment. "Been eight years."

It wasn't an unexpected greeting.

"Hello, Monica. I'd like to introduce you to Tori Hunter."

Tori extended her hand which Monica took slowly, a wary look.

"You better come in." Monica gestured to the couch and slowly took a seat in a chair across from them. Eight years of anger stared back at them. "Cardellini called me and asked that I sit down with you. Given what's happened today, and the fact you're here, I wasn't sure I should. Another cop dead and here you are."

"I don't blame you," Braddock said. "I let you down eight years ago. I'm here to try and make things right."

"Or tie up loose ends," she asserted. "Hide the last of what you did to my husband. That's if what all these people are telling me is true. Ray Lange comes out to Minnesota and ends up dead. You're here in New York City and Ira Renko is dead. My husband is dead. My nephew is dead. Others are needlessly dead. Need I continue? It's following you everywhere, Will."

"Monica, I—"

Tori jumped in. "You know what I appreciate?"

"What?" Monica snapped.

"Directness. No bullshit. Let's just cut right to it."

"Who are you to him?" Monica asked Tori. "His partner?"

"Professionally and personally," Tori replied, resting her hand on Braddock's thigh. "I'm a retired FBI special agent. It's a long story, but I spent most of my Bureau career in New York City and then moved back home to Minnesota a few years ago and... found Braddock. He screwed up plenty eight years ago, and some again this week, but he's not your enemy. And spending just a few minutes with you, I don't think you really believe that either."

"I just don't know anymore," Monica replied after a moment. "I just... don't know who is worth trusting anymore."

"I knew your husband."

That caught Monica by surprise. "You did?"

Tori nodded. "I worked a couple of cases with him. I liked and respected him. I was at his funeral." She paused. "It's been a shock to my system as well that the last week of my life has been consumed with this case."

Monica nodded. "Then you know that a lot of people have told me the last couple of months that Will is involved."

"He is," Tori said flatly. "But not in the way they're insinuating." She turned back to Braddock. "Tell her. All of it. You owe her that."

"Tell me what, Will?" Monica said.

He nodded, leaning forward, his hands clasped. "I know I told you I would dig into what happened across the street, but then abruptly left New York and moved to Minnesota before I had," Braddock said. "And I know that the reopened case has focused on me in part because of that and some other—" he struggled for the term "—events that have occurred."

"Events. Is that the polite term for murders?"

"Fair. I know I told you I hadn't done much on what happened to Dan when I left eight years ago. I lied about that. I had done and learned plenty, too much in fact. I was making progress figuring out who was responsible for his murder, but I stopped."

"Why?"

"I had to. I was... forced to."

"Forced? By whom?"

Braddock opened a folder and took out the photo of him and Quinn.

"Oh, Quinn." A slight smile creased Monica's lips at the sight of him. Monica had a daughter of a similar age, and she and Quinn played together a few times back in the day. "How old is he now?"

"Just turned fourteen. Starting eighth grade."

"Plays hockey, nonstop," Tori added. She took out her phone and stepped over to Monica's chair to show her a picture of Quinn and her standing on the dock at home.

"He's so tall," Monica said, her sullen demeanor fading for just a moment.

"Towers over me."

"That picture I handed you, I came home and found that had been slipped under my apartment door," Braddock said. "Flip it over."

Monica turned the photo over and they both watched her lips read the message, her eyebrows jumping and jaw dropping just a little and then looked at Tori. "Is this real?"

"My reaction was just like yours," Tori said. "I'm not Quinn's mother, but I love him. I know what I felt when I saw it. Rage." She turned to Braddock. "Braddock couldn't allow himself to have that back then. Not with Meghan having died."

Monica's shoulders slumped. "Oh, Will. I'm so—"

Braddock stopped her. "I'm sorry. I had to walk away. I just... I had to protect Quinn."

"And now?"

"They've come after me, after Tori, they'll come after Quinn. I'm going to finish what I started eight years ago." Braddock explained the last week from his perspective, including the attempts on his and Tori's lives. "Dan was murdered. He was murdered by cops, who are likely now ex-cops, and they'll do whatever it is they have to do to protect themselves. They've shown that time and again."

"Why murder Detective Lange or Renko?"

"As to one of them, you answered that question a few minutes ago," Tori said. "Tie up loose ends."

Monica looked from her to Braddock and back. "Which one? Which one was responsible for Dan?"

"Monica—"

"No, Will. People have been throwing your name under the bus, me included. It's your turn. Who?"

"The investigation isn't there yet, but we think Renko," he replied. "I didn't get the job done on your nephew's case. Had I, none of this probably would have happened."

"Meghan was dying."

"That's my excuse, but that's no excuse. Meghan wouldn't have let me use that then, and I'm not going to do it now. I missed it. Renko didn't miss Dan's case, he manipulated it, he couldn't find the shooters because if he did—"

"He'd have exposed himself," Tori finished. "But if Detective Cardellini finds what we think she's going to find, the spotlight will find its way back to Renko, eventually."

Monica nodded. "But they're still looking at you, Will. And you're here and now Renko was murdered. You'll be a suspect."

"That's why we're here to see you. Tori and I know something nobody else knows. I came here to see if you would make a connection for me."

"What connection?"

"I think we're looking for an ex-cop or ex-cops who worked narcotics in the NYPD. Now, Dan was working homicide his last three years or so after his tour with the JTTF, but before that, he made a name for himself in narcotics, and I know he remained very close with some of the cops he worked with back in those years. I think we're looking for people of that era."

"Yeah, he did. I still see and hear from some of them to this day. But you don't think his good friends killed—"

"No. But I need their help, and they might give it to me if you'd ask them too. We are looking for someone in particular."

"Why not have Cardellini help with that?"

"I don't want to tip these guys off about him," Braddock said. "We need to keep it close."

"Who are you looking for?"

"Monica, do you know what a port-wine stain is?" Tori said.

Monica nodded. "A birthmark, right?"

"Yes." Tori held out her left arm. "We're looking for someone with a port-wine stain that runs from the forearm—" she pointed with her finger "—all the way down over their left hand. We're wondering if..."

Monica sat back, as if she'd been hit by a thunderbolt.

"Monica, what is it?" Tori asked.

"I've... seen that somewhere before," Monica muttered, jumping out of her chair, running her hands through her long straight black hair. "I've seen it. I've seen it." She looked at them both, her eyes wide, excited. "I've seen it."

She turned and ran down the hallway. Tori and Braddock took off after her, finding her in the master bedroom. Monica was in the closet, digging out boxes until she seemed to find the one she was looking for. She set it on the bed and took the top off. It was full of photos, some framed, some not, but all included Dan. Tori glanced to the other boxes, and they were all marked 'Dan.'

Monica started frantically searching through the photos. "No, no, no... no... no..." She kept checking them and then tossing them aside.

"No, no, no... no."

Braddock started helping. "What am I looking for?"

"Newspaper photo, I think," Monica replied. "It was a big drug bust. No." Toss. "No." Toss. "No, no, no... no... n... wait. Here." She handed the photo to Braddock. "Will, there."

It was a framed newspaper photo, in color. There were twenty or so men, two rows deep, pictured standing behind stacks of cocaine on a table. It was a large drug seizure from seventeen years ago. Dan was standing in the back row left.

"There," Monica said. "Him."

In the front row on the far right, standing, turned somewhat sideways toward the camera was an officer with a bushy black mustache, black hair, his navy-blue dress shirt sleeves rolled up to the elbow, but from mid-forearm down, only covered in part by his wristwatch, was a port-wine stain.

The officer's names were listed under the photo.

Braddock traced with his finger, running along the names left to right, to the last one of the front row.

"Salvucci. Detective Phil Salvucci."

TWENTY-FIVE

"YOU KNOW WHO ELSE WAS FIFTY-FIVE."

In the past eight years Boo visited his 24/7 storage facilities quarterly to check, re-check and update the contents. He had three now, all under different names. But the first had been rented for altruistic reasons years ago to store his mother's furniture after he'd had to move her into a nursing home. It was supposed to be a temporary solution until he found the time to sell the furniture. He had no intention at the time of having it for ten years. However, after they had pulled the jobs, it had proven fortuitous.

Hidden deep behind the behemoth of a wooden desk, the bookshelves, lamps, end tables, the dining table, portraits, and rows of stacked chairs was the safe. He tapped in the six-digit combination and opened it. In the upper left-hand corner of the top shelf was a large plastic bag that he retrieved and then spread the contents out on the table next to the safe.

There was a passport, a driver's license, two credit cards, a phone and two small clips of cash. The quarterly visits had always been to replace the flash drive with an updated one that contained the updated banks and account numbers and to make sure the burner phones were charged. Along with that he retrieved two Sig Sauer P226s with additional magazines, stuffing them into the duffel bag. There were six stacks of cash sitting on the top shelf, he grabbed them as well. No sense leaving sixty grand behind if the idea was to clean this safe out. He put the contents back in the bag, pulled the storage door closed and drove home to his condo.

They had all set up their escape plans and go-bags separately, plus banking accounts and business relationships in different countries. He had chosen Panama for his own banking and had used one of the identities to travel there on occasion to look in on it and evaluate future property options.

Over the years they had been careful not to flash too much money, but between their private security business and not being overly greedy, they had all given themselves a bit more comfort in their lives. In his case, three years ago he had bought his condo, a spacious one on the third floor of a four-story building in a row of connected red and brown brick buildings in Brooklyn. Vooch had bought a similar condo a mile to the northeast and Conn rented out the side of a newly remodeled duplex on a nice street in south Queens. The three of them were within a few miles of one another.

He retrieved a bottle of iced tea from the refrigerator and decided to go up the stairs to the roof. They weren't supposed to go up top, but people did it all the time. It was just after 6:00 p.m. The sky was a hazy muggy blue in the late-day warm western sun.

He breathed in the warm evening air, his eyes drawn to the south Manhattan skyline, especially One World Trade Center. He took a drink of the tea and looked to his right. Another interesting part of being on the roof was he could, with a bit of climbing and jumping effort, cross from building to building.

He walked to the north, hopping over the short barriers for each building. He glanced to his right to the street below, the pedestrians walking along, including a group in hospital scrubs loudly talking and laughing like people who might have stopped for a cocktail or two after their shift. New York-Brooklyn Presbyterian Methodist Hospital was just a few blocks away, as were many a watering hole between here and the hospital. The group he observed was heading to one of the stairways down to MTA subway station underneath the street.

His pocket buzzed. Vooch. He answered, "Yeah."

"You make your checks?" Vooch asked.

"Yeah, you?"

"Done. Conn as well. The Yanks are out on the west coast, playing the Dodgers later. Mets are playing late as well. Meet at ten at Sweet Sally's for the opening pitch?"

"I'll be there."

"I'll pick up Conn and meet you."

* * *

Cardi, along with White, had a sit down with MCS detectives, updating them on the status of the case, including all they had learned in Minnesota. Yes, Braddock had been their primary person of interest, and you couldn't ignore how he seemed to be connected to the key events and people in the case. "He shows up time and again. There is no denying that. It's why there has been intense focus on him the last few weeks."

"What did you think when someone took a shot at Braddock in Minnesota?" an MCS detective asked.

"Renko thought that meant Braddock's partners wanted to silence him before he spoke."

"And you?"

She took a moment, couching her words. "Chief Renko and I weren't aligned in that view."

"Where were you aligned?"

"In the fact that Will Braddock was a key person in the case.

I wasn't yet convinced of his guilt. Renko, and even Lange to a degree, both were."

"There was this... confrontation in Minnesota between Renko and Braddock. I understand Renko took the worst of it."

"I witnessed it," Cardi replied. "Chief Renko antagonized and provoked him. It was a mistake, on *both* their parts."

"And now Renko is dead. And Lange and Gonzalez murdered in Minnesota, after Gonzalez called Braddock," the detective pushed. "How is he not a prime suspect, Detective?"

"Proof," Cardi replied calmly. "Circumstantial evidence made him a person of interest. It's proof that would make a suspect. We don't have any more proof after Renko's murder than we did before. And if you're suggesting that Braddock is involved with others and they killed Renko, ask yourself this. Wouldn't killing Renko heighten the intensity of the focus on them, not decrease it?"

"Your point?"

"Braddock is still of interest in large part because his name stretches back eight years on this case, but his isn't the only one, is it? Maybe we ought to ask ourselves why Renko was shot?"

"What are you implying?"

"I'm simply asking a question about the motive for the murder of one of the victims this morning. Why Renko? Is it just because he was investigating this case or was it something more? Seems a prudent inquiry."

What she left out for now were the parts about Braddock and Hunter finding Ana Gonzalez in Toledo and the name of Stagliola. Braddock and Hunter wanted to keep those facts close to a select few for at least another twenty-four to forty-eight hours while they hunted on their own. They'd only play those cards if they needed too.

After she'd finished with the MCS detectives, she started on Carmine Stagliola. He wasn't answering phone calls. She'd made a discreet check on his house in Bulls Head on Staten

Island, but all was quiet. A quick chat with neighbors and they said they hadn't seen him in a week if not more.

After her late-afternoon field trip, she engaged in a deeper dive and learned that Stagliola had lived almost his entire fifty-five-year life at various places on Staten Island, from his child-hood, through his marriage and divorce and until now.

"You know who else was fifty-five," she murmured to herself as her fingers danced over the keyboard, typing in the name of Ira Renko. Once she did, it took her five minutes to find it.

Beekman Street.

Stagliola and Renko were the same age and grew up on the same one block that was Beekman Street in Port Richmond on Staten Island.

Renko was dead.

Stagliola unreachable.

Braddock and Hunter were probably right. Stagliola was dead too.

And what was the description of the man Gonzalez saw Stagliola talking to that he thought was a cop? Black hair, round head, wearing a suit and driving a plain silver sedan. Renko's black hair now was speckled with heavy amounts of gray but back then, likely was just black. And what was he driving? Silver sedan. She did a quick New York DMV check. Eight years ago, Ira Renko was driving a gray 2016 Nissan Altima.

She took a quick look around and realized that most everyone had departed for the day, including White. And then it dawned on her: *Cardi, nobody is around because it's Saturday night. Go home.*

After a stop for takeout, she retreated to her apartment. If there had been one decent outcome of her recently ended second marriage it was that her second husband was successful on Wall Street. Their marriage had seemed good, lasted five years until he came home one night, told her he'd had an ongoing affair with a co-worker, she was pregnant, and he decided he wanted to be a father. This after he'd told her, repeatedly, using up her own child-bearing years in the process, that he didn't want children.

She made him pay.

In addition to ongoing maintenance, he bought her a three-bedroom south Manhattan apartment in a newly constructed amenity-filled building that she turned into her own little personal oasis. She had converted the third bedroom into an office. It was there she started reviewing the entirety of what she had found on the day and what she knew of the case while she ate takeout. When she'd finished dinner, she thought it was time to make a call, selecting the number she'd dialed earlier in the day.

"Detective Cardellini," Tori Hunter answered.

She could tell they were in a moving vehicle. "Tori, we need to meet."

"We do but we're working on something at the moment."

She looked at her watch. "Want help?"

TWENTY-SIX

"NO DRINKING ON THE JOB."

Vooch pulled to a stop in front of the driveway and waited. Conn exited the house from the side door along the driveway. He stumbled on the last step and had to catch himself.

"Ooh. Careful, Conn," he murmured.

As he was walking toward the car, Vooch could tell that Conn was favoring his shoulder, holding it close to his body, grimacing a bit as he reached for the door handle.

"Man, are you okay? I saw you stumble."

"Yeah," Conn moaned as he got in. "Just need to keep it in the right position is all. I tripped on the last step coming down."

"Slow down. Be more careful."

"Yeah, yeah."

"How's the wound?"

"The stitches itch but news at ten, scratching at them is a bad idea," he replied. "I found that one out the hard way. We're going back to Sweet Sally's?"

"Yep. I can never have too much barbeque."

Creatures of habit, the three of them had four or five bar restaurants they regularly frequented in Brooklyn and Queens, places where they were considered regulars, were recognized by the servers and bartenders and were looked after. Sweet Sally's was often the choice if they were watching a ball game and tonight the Yankees were in Los Angeles to play the Dodgers. The Mets were in Seattle playing the Mariners as well, so they had ballgames on all the screens and sweet saucy barbeque. Boo had beat them there and had a table in the corner, a tall beer in front of him, perusing the menu.

The server stopped by, chatted them up for a bit and took beer orders and returned quickly with them and then took the first of their food orders. They planned to hunker down for a few hours.

"Heck, we even have a couple of preseason football games on tonight," Vooch said. The bar had televisions all around the top of the bar, which was set in the middle of the place and then up high in several other places, along with a wall with a bank of televisions in two rows. It was a popular place on a weekend night though there were a few tables open in their general vicinity. A couple was taking one of them.

"Anything new tonight?" Conn said almost under his breath.

Boo shook his head and then put his beer close to his mouth, as if to cover his lips. "No. I'm getting it third hand but there are no witnesses and no probative physical evidence. We got away clean."

They could hear it in the tone of his voice. There was concern.

"That was the good news. What's the bad news?" Conn asked.

"It's the risk we assumed all along," Boo replied. "The one we might have to ride out. With Renko gone, the person most focused on Braddock is gone. Fresh eyes on the case and some focus will turn to Renko."

Conn shook his head. "Who knows if he was careful

enough? He and Carmine weren't careful enough in the first place. Did they cover their tracks?"

"And at some point," Vooch noted, "someone will look for Stag."

"They will," Boo said, looking to the couple at the table, who were locked arm in arm as the server took a picture of them. He heard the woman bellow, "It's our anniversary!" She took the phone from the server and looked at the photo. "Honey, isn't that a nice picture!"

Vooch turned to the couple. "How long have you been married?"

"Twenty-seven years," the man, tall and angular, replied with a smile.

"Well, congratulations to you both."

"Thank you."

He turned back to Boo and Conn. "I'm not sure if you put the three of us together, we got twenty-seven years of marriage."

They did the quick calculation and determined they had thirty-three years among them. Conn was the leader with sixteen.

"You know, if all these dating apps existed twenty-five years ago, I doubt I'd have ever gotten married," Boo said. "I could just go match-up on one of those apps and have company three nights a week. That's what Renko was doing last night, that woman who was with him he met through an app."

"She should have swiped left," Vooch said. "Not right."

* * *

Braddock and Tori were in the Tahoe, and Oliver and Connie in their BMW sedan, alternating the tail of Salvucci from his condo in Brooklyn as he drove east on Atlantic Avenue. Just as he'd crossed over into Queens, Salvucci turned right. Oliver followed and Braddock did the same.

Three blocks ahead, on a street of duplexes, Salvucci pulled to a stop on the right side. Oliver turned left the block before to loop around while Braddock pulled to the right side of the street just short of the corner and turned off his headlights. They could see the glow of Salvucci's headlights a half-block ahead on the right, waiting at the end of a driveway.

Tori saw him first, a man walking slowly down the drive-way. "Are you seeing what I'm seeing?"

"Yes," Braddock said, watching the man walk slowly and favor his left arm, holding it close to his body. "See that adjust-ment where he reached over with the right hand?"

"As if to hold or steady his left arm."

The man got into the Equinox and Salvucci pulled away, heading south. Braddock pulled down the street to follow and Tori took down the house number as they drove by.

Braddock accelerated ahead, keeping the Equinox in view as it took a right turn onto 101st Avenue and was now heading west back into Brooklyn. Just as 101st merged into Liberty Avenue, the burner phone rang.

"Interesting," Tori said, putting the phone on speaker. "Detective Cardellini."

"We need to meet."

"We do but we're working something at the moment."

"Want help?"

Tori glanced at Braddock with a look of: *what do you think?* Braddock nodded. "Yeah. I have an address for you."

"Shoot."

Tori recited the address to her.

"I'll make a check," Cardi said. "Are you two up to something?"

"Always."

"Who?" Cardi asked. "No, wait. Did you find the man with the port-wine stain?"

"Cardi," Braddock replied. "Run that address and call us back. Then we'll talk."

"That's a yes," she replied excitedly. "Okay, let me run this."

Fifteen minutes later they were back west a few miles into the heart of Brooklyn, parking in time to see Salvucci and the other man walk in the front door of Sweet Sally's. "I bet we passed a hundred bars to get back here. You only come back this far because they're meeting someone else," Tori said.

"Let's find out," Braddock said.

"We can't go in there."

"Your friends can. They're plenty smart and eager to play."

Tori smiled. "They are at that." She reached for her walkie-talkie. "Connie?"

Connie and Oliver were thinking just as they were. "Tori, coming all the way back here, they have to be meeting some-body in there. Only thing that makes any sense."

"Want to let us know who?"

"Thought you'd never ask," Oliver said, and she could just envision him smiling. "This place has good barbeque. What do you say, darlin'? Should we go in and celebrate our anniversary a few months early?"

"Why yes, Oli, I think we should."

"No drinking on the job," Tori needled.

"*Riiiight*," Connie retorted.

Two minutes later, Connie and Oliver, who had parked further down and on the opposite side of the street came walking hand in hand down the sidewalk and then into the bar.

Bzzz. Bzzz. Bzzz.

"Cardi, I'd imagine," Braddock said before answering. "What have you got?"

"The address is for Conn Dent. NYPD, retired four years ago. He was a narcotics detective."

"I'm detecting a theme here."

"Dent? You said Dent, right?" Tori replied, excitedly.

"Yeah."

Tori had a copy of the photo from earlier in the day on her phone. She tweezed the print larger and was looking through the names. In the second row, just to the left of Salvucci was officer Conn Dent. She showed the photo to Braddock, her index finger just above Dent.

"Looks like the guy, doesn't it?"

"Oh yeah."

"Will?"

"Yeah, Cardi."

"Dent was born and raised in Port Richmond. As was Ira Renko and Carmine Stagliola. In fact, Stagliola and Renko were the same age, and grew up on Beekman Street. The street is one block long. You were right about them, and you were right about ex-narcotics officers when it comes to Dent."

"Cardi. We have another name for you. Phil Salvucci. Narcotics detective. Do a quick check on him."

"I can do that. Then what?"

"How long for you to get to Sweet Sally's in Brooklyn?"

"Not long."

* * *

"For the lady, on her anniversary no less?" the server asked.

"One of your fine Palomas," Connie ordered.

"And you, sir?"

"Bourbon Old Fashioned."

Connie pulled out her phone and texted Tori that they were inside, and she allowed her eyes to look up and just over Oliver's left shoulder to the three men sitting in the booth. She turned her camera up and took a couple of photos and checked them on her phone. They were a little distant and not as clear as she'd like as the camera focused more on Oliver.

"A Paloma for you. An Old Fashioned for you," the server

said upon his return, sitting the drink down in front of Oliver. "Happy anniversary."

"Thank you," Connie replied. "We need a picture," she said, standing up and moving over to Oliver's side of the table. "Would you?"

"Of course," the server said. "Hold your drinks up."

"Take several," Connie said, holding up her drink, smiling as was Oliver. "And get the background so we can tell we're here at Sweet Sally's."

The server did as she requested, having snapped several photos. "Let me know if that's good."

She swiped through the photos and saw several possibilities. "Thank you, perfect."

One of the men at the table turned around, which caused Connie's heart to skip a beat. Had they been caught. "How long have you been married?" the man asked.

"Twenty-seven years," Oli answered, smiling.

"Well, congratulations to you both."

"Thank you." Oli took his seat again, raised his drink glass close to his lips before asking: "Did you get a few good ones over my shoulder?"

"Three possibles." She looked up to him and then the three men in the booth behind. "I'll be right back," she said, smiling. "I'm going to go powder my nose, dear."

"Powder away."

Connie went to the ladies' room and took the stall on the end, closing and locking the door. She sat down and selected a photo. Their daughter worked in advertising and did a lot of photography work with her phone and was incredibly proficient at using the editing tools to crop, enlarge, and lighten photos and shared many tricks of the trade with her. It took her a couple of minutes, but she managed to enlarge one photo that would allow Tori and Braddock to see the man they had not yet identified. She called Tori who answered right away.

* * *

Cardi's sporty fully loaded Lexus NX 300 Sport was another outcome of the divorce. It let her easily weave through the Saturday night traffic on the Brooklyn Bridge. Once over the bridge it was another ten minutes for her to get to the bar. She'd been to Sweet Sally's a few times, driven by hundreds more. Spotting what she thought was the black Tahoe, she made a U-turn and squeezed into a parking spot three vehicles back. She took a moment to get a sense of the area and if anyone was watching or observing her. Was she being overly cautious? Perhaps. But at the rate bodies were dropping she couldn't be too careful.

Patting for her service weapon and then phone, she got out and then stepped across the front of her car up to the sidewalk, eyeing up the bar and the big marquis sign with a small horizontal Sweet in neon-blue cursive and a large vertical red block Sally's beneath it. She saw Hunter's ponytail swing around in the front seat. She got into the back seat and slid to the middle. "Well, ain't this some shit," she greeted heartily. "Collaborating with the suspects."

"Ain't it though," Tori said, this time offering her a bit of a smile.

"You're trusting me now?" The question was directed at Tori.

"You're trusting us?"

"Seems so," Cardi mused. "You two have gotten further on this in a few days than we got in months."

"We didn't exactly start from scratch," Braddock said. "Eight years ago, I had suspicions on Renko because his investigation of Dan's murder was as suspect as mine of that damn warehouse. My work was compromised by grief. Renko's was compromised because he was responsible for it."

"You still need proof, Will. I argued with Renko, with

Lange, even to MCS, there was no proof of *your* complicity in this, no direct evidence, just innuendo. You don't have that on Renko either," Cardi said. "Do you?"

"That is why we are here. To find the others."

"Besides Dent, who is inside?"

"Port-wine stain man, otherwise known as Narcotics Detective Phil Salvucci. What did you find out about him?"

"He's retired, four years. He too was born and raised in Port Richmond. Dent and Salvucci are three years younger than Renko and Stagliola, but they're all from the old neighborhood. How did you identify him?"

"Monica helped us identify him by name," Braddock replied and explained how.

"It's them," Tori asserted. "Too many squares on the bingo card are getting filled. These are the guys."

Cardi nodded. "How is this all connected?"

"Thanks to what you found, Cardi, at least to four of them, it starts with Port Richmond, Staten Island," Braddock replied. "They're all old friends, acquaintances. Salvucci and Dent were narcotics officers. Stagliola at the port. Renko, Stagliola's neighbor and old friend, was down at the port eyeing up the deliveries with him. That's what we think. As you said, we can't prove that—yet. I do think, however, we might be getting to the point where we could prove they were in Minnesota."

"That would be a start," Cardi replied. "Why here? This bar?"

"Dent and Salvucci are inside with someone."

"How do you know?"

"We have two sets of eyes inside," Tori replied.

"And who is it they're meeting with?"

"I'm thinking, or more hoping, that's it's the third man at Espinosa Warehouse," Braddock said. "The third man involved in Dan's murder. A third man who was up in Minnesota last week."

"Who do you have inside?"

"Our alibi from last night. Old Bureau colleagues of mine," Tori said. "Retired married couple."

"People of unassailable character who can vouch you two were sleeping in their guest room last night?"

"Indeed," Tori said and then her phone buzzed. "Speaking of which," she said, putting the phone on speaker. "Hey, Connie?"

"I'm texting you a couple of photos. Three men total, so a new face. He looks to be a bigger, more... menacing fellow. At least that's my take." The phone clicked off.

"Sounds ominous," Cardi quipped.

"Will our mystery guest please sign in," Braddock murmured as he leaned over to look at Tori's phone, Cardi leaning over from the back.

Tori tapped on the photos, swiping through them. The third was an enlarged photo. She could only make out the profile of Salvucci. Dent they were seeing straight on and then a third man. "She's right, a big guy," Tori said and held up her phone and looked to Cardi. "Look familiar?"

"No, but as you said there are thirty-five-thou—"

"That's... Boo," Braddock said.

"Boo?" Tori said.

"John Boo Coollee."

"Whoa, are you sure?" Cardi said, looking at the picture more closely. "I've heard the whispers over the years, but I never actually saw him in person."

"Who is he?" Tori inquired.

Braddock exhaled. "He was a narcotics cop, worked a lot undercover, but he was also the guy you called in to scare the shit out of people." He paused. "You'd hear about cops like this. Ones who were willing to do anything to make a case. *Anything.*"

"Goon?"

"No, he was far more dangerous than that. Goons and thugs with personnel files filled with brutality claims and suspensions are a dime a dozen. They're the ones who end up on the news and the department pays settlements on because they're stupid. Boo Coollee was a phantom. As shrewd as he was ruthless."

Cardi agreed. "The legend is that he'd scare people, making them believe bad things would happen to them if they didn't do what he wanted."

"And nobody ever reported him? Laid a finger on him?" Tori asked in disbelief.

Braddock turned to them both. "I was with the JTTF and there was this investigation we were on the periphery of. The case was run by Manhattan North Homicide detectives. We knew who the two murderers were, but the detectives didn't have enough evidence to charge and the chances of them developing it looked bleak. Then a few days later, no new evidence, no new witnesses, no new pressure by the investigating detectives, but one of them suddenly flipped. He took twenty years and testified against the other guy who got a life sentence."

"What happened?"

"All I heard were whispers."

"Which were?" Tori pressed.

"It was Boo. These two guys were out on bail, walking the streets and he got to one of them."

"Boo. Hmpf," Tori scoffed. "Like Boo Radley in *To Kill a Mockingbird*."

"More like Boo as in a ghost," Braddock said. "One night, at a bar, in a dark corner, I'm having a drink with a fellow detective who I worked that case with when Boo Coollee walked into the bar. My fellow detective told me he had heard that Boo had a *visit* with the guy. Now what Boo threatened to do, nobody knows but the guy. All I know is that with his lawyer present advising him not to take the deal, he took the deal."

"And he never said a word about this Boo Coollee guy?"

"Nada. The guy had a wife and a daughter. If the legend is true, Boo convinced this guy some tragedy would befall them if he didn't play ball. He played ball."

"And what if the guy didn't flip, what then?"

"Who's to say," Braddock replied.

"That's... just..." Tori stuttered. "The ends don't justify the means."

"I agree," Cardi said.

Braddock sat there quietly for a moment until he looked back to Cardi. "What else did you bring?"

"Current Guerero investigation file," she said. "Thought you might want to take a look at a few things."

"I want to see Dan's notes."

For an hour, Braddock and Tori read through various parts of Cardi's investigative file.

"Pretty thorough review of your finances," Tori said to Braddock. "They concluded you were a very wealthy man." She smiled. "I feel so cheated."

"He's not that wealthy?" Cardi asked.

"He's comfortable."

"Tori has more money than me."

"The timing of your move. The lake house initially, then the expansion and the boat. And then a search of property around you raised additional questions. The home values on your lake are only exceeded by those on a lake outside of Minneapolis."

"That's Lake Minnetonka," Tori said.

"When we came out to Minnesota, to Manchester Bay after Lange's murder, some assumptions were made because they fit a narrative," Cardi said. "They were made without truly knowing some key information, such as how you came to own the house." She paused. "Will, I was part of that. I'm truly sorry."

Braddock nodded but didn't say anything.

"I see a lot in here that matches what you have," Tori said to Braddock. "You and Dan were on it. He was a bit further it seems, but his notes are very cryptic."

"As were yours when I saw them on your desk," Cardi noted.

"Intentionally so," Braddock said. "If you're investigating dirty cops, you're not writing down names. You're writing pieces that mean something to you. Like Dan wrote here: Stag/Port. We know what that means now, but Cardi I bet you looked at that and had no idea what Dan was talking about."

"No. I didn't."

"He wrote in code," Tori said. "Or snippets that mattered to him. Like the LP Boys. What does that mean? Or..." Tori laughed out loud. "He wrote down 'Ghost.'"

"That's probably Boo. He knew who he was up against."

"He was close, Braddock."

"Dan was a smart guy, he just wasn't careful enough. He either didn't sense they were onto him, underestimated what they would do, or just didn't think they'd do him in broad daylight at a bodega."

"Here's my question," Cardi said to Braddock. "Why didn't they kill you?"

"If they'd have killed Dan and then me for digging into Dan's murder, and into Espinosa Warehouse, and the other robberies, that would have brought too much heat. They tried something else with me."

"What?"

"I'll show you," Tori said, reaching across Cardi for the backpack behind Braddock's seat. She took out the envelope and handed it to Cardi. "That was slid under his apartment door."

Cardi opened the envelope and took out the photo and then flipped it over. "Those bloody bastards."

"Uh huh," Tori murmured.

"That's why I left, Cardi," Braddock said. "Because if I didn't, I'd have ended up like Dan."

"Damn," Cardi said. "I'm sorry, Will." She held up the photo. "About all of it."

"I get why you guys thought what you thought. I'm not happy about it, in fact I'm still very pissed, and my ribs ache, but in an objective sense, I get it. I always worried about it."

Tori's phone buzzed. It was a text from Connie. "Connie and Oliver just settled up, and she indicated the three of them are doing the same."

"What's the plan?" Cardi asked.

Braddock thought about what they had seen, who was involved and what they had talked about. "Cardi, follow Coollee. See where he goes. At this hour, I'd assume home but all the same, let's see."

"On it."

"The four of us will take Dent and Salvucci home."

Cardi reached for the door.

"And, Cardi," Tori said, "if this guy is as canny and vicious as you two say, be careful, huh."

"Hey, Will, she called me Cardi," Cardi said, smiling, a twinkle in her eye, as if she were having fun and perhaps, she was. "We're practically friends now."

She left and Braddock laughed.

"What?" Tori retorted.

"Don't *what* me. I will not be *whatted*!"

"Your point?"

"Try as you might not want to, you kind of like her."

Braddock wasn't wrong. "She's real police, that's for sure. Always have to respect that."

"Well, she ought to be." He turned to her with a wry smile. "She's third generation. There are more than a few Cardellini members in the department. Her father was a commander. An uncle who was a captain. It's the family business."

"And that's why you trusted her."

Braddock nodded. "It's a big reason why people trust you back home, isn't it?"

"Because of Big Jim," Tori replied, taking the point. She nodded to the front door of Sweet Sally's. "There they are."

Taking their own advice, sitting low and still in their seats, only their eyes moving as they kept watch on Coollee, first as he walked along the sidewalk on the opposite side of the street and then cut in front of a parked car and then doubled back four cars to his own.

"Hmm," Tori murmured, having carefully turned her head.

"Tori," Braddock said in his low voice, watching in the side mirror as Coollee dropped down into his vehicle. "Does an innocent man check his six like that after leaving a bar at midnight on a late summer Saturday?"

Twenty minutes later, they put Dent to bed. While Tori and Braddock observed at distance, he too was checking out his windows.

"Paranoid much," Tori murmured.

"These guys sure seem worried someone is watching."

"What now?"

"Sitting outside Sweet Sally's for three hours made me hungry," Braddock stated. "Let's go eat. See if everybody else wants a bite."

They were all game for a bite.

Bernie's Delicatessen on the west side of Manhattan was open twenty-four-seven. Cardi was introduced to Oli and Connie, and they all ordered. Braddock and Tori had sandwiches, the others opting for dessert. Everyone had coffee.

Braddock took a massive bite of his sandwich, drips of mayo and mustard dirtying his thick stubble. "Ahh, *real* pastrami," he said, savoring the flavor. "*This* I miss about New York."

Tori nodded, equally satisfied with her corned beef. "We can get a reasonably good sandwich in Minnesota but this..." She smiled, wiping her mouth with a napkin. "We can't get this, especially at one thirty in the morning. Not in Manchester Bay." She dove in and took another bite. "God, that is so good."

"What did you learn tonight?" Connie asked, poking her fork into her piece of cherry pie.

"That Coollee and Dent were watching their backs," Tori said, recapping their observations. "They at least think someone could be watching them for some reason."

Oli reached over for a gooey cherry off his wife's pie. "How are all these four or five people connected?"

"Port Richmond, Staten Island," Cardi said, tipping her head to Braddock and Tori. "That started with the connection between Renko and Stagliola growing up on the same block. Dent and Salvucci are from Staten Island."

"And Coollee worked narcotics, as did Dent and Salvucci," Tori noted. "And I wouldn't be at all surprised if he wasn't from Staten Island."

"Score one for Tori," Cardi said. "He is. And I think I can do you even one better. Before I came over here, I made a quick check. Guess who graduated the Police Academy together, same class?"

"Renko and Coollee."

"Gold star, Tori."

"And now you can draw a circle around all five of them."

"I prefer a Venn diagram," Braddock quipped.

"Ha, well you might get part of it. There is a gathering at Lou's Pub in Port Richmond tomorrow night, an Irish wake of sorts for Renko. I'm told it's an old tradition for cops from out that way," Cardi said. "I plan on going."

Braddock chuckled, a wry smile spreading across his face.

"What?"

"Dan, you were a beauty. God, he had it, all of it."

"I'm not following."

"Dan's notes. There was one for LP Boys. Lou's. Pub. Boys," Braddock said, smiling. "I'm betting all of them frequented it."

"What do you want to bet all three of them will be there tomorrow night?" Cardi said.

"That's chutzpah if they're guilty of what you think they are," Oli observed.

"True that, but, you also gotta keep up appearances," Tori said. "If they didn't show—"

"*That* would be noticed," Cardi said and then smiled, self-satisfied. "We know who it is now. We just dig in on them. I've started on Stagliola. I can tie him to Renko. You have this port-wine stain piece of evidence on Salvucci and Dent is favoring his left arm and shoulder. I could talk to White, tell him what we know, and go deep on these guys. Work it from my end, while MCS works it from theirs and we get there, eventually. Put people on them, watch them, see if there's anyone else involved."

Tori thought what Cardi said made sense from a conventional investigative perspective, and it would get she and Braddock out of it, free and clear. She turned to Braddock, who had a distant look in his eyes, the one he often said she had when she was deep in thought. "You're awfully quiet all the sudden."

He shrugged.

"Care to share your thoughts with the class?"

"Go easy on me, Professor."

"You've got something on your mind. Spill."

He nodded and took a deliberate sip of his coffee. "Coollee's and Dent's behavior tonight was... twitchy."

"Meaning?"

"I'm betting Coollee, Dent, and Salvucci were the men in Toledo. They know we spoke with Ana. They know Ana probably gave us Stagliola and maybe Renko. So they took them out. In doing so, they had to know it would cause a shit storm."

"It has. So?" Cardi led.

"They're on edge. They're sitting on millions. They have to be thinking of disappearing." He took another sip of coffee. "Cardi, you're right from the normal investigative standpoint: build the case, but my worry is, one, it will take too long and two, these guys will vanish the second they get wind of it."

Tori heard the tone. "You have a move in mind, don't you?"

"I do."

"Which is?" Cardi asked.

"Sometimes the ends do justify the means."

TWENTY-SEVEN
"THIS IS WHERE I NEED SOME ROPE."

Tori pushed herself up and then rolled off Braddock and onto her back, panting heavily, feeling a little perspiration on her body. "Well..." she exhaled. "Hoo... mmm. They say make-up sex is always the best."

"I don't know who 'they' is, but I'd find it hard to argue the point right now," Braddock said, before letting out a slow relaxed breath. He looked to the closed bedroom door. "I'm hoping you didn't wake your friends."

"Oh please," she replied with a laugh, sliding the bed sheet off Braddock and rolling her naked body back on top of him, leaning in and kissing him, whispering, "I wasn't *that* loud."

"The moaning."

"I breathe, I don't moan... much. And those might have been groans, I still hurt all over, although—" she leaned down and kissed him again "—I do seem to be improving. As do you," she added, tickling him just below his wound on the rib cage.

"Ow, don't do that."

"Wimp."

He laughed at that as he brushed the hair away from her face, so he could see her deep green eyes and smile. It's what always stopped him, her eyes and bright smile. It was an irresistible combination that could take his breath away when she walked into a room and caught his eye or at times like now, lying comfortably on him, her chin resting easily on her clasped hands, her legs casually dangling, relaxing, her eyes locked on his, leaning in, smiling, likely to kiss him at any moment. "I do rather like it, darling, when you do moan."

"Well, you did ravage me so," she said lightly, delighting in their brief respite, a needed healing reconnection after the last week. "Though I think the bed frame was louder than me. It's kind of squeaky." She rested her forehead to his. "And you can call me 'darling' more. I do like that."

"I shall endeavor to do it more often then, my darling."

"'My darling' is even better," she whispered, her lips softly on his.

He let his fingers very lightly caress the soft tanned skin on her back, contented that he was back in her better graces. "I'm sorry we're here. I'm sorry for all of this."

"Darling."

He nodded. "I'm sorry for all of this, darling."

She tapped his nose lightly with her finger and then brushed his hair away from his eyes. "I guess you'll just have to make it up to me somehow."

"Well, Victoria Hunter, I think you're very much in a name-your-price position."

She smiled. "And I plan to name it. In time. One must fully consider their options when they have one so over the barrel."

He laughed lightly.

"I like that you smiled and laughed just now. Not a lot of smiles this week."

His phone buzzed again. It had buzzed twice while they had been otherwise occupied. He checked the phone. "Hmm."

"What?"

He turned the phone so she could read the missed calls.

"NYPD is persistent. They called yesterday. Twice today already."

Clicking over to voicemail, he read the transcription of the morning messages. "Major Case Squad would like to have a word," he said. "Oh, I bet they would, especially if they knew I was here."

"How do you want to handle it?"

"Ignore them for now. It'll make them *more* interested in me."

"And that's a good thing?"

"For now, it is. We've put something in motion. I want to see it through."

There was a knock on the door.

"Oh, oh," Tori blurted as she rolled off him and scrambled to pull up the bedsheet. "Come in."

"So," Connie said, smiling as she peered around the door. "Would you two lovebirds like some breakfast?"

"That would be great," Tori replied, the sheet pulled up to her neck.

"I'll get started then." Connie pulled the door closed though they could hear her cackling down the hallway.

"Told you they heard," Braddock said.

Connie prepared an egg soufflé, fruit and coffee. Oli had the *New York Times* Sunday edition, and they all took sections of the newspaper to read, passing them around as they ate. Then, they all sat around having another cup of coffee, chatting as if they were on vacation somewhere, not a care in the world. A little stretch of normality.

Then Boe called.

Braddock looked to Tori. "We better take this." To Oli and Connie, he said, "If you'll excuse us. Time to put out a fire, I think."

"It seems as if that's all you two do," Connie needled with a wry smile.

They retreated to the bedroom. "Jeanette, let me guess. NYPD is calling you," Braddock said.

"How do you know?"

"I've been ignoring their calls since last night."

"Two detectives with their Major Case Squad called me, looking for you."

"And you told them what?"

"You were suspended and that as far as I knew, you and Tori had taken some time away. They told me they've tried to reach you, but that you don't answer."

Braddock chuckled. "Well, they're right, I haven't. I don't want to talk to them just yet."

"Is that wise?"

"If I don't talk to them, I don't have to lie to them."

"Heck," Tori said with a chortle. "Right now, get this, we have the Cold Case Squad lying to the MCS, *for us.*"

"They're helping... you? Why?"

"They want to close their case," Tori said. "Cardellini is fully on board."

"So, they're lying, and you got me lying," Boe replied. "You get a lie, and you get a lie, it's Oprah Christmas."

"Call it withholding pertinent information."

"Or lying for short."

"Jeanette, are you lying? I've taken some time away. Toledo was lovely," Braddock said breezily. "Or just tell them that you've heard that Tori and I went for a four-day canoe trip in the Boundary Waters to commune with the bears. No cell phone service up there."

"Dammit, Braddock, this isn't funny."

"It sure as shit isn't," Braddock replied darkly. "Jeanette, we know who is responsible. *We know*. It's solved. Tori and I just need another twenty-four hours to prove it. If I get bogged down with the Major Case Squad right now, we might miss our shot. I don't want to risk it. If we can't bring this home in that time, then I'll go to the Major Case Squad, clear my name and let them go after these guys."

"Friday night, Renko was shot and killed."

"Yes, he was," Braddock replied without a hint of regret. "And before you ask, yes, Tori and I were in New York City by then."

"Cripes. That doesn't help."

"We have an alibi," Tori said. "We're staying with friends of mine, former Bureau colleagues. It's where we're calling you from."

"That helps only so much," Boe said. "You two have said it yourself, this isn't some one-man operation. There are many involved."

"There are five to be exact. And they want me to name names," Braddock said. "And one of them would be Ira Renko."

"You're sure."

"We are sure," Tori replied. "But, even if he's dead, you can't just accuse the Chief of Internal Affairs without proof. Tonight, we're going to try and get it."

"How?"

"That plan is evolving."

"Evolving?"

"We're putting the pieces in place. We're counting on a couple of things to happen and Cardellini needs to come through," Braddock said. "I think she will."

"In the meantime?"

"Stall."

* * *

Cardi arrived at work, sunglasses covering her eyes, a large double-shot espresso in hand. She sat down at her desk, powered up her computer, flipped her sunglasses on top of her head and took a long drink of the coffee and contemplated where things were at.

What Braddock had in mind was both highly risky and perhaps the one way to truly prove the case from the inside—if it worked, and they skirted some of the questionable legality of it. And then, would the boss even go for it? She let out a big yawn as she waited for her computer to fire up.

"Late night?" White asked as he strolled to his office door.

"Yes." And now she had to go to work. "I need to tell you about it."

He caught the tone and nodded for her to come inside. She walked in and he closed the door behind them.

"Cole, do you trust me?" she asked as White sat down in his chair.

White eyed up his detective. "Cardi, what's up?"

"It's... it's..." She struggled for the metaphor. "Cole, it's kind of like a three-legged stool. One leg is, don't be angry—yet. Second leg, you're going to need to give me some rope to maneuver. Third leg is I'm going to need your help."

"Uh... okay. You're being oddly cryptic here."

"I am."

"Care to tell me why?"

"Hypothetically—"

"The three-legged stool analogy tells me this isn't hypothetical, Cardi. Just get to it."

She exhaled. "Yesterday, with my help, Will Braddock and Tori Hunter found who is responsible for all of this."

"Wait a second?" White held up his hand. "Your help?"

"Yes."

"Braddock is—"

"Not the one responsible for all this. But he, Hunter and I know who is."

"All of this? What... all of this?"

"Our case, the case. Guerero, Lange, Espinosa Warehouse, Malik Muhammed, Julio Gonzalez, *that* all of it."

"Who?"

She shook her head. "This is where I need you to trust me, and I want you to have some plausible deniability."

White eyed her up. "And I would need plausible deniability, why?"

"Because there was one name I left out of the 'all of this.'"

"One... name," White said, looking at her quizzically, then his eyes widened. "Wait. And you left... No..."

"Yeah."

"No."

"Oh yeah, Cole."

"Renko?"

"Yeah. He was involved in all this, fully involved."

White's face turned exactly that, white. "You're telling me that the Chief of Internal Affairs in this department was responsible for the murders of Dan Guerero, Ray Lange, and all the others?"

"He wasn't the trigger man most likely, but he was involved. He and another man named Carmine Stagliola." She told White about the connection between Renko and Stagliola. "And there are three others."

"And you can prove all this? Renko, this Stagliola?"

Cardi nodded. "Some of it."

"And you know who these men allegedly are?"

"We confirmed all three last night."

"Who?"

"Not yet," Cardi said. "This is where I need some rope. And your help. Braddock has an idea—"

"Damnit, Cardi! Braddock is under investigation. Regardless of what you think you know, he's still a prime focus of the investigation. MCS is trying to track him down as we speak."

"I bet Boe is running interference for him."

"She may be. But, Cardi, when they find out he's been here the last two days, that he was here the night Renko was murdered, they're going to come down on him and anyone around him. And you're setting yourself up to be anyone. How about we go to Major Case with all of this? Give ourselves some cover."

"Braddock fears that if he does that now, these guys will spook and run." She related Braddock's theory that these men likely had sources inside the department and were also likely ready to disappear at a moment's notice. "We just need another twenty-four hours. If we can't prove it by then, Braddock will go to the Major Case Squad himself with what we have. I just need you to trust me a little longer."

"How do you know you can trust Braddock?"

"I just... do."

"Not good enough."

"Cole, he and Hunter have this thing. *They've* found them. They are—" she held her index finger and thumb a centimeter apart "—this close to proving it. I just can't tell you who... yet."

"I need more. Especially given what Braddock is under investigation for."

"Braddock left New York eight years ago because he was under threat."

"From?"

"The same men who killed Dan Guerero, Ray Lange, and everyone else." She related the story about the picture. "He was getting close to them then and they threatened him, and his son. That's why he left. And that's why he's being so careful right now."

"And you saw this photo?"

"Yes."

"And you buy that?"

"I one hundred percent do."

"How can you be sure he's not playing you?" White pressed. "You want my help. Convince me I should give it."

"I buy it because Tori Hunter buys it. You know her history, what she's all about, her Bureau record. Part of my assessment of him, is hers."

"Cardi, she's not objective. She and Braddock are a thing."

"You think she's going to cover for him? I'm third-generation cop, she's second."

"Second?"

"Her father was sheriff of Shepard County for twenty years. He's a legend there."

"Meaning?"

"Do you think I'd harbor a cop killer? You think she would? Really?" Cardi shook her head. "No way. No fucking way. She'd shoot Braddock herself if she thought he'd done any of this. You haven't been around her. She's one tough cookie, let me tell you. If she trusts him, I trust him."

"That's the best you can do?"

"What more do you want, Cole?" Cardi pleaded. "They know who is responsible. Braddock and Hunter have shown me what they've found. I've talked to the detective in Toledo who helped them with Ana Gonzalez. Braddock and Hunter put her in protective custody, Cole. That triggered the move on Renko and I suspect this Stagliola as well." She paced in front of his desk. "I've connected the three men—whose names I'm not giving you yet—to Renko and Stagliola. Who Braddock and Hunter have their sights set on are the guys we're after. I know it, Cole, I know it. We need just one extra thing to bring them all down and that's where you come in." She leaned on his desk. "Are you going do me this favor or not?"

"What do you need?"

"Something I know you can arrange." She told him what Braddock and Hunter wanted to do. "That's how we prove it for sure."

"They need about six things to go right for that to work," White said, shaking his head.

"You going to step up or not," Cardi pressed.

"So, I'm being asked to provide this, but you're not going to tell me exactly who we're after."

"Like you said, a few things have to go our way. We just need people in the right position who will do what we need them to do." She went in for the final sale. "Cole, if this works, we could bring this case home—big time. Our unit, not Major Case Squad. And that isn't nothing, for you and me."

White snorted a laugh, and she knew she had him. He couldn't resist the upside. He couldn't really say no to the chance to bring it home. "Is there anything more you can tell me?"

"You should go to the event for Renko tonight at Lou's Pub out on Staten Island."

"They'll be there?"

"We're banking on it."

TWENTY-EIGHT
"PLEASE FOLLOW MY INSTRUCTIONS."

Vooch and Conn strolled through the parking lot outside Lou's pub. "There's Boo's SUV," Vooch said as they approached the front entrance. They could hear the rumbling din of the crowd inside. The sound hit them in full when Vooch opened the door. Just inside the vestibule was a wide placard sign on an easel for the memorial gathering for Renko.

Vooch led Conn into the mass of people.

"Lots of familiar faces," Conn said, as a woman carrying two glasses of white wine bumped his left shoulder, and he grimaced, trying not to react.

"Oh, I'm so sorry," she said. "I'm so, so, sorry. It's just so crowded in here."

"It's... okay."

It wasn't. Not only had some wine splashed on his sport coat but he felt the scorching jolt of pain down to his toes, doing all he could to suppress a scream.

Vooch saw his reaction, much as he tried to hide it. "Sorry, man, I completely spaced that when I led you this way."

"I'm going to have to find some more open space."

Vooch cut a wide swath as they made their way over to an

open area near the far windowed wall. "Hang here. I'll go get us a drink." Vooch was back a few minutes later with beers when a familiar face strolled up, carrying a beer of his own.

"Pauly, look at you," Vooch greeted with a warm handshake.

"Conn! Vooch! Haven't seen you two boys in a couple of years," Pauly said. A Staten Island boy they went back years with him and he was now a detective with the Major Case Squad. "I wish I was running into you guys under different circumstances. I know you were both friends with Renko."

"I hear you," Vooch said. "It's a shock man. Right on top of Ray Lange too. Are you on the case?"

"Yeah, I'm working it some. You guys see Renko anytime recently?" Pauly asked. "You two used to bowl with him once upon a time?"

"For a few years we did on one of the teams Lou's sponsored," Conn said and then looked to Vooch. "I haven't seen Ira in a good year, though. Had you?"

"Maybe six or seven months ago in here one night, in fact," Vooch said. "He was meeting some other friends, but we had a quick drink together and caught up. We talked about retirement as I've been and he was musing about it, though he was also talking about maybe another promotion, maybe to Chief of Department. I got the impression he was in the mix."

"Did he have a distant eye on the big chair, you think?" Conn said.

Vooch shrugged. "He was the type who would. Renko was a climber, always was, so, who knows. What happened to him? We've just heard rumors of stuff."

"Someone walked up on him and his lady friend in that alley and just mowed them both down," Pauly said, shaking his head. He peeked around before leaning in. "It was in cold blood, I'm telling you, cold fucking blood. Renko never even got his hand on his service weapon. And that's after Ray Lange last weekend out in Minnesota."

"Any leads?"

"Not from the scene." And then Pauly leaned in again. "It may be part of something else. The Cold Case investigation of Dan Guerero's murder is now part of our investigation. Ray Lange was shot out in Minnesota and Internal Affairs was part of the group digging into that, Renko included. Could just be a coincidence though I don't believe in them, not on something like this."

"Did they have a suspect?"

"Don't know but that doesn't get folded in unless someone thinks there's a strong connection. If there is, the case will move fast. Too many dead bodies for those responsible not to reveal themselves." Pauly glanced around. "I saw Coleman White a few minutes ago. He's the Commander of the Cold Case Unit. He was at the scene this morning. And Adrienne Cardellini, Cold Case Detective, she was there this morning too." He leaned back in. "Cardi's a little hard to not notice, you know."

"I don't know her," Conn said. "Who is she?"

Pauly looked around and nodded across the room, to an area up on a riser near the wall filled with pictures of Lou's Bar history, "She's over in that group there, the tallish one with the long black hair."

"Ah, I see her," Conn said.

"Interesting," Vooch said. "If you hear anything else, Pauly, I'd like to know. I'd lost some touch with Ira, but he was a good friend."

"I'll see what I can do."

As Pauly drifted away, they both saw Boo making his way through the crowd, three bottles of beer dangling in his thick fingers.

* * *

Cardi peered at the photo on the wall and then turned and looked out to the room before she took out her phone and snapped a quick photo, checked it and then texted it. She slid the phone into her blazer pocket and turned back to the rest of the room, taking in the massive crowd, able to see Coollee talking with a couple of other men at the bar.

She took a drink of her club soda and felt the phone vibrate, twice, reply text messages.

The first reply: *Great photo.*

The second reply: *Two bogeys coming in.*

She sent a text of her own and then made eye contact with the recipient at the bar, who gave her a nod back.

A few minutes later Phil Salvucci and Conn Dent stepped inside and immediately waded into the crowd, making for the bar. Then she saw Roz, two wines in her hands, bump into Dent, wine splashing out of the glass onto him.

Roz, you're a beauty.

The flinch and wince, it was slight, but there.

After Roz drifted away, the two men made a ninety-degree turn toward the side of the room, getting out of the mass of crowd to a more open area.

"Ladies and gentlemen," a voice boomed from the stage area. "I'd like to say a few words about my friend, Ira Renko."

As she listened to the speaker sharing a story, White approached, a beer in hand, his tie loosened at his collar. "Detective," he said quietly.

"Sir."

"Is everything set with my guys?"

"It is."

"Do you know your target?"

Cardi grinned. "We do now."

"Then I'm done with plausible deniability. I want to know."

She leaned in. "Turn around very slowly..."

* * *

It was after 11:00 p.m. when Boo led the two of them out the front door of Lou's and they walked to his SUV. "You boys hear anything tonight?" he said as he stopped at his Tahoe.

"Conspiracy theories galore," Conn said. "But Pauly spilled the tea a bit on MCS and the Guerero case now being folded in. There's a lot of people investigating this case now. Lots of profile because it involved Renko."

"As long as Renko was careful with his money, there will be no paper, or at least no paper that leads to us, and it ends there," Vooch said.

"I don't know," Conn said. "Something Pauly said, about too many bodies for the connection not to be found. It got me thinking about what we did on Renko."

"I'm not that worried about what *we* did on Renko," Boo said. "And I know he was careful with the money."

"What are you worried about then?" Conn said.

"What did Braddock and Hunter learn from Julio's wife? Julio must have given the cops Stag. Stag and maybe Renko. They went to Toledo. They found her and talked to her. What exactly are they doing with that information? I had an MCS guy actually tell me they want to talk to Braddock, but they can't find him right now. Where is he?"

* * *

"Is Boo overreacting?" Vooch said to Conn as they drove into Brooklyn.

Conn took a minute to think. "No. I get the concern, the worry. They were in Toledo and that changed things."

"Sure, for Stag and Renko. But how do they get from those two to us?" Vooch said. "That's what I don't see."

"Braddock is a capable guy. Hunter too."

"What are you thinking?"

"What we've been thinking. That it's time to go, Vooch. Boo said it the other day. You and I could go at any time. We've reached any time. I grabbed my stuff the other day. You did too. Why stick around?"

"You've got kids? Grandkids."

"I don't want to leave them, but I don't want the alternative either. If the storm passes, we can come back. If not, we're gone. I'll worry about the rest later."

Vooch contemplated what Conn was saying. "I know Boo thinks he needs to stick around for appearances, but I think he should bail too. Help me convince him tomorrow."

"Sure. But then I'm hitting the road, pal," Conn said. "And you should too."

"Agreed. I'll call Boo in the morning. Lunch? Get together and make the plan then? We all still need to stay in some touch."

"Yeah. How about the Peach?"

"Noon?"

"See you then."

Conn dropped Vooch off and pulled away. He turned up the music as he cruised east on Atlantic Avenue. All he wanted to do was get home, take a painkiller, apply some ice to his shoulder and get his left arm in the sling. He'd slept in the recliner last night and being a bit more upright helped with some support behind his left shoulder. It did make him feel a bit like an old man, sleeping in the recliner, waking to find the remote for the television in his right hand, empty beer cans on the light stand. In the morning, he'd pack a bag, then meet Boo and Vooch for lunch and by the end of the day, he'd be on a plane.

Letting out a big yawn, tired, he drifted a bit lazily into the right lane, jerking the wheel abruptly and then all the sudden there was bright flashing lights behind him. He looked up in the rearview mirror. "Ah shit. Shit, shit, shit."

The flashing blue and red lights from the light bar and grille filled the rearview mirror as the patrol unit pulled up on him. He took an immediate right turn into the parking lot for an auto repair shop and pulled to a stop.

The patrol unit pulled in behind him, stopping fifty feet back. The spotlight was on, filling the inside of the car with light. Checking the rearview mirror, he saw an officer slowly approaching and he powered down his window. As he looked up in the rearview mirror, another officer was outside the vehicle on the passenger side, his flashlight out, shining it in the back. *How many beers had he had?*

A uniformed officer stepped to the side of his car.

"Officer," he greeted.

"Sir. Do you know why I pulled you over?"

"Uh no."

"You were weaving in and out of your lane and then just changed lanes erratically and without signaling."

"Uh, sorry, Officer. I have a broken left collarbone. It makes it a little difficult to drive at times. I do apologize for that." He pulled back his shirt to reveal his brace. The officer leaned down for a close look, examining the left shoulder.

"Looks painful."

"It is."

The officer lingered for a moment before he stood back up. "Sir, I smell alcohol. Have you been drinking this evening?"

That was the question he was dreading. "Officer, my name is Conn Dent, NYPD retired. I was on the job twenty-five years. I'm eight blocks from home."

"Sir, that isn't an answer to my question."

"I'm asking you to do a brother in blue a solid here, huh? I was at an event tonight for Chief Renko, who was murdered on Friday night. It was a tough deal to be at."

The patrol officer peered down at him, searching the vehicle with his flashlight. "Sir, I need to ask you to step out of the vehicle."

"Really?"

"Sir, I'm requesting you get out of the vehicle," the officer said, this time his right hand resting on the handle of his service weapon.

They were going to put him through it. He nodded, reaching across his body to open the door with his right hand. He shoved the door open and then deliberately lifted himself up out of the vehicle and then made a show of gingerly holding his left arm close to his body.

"Please step to the back of the vehicle," the officer requested.

He did so slowly, judicious with his movements.

"When did you break your collarbone, sir?" the officer inquired.

"Oh... umm... a week ago."

"How did you do it?"

"Oh, I... uh... I... I slipped and fell. You know, landed hard on my shoulder."

"You sure about that?" the other officer asked. "You seemed a little uncertain."

Conn eyed up one officer and then the other. "Like I said, Officers, I'm a retired detective. I worked narcotics, tough stuff that work."

"I'm sure it was," the first officer said and then held up a pen. "Sir, please follow the pen with your eyes." The second officer kept his flashlight on him.

"Really, we're going to do this?"

"Sir. Please follow my instructions."

Conn sighed. "Yes, Officer." He stood still, focused on the

pen and let his eyes follow it as the officer moved it left, right and then slowly back left again. The officer put his pen back into his shirt pocket.

The second officer walked to a spot twenty feet away.

"Sir, please take nine steps heel-to-toe in a straight line to the officer," the first officer explained. "Then turn around and walk the same way back toward me."

Conn did as he was told, heel-toe walking deliberately, trying to keep his left arm still but he felt it, he was a bit unsteady as he made the walk, stumbling just a bit when he made the turn and slowly walked back to the first officer.

"Sir, are you taking medication for your broken collarbone?" the first officer asked.

Conn eyed the officer up. "I'm on pain medication for it, yes."

"Is that a prescription you have for it?"

"Uh... uh... y-yes."

"You sure about that," the second officer queried, putting the flashlight back up to his eyes. "You don't sound so certain."

"What is this shit!" Conn snapped. "I'll be talking to your commanding officer."

"Sir, you're free to do that," the first officer said evenly. "However, right now, I need you to stand on one leg and raise the other six inches, like this." He demonstrated the test. "And I'll need you to count, one-one-thousand, two-one-thousand, until I tell you to stop."

Conn shook his head. They were putting him through the paces. He contemplated which foot to use and settled on his right, thinking it was his stronger foot. "One-one-thousand. Two..." He got to eight-one-thousand and felt himself leaning a bit right. He tried stabilizing but overcorrected and felt himself teeter left and he dropped his left foot.

Shit.

ROGER STELLJES

"Sir, I'm placing you under arrest on suspicion of driving while under the influence."

"For this? Come on."

"Please turn and place your hands behind your back," the second officer said.

"I can't," Conn replied, closing his eyes. "I can't put my arm behind my back. Only in front."

"Very well," the officer replied and first cuffed his right wrist and then was cautious with his left wrist and then led him to the patrol cruiser and eased him down into the back seat and slammed the door closed.

They took him to the 75th Precinct. The first thing they had him do was take a breathalyzer test, administered by a bespectacled woman officer who couldn't have been all of five feet tall. She had him blow in the tube and then read the results.

".o8," she said. "That's over the legal limit. Sorry."

He was booked, photographed and fingerprinted. Two officers took him down to the holding cells.

"Sir, you'll need to take off your clothes and get into this gray jumpsuit."

Conn sighed. "Really? For this?"

"Sir, please follow the instructions," the officer implored. "And I will need to look under your brace, just to inspect for safety. I'll be careful."

Conn shook his head, rolled his eyes and then complied with the request.

The officer checked the right side first, looking under the brace and then the left side. "What's the bandage for?"

"When I broke my collarbone, I got cut as well. It's stitched."

The officer pulled the bandage away.

"Is that really necessary?"

"Just a precaution," the officer replied flatly, peeking quickly under the bandage. "It looks painful," he said as he carefully put the bandage back in place. "Please pull on the jumpsuit. You'll get your clothes back when you process out."

At this point, he would be in jail until he could get before a judge, probably in the afternoon. He laid down on the musty bed and let his eyes drift closed.

Conn's eyes fluttered open when he heard the cell door loudly slide open.

The officer came in with something that appeared to be a breakfast, a roll in a cellophane wrapper and a plastic bottle of juice. "I don't suppose I could get a cup of coffee?"

"I'll see what I can do," the officer replied. And he did, coming back a few minutes later with a short coffee with a plastic top.

"What time is it?"

"7:47 a.m."

After he downed the breakfast, the juice and the coffee, he laid back down on the cot, listening to the rhythm of the jail, the opening and closing of doors, the light conversation, the occasional loud warning. There was a holding cell down the way that sounded as if it had several people inside. He wondered about having a cell to himself but suspected that while the officers last night didn't cut him any slack, at least here at the precinct they'd offered some accommodation, not housing him with other suspects.

He heaved a sigh, lying back, closing his eyes, trying not to breathe in too much of the stench of the bed, mattress and cell.

Just get through this, get released and then get lost.

.   .   .

The wait had been another two hours, when his eyes slowly opened at the sound of his cell door opening.

"Sir, if you would come with me."

He pushed himself slowly up off the mattress, careful not to jostle his left shoulder. "What time is it?"

"10:33 a.m."

The officer led him down to a room with a table with two chairs, one on each side. He was directed to take a seat on the far side of the table, opposite a two-way mirror.

This seemed odd to him. What questioning would be left? He'd expected he'd be part of a cattle call of some kind to go in front of a judge and make a plea. "Why am I in here?"

"Just procedure, sir. I think someone realized who you were." The door closed.

I think someone realized who you were. It's about time.

Conn closed his eyes and let the same mantra roll through his mind: Just get out of here, go home, and get lost. By this time tomorrow, you'll be thousands of miles away.

He heard footsteps in the hallway and then keys in the lock.

The door slowly opened.

He would not be leaving the country at all.

TWENTY-NINE

"I'M THINKING ALL BAD THINGS."

Braddock, Tori and Cardi walked into the room. Dent stared back at them, his mouth agape.

"*Surprise!*" Tori taunted.

"Oh boy, you don't look happy to see us, Dent," Cardi said as she took a seat in front of him.

Tori leaned against the wall to his left and Braddock had walked behind him and rested his left hand on Conn's left shoulder, at first lightly but then he applied just a little pressure, enough to make Dent wince. "Hands off."

"Tender still, eh, Conn?" Braddock kept his hand there, letting his fingers rhythmically tap the damaged area of his shoulder. "We'll get to the cause here shortly."

"Who the hell are you guys?" Conn blurted.

Tori smiled, a big toothy grin. "Oh, Conn, come on. You *know* who we all are. It was written *all* over your face when we walked in here."

"And the look said: I'm screwed," Cardi said, but not smiling. "And you're right, you are."

"And the beautiful thing is, you set yourself up, dumbass," Tori needled. "Don't drink and drive."

"I'm thinking it was probably that third beer or maybe the fourth I saw you drink at Lou's that put you over the top," Cardi needled. "You made it easy for us."

"And then he smelled like a wino too," Tori teased.

"Made what easy?" Conn said. "What the fuck are you all talking about?"

"I'm talking about twelve murders, two attempted murders, and three drug robberies committed by you, former Terminal Operations Manager for the Port Newark Terminal, Carmine Stagliola, Chief of Internal Affairs, Ira Renko, former NYPD Narcotics Detective Phil Salvucci, and former Narcotics Detective John Boo Coollee," Braddock charged.

"The five of you," Cardi said, holding up her phone, showing the picture she'd taken at Lou's Pub. It was a photo from the wall, Stagliola, Renko, Coollee, Salvucci and Dent, a bowling team sponsored by the bar. "You all go *way* back."

"We know all of it, Conn," Tori said. "But most importantly for your purposes, you need to understand, we have *you* dead to rights. You're going to have to make some decisions and make them fast."

"I ain't saying anything without—"

"A lawyer?" Cardi said, holding up her hand. "And that's your right. However, I think you'd be wise to listen for a few minutes before you significantly delay matters by bringing a lawyer into this."

"I said—"

"You don't have to say a word," Tori asserted. "In fact, we don't want you to. Not yet anyway. We just want you to listen. A free preview of coming attractions, if you will."

Braddock sat on the edge of the table and leaned in on Conn. "Let me give you the facts there, Conny Boy. Last Sunday night, you were ten miles northwest of Manchester Bay at a hunting cabin out in the woods. At the cabin, *you*, along with Carmine Stagliola, Phil Salvucci and John Boo Coollee murdered NYPD Cold Case Detective Ray Lange and Julio Gonzalez, a witness. And I know this because they fought back against you and your friends and as a result you were shot in the left shoulder and were treated a few hours later by Doctor Julian Vance in St. Cloud at his clinic on Division Street for a gunshot wound to the left shoulder and a fractured clavicle. You paid Vance twenty-five thousand dollars cash for the treatment. The stitched wound on your clavicle is a rough V-shape because of how the skin tore from the gunshot wound. And two to three inches right of the wound are two round moles. How am I doing so far?"

Conn simply stared straight ahead.

"Now maybe you either don't know this part or didn't think it through, but we found blood at that scene, on a tree on the left side of the driveway," Tori said, piping in. "It wasn't much, but you don't need much for a DNA sample. Now all we needed was something to match it to." She paused for effect. "Did you know that we can get DNA from the saliva on the mouthpiece from the breathalyzer you took? The CSI who took that sample, was very, *very* careful."

Conn tried to give off an unworried vibe, but his eyes flinched, and he looked away from Tori. Problem was when he looked away from her, he looked right at Braddock.

"You didn't know, did you?" Braddock said, grinning.

"Oh, I don't think he did," Cardi chimed in.

"Rapid DNA analysis is a beautiful thing when you have two samples to compare," Tori explained as she stared down at Dent.

"We had to wait for some folks to get in for work here and in Minnesota, but they did, and you know what, Conn?" Braddock paused for a moment. "The DNA for your saliva was a perfect match to the DNA from the blood. You were there Sunday night." He gestured to Conn's left shoulder. "You were shot right there. I've got the doctor who treated you who can identify the scar and your two moles. And then, while we were awaiting the DNA results, we discovered the little security business you, Salvucci and Coollee are running. You papered it over pretty good."

"But we've got a crackerjack detective who is an absolute bloodhound on the paper trail, and she found you," Tori added.

"And with that business name, my detectives back in Minnesota chased down flight manifests for a private plane landing in Superior," Braddock continued. "That same plane then flew from Superior, Wisconsin to Detroit, arriving last Thursday night and then it flew out first thing this past Friday morning to Morristown airport over in New Jersey. Oh, and the personnel at Morristown airport were able to identify you as one of the people who got off that plane. In fact—" Braddock gestured to Cardi who put a surveillance photo on the table "—the people at the airport verified it was you, Salvucci, Coollee *and* Stagliola who all got off that plane."

"And those are the last people we have found that have seen Carmine Stagliola," Cardi said. "He has been missing since. He either flew the coop, or you all killed him because he was a liability because you know these two spoke to Julio Gonzalez's wife. In fact, not only did you ice Stagliola, but you did Renko too for the same reason."

"I think another relevant question is where do retired cops come up the scratch for private planes, I wonder," Tori mused. "The pensions for NYPD must be awfully good." She looked to Braddock. "You shouldn't have left."

"We'll get to my reason for leaving if we have to." Braddock turned back to Dent. "They can afford it because they made millions, *millions*, from the drugs they stole, like at Espinosa Warehouse. And you guys played it mostly smart, you know. Living nicely, but not too nicely, not in a way that would raise suspicion."

"Until Detective Ray Lange and I reopened Dan Guerero's

homicide investigation and found Julio Gonzalez in Superior," Cardi explained. "When that happened, you all had to activate. You couldn't have Lange talking to Julio, that would start the dominoes."

"And it did," Braddock continued. "You've been scrambling to cut all ties back to you ever since, but we found you and have now proved you were there and murdered Ray Lange and Julio Gonzalez. And now, that money, Conn? It's all gone. It's. Gone. You're never going to see any of it. It's over. At this point there is only one question left for you to answer."

"Yeah," Conn said, looking up at Braddock. "What's that?"

"How do I avoid going to a maximum-security prison on a life sentence as a cop."

"Because, Conn," Tori said, leaning on the other side of the table, "that's where you're going. I revel at the thought of what'll happen to you in the general population at Attica," she said, smiling. "I'd love to just sit with a bag of popcorn and watch them all tear you apart piece by piece."

"Ouch," Cardi taunted.

"You know the drill, Conn. The first one to talk gets the deal," Braddock declared. "And just so you don't think you can run out the clock or get a lawyer in here to get you released there is something else you need to know."

"Oh, I love this one," Tori said.

"You remember the officer that checked under your brace and saw the wound in your left shoulder, the V-shape of the stitches and the two moles to the right of it. That is just as Doctor Vance described to me last Thursday. That visual inspection, along with the DNA match, got us a search warrant for your house. We've been there the last couple of hours."

Tori stepped over and knocked on the two-way mirror. A few seconds later the door opened, and an officer handed Braddock a large evidence bag.

Braddock held up the evidence bag to Conn. "Does this

look familiar?" Braddock started laying out the contents of the bag. "We have the fake passport, the fake New Jersey driver's license to go with it, a nice stack of cash, two Visa credit cards for Edward Luck."

"Edward Luck," Tori snickered. "Is the middle name Bad?"

"It sure as hell ain't Good," Braddock continued. "I suspect the most important thing is this flash drive." He held it up to Dent's face. "I bet this has all your offshore bank account information on it. At least that's what the CSIs will find when they plug it into a laptop. I'm thinking you probably have a few different stash locations of this stuff, right? Probably within five minutes, ten at most, from your home at someplace you could access twenty-four-seven so that you could bolt at a moment's notice. You've probably had these just in case locations for years."

"Then Toledo happened," Tori said. "You had to take out Stagliola, and then Renko, and that poor woman friend of Renko's, Rita Hanratty, was just in the wrong place at the wrong time."

"Now, shit just got real and you might have to run. And soon. And I bet all three of you are thinking the same thing too. I bet Salvucci and Coollee retrieved their go-bags too, right? Right, Conn?"

Conn's eyes betrayed him, at first widening and then closing. They were right on this point. Salvucci and Coollee were both prepared to go.

"I thought so," Braddock said.

"It has to be just killing you." Tori chuckled, smiling. "You were this close, *this close*, to being gone, enjoying millions somewhere in the Caribbean, sitting on the beach, drinking umbrella drinks, finding a nice senorita for company when you wanted one."

"Poof," Braddock said. "All this—" he gestured to the

contents of the plastic bag "—will not save you now. The only question is where you go from here."

"And you're offering what?" Conn said.

Braddock looked to Cardi. "What is the NYPD offering?"

"You tell us everything, down to the last detail about every robbery, every murder, every nickel, all of it. In return, we will get you federal prison with a new identity. Western part of the country where nobody would recognize you. It'll be a life sentence, of course, but not maximum security and not as a cop. Your last days on this earth will be in prison, but you'll be able to serve your time without the worry of being turned into the prison bitch."

"That's it?"

"Or roll the dice. You're all going down for this one way or another."

"That's not much of a deal," Conn said.

"You've got twelve murders on your resumé. What do you expect?"

"If you're all so confident in your case, why offer *me* a deal at all?"

"Closure," Cardi replied. "Closure for Monica Guerero. Closure for Lange's family. Closure for all the victims' families. And—" she looked to Braddock "—closure for Braddock, his son Quinn, and Tori, for Ana Gonzalez and her daughter Emma."

"And one other thing," Braddock said.

"What's that?"

"You had this go-bag. Salvucci and Coollee probably have the same thing. If they run before you talk, no deal."

Conn took a moment, contemplating all that had been put in front of him. "Better get me a lawyer to walk me through this."

In the hallway, they found Coleman White waiting for them. "Public defender will be here soon."

"How many people are watching Coollee and Salvucci?"

"A two-man team on each of them."

"That's not enough. Double, triple it up," Braddock demanded. "And get an Emergency Services Unit teed up."

"You think they'll throw down?" White asked.

"After all they've done to get to this point," Tori replied, shaking her head, "they won't go quietly."

* * *

Vooch pulled the door open, and Boo stepped inside the Peach and looked for Conn.

"Where is he?" Boo said, slipping off his sunglasses. "You see him?"

"No," Vooch said. "He must be running behind."

"We're ten minutes late."

"So is he."

A hostess arrived at the stand and showed them to a booth. A server was there quickly with menus and took their drink order.

The Peach was a place they would go to from time to time and neither of them needed much time with the menu. They had each ordered iced tea which the server brought. They asked for a bit more time to order. "We're waiting on a third."

The server drifted away, and they talked for a bit, constantly checking their phones. "Give him a call," Boo directed.

Vooch tried calling him, but the call ended up in voicemail. "Where are you? The Peach at noon, remember?"

"How was he when he dropped you off last night?"

"Seemed fine. Tired. I think his shoulder was bothering him. He complained about it."

Boo checked his watch. Conn was over a half-hour late and he was, if anything, someone who was punctual. "Any chance he mixed his meds and booze too much?"

"Ooo," Vooch grimaced. "I didn't think of that. You want to go check?"

The server approached again. "Are we still waiting on one more?"

"We were," Boo said, "But we have to go."

* * *

The public defender spent fifteen minutes talking Dent through his options. He came back to find them.

"Twenty years in a federal minimum-security prison camp in a southern climate," the attorney said. "Give him that, he'll tell you everything."

"No," Cardi growled. "Twenty years? We're talking about a dozen murders, two of which are good cops plus attempts on Braddock and Tori. Club Fed, are you serious?"

"He's got kids—"

"So did all the cops he killed," Braddock railed and then gestured to Tori. "And so do we!"

"He's got grandkids too," the public defender insisted.

"With what they have on him?" the assistant district attorney replied to the attorney. "It's life with the possibility of parole after twenty-five years. And we'll go medium security and if he behaves himself, in five years, we'll get him moved to low security, but he's not going to Club Fed. He's not a financial fraudster. He's a killer who is going to prison."

The attorney sighed. "I'll be back."

After he left, Tori turned to Braddock. "*We* have kids?"

"Yeah, *we* do."

* * *

Boo pulled up in front of the duplex. Conn lived in the left-side unit. He and Vooch walked up to the front door and Vooch pressed the doorbell. They listened but they didn't sense any movement inside, even after pressing the doorbell again.

Boo looked up. "The porch light is still on."

"On for the garage too," Vooch said and walked further up the driveway to the detached garage and peeked in the one of the windows. "His car isn't inside."

Boo took out his phone and was going to try calling him again.

"You're back again?" a neighbor said from behind her back-screen door.

"Again?" Boo said, holding up. "What do you mean?"

"Well, there were police here earlier, or at least I think they were police," she said. "They went in Conn's side, were around for maybe twenty minutes, a half-hour and then left. They didn't make a big show of it, but I could tell they were police."

"You don't say," Vooch replied.

"Who are you guys if you're not cops? You sure look like cops."

"Friends of Conn, just looking for him," Boo replied. "Have you seen him?"

"No. I haven't. Not since about this time yesterday."

"Thanks for letting us know."

Boo and Vooch walked purposefully back down the drive-way, their faces straight ahead but their eyes carefully darting about. "Assume we're being watched," Boo murmured.

They got into the car.

"What are you thinking?" Vooch said.

"I'm thinking all bad things," Boo replied as he pulled away, his eyes drifting up to the rearview mirror, driving back north to Atlantic Avenue. "He's in custody. If detectives searched the house, they had a search warrant. If they had that, they got something pretty good on him. Something to break him with."

"He won't say shit," Vooch replied.

"Don't be so sure. We're all staring down a life sentence

here. Is everything you need at your condo?" Boo asked. "I mean in and out in just a few minutes?"

"We're bailing."

"Right now."

"I've got it at my place, or we could go to one of the backups at the storage lockers."

"I could do that too, but if they are watching and we do that—"

"They jump us."

"That's what I'm thinking," Boo replied, peering up. There was a dark four-door sedan just a few cars back. He'd seen it since he'd turned back west on Atlantic Avenue. There were two men in the front. Vooch, slumped down in the front passenger seat, was eyeing the side mirror and he'd seen it too.

"We have company."

"I think so. I've got this covered," Boo assured and took out his phone, "Stella, it's John. Remember that favor I said I might need? ... Yes, the one I left you money for... Drop whatever you're doing and do it right now."

* * *

It felt like it took the lawyer another hour. It was only another fifteen minutes. "He'll take the deal."

"Let's lock this in," White said. "At least generally. Then we move on Coollee and Salvucci."

Braddock, Tori, Cardi and this time White and the assistant district attorney went back into the room along with Dent and the public defender.

"We're going to need days to get all the details down, but I'm going to make this quick," Braddock said. "The Espinosa Warehouse. That was a five-man operation. Carmine Stagliola and Ira Renko at the port, you, John Coollee and Phil Salvucci at the warehouse, correct?"

"Yes," Conn said.

"Why did you kill the six people at the Espinosa Warehouse?"

"It was not the plan. However, the gang guys showed up early. We were going to walk but then they saw us. Boo made the call like that and we smoked them."

"Coollee made the call?"

"Yes. This whole thing was his operation from the get-go. He had the leads on the drug deliveries through contacts from his undercover work. He gave some of those contacts a taste of the proceeds."

"And you took down how many of those?"

"Three. Espinosa, another one in Manhattan, one out in New Jersey. You know the ones. You had them pegged when we warned you off."

"Who killed Dan Guerero at the bodega?" Braddock asked.

"Salvucci was the decoy at the register to draw Guerero's attention. Boo came in the back and shot him. I was the driver," Conn answered.

"And Renko, he ran and hindered the investigation on Guerero's murder," Tori led.

"He directed it away from us for sure."

"He knew you were going to do Guerero?"

Conn nodded. "He did. He left the details to Boo."

"And then when I started digging into it, why warn me off? Why not kill me too?" Braddock asked.

"Boo wanted to, but Renko said no," Dent replied. "He said that if we killed you after Guerero, it would bring way too much heat and the Guerero case would get life again. So, we warned you off. When you moved away, we thought it was all done, other than Julio. He was a loose end. We tried to track him down for years, but he was elusive and then enough years passed that the urgency waned. That ramped up again when the Guerero investigation was reopened. But we couldn't find him. Then Renko learned Julio had been found too late for us to get to him before Lange did. In Manchester Bay, Lange and Julio were in the same spot. It wasn't much of a choice."

"Who shot Ray Lange?" Tori asked.

"Boo."

"But you and Salvucci were there, covering the driveway. You two were firing at the cabin?"

"We were."

"You were on the left," Tori gestured. "And Salvucci on the right?"

"That's correct."

"And you were shot in the left shoulder?"

"By Lange. He had left the cover of the cabin for his car. I think his gun, or a backup piece was in the car."

"Did you dump the bodies of Lange and Julio in the river before or after you went to get treatment for your wound?" Braddock asked.

"During. I was getting treated. Boo and Stag dumped the car and bodies in the river."

"And Doctor Vance treated you and Salvucci was with you, yes?"

"Correct."

"Who shot me?" Braddock asked.

"Salvucci. I was his driver."

"And the attempt on Tori?" Cardi asked.

"Boo was driving. Stag was with him."

"And what was your thought in attempting that? Why try to kill them?"

Conn shrugged. "Braddock was *your* primary focus. If we killed Braddock, he would still be your focus. If we only killed Braddock, we worried Hunter would dig into this, which we didn't want, so we thought take her too."

"And who murdered Chief Ira Renko and his friend Rita?" Cardi said.

"Boo and Salvucci. I drove."

"Why kill Renko?" Tori asked.

"You and Braddock," Conn replied. "You got to Ana Gonzalez in Toledo before we did. We figured she gave you Stagliola's name and maybe a description of Renko. It was kill them, or all of us go down."

"And what are Salvucci and Coollee's plans?"

"I don't know. We were going to discuss it today."

"When?"

"What time is it?"

"It's 1:20 p.m."

Conn winced. "I was supposed to meet them for lunch at noon."

"Where?" Braddock asked.

"The Peach."

"On Atlantic Avenue?"

"Yes."

"You should have said something," Braddock growled before nodding for everyone to step into the hallway. He looked over to the assistant district attorney. "That's enough on Coollee and Salvucci, isn't it?"

"For now, yes. Like you said, we'll need to nail down more of it later."

"What are you thinking?" Cardi asked.

"That we need to get moving, and right now."

THIRTY

"THE CYCLONE."

"Are they still back there?" Boo inquired as he turned right off south 7th Avenue to 9th Street.

"Yes," Vooch replied, having adjusted the side mirror for a better line of sight. "I make two cars now, rotating, one black, one silver. Two men in each."

The side streets in his neighborhood were one-ways running east and west. Boo turned left off 9th Street onto 6th Avenue, drove south one block and then turned left onto the narrow 10th Street, which was a one-way running back east. It was a tightish squeeze with vehicles parked on both sides of the street. Vooch peered back to see a silver sedan make the turn and then immediately pull to the right side, parking partially in the crosswalk.

"Hard to follow on these streets, isn't it?" Vooch muttered.

Boo found a parking space on the left side of the street close to the intersection for 7th Avenue. They were both carrying, and each chambered a round before they got out. Vooch grabbed his duffel bag from the floor. They walked along the sidewalk. At the corner they turned left onto the 7th Avenue sidewalk and walked a quarter of the block to the entrance to the building and went inside.

"I think the black sedan that was following us is parked up the block on 7th," Vooch said as they stepped inside the door.

"See any others?"

"No, but you know they're out there."

They took the steps to Boo's second-floor apartment. Inside Vooch went to the right side of the front window and careful not to disturb the curtains, carefully peered around the corner of them. He could see the black sedan and then, not that he needed confirmation, he got it. The man in the passenger seat raised up a police radio. "What's our move here?"

Boo came out of his office with two black backpacks, and wearing a blue bucket hat and tossed a blue baseball hat to him. "Come on."

* * *

"We have two units but two more on the way to join in. Coollee and Salvucci are together in Coollee's vehicle," White stated as they got ready to depart the precinct building. "They just made their way around Grand Army Plaza and are driving south on Prospect Park West."

"They have to be going to Coollee's apartment," Tori said. "His building is on 7th Avenue."

"Agreed," White said. "ESU is on route. Cardi and I need to get over there," he added as he and Cardi pulled on their Kevlar vests.

"What about us?" Tori said. "We want in."

"You don't have the gear. Once they're in custody, you'll get your shot. We'll handle them like we handled Dent, but we're taking no chances with anyone else. If you two are right and these two won't go down without a fight, then I'm keeping you out of the fray."

"Fine but we're still driving over to watch," Braddock said.

"Watching's acceptable but I better not see you anywhere near the building," White said and tossed Braddock a small police radio. "Just listen."

Braddock and Tori followed White and Cardi, who were zooming through traffic with lights and sirens. Braddock barely kept up with White ripping through intersections. He laid the horn on more than once to keep an intersection clear.

As they finally turned left onto 7th Avenue and drove south, White turned off the lights and sirens. The radio burped that ESU was staging two blocks north at New York Presbyterian Brooklyn Methodist Hospital. White turned left to meet up with them. Braddock drove ahead another block, finding an open parking space on the right side of the street just short of the intersection of 7th Avenue and 9th Street, next to the entrance down to the subway. "Coollee's place is up on the right close to the other end of the block?"

"It is. We can *watch* from here," she said sardonically. It almost seemed anticlimactic to be in the observing position. She took in their surroundings, 7th and 9th being a busy corner with a lot of pedestrian traffic on Labor Day. Immediately to their left on the northeast corner was Smiling Vittorio's Pizza Pad that appeared to be popular with the locals. "I've never eaten there. Have you?" Tori asked.

Braddock smiled. "Many, many a time in my youth. Vittorio's has been around forever. My folks brought me there, I went there with high school and college friends."

"Meghan?"

"One time. We were coming back from Coney Island. We'd taken a day trip down on the subway. Walked the boardwalk, played some games, went on all the rides."

"The Cyclone."

"Oh yeah, Thunderbolt, Soaring Eagle, Steeplechase, The Tickler! We took a ride on all the coasters."

"You remember all the names of all the rides!"

"Oh, hell yeah. I've told you many times, my parents weren't much for venturing far from Long Island. They were home bodies. But they loved Coney Island. We came down at least once a summer and the old man who was pretty darn frugal, was more than happy to keep shoveling out the dollar bills to pay for me to go on ride after ride or play the arcade games. For some reason he got a kick out of that. He and Mom would sit on a park bench, eat an ice-cream cone and watch me go again and again. So, I wanted to show Meghan that. Then at the end of the day, she was hungry for pizza, *good* pizza."

"And you knew just the place."

"We took the F train back to here." He gestured to the steps leading down to the Subway for the F and G trains. "We came right up those steps and went and had pizza at Vittorio's."

"Did she like it?"

"Oh, maybe not as much as me but like Coney Island, it was one of those things that was part of my childhood that I wanted to share with her."

Tori smiled. "Sounds like a great day."

"It was a good, *good* day. It wasn't long after that, we found out she was pregnant with Quinn."

"Another good day."

"Yeah."

"I'm glad to hear you talk about good days from back then because I have to think this whole thing has brought back memories of a lot of bad ones."

Braddock nodded. "I had something this time I didn't have last time I was dealing with this... case. With Dan's murder."

"What's that?"

"You."

The police radio crackled that ESU was moving.

"Here we go," Braddock said.

"I hate not going in," Tori muttered. "Feels very—"

"Unsatisfying."

"Yes," Tori said emphatically. "You and I should be putting the bracelets on these two."

"I'll take the win."

"Have White and Cardi informed MCS about any of this?"

"I don't think so," Braddock said. "They've played it close to the vest to get it here."

"That could be a problem for them."

Braddock snorted a laugh. "This is their case. Fuck MCS."

Tori looked back and saw the black NYPD ESU unit truck that looked like a tank roaring up the street. White and Cardi were right behind as they pulled to a stop in front of the apartment building. The ESU officers in their tactical gear jumped out the back and raced to the door to the building and then inside, Cardi and White right behind.

"When's the last time White went in on something like this, do you figure?" Tori said.

"Years, but a case like this," Braddock said, with a sly grin, "that's too tantalizing to pass up. Plus, these guys killed his detective. I'd want to be there for that. Especially if it was a turncoat cop who did it."

Tori looked ahead, watching the apartment building, waiting on news from the radio.

"We're in position," a voice reported.

"Go!" White ordered.

They waited, staring intently at the apartment building. Pedestrians stood back, curious at the sudden police presence. A woman scurried away with her daughter. Two men exited a neighboring apartment building and walked swiftly toward them in medical scrubs. Two women in their twenties hustled out of the way, though they looked back in interest. A crowd of curious onlookers had started gathering on the corner in front of them as well as across the street at the pizza place. One could sense the murmur of excitement pulsing through the throng.

"They're not here!" the radio cackled.

"What?" Braddock blurted, turning to Tori. "Not there."

"The apartment is empty," the voice on the radio reported. "I say again, the apartment is empty."

"Coollee," Braddock muttered in disgust. "He saw this coming."

Tori peered through the crowd on the corner. Across the street she saw the two men in medical scrubs again. The taller wider one wore a blue bucket hat pulled down tight. The other had a faded Brooklyn Dodgers baseball cap on. Both men ignored the activity behind them as they carried backpacks and descended the steps down one of the 7th Avenue entrances to the subway station below.

"Lock the building down," White ordered. "Start a search. Two-man teams."

Tori reached for the door handle.

"Where are you going?"

"I think..." She looked to the subway station entrance to their immediate right. In fact, there were subway entrances on all four corners of the intersection with the F & G subway lines both running under 7th Avenue.

"What?"

"Come with me," she said and jumped out.

"Tori?"

"I saw two men in medical scrubs exit the building north of Coollee's," she said.

"Yeah, I caught a glance of them too," he replied as he got out.

"They went down to the subway station."

"So?" He gestured to the hospital. "They were going to work."

"Are they? The hospital is only two blocks north of here so why go down to the subway? This is the hospital stop. But in this area, dressed in scrubs they wouldn't—"

"Look out of place," Braddock said, walking around to the sidewalk. "They'd blend."

"Coollee and Salvucci knew they were being followed?" Tori said, stepping to the subway steps.

"Dent didn't show at the Peach," Braddock observed. "That put them on guard. And who's better at spotting cops than—"

"Cops," Tori said.

"We're not doing anything here. Let's go see," Braddock commanded. They hustled down the steps beneath the ground to the subway station.

"The turnstile?" Tori said.

"Hurdle it," Braddock said as he threw himself over.

Tori leaped over and they rushed through the iron gates onto the long, wide platform just as the nose of the southbound train pulled into the station, the brakes whistling as the long train of cars slowed.

They both scanned the pending riders on the busy platform as they waited for the train to stop and the doors to open.

"Do you see them?" Tori said, straining to see around and over people. It was moments like these that five-foot-five in sneakers was not tall enough.

"Not yet."

The train doors opened.

It was chaos.

A wave of riders spilled out as new riders jockeyed for position to get onto the train. The number of people to sift through had instantly doubled. It was a mass of people bumping into one another on a Labor Day Holiday Monday at a busy multi-track subway station.

Braddock used a wide pillar for cover while he scrutinized the riders on the platform. If they came down the steps on the south side of 7th, they would most likely be on the other end of the platform at the front of the train.

"Do we get on?" Tori said urgently, moving toward the last

car of the train. Most everyone was off the train, and now most had gotten on, the crowd on the platform thinning.

"*Do we!*"

* * *

Boo had led Vooch to the roof of his building. They worked their way north, over seven waist-high dividing walls for other apartments, until they reached the last apartment building of the same height. Boo had a key to the emergency door for the building and led Vooch down to another apartment on the second floor, unlocked the door and they stepped inside.

"Whose place is this?"

"Stella's unit," Boo replied. "She's my renter and she and I occasionally, you know."

"Yeah, yeah."

"Change into the scrubs in the backpack and transfer all your stuff in there," Boo said, while he too changed into his own pair of scrubs and then pulled on the bucket hat. Vooch pulled on an old navy-blue Brooklyn Dodgers baseball hat.

Boo was at the front window and now had a view of the back of the black sedan. Then he looked north and saw the black ESU truck coming south. "Let's go."

At the bottom of the steps in the vestibule for the entrance to the building, Boo looked to his right and waited for the ESU officers to charge inside the building for his apartment.

"Come on. Rush but don't hurry."

* * *

Braddock looked over the heads of riders. It was times like this being six-foot-four was helpful.

A man in a blue bucket hat came from behind a far pillar, along with another in a blue baseball cap. *Was it them?*

"Braddock!"

They'd have to find out.

"Get on the train!" Braddock said, rushing over, grabbing Tori by the arm and getting onto the last train car as the doors started closing.

"Where are they?"

"First car, *I think*.

"You think?"

"I saw the blue bucket hat, so if that was him, they got on."

"*If* that was him?"

"I took a chance. We'll have to move forward and confirm."

Braddock moved to the front of the car and looked up to the map and video display board.

"Prospect Park stop is coming up quick," Tori said. "Like, two minutes."

The train pulled into the station and Braddock and Tori moved to the sliding door. The second it opened they stepped out onto the platform and walked toward the front of the train, slowly working their way through the departing and entering crowd, eyes on the first car ahead. Braddock was able to see over the crowd as they pressed ahead from one car to another as the crowd thinned, they stepped into the fourth subway car.

"You didn't see them get off?"

"No," he replied. "If it's them, I'm thinking they want to put some distance between them and the condo." He looked up to the subway map. The next stop was Church Avenue, a few minutes away. At that stop, they slipped out of the front of the fourth car, passed the third car and darted immediately into the back of the second car and hung by the open door, both watching the first car but they didn't see them exit.

The doors closed and the train pulled away again.

Tori, with Braddock following, made her way to the front of the train car and went to the left side of the small front door and peered around the edge. Braddock, who'd been right behind her, took the right side. Tori, crouched low, took a careful peek, looking through the window from their door and through the window of the rear door of the front car. "I think I can see Coollee. What do you think?"

"Yeah. I see Salvucci too, blue baseball hat, hospital scrub pants," Braddock said, ducking back, and reaching for his police radio.

"Don't use that," Tori whispered, looking back to their full train car. "You'll freak people out." She took out her phone and called Cardi. It took a few rings for her to answer.

"Tori, we're searching the building. Stay outside. I'll call you back."

"Hold on! *Hold on!*" She halted for a second, lowering her voice to a whisper. "You're not going to find them there. Coollee and Salvucci are on the F train heading south. We've just pulled out of Church Avenue Station."

"We? You and Braddock are on the train. H-H... How?"

"I'll explain that later. What matters is we don't know where they're getting off, but they have a destination in mind."

"Ahh, for fuck's sakes," Cardi groused and then Tori heard her yell. "We've been suckered."

* * *

Coollee answered the call from Stella. "Where did you park it? ... Alright, that works... Good girl." He hung up.

"The car?"

"We're set. Not even a five-minute walk from the train station."

Their subway car was perhaps three-quarters full, a large group of people who appeared to be good friends were riding at the far end, talking, hollering, laughing, having a good time. As the train rolled south, they passed through a couple of stations that had nobody on the platforms and stopped only briefly at other stations that had a few people waiting on the platforms. Fewer and fewer people were getting on or off the further south into Brooklyn they went. The doors only stayed open for fifteen to thirty seconds before they closed, and the train rolled again. Given what they could see, they suspected many in their car were going to the same destination they were.

*　*　*

After Church Street Station, the train came above ground up onto elevated tracks, McDonald Avenue running directly beneath them. Warm afternoon sunlight filled the train cars with light.

"I liked it better in the tunnel with less light," Braddock murmured. "Be careful, sit back, it's easier to see."

Tori leaned back, still on the phone. "We just blew by King's Highway Station," she whispered to Cardi. "The train barely slowed. There was nobody on the platform."

"What's the next stop?"

Tori looked up at the F Line map. There weren't many stops left but the one at the end was a big one.

"Tori?"

Tori whispered to Braddock. "Are they going where I think they're going?"

He was checking the map as well. "We've come this far."

"Where?" Cardi asked.

"Coney Island Station," Tori said. Braddock waved for the phone and Tori handed it to him.

"Cardi, it's Labor Day. The station will be a zoo, as will the beach and amusement park. They can get lost in the crowds, especially if they split up. It's a short drive to JFK International from there. They could get on a boat in Sheepshead Bay. Lots of transport options and ways to disappear from there."

"Car," Tori said. "They could have a car waiting."

Braddock nodded. "That's a thought. They probably do. Cardi, where are you?"

"We're coming, but probably still ten minutes away even with lights and sirens. Like you said, its Labor Day, in New York City."

"Call in some patrol units to the area around Coney Island Station, but don't converge until we know where they're going. Let's get them away from crowds if we can."

"Copy that."

* * *

They reached the stop at Neptune Avenue. To Boo's surprise, the big group at the back of the car got off. He thought for sure they were destined for the amusement park. A man and a woman stepped onto the train in their place. The woman was very fetching in a low-cut summer dress that left little to the imagination. He let his eyes linger on her for a moment as she sat down on the bench with her beau.

"He outkicked his coverage," Vooch muttered.

"Indeed," Boo replied as they pulled away from the station and sunlight again filled the train car—and then it filled the car behind them with light, and he froze. She was staring right at him, if for but a second or two before she pulled back.

"Vooch," he whispered.

"Yeah," Vooch said.

"The other end of the car, at the door, peering through from the other car."

"What?"

"Someone is watching?"

Vooch pulled down the brim of his ballcap and leaned down to fiddle with his backpack at his feet and let his eyes drift left, unzipping the top of his backpack. It took fifteen seconds. There was a woman, being very careful but she was sneaking a peek at the right side of the window. "It's a woman. She's interested."

"I've got a man looking too on the left side," Boo added, looking down at his backpack, pulling out a zip-up hoodie. Vooch took his out as well and pulled it on.

* * *

"They saw me," Tori muttered. "Dammit."

"They both were looking back," Braddock replied calmly. "They were going to see us sooner or later."

"I was hoping for later."

"They're pulling on hoodies," he said. "You don't need those when it's eighty-six degrees outside. They're going to be making a move." He unbuttoned his sport coat.

Tori raised her phone to her ear. "Cardi. Stand by."

"What's happening?"

"Something."

The train started to slow. They were coming into the Aquarium Station, the last stop before Coney Island Station which was another half mile away. Braddock moved to the nearest door. No sense hiding now. Tori peered around the corner, through the windows into the front car. Coollee and Salvucci were still sitting, holding their backpacks.

* * *

Boo peered back to the rear emergency door. The woman knew that she had been seen and in another flash of sunlight that hit her face, he recognized her.

"It's Hunter," he said under his breath. "It's Braddock and Hunter. Should have known."

"If it's just them," Vooch said. "It's two on two then."

The train slowed as it arrived at Aquarium Station. Boo

contemplated their options. If they'd been watching now since 7th Avenue, they had to have figured their final destination.

The train pulled to a stop.

"Boo," Vooch muttered.

"Hold."

A half-dozen people got out of their train car and others were disembarking from the other cars. Some crowd cover.

"Boo," Vooch uttered more urgently. "It's gonna close."

Three... Two... One...

"*Go!*"

* * *

The train slowed coming into Aquarium Station. She had been here at least once, maybe twice though it had been years. It was an open-air station on elevated tracks. There was a long stairway down to street level. Braddock stood by the open door, Tori still peering into the first car. Coollee and Salvucci each stood, holding a vertical bar, as if they were going to stay on the train. She could feel the countdown, most everyone off the train now, nobody new getting on.

Coollee darted for the door, Salvucci right behind.

"They're getting off!" she said as she bolted from her seat.

Braddock held his body against the sliding doors as they started to close. She turned sideways as she jumped through and then grabbed Braddock's hand, pulling him away from the closing door.

"Where are they?"

"They're going down the steps," Tori said and the two of them jogged ahead, turned right and peered down the long run of steps.

"Cardi, they got off at West 8th Street. The Aquarium Station," Tori reported.

Coollee and Salvucci were two-thirds of the way down the steps. Salvucci looked back up.

* * *

"They're coming. Hunter's on the phone," Vooch reported.
"We gotta hustle."

* * *

Braddock saw the two of them take off and then veer left at the bottom of the steps. "They're running!" He took the steps down rapidly two at a time.

Tori followed. "Cardi, they're running."

"Where?"

"Stand by."

At the bottom of the steps, they turned left, emerged from under the canopy for the steps into the sunlight and could see Coollee and Salvucci running south, toward the ocean visible in the distance. They turned right at the intersection. "What street is that?"

"Surf Avenue," Braddock said as they jogged ahead.

"West on Surf Avenue. They're in dark hoodies, light-blue medical scrubs for pants. Coollee's wearing a blue bucket hat. Salvucci a blue Brooklyn Dodgers hat."

They could hear sirens in the distance.

"Tori, patrol units are coming. We're coming, we're about a mile away."

The Cyclone roller coaster towered in the air on the opposite side of the street, framing the east end of amusement park.

* * *

White maneuvered through the congested afternoon traffic, ESU a block behind them as they raced south on Ocean Parkway. Another patrol unit turned left onto the road ahead and Cardi caught a glimpse of another turning onto the road behind them, coming up on the ESU truck.

"Tori, we're coming down Ocean Parkway. We'll be coming in behind you." She flipped to the radio. "Units converging on Coney Island Park..." She provided the description of who they were looking for.

"Describe Braddock and Hunter," White said.

"Be advised, two plain clothes officers are in pursuit of suspects on foot. One male, Will Braddock, six-four, black hair wearing a dark-blue plaid sport coat and blue jeans. The other a woman, Tori Hunter, medium height, light-brown hair in a ponytail, wearing a linen gray blazer."

* * *

Boo sprinted ahead, the historic Cyclone wooden rollercoaster on their left, the cars roaring and voices screaming as the cars raced down the rails from the top of the coaster. The amusement park was packed. "Come on."

He sprinted across the street, in between cars going east-west, honking as he and Vooch weaved their way through. Once on the sidewalk they ran past the end of the Cyclone and turned left.

* * *

They were fifty yards behind them as Braddock led them through the traffic, holding up his arm to hold off the east bound traffic, ignoring the honks, profanity and gestures.

"They just ran into the park."

"Cardi," Tori reported. "They're in the amusement park. East end. We're coming in behind them."

Braddock reached for his gun, leaving it in the holster, as they approached the corner of Surf and West 10th Street and he peeked around the corner. Coollee looked back before he and Salvucci turning right into the park.

"They're in the amusement rides, just west of the Cyclone," Tori reported.

"Half mile out," Cardi answered.

* * *

There were people everywhere. The sounds of the rides and people combined for a roaring cacophony of sound.

Boo looked back. "We have to shake them loose," he said as they hustled past the Hang Glider ride. "The car is on the south end of West 15th. Four blocks. A champagne-colored Honda Accord. Keys under the seat."

"Got it," Vooch said.

"I ain't going to prison, man," Boo said, eyeing his partner up. "You hear me? I ain't fucking going."

"Me neither."

* * *

Braddock reached the public entry and cautiously peeked right around the corner. "I see them." He turned the corner, Tori on his right hip and they instantly saw them split, Coollee left, Salvucci right. "I got Coollee," Braddock said and shuffled to the left.

"Cardi, they've split up in the middle of the park. They're moving west, we'll keep pushing them that way. I gotta hang up."

"Tori—"

She veered to the right of the Hang Glider ride and saw Salvucci going left around the Tickler roller coaster. She followed, stopped at the corner of the roller coaster barrier, and peeked left to see Salvucci look back as he ran into a narrow arcade walkway.

Tori fast walked ahead in a crouch, holding to the left side of the walkway, her right hand inside her blazer, fingers loose on the gun grip. She had zero desire to pull. Despite the carnival-like sound assault on her ears, the sirens in the distance told her help was coming. She just had to stay on him.

Salvucci turned left and she sped ahead to the corner and peered left around the corner into the crammed corridor of arcade games.

* * *

Vooch turned left and instantly wadded into a mass clustering of people hovering around the arcade games, gift, and concession stands. Up ahead was another turn to the right. Just as he turned, he looked back and saw her again, peeking around the corner, getting closer. He pulled his gun out of his pocket and pivoted.

* * *

Tori saw Salvucci swing around. *Oh man.*

"Gun! Get down! *Get down!*"

She ducked back.

Crack! Crack! Crack!

"This way! This way!" Tori yelled, crouched, waving people toward her, grabbing a little girl by the arm and pulling her around the corner.

She peeked back around the corner. A woman was lying on

her back on the ground, and she could see that she was wounded in the chest.

People fled, yelling and screaming.

Tori pulled her gun, sprinted across to the other side and moved forward, her gun up, as she approached the corner where Salvucci turned right. She took a quick look around the corner onto Bowery Street and saw Salvucci running across the street in the distance.

She turned the corner and pushed ahead, her gun in her right hand, hanging low, both moving with and against the fleeing crowd, keeping to the right side where there was more cover.

* * *

"Tori! Tori!" Cardi looked at the phone. "Dammit."

"She hung up?"

"Coollee and Salvucci split up," she replied. "Get there!"

"Working on it."

* * *

Braddock saw Coollee run past the Flyer ride, go through an archway and then turn left at the Thunder Bolt roller coaster. He knew that led to the narrow walkway between Skee-Ball and Bumper Cars. After he took his own left, his height allowed him to see Coollee and his bucket hat bob along as he weaved through the crowd. Braddock pushed to move up on him, shuffling to the right side, hewing close to the railing, passing slower walking people. He was closing on him, forty feet, and he darted over to the left side as Coollee passed the Ferris Wheel ticket booth on the right, the walkway narrowing into a tight corner where only a right turn was possible.

Crack! Crack! Crack!

The shots were from behind him.

The crowd in the walkway halted, looking around nervously.

He kept focused on Coollee, seeing his right shoulder and arm move. Coollee ducked right, disappearing behind the support pillars for a ticket booth.

Two more steps forward he caught the flash of movement at the end pillar on the right. Coollee.

"Gun!"

Boom! Boom!

He dove over the counter of the Ice-Cold Drink stand, grabbing the server as he did, dragging him to the floor.

Boom! Boom! Boom! Boom!

"What the fuck, man!" the server yelled, the soda dispensers leaking on them.

"Stay down." He pulled his gun and looked up over the counter, but Coollee was on the move again.

* * *

"Be advised," the police radio burped. "Shots fired. Luna Park at Coney Island."

"Dammit!" White said, racing on Surf Avenue, passing the Cyclone. "Where are they?"

"Tori said they were pushing them west. Go to the far side of the park."

* * *

Tori had her eyes on Salvucci as the crowd was thinning, people fleeing mostly running north toward Surf Avenue now and out of the park.

She ran across 12th Street, Salvucci still running straight, but each time he looked back, he slowed down just enough that she could close the gap, and she could tell she was moving faster than him to begin with.

Boom! Boom!

That was south.

Braddock.

Boom! Boom! Boom! Boom!

She crossed the street, Salvucci a half block ahead, the white and red loops of the Thunderbolt roller coaster visible in the distance. He looked back again, and they eyed each other up. She was closer yet now she realized, too exposed.

Salvucci spun around.

Dumpster to the right.

She dove for it.

Crack! Crack! Crack! Crack!

The shots pinged off the dumpster and cement of the building overhead. She rolled up onto her knees and peeked around the edge. He was running again. She stood up, then shuffled left, setting her feet. She had a clear shot.

"Damn."

There were too many people in the background.

She ran ahead. Salvucci was almost to 15th Street, and he was angling to the left side.

You're taking a left aren't you.

There was a gate open in the fencing up to the left and she ran through it. The path ran at a forty-five-degree angle to 15th Street and at the end was another gate open to the street.

* * *

Crack! Crack! Crack! Crack!

Vooch turned and sprinted ahead. It was 15th Street. The car was at the south end of the street, a champagne-colored Honda Accord.

Turn left.

Tires squealed to his right. He glanced back.

* * *

The crowd in the street parted as White turned hard left off Surf Avenue onto 15th.

"There! That's Salvucci!" Cardi yelled, pulling her gun.

White screeched to a stop, his car door flying open.

Salvucci pivoted.

"Duck!" White yelled, pushing Cardi out her door.

Crack! Crack! Crack! Crack!

"Ahhhh!" White groaned out.

* * *

Vooch kept firing.

Crack! Crack! Crack! Crack! Crack!... Click!

He turned and ejected the magazine and pulled another out of his sweatshirt pocket and slammed it in.

* * *

Tori heard the firing to her right.

Crack! Crack! Crack! Crack!

At the gate opening she pivoted right. Salvucci turned right at her, his gun up.

Bap! Bap! Bap!

She hit him three times.

Salvucci crumpled to the street.

Tori shuffled forward, her gun up.

Salvucci grunted, rolling onto his left side and tried to push himself up.

"Stay. Down!" Tori called.

He pushed up to his knee, raising his gun.

Bam! Bam! Bam!
Tori glanced to her right. Cardi. She'd finished Salvucci off.
"Behind you!"

* * *

Braddock peered around the corner of the Ferris Wheel ticket booth.

Coollee was running, tossing away his bucket hat, rushing through the crowd, getting to the end of the tight walkway.

Crack! Crack! Crack! Crack!

Those shots were to the north.

"*Go! Go! Go!*" Braddock urged as people rushed by him. "Keep going. Keep going."

Coollee turned right.

Following him wasn't working. Any support coming was coming from the north. The play was box him in from the south.

* * *

Boo looked back at the end of the arcade corridor and didn't see Braddock. He turned right, ran a half block and then turned left, glanced back and then turned and ran through a walkway with picnic benches, across Stillwell Avenue and on a narrower path between park areas that were being remodeled. At the end of the path, across the street he saw it.

The Honda.

Bam! Bam! Bam!

He came out of the opening and glanced to his right and turned that way.

* * *

"Behind you!"

Tori spun around. Coollee. He was right there, gun up. She whirled left, took three running steps, firing as she did.

Bap! Bap!

Boom! Boom! Boom!

She dove through the gap in the fence and rolled on the pavement, landing against another chain link fence.

* * *

Cardi fired.

Bam! Bam!

She grazed Coollee but he fired back.

Boom! Boom! Boom!

Her right leg gave out instantly. "Ahrg!" She crumpled to the ground, the burn searing through her body.

* * *

Boo had been hit twice but he hobbled to the car and started it. He backed out rapidly, swinging around and accelerated north, driving right at Cardellini.

* * *

Braddock rushed ahead and instead of going right, went left. "Police! Police! Out of the way! Out of the way!" he called out, pushing his way past people up to the Coney Island Boardwalk. He ran ahead freely in the more open space of the boardwalk.

At Stillwell Avenue he glanced north. He saw police lights fly by on Surf Avenue, and he caught a glance of a big man, light blue pants, backpack, running west.

Crack! Crack! Crack!

Bap! Bap! Bap!

More of the gunfire he heard earlier.

"*Move! Move! Police!*" he yelled, the confused and panicked crowds parting for him. "Out of the way! Out of the way!"

Bam! Bam!

Boom! Boom! Boom!

That was just ahead.

He reached 15th Avenue, stopped at the corner of the Pop-a-Shot game and peered around the corner. Coollee was getting into a car. In the distance he saw a woman in a navy-blue pant suit lying in the street. Cardi.

Braddock ran down the narrow right-side planked walkway.

Coollee backed out quickly, swinging the front end to the right and racing away north.

Braddock set his feet to shoot but held up.

ESU.

* * *

The black tank-like truck drove right at him.

Boo yanked the wheel hard left, throwing the back end around and he hit the gas. The only way out now was the boardwalk.

* * *

Coollee was coming right at him.

Braddock stepped to his left, standing high on the board-walk which was elevated over the barricaded end of 15th Street as it reached the beach. He could cover either the left or right ramp. Coollee veered to the left ramp.

"*Get away! Get away! Get back! Get back!*" Braddock yelled, tracking the car.

The Honda reached the bottom of the ramp.

He fired.

Bam! Bam! Bam! Bam!

The Honda kept coming. He rotated left with it.

Bam! Bam! Bam! Bam!

Out of control, the car flew off the end of the ramp, catching air before crashing onto and then across the wood planks of the boardwalk, running head-on into a green wrought-iron ornate streetlamp. The streetlamp slowly tipped backward and then crashed down on the roof of the car, collapsing part of the passenger compartment.

Braddock slowly stepped out to his left, giving himself a wide berth from the car, smoke and steam billowing from the engine, the front end crumpled, the top of it crushed by the light pole.

"I'm a police officer. Get away! Get away! Get back! Get back!"

The driver's side door creaked open.

"Boo, you're done!" Braddock called, gun up, ready. "Don't move! Don't. Move!"

Coollee, his face filled with blood, stumbled out, raising his gun.

Bam! Bam! Bam! Bam! Bam!

Coollee crumpled to the ground, the gun falling from his hands. Braddock rushed up and kicked the gun away while keeping his pointed at the now bloody, unmoving mess that was John Boo Coollee.

"Move! Move! Move!" voices called from his right. ESU officers fully geared in all black with automatic weapons came rushing, guns up to the car.

"Where have you guys been?" Braddock cracked.

"Are you Braddock?" one of the officers asked, while another went to check Coollee for a pulse. The officer looked up and shook his head.

"Yeah, that's me."

"Seems you and everyone else took care of things. Was there anyone else beyond the two dead men?"

"No. If we have two dead, we're done. How many others were shot?"

"Some civilians and two cops."

"Which cops?"

"White and Cardellini."

"Ah shit," he grimaced and glanced to his right. Tori emerged through the crowd and jogged over to him. The officers turned around, wary, seeing someone with a gun. "Easy, she's with me."

"Got him, huh?" she said, breathing hard.

"Yeah," Braddock replied. "Eight years too late." He threw his right arm around her, pulling her close. "Are you alright?"

"I think Meghan got the better day with you at Coney Island."

Braddock and Tori made their way back north on 15th Avenue and the mass of police officers who had now arrived on scene.

"Where were all of them when all the fun started?" Tori remarked sarcastically as they walked swiftly toward an ambulance stopped in the middle of 15th.

"It all went down fast. It was a couple of minutes from when we got off the train until it was over."

Flashing police and emergency vehicle lights were all about. The sound of sirens filled the immediate area. At the far end of the street media trucks had arrived and cameramen were taking in footage of the scene.

Cardi lay on a stretcher, her right leg immobilized. The paramedics were preparing to load her into an ambulance.

"Hey there," Braddock said, reaching for Cardi's hand, taking a quick look at the bloody mess that was her right thigh. "That's gonna leave a mark."

"Seems like we all had to take our turn getting shot on this one," she said through gritted teeth. "It's a first for me though."

"Thanks for covering me," Tori said. "I didn't see Coollee behind me."

"Right back at you," Cardi said as they lifted her stretcher up.

"And White?"

"Shot twice. It wasn't good."

"Where are they going?" Tori asked the paramedic.

"Coney Island Hospital."

* * *

Before they could go to the hospital, there was the matter of the post-shooting incident statement.

Braddock and Tori turned over their weapons and were put through the paces by the Chief of the Major Case Squad, who expressed he was none too pleased with how White and Cardi had iced others out.

Braddock laughed at the chief.

"Did I say something funny, Braddock?"

Tori threw her head back. "Oh, I think he has zero fucks left to give at this point."

"I don't," Braddock sat forward in his chair. "It kills me that your first thought is chain of command, not all the innocent people dead at the hands of Coollee and his boys or the giant shit stain this thing is for the department."

"That's for damn sure," Tori agreed and then found her voice rising. "It was cops and ex-cops of this department who were responsible. They killed all these people, stole those drugs and tried to pin it all on him. They were either trying to kill him or set him up, or both."

"Look, I understand you're both upset about that, but—"

"We're upset," Braddock replied, bemused, turning to Tori. "This fucking guy. Chief, they were getting information from inside the department, from inside this investigation, and I don't know if that was limited to Renko, or if someone inside your unit was feeding them intel too."

"Now hold on."

"I don't know," Tori said. "According to Cardi, one of your detectives was all buddy-buddy with Salvucci and Dent at the event for Renko last night. Maybe instead of you interrogating us, we should be interrogating you."

"Not to mention, this department—your investigative unit, despite the attempts on my and Tori's life last week—still considered me a suspect."

"Not without reason."

"Fuck you, asshole," Braddock charged, all his anger pouring out. "I've had this threat hanging over my head for eight years."

"Look—"

"No, go fuck yourself, Chief. I don't work for you."

"Hey, fuck you back, Braddock! You were off the grid. Your sheriff was covering for you. You weren't answering your phone. We didn't know where you were. You assaulted Renko last week. You're all over this case and not in a good way. What do you expect us to think? What do you expect us to presume?"

"And you sit here dumbfounded as to why I didn't trust you or hardly anyone else with NYPD," Braddock replied, exasperated. "And that's after all the years I gave this department."

"You trusted Cardellini."

"I needed someone on the inside."

"Why trust her?"

"Because she was a Cardellini," Braddock replied. "And Tori trusted her and there's nobody I trust more than Tori. I needed to know what was coming at me for once on this case. And Cardi came through. She and White, who are now both in the hospital. You damn well better find room in whatever report you're writing that *clearly* and *unequivocally* states that her performance here was exemplary and she and White better get proper credit for bringing this home, regardless of whether they kept you in the loop or not."

"Worthy of the highest honor this department has, if you ask me," Tori affirmed.

"Chief, I have zero desire to speak to any reporters, to talk with any media. None. Zero. I just want to go home and get back to my life, but I swear to God, if someone from this fucking department isn't out front lionizing those two, I will have a lot of things to say about the case and about the department. And you think I'm angry now? Just fuckin' wait. I will take a flamethrower to everyone. Every fucking person I can think of."

The chief closed his folder and sat back, clasping his hands in his lap. "Detective Braddock, Special Agent Hunter, I don't think that'll be necessary."

They left the office and as they walked down the hall, Tori said: "Nobody you trust more?"

He stopped and looked her in the eye. "Thanks for having my back on this."

"There's no place I'd have rather been," she replied, pecking him on the lips. "Though my price keeps going up."

"Oh, I bet it does," he replied, kissing her back. "I might actually have to become a dirty cop to afford it."

"Now that's funny."

* * *

White was in the Intensive Care Unit following his surgery. He was in a serious condition but there was optimism he would pull through.

"He'll make it. He's tough as nails," Cardi said, lying back against her pillow, having awoken from surgery on her right thigh. She was going to be on the sidelines for a few months. "I heard the chief of the Major Case Squad was displeased he'd been kept in the dark."

"Braddock was more displeased," Tori said. "And voiced that rather," she paused, trying to find the word, "colorfully."

"I can only imagine." Cardi offered a wan smile. "You're cleared now."

"Yeah," Braddock replied and his phone rang. "It's Boe. I should take the call and let her know we're okay and that she can stop lying to the NYPD now."

"Go," Tori said, and Braddock walked out of the room. "Hey, Jeanette, we're okay…"

Cardi chuckled, her voice weak and hoarse. "I came to Minnesota, knowing about your relationship with him, absolutely certain I would hate you."

"Yeah," Tori replied with a smile. "I saw that hug you gave him in Boe's office when you arrived and I knew then and there, there was something between the two of you back then. So, you could say, I instantly hated you."

"In all honesty, that hug had a purpose."

"I'm sure it did," Tori replied. "But, you know, sometimes if you give a person half a chance, they'll surprise you."

"No kidding," Cardi replied, letting out a breath. "I could see us as friends, you know, if you still lived here."

Tori smiled. "We are friends now, Cardi. You don't go through something like this, survive it, and not end up being at least friends."

"Even after the stuff with—"

Tori shook her head. "It happened—eight years ago. Long before I arrived on the scene. And I'd be a pretty big hypocrite given all my own mental baggage, if I judged either him or you for your little two-week affair when you were both not at your best."

"Baggage," Cardi replied, her voice slow, scratchy. "I've got plenty of that. Another divorce," she said, shaking her head in dismay. "My taste in men is… mostly disastrous, so I know a little something about not so good guys, Tori," she said and then looked Tori in the eye. "You have a rare one. Men like him are hard to find for women like us."

"Yeah, they are."

"This won't be over for him yet, not for some time. You don't just wave away eight years."

"No, it'll linger, I think."

"Take care of him."

"You can count on it."

* * *

Ring! Ring! Ring!

"Hello?" the voice called over the intercom.

"Monica, it's Will Braddock and Tori Hunter. I know it's late, but can we come up?"

The buzzer went off and the front door popped open. Monica was waiting for them with the door open. They all took the same seats they had on Saturday afternoon.

"Did that man we identified in that photo, did that help?"

"It did," Tori said. "We wouldn't have solved it without it."

"Solved it?" Monica asked, surprised, looking from Tori then to Braddock.

"Phil Salvucci was one of the men responsible for what happened to Dan," Braddock said. "Did you see the news, the shooting out at Coney Island today?"

"I did. Was that you?"

"Yes," Braddock replied. "We got them, Monica. Every man responsible for killing Dan, we got them. Four of them are dead and one is going to prison for a long, long time."

Monica's lips trembled and her eyes watered, no longer having to wonder after eight years. "Oh, Will? Really? It's over. You know what happened to Dan."

"Yes. Another time, I can tell you the whole thing if you want. But... I'm just so sorry it happened. I'm sorry I didn't do my job better back then," Braddock said, his own eyes watering, his voice wavering. "I'm just... sorry."

Monica stood up and walked to Braddock, who slowly stood. She gently cupped his face in her hands, tenderly wiping away the tears running down his cheeks, "Thank you, Will. Thank you."

* * *

It was just after midnight as they fought the Manhattan traffic driving south back to Oliver and Connie's.

"Hey, hey, pull over," Tori demanded, pointing to Uncle Paulie's pizza. "Uncle Paulie's is the best and I'm starving. Aren't you?"

"I could eat. A big pizza. Maybe Oli and Connie will want some."

She purchased a large pizza and a six-pack of beers, holding them up as she got in. "I know you're still processing it all, but there is cause to celebrate. Just a little."

* * *

At Oli and Connie's, while they ate pizza and drank beers, they called Ana Gonzalez, who was hiding out in San Diego under the hospitable and watchful eyes of Eddie Mannion and his wife.

"I'm safe?" Ana asked. "No more running?"

"No more running," Tori said. "You'll not ever have to worry about this again. Now, you can think about Emma and what you'd like to do and where you'd like to do it. Have you given that any thought?"

"Mr. Mannion and his wife—"

Tori laughed. "What's this 'Mr. Mannion' stuff?"

She heard Eddie laugh loudly in the background. "Damn right I'm Mr. Mannion!"

"Well, Eddie and his wife were talking with me about that.

I'd like to go back to nursing. He said he knew people at the hospital in Manchester Bay. They're always looking for nurses and he said he thought he could get me hired there and we'd figure out what I needed to do to get re-certified."

"So, you're thinking Manchester Bay?"

"Yes. We lived in Superior the last four years, and I didn't mind the winters and Mister... well, Eddie, said Manchester Bay is a good place to live."

Thinking of her own life experience, Tori said, "It can be a good place for a fresh start."

Oli and Connie retired to bed, but Braddock wanted to stay up and have one last beer and wind down. They sat out on the small patio for the apartment, the air cool and comfortable. Braddock was mostly quiet and distant, sipping his beer.

"What are you thinking?" Tori asked, before taking a sip of her beer.

"I don't know," he said. It was a lie. She prodded him. As much to get him talking so that he would provide the openings to say the things she wanted to say.

"We solved it. We finished it."

"There wouldn't have been the need to solve or finish anything had I done my job years ago," Braddock replied. "All the deaths..." His voice trailed away. "Dan, Lange, Malik, Julio, almost you, almost Cardi and White. The carnage it all wrought."

Tori stood up and walked over to him, nudging his left leg more open so she could sit on his lap. She threw her right arm around him and with her left index finger tipped his chin, so he was looking her in the eye. "I've been around this job my whole life."

"I know."

"Even under the best of circumstances, this is a hard, hard

job we do. And eight years ago, you were not operating under the best of circumstances. You were grieving, and struggling, and lost. Cut yourself just a little bit of slack."

"But—"

"I know you feel responsible," she said, as he leaned his head into her. "My father was like that. He had that dedication to do right by people."

"I see the same thing in you."

"I got it from him. You said earlier you trusted me more than anyone else."

He looked her in the eye. "I do. You know I do."

"Then trust me, *trust me*, when I say this. It wasn't all your fault."

"Tori—"

She put her finger to his lips. "*Shhhhh*. You didn't steal all those drugs and profit from it. You didn't shoot the six men at Espinosa Warehouse. *And* you didn't make Dan Guerero go investigate all that either. He chose to do that. Dan was a big boy, who knew what he was getting into. If he were sitting here right now, I'm certain he would agree with me. And he would thank you for getting Monica closure after all these years. I know you've carried this and will continue to carry it because that's who you are, but there is no more guilt here for you to bear."

Braddock didn't say anything for a minute, just breathing, his left arm wrapped around her waist. "What do we do now?"

She leaned down, cupped his right cheek gently in her left hand and kissed him, leaning her forehead against his. "You take me to bed."

"And tomorrow?"

"We go home."

A LETTER FROM ROGER

Thank you for choosing to spend some of your hard-earned money and valuable free time reading *Trust No One*.

I hope you enjoyed it. If you did, I'd like to keep you up to date with all my latest releases, just sign up at the following link. Your email address will never be shared, and you can unsubscribe at any time.

www.bookouture.com/roger-stelljes

I write these books for you, the reader. I hope you have as much fun reading them as I do writing them. Where does the fun come from for me? From curating this world of Tori, Braddock, Manchester Bay and all the characters in it. Every book provides the opportunity to think about my characters and what little idiosyncrasy I can add and what new intriguing pieces of backstory could build their legends. And the backdrop of Manchester Bay, of Minnesota lakes country, provides the ideal visual canvas to tell a captivating story. And this time, I was able to take the story on the road to New York City, a place so central to the life stories of both Tori and Braddock. I truly hope you enjoy reading the adventures of Tori, Braddock and all the rest every bit as much as I do the process of crafting them.

One of the best parts of being an author is seeing the reaction from readers, both those who have read all my books and those new to the Tori Hunter scene. My goal every time I write is to give you what I have always looked for in a book myself.

That's an exciting story that draws you in, puts you on edge, makes you think, on occasion pulls at the heartstrings, and always, *always*, makes you want to read just one more page, one more chapter, because you just couldn't put it down. That is my litmus test for a good book. It is my credo as a writer. I endeavor to deliver it to you, the reader, every time.

If you enjoyed *Trust No One*, I would greatly appreciate it if you could leave a short review. Receiving feedback from readers like you is important to me in developing and writing my stories but is also vital in helping to persuade others to pick up one of my books for the first time.

If you enjoyed *Trust No One*, and it's your first time with Tori, Braddock, and their friends, they can also be found in *Silenced Girls*, *The Winters Girls*, *The Hidden Girl*, *Missing Angel*, *The Snow Graves*, *Their Lost Souls* and *Taken in the Cold*, and in more stories to come.

Thank you,

Roger

www.RogerStelljes.com

facebook.com/rogerstelljesbooks

x.com/RogerStelljes

instagram.com/rogerstelljes

ACKNOWLEDGMENTS

While the author's name goes on the cover, every book has a team of true professionals behind it. I wish to thank the entire publishing team at Bookouture for all their work in bringing *Trust No One* to the readers.

I'd especially like to thank my editor, Ellen Gleeson, who brought me to Bookouture in 2020. It's our eighth book together and I look forward to many, many more. Also, many thanks to my copyeditor, Jane Eastgate, who gets the little idiosyncrasies of my writing style and lets them survive the editing cut. And again, I can't thank enough the remainder of the publishing team for bringing the latest and greatest Tori Hunter adventure to the readers.

Cheers to you all.

PUBLISHING TEAM

Turning a manuscript into a book requires the efforts of many people. The publishing team at Bookouture would like to acknowledge everyone who contributed to this publication.

Audio
Alba Proko
Sinead O'Connor
Melissa Tran

Commercial
Lauren Morrissette
Hannah Richmond
Imogen Allport

Cover design
Ghost

Data and analysis
Mark Alder
Mohamed Bussuri

Editorial
Ellen Gleeson
Nadia Michael

RAISING READERS
Books Build Bright Futures

Dear Reader,

We'd love your attention for one more page to tell you about the crisis in children's reading, and what we can all do.

Studies have shown that reading for fun is the **single biggest predictor of a child's future life chances** – more than family circumstance, parents' educational background or income. It improves academic results, mental health, wealth, communication skills, ambition and happiness.

The number of children reading for fun is in rapid decline. Young people have a lot of competition for their time, and a worryingly high number do not have a single book at home.

Hachette works extensively with schools, libraries and literacy charities, but here are some ways we can all raise more readers:

- Reading to children for just 10 minutes a day makes a difference
- Don't give up if children aren't regular readers – there will be books for them!

- Visit bookshops and libraries to get recommendations
- Encourage them to listen to audiobooks
- Support school libraries
- Give books as gifts

There's a lot more information about how to encourage children to read on our websites: **www.RaisingReaders.co.uk** and **www.JoinRaisingReaders.com**.

Thank you for reading.